"WE'RE PUTT ." SULU SAID. "N

Asher, take us into the path of those blasts, between the Neyel ship and the Tholian settlement."

Chekov moved toward the command chair and leaned in. "Please tell me you a have a plan," he said quietly.

"If we lost only seven percent of our shield capacity from the previous attack, then we ought to be able to sustain another few direct hits without serious damage. And that may buy some time for the Tholians down there."

"You hope," Chekov finished for him. "If that first volley they fired at us really was only a warning shot . . ."

"I can't just allow the wanton slaughter of those people down there, Pavel. And if we can stop the attack without having to open fire ourselves . . ."

"Big gamble," Chekov said.

"I know," Sulu told him. He studied the viewer as the Neyel ship, with its long, weapons-festooned hull, loomed steadily larger in *Excelsior*'s flight path. He wondered for a moment if any sort of parley or peace was even possible with such apparently hate-filled people. After all, the Neyel with whom he had spoken had referred to the Tholians as an "infestation."

I just hope I'm not placing my ship and my crew in jeopardy over a lost cause.

STAR TREK®

THE LOST ERA

THE SUNDERED

2298

MICHAEL A. MARTIN
AND ANDY MANGELS

Based upon STAR TREK
created by Gene Roddenberry

POCKET BOOKS
New York London Toronto Sydney Singapore Oghen

An *Original* Publication of POCKET BOOKS

POCKET BOOKS, a division of Simon & Schuster, Inc.
1230 Avenue of the Americas, New York, NY 10020

This book is published by Pocket Books, a division of Simon & Schuster, Inc., under exclusive license from Paramount Pictures.

ISBN: 0-7434-6401-X

First Pocket Books printing August 2003

10 9 8 7 6 5 4 3 2 1

POCKET and colophon are registered trademarks of Simon & Schuster, Inc.

Cover design by John Vairo, Jr.

Manufactured in the United States of America

For information regarding special discounts for bulk purchases, please contact Simon & Schuster Special Sales at 1-800-456-6798 or business@simonandschuster.com.

For the gallant crew of STS-107, the proud handful of achievers who flew into Eternity aboard the Space Shuttle *Columbia*: Michael Anderson; David Brown; Kalpana Chawla; Laurel Clark; Rick Husband; William McCool; and Ilan Ramon. Your courage is writ large across the sky, through all the eras, lost or otherwise.

—M.A.M.

For Kehvan Zydhek, a good friend and a pretty darn good webmaster as well. Thanks for your friendship, support, and help. Live Long and Prosper!

—A.M.

ACKNOWLEDGMENTS

The authors' heartfelt thanks go to Dr. Al Globus of the NASA Ames Research Center. His keen insights into the construction of off-world orbital habitats was invaluable to us both.

Thanks are also due to the dean of science fiction, the late Robert A. Heinlein, for penning the novellas *Universe* and *Common Sense*, and the short story "The Green Hills of Earth," which is (mis)quoted very briefly in Chapter 25 (granted by permission of the Robert A. and Virginia Heinlein Prize Trust).

One doesn't discover new lands without consenting to lose sight of the shore for a very long time.

—André [Paul-Guillaume] Gide (1869–1951)

If it were all so simple!
If only there were evil people somewhere
insidiously committing evil deeds,
and it were necessary only to separate them
from the rest of us and destroy them.
But the line dividing good and evil
cuts through the heart of every human being.
And who is willing to destroy a piece of his own heart?

—Alexsandr Solzhenitsyn

HISTORIAN'S NOTE

This story is set in the year 2298, five years after the presumed death of Captain James T. Kirk aboard the *U.S.S. Enterprise*-B in *Star Trek Generations*, and sixty-six years before the launch of the *Enterprise*-D in "Encounter at Farpoint."

PART 1

ALIENS

Chapter 1

After bowing respectfully before his opponent, Captain Hikaru Sulu straightened, tensing his wiry form as he raised his épée to the ready position. "*En garde!*" he shouted, then lunged forward, the slender blade flashing before him.

With a grace that belied her considerable size, Lieutenant P'mu'la Hopman deflected Sulu's foil toward the captain's left with a deft parry sixte. Sulu tried to conceal his surprise at how quick the muscular exosociology specialist was on her rather large feet. Though less than twenty years Sulu's junior, Hopman moved like someone far younger. On top of that, she was in her male phase this morning. Sulu had become accustomed to sparring with Hopman when she wore her female form, which was more equivalent to Sulu's own mass.

Recovering quickly, Sulu renewed his attack, stepping forward, then back, then forward again, all the while probing his opponent for weakness or hesitation. He thrust, cobralike. Hopman countered him once again with a quarte parry, melding fluidly into a forward-lunging riposte that Sulu easily sidestepped.

"You're not going easy on me just because I'm the captain, are you, Lieutenant?" Sulu said, wishing he could see his opponent's expression through the white duranium-mesh facemasks.

Hopman drew a languid circle in the air with the tip of her foil. "The captain is being entirely too modest about his skills," she said, the smile behind her mask clearly audible.

Sulu recalled how Hopman—a variable-gendered Thelusian who still carried the surname of a human ex-spouse—had recently stared at the platinum belt he kept on the wall of the situation room. The trophy had hung there for so long that Sulu rarely thought about it anymore. It had been years since he'd bragged to anyone about having swept the Inner Planets championship tournament as a Starfleet Academy cadet.

On the other hand, he was far from ashamed of his prowess with the blade. After all, those talents had saved his life years earlier, when he'd been forced into *bat'leth* combat during Curzon Dax's impulsive *hajj* into the Klingon Empire. *But it's nice not to have the burden of defending a current championship title,* Sulu thought. Command of *Excelsior* was responsibility enough.

"I know that flattery doesn't work on you, sir," Hopman said, now standing motionless except for the slow twirl of her blade tip.

Sulu grinned. "Really?"

"Yes, sir. At least that's how Lieutenant Tuvok tells it."

Sulu's throaty chuckle resonated through the otherwise empty gymnasium. If any member of his senior staff was above the giving or receiving of flattery, it was Lieutenant Tuvok, his Vulcan senior science officer. Five years ago, shortly after coming aboard *Excelsior* as part of a contingent of junior science specialists, Tuvok had brought a cup of Vulcan tea to the bridge and presented it to Sulu. The subtle blend of flavors had been delightful, and Sulu had wondered for more than a year afterward why Tuvok had never repeated the gesture—until Janice Rand finally revealed that she had ribbed Tuvok that very day by suggesting that his gift of tea might have been taken as a career-advancement tactic. Sulu, too, had made a similar mock-serious observation in Tuvok's presence even as he'd taken his first sip of the proffered beverage.

Ever since that day, Tuvok never again made another unsolicited gift of any sort to a superior officer, no doubt intent on making it crystal clear that he wished to receive no unearned favors.

"And I wasn't going easy on you, sir," Hopman said earnestly, her wide shoulders slumping. Sulu thought the mannerism might have been unconscious. "I just feel more comfortable when I'm . . . smaller."

Sulu raised his foil again. "That additional mass you're carrying at the moment gives you a strength advantage, Pam. Why not use it?"

With that, Sulu renewed his assault on Hopman. She parried, prompting Sulu to attempt a counterparry. The bulky lieutenant spun into a counter-disengage before Sulu could find an opening. The deck seemed to shudder slightly beneath Sulu's feet. The effect was nearly imperceptible, but it distracted him momentarily nonetheless. *We've changed speed.*

Suddenly, Hopman's blade scored a solid touch against Sulu's padded fencing jacket.

Hopman lowered her foil and doffed her facemask, releasing her long, sandy hair. A grin spread across her wide, masculine features. "*Now* who's holding back?"

Sulu lowered his blade. "You wound me, Lieutenant. Almost literally. Be careful, or you might turn this into an affair of honor."

"Best two out of three?"

Sulu shook his head. There was the little matter of *Excelsior's* apparent change in velocity—and the disconcerting fact that no one from the bridge had called him yet with an explanation.

"Another time, Lieutenant," he said as he removed his mask and mopped the sweat from his brow with a long, white sleeve. "Duty calls."

Just as Sulu reached the bulkhead companel, the gymnasium doors immediately beside it whisked open. Sulu turned and saw Commander Pavel Chekov, *Excelsior*'s executive officer, standing in the threshold.

The slight frown that creased Chekov's forehead plainly told Sulu that his old friend hadn't come down for a workout.

"The Tholians have changed the time and place of the meeting," Chekov said.

Sulu handed his foil to Hopman, but kept his eyes fixed on his old friend. "Don't tell me they want to postpone."

"No, sir," Chekov said. "In fact, they've moved the rendezvous up, to tomorrow morning at 0930 hours. They want us to meet them near the 15 Lyncis system."

Ah, Sulu thought. That explained the velocity change that he'd felt thrumming through the deckplates. Despite the good-natured puzzlement of Chief Engineer Azleya, Sulu had never allowed her to refine the inertial dampers to the point where they rendered such adjustments completely unnoticeable. After all, *Excelsior* was a ship of the line, not a luxury liner.

"I trust Commander Lojur and Lieutenant Docksey already have us under way," Sulu said, though he already knew the answer.

"Aye, sir. We certainly don't want to keep our clock-watching friends waiting." The Tholians were notorious for the meticulous attention they paid to their itineraries. Perhaps especially so when they were altering them.

Sulu nodded. He recalled the position of the 15 Lyncis system from his decades of helm duty. It lay a good ten light-years outside of the vast, meandering volume of space claimed and defended by the extremely xenophobic Tholians.

Starfleet Command's original orders had called for *Excelsior* to rendezvous with the *Jeb'v Tholis*—Tholian Admiral Yilskene's flagship—late the following week in the Qilydra system, nearly two full parsecs inside what was generally agreed to be Tholian space. *Excelsior* would have to accelerate to warp nine to make the rescheduled appointment on time.

"Apparently something's persuaded the Tholians that it's no longer a good idea to invite us across their border," Sulu said.

"They haven't canceled the meeting, though," Chekov pointed out. "They've only changed the time and place."

"But why?" Sulu wanted to know.

Chekov shrugged. "We've watched the Tholians for a long time, Hikaru. They're usually as territorial as Klingon *targs.* It's not surprising that they don't want us coming too close to their homeworld. I don't think the crew will be too disappointed about meeting with them elsewhere. From everything I've read, Tholia and the rest of the N-class planets the Tholian Assembly controls aren't exactly competitors of Wrigley's Pleasure Planet."

Sulu nodded. "When the Tholians asked for a diplomatic meeting *inside* the boundaries of their own space, it looked like a pretty hopeful sign. Maybe an indication that they were finally beginning to look beyond their ingrained xenophobia."

"Looks like that hope might have been premature," Chekov said. "After all, it's not easy to overcome almost one hundred and fifty years of mutual suspicion."

Sulu grinned. "That's uncharacteristically diplomatic of you, Pavel."

"Don't get me wrong," Chekov said, scowling as though he'd been insulted. "Their waffling as to where and when to meet us doesn't exactly fill me with confidence. Something very strange may be going on inside the Tholian power structure. Until we know what it is, I suggest we be very, very careful around them."

Over the years, Chekov had regaled Sulu with countless tales of the many wars and invasions his Russian homeland had endured through the centuries. Sulu knew that suspicion came quite naturally to Chekov. In fact, it was an asset that he frequently relied upon in making critical command decisions.

"I agree," Sulu said. "All we know is that the Tholians appear to have suddenly fallen back into their old habits, but without any more explanation than they offered when they asked to meet with our diplomats in the first place. So the question remains: why?"

"It might not add up to anything sinister," Lieutenant Hopman said, breaking her silence as she leaned her foil alongside Sulu's against the gymnasium wall. "You've already mentioned the renowned Tholian penchant for xenophobia. Perhaps that's all this is."

But Sulu wasn't buying it. "The Tholians are renowned for a lot of things, Lieutenant. Dithering isn't one of them."

"Their society is made up of multiple castes," Hopman said. "Perhaps the castes are in fundamental disagreement about how best to deal with the Federation."

Sulu nodded. "Maybe they aren't all in agreement that they even *should* deal with the Federation."

"A distinct possibility," said Hopman.

"Well, maybe *this* will shed some light on the matter," Chekov said, holding up a memory chip, which he then handed to Sulu. "Janice received this just before I left the bridge. It's an encrypted message from Starfleet Command. It's scrambled and marked 'for the captain's eyes only.' "

Sulu contemplated the palm-sized piece of translucent red plastic he held in his hand. This far from a starbase, real-time subspace communication with Starfleet brass simply wasn't practical. So the message's arrival, by itself, was no cause for concern. However, its "eyes-only" classification concerned him. It obviously contained sensitive information, and its appearance on the eve of the first major rapprochement between the Tholian Assembly and the United Federation of Planets had to be significant as well.

"Do you want me to alert the Federation special envoy

about the change in schedule?" Chekov said, a faint look of distaste on his face.

Sulu shook his head. "Not yet. Let me see what Starfleet Command has to say first. Then I'll talk to Ambassador Burgess about the change in plans."

Chekov looked relieved not to have to handle the Federation representative himself. For his own part, Sulu did not relish the prospect either. True enough, Aidan Burgess had been more than cooperative in furnishing Lieutenant Hopman and the rest of *Excelsior*'s senior staff with valuable information about the Tholians during the two days since the *Enterprise* had dropped her off. But the ambassador's frantic preparations for the impending diplomatic meetings had run many of the ship's support personnel ragged.

Sulu had done his best to make certain that most of Deck Eight had been converted for the Tholians' use, including the installation of forcefield-reinforced transparent aluminum walls capable of holding a Tholian-friendly N-class atmosphere at 200° C and twenty-two bars of pressure. Chief Engineer Azleya had overseen the technical details of the hasty environmental modifications with her usual Denobulan good humor.

It had been the quartermaster and his staff who had probably endured the biggest hardships because of Burgess's presence; she had browbeaten them into fashioning a ceremonial gown for her upcoming meeting with Tholian ambassador Kasrene. Not only were Burgess's specifications exacting, but she had also insisted upon using a peculiar metallic fabric for the job. It was evidently something that she had only very recently acquired, at considerable cost, and it appeared to be resistant to any tool short of a mining drill.

But since Starfleet had explicitly ordered him to indulge the ambassador's eccentricities, Sulu was determined to be as obliging as possible in the interests of the mission. Diplomacy, he knew from long experience, was a very mixed bag—as were diplomats. Maybe Burgess didn't possess quite the same quiet dignity as a Sarek or a Spock. Who did? Sulu knew he could at least be thankful—so far, at least—that she wasn't a martinet like Robert Fox, or a loose cannon like Curzon Dax. *Things could always be a whole lot worse,* he thought.

"I'll assume you're taking a rain check on the rest of our workout, Captain," Hopman said as she retrieved her foil from where she'd left it leaning. Sulu dismissed her, and she raised her blade in a fencer's salute before departing.

Sulu turned to Chekov. "You'd better advise the quartermaster about the schedule change right away. If Ambassador Burgess's tailoring job isn't ready before 0900 tomorrow, I don't want her jumping down my throat about it."

Chekov began moving toward the door, a wry smile on his face. "I'll make sure he either finishes on time, or else perishes in the attempt."

After Chekov exited the gym, Sulu grabbed his épée and made his way toward his quarters. He looked forward to a hot shower, a change of clothes, a steaming cup of Darjeeling—and discovering the contents of Starfleet Command's mysterious "eyes-only" message.

Sulu stripped down for the sonic shower as the computer terminal in his quarters displayed the Federation emblem. Slowly stretching the muscles in his back, he spoke his security access code to the computer and instructed it to display the newly arrived message.

"Working," the computer said, speaking in a soothing, feminine alto. One of the first things Sulu had done after assuming command of the *Excelsior* was to get rid of the booming male computer voices that his immediate predecessor, Captain Styles, had favored.

Sulu felt a twinge in his left shoulder as he removed his fencing jacket and tossed it into the clothing 'cycler. *Must have pulled something during the workout. Or maybe I'm just beginning to feel my age.*

In the mirror, he could see the irregular, vaguely star-shaped traceries of scar tissue that covered his left shoulder like a worn piece of braid. Over the past three decades, several doctors had offered to repair this superficial blemish. Sulu had always politely declined.

He had received those scars on a long-abandoned Kalandan outpost, at the hands of a lethal re-creation of Losira, a beautiful woman who had died some ten millennia earlier. The mere touch of the mournful-eyed siren had already killed one member of an *Enterprise* landing party, blasting each of his cells from within. In an effort to protect her small domain from a perceived invasion, she also tried to kill Sulu in the same fashion. The scar where her fingers had brushed him was now all that remained not only of Losira, but of her entire civilization.

The thought of removing those jagged white markings struck Sulu as somehow disrespectful.

"*Message decrypted, Captain,*" said the computer, interrupting Sulu's reverie. The scowling visage of Admiral Heihachiro Nogura replaced the U.F.P. seal. Sulu took a seat at the foot of his bed, listening attentively.

"*Captain Sulu, you and your crew are about to become involved in a matter of the utmost delicacy. I'm sure it's not news to you that ever since humans first came into contact with them nearly a hundred and fifty years ago, the Tholians have always been xenophobic, territorial, and almost completely uninterested in either trade or cultural exchange with other species. That, of course, makes their recent détente overtures extremely surprising. But that's only part of the story.*

"*Starfleet Intelligence has recently learned that the Tholians have stepped up their energy-weapons development programs over the past few years. While they have yet to attack any of our outposts along our shared border, Command is concerned about their unexplained defense buildup. It is entirely possible that the Tholians' current peace initiative is really an effort to lull us into letting our guard down as a prelude to an aggressive blitz into Federation territory."*

While Sulu found this news disquieting, he was also strangely relieved to hear that his superiors weren't afraid to look askance at the Tholians' olive branch. He and Pavel Chekov had both been on the bridge of the *Enterprise* when the Tholians had attacked with one of their devious energy webs. Sulu suspected that only a very few other currently active Starfleet officers—perhaps as few as Chekov, Captain Uhura, and himself—truly understood just how dangerous the Tholians could be when they felt threatened or cornered.

Nogura continued: *"Our choice of* Excelsior *to ferry Ambassador Burgess and her party to the meeting requested by the Tholians was no coincidence. We expect your previous experience with the Tholians to be invaluable. We are also hoping that your vessel's unique sensor capabilities will help us learn in detail the nature and extent of the new Tholian defense buildup."*

Nogura's reasoning made perfect sense to Sulu; he recalled vividly how *Excelsior*'s sensitive instruments had assisted in protecting the first Federation-Klingon peace efforts at Khitomer by helping to detect and destroy the renegade Klingon general Chang's vessel, a prototype bird-of-prey capable of firing its weapons while cloaked.

"You are hereby ordered," the admiral continued, leaning forward as if to emphasize his words, *"to use whatever resources are necessary to conduct a discreet investigation, even as the diplomatic meeting proceeds. And I do mean* discreet. *Ambassador Burgess is* not *to be made privy to your orders. I cannot emphasize enough how disastrous it could be for the Federation should the Tholians discover your covert surveillance activities. They might well try to use it as a justification for war. For that reason, Starfleet Command will disavow any*

knowledge of your actions should the Tholians learn what you're up to.

"I'm sorry you have to shoulder this responsibility alone. But you've never given me reason to be anything less than confident that you'll pull off a flawless mission.

"Good luck, Captain," Nogura said just before his image vanished from the screen.

Alone in his silent cabin, Sulu swallowed hard. He was an explorer at heart, and always had been. It had been several years since he'd done any work specifically for the purpose of gathering military intelligence. He hadn't missed the shadowy world of galactic espionage one bit.

Damned if I'm going to face this without some expert help, he thought. After all, he wasn't the only officer aboard whose prior experience with the Tholians—and with espionage—might prove beneficial to the mission.

A long, relaxing shower was now out of the question. Rising from the edge of his bed, Sulu crossed to the companel mounted on the wall outside the bathroom.

"Sulu to Commander Chekov."

"Chekov here, Captain." Sulu could hear various bridge instruments beeping and chirping in the background.

The captain was grateful that he could leave the bridge in Chekov's steady hands. And though he deeply regretted having to place his closest friend onto the hot seat with him, he also knew it couldn't be helped.

"Hikaru?" Chekov prompted, concern audible in his voice.

"Pavel, I need to see you in the situation room. I'll be up there in ten minutes."

Chapter 2

The next morning, Sulu stood at attention in Transporter Room One, where the lights were already dimmed to half their normal level, in deference to the soon-to-arrive Tholian diplomatic party. Chekov stood ramrod straight at Sulu's side, at the head of the senior officer delegation.

The captain's long, crisply pressed maroon dress jacket constricted his chest. The seldom-worn formal garment made him feel as though he were preparing for another fencing match. *But it's not* my *match,* he reminded himself, glancing across the room at the special Federation envoy and her retinue. *I'm just Burgess's driver.*

Flanked by a quartet of aides in gray civilian attire, Federation Ambassador Aidan Burgess cut an imposing figure in the simple, ankle-length, metallic-looking gown the weary quartermaster's ceaseless efforts had finally yielded. The ambassador was tall, towering perhaps half a head over Sulu. Her shoulder-length auburn hair presented a startling contrast to her silvery raiment, which somehow deemphasized the freckles that spangled her fair, slightly weather-beaten skin. Sulu estimated her to be about a decade his junior. He couldn't help but admire the air of calm authority she presented while awaiting the arrival of the Tholians.

Standing at attention behind the diplomatic party, and

flanking Sulu and Chekov, was the remainder of *Excelsior*'s senior staff, all turned out in their maroon dress uniforms: Dr. Christine Chapel and Commander Janice Rand, both fellow alumni of the late Jim Kirk's crew; Lieutenant P'mu'la Hopman, now once again in her more demure female form; Chief Engineer Terim Azleya, a garrulous female Denobulan who clearly would have been more comfortable in a jumpsuit fit for the cleaning of plasma conduits; Lieutenant Tuvok, the dark and dour Vulcan senior science officer, a portrait of cool dignity; Lieutenant Commander Lojur, the black-goateed Halkan navigator; Lieutenant Shandra Docksey, *Excelsior*'s petite helm officer; Scott Russell, the fastidious young petty officer who ran the galley, and who was charged with keeping the Tholians fed for the duration of their stay; and the towering Lieutenant Leonard James Akaar, the ship's chief of security, who looked as though he felt naked without a visible sidearm. Akaar's straight blonde hair was pulled back in a simple warrior's braid that hung halfway down his back.

Sulu glanced down at his wrist chronometer. Less than one minute remained until the time designated for the beam-over from Admiral Yilskene's flagship, the *Jeb'v Tholis,* which was keeping station a few dozen klicks off *Excelsior*'s starboard side. Whatever unforeseeable turns this mission might take, Sulu was confident at least that he wouldn't offend the Tholians by being tardy.

After exchanging quick glances with her aides, Burgess met Sulu's gaze.

"It's time," she said, her mien serious. "Whatever happens next, please follow my lead."

Showtime, Sulu thought, noticing the questioning look on the face of his giant Capellan security chief. Sulu answered with a subtle, prearranged hand signal. Though the young lieutenant looked skeptical, he nodded his acquiescence. *Keep the phaser hidden until and unless I say differ-*

ently, Sulu had told him. Both of the young man's large, callused hands remained in sight and empty, but Sulu was well aware of how quickly that could change.

The Tholians have finally reached out to us, he thought. *Yet we still have to prepare for the worst, and do it in secret. How sad.*

Sulu found it hard to believe that five years had passed since the signing of the Khitomer Accords. In addition to establishing the framework of the first real, long-term peace between the Klingon Empire and the Federation, that historic document had also yielded an important unintended consequence: a quiet yet very real "cold war" had recently begun to rage within the Federation's innermost circles of power.

Ever since Khitomer, the tension between the civilian and military spheres of Federation government on matters of foreign policy had been slowly but steadily ratcheting up. It often struck Sulu as ironic that the price of peace with the Klingon Empire was political unpleasantness within the Federation. In fact, it appeared to Sulu that all the major Alpha Quadrant powers had become increasingly uneasy of late. The Tholians were merely the latest additions to the list. It was as though the Federation's internal disagreements about how best to deal with the opportunities and dangers created by the wrenching changes of the last few years had sent a sympathetic vibration across the entire quadrant.

Akaar's evident readiness to reach for his weapon seemed illustrative of this new pervasive sense of wariness. It made Sulu wistful. Back when the Klingons had been predictable, dependable villains, Starfleet had largely concerned itself with pursuing mankind's noblest dreams, chasing knowledge for its own sake. The Federation's ideals had been sharply limned by the contrast it drew between itself and its most dogged adversaries.

But after Khitomer, the Federation's self-definitions had been forced to adapt to changing circumstances. *Change can be frightening. And if change can frighten key Starfleet, Klingon, and Romulan officers into betraying their governments, then it can frighten just about anyone into doing just about anything.*

Sulu glanced quickly at the poker-faced Chekov, who appeared to have watched his entire exchange with the security chief. Looking to Burgess, he saw that she and most everyone else present seemed to have focused all their attention on the empty transporter stage.

Sulu turned to nod at the transporter chief, who immediately busied herself touching the console's control surfaces. The chamber began resonating with a whining hum that rose to a swift crescendo.

Five figures began shimmering into existence on the pads, bathed in golden columns of light as their molecules coalesced and solidified within the harsh radiance of the confinement beam. A moment later, a handful of envirosuited Tholians stood aboard *Excelsior.*

Sulu's hackles rose involuntarily as he regarded his guests, who looked for all the world like giant spacesuited scorpions with large, polyhedral heads. The Tholians' amber-colored suits seemed to be made from a material similar to that of Burgess's gown, and ballooned up from the internal pressure of the dense, superhot atmosphere necessary to sustain their lives. The movements of their multidirectional, arthropodlike joints evoked an instinctual revulsion within Sulu, who presumed he wasn't the only one present who felt it. He forced the emotion down, immediately ashamed of it.

This is only a little taste of the diversity and mystery that the Universe still has in store, Sulu reminded himself, and a sense of wonder gradually began to eclipse his initial reaction to the physical presence of the Tholians. *This is why*

I worked so hard to become a part of Starfleet in the first place.

Thanks to Ambassador Burgess's input, Sulu had taken the precaution of dispensing with the traditional electronic boatswain's whistle that was used to "pipe aboard" new arrivals. Tholians, Sulu had learned during the ambassador's briefings, were notably sensitive to loud, high-frequency sounds. Sulu was never one to object to the shucking of ceremony and protocol whenever an opportunity to do so presented itself. Especially if said protocol might have been regarded as an insult, or perhaps even an act of agression.

Despite his efforts to overcome his first impression of his alien guests, Sulu felt his entire body tense involuntarily as Burgess approached the foremost Tholian. The creature stood nearly two meters tall on its hindmost legs, its great, lethal-looking tail switching to and fro behind it.

Though Sulu found the five Tholians virtually indistinguishable one from another, he assumed the individual in front had to be Kasrene, the Tholian ambassador. Like Commander Loskene, the first Tholian Sulu had ever laid eyes on, Kasrene and her retinue seemed to exude menace, despite the fact that their protective garments almost entirely obscured their bodies.

Burgess stopped less than a meter from the great insectile creature and bowed her head.

Kasrene's tail flashed like a whip, attaching itself to the Federation ambassador's back. Akaar tensed, his hands moving toward his concealed phaser. Sulu locked eyes momentarily with the huge Capellan, shaking his head.

I'm trusting you, Ambassador, Sulu thought, noting that Burgess seemed unsurprised by Kasrene's movements. *I just hope my trust doesn't get you killed.*

A pair of Kasrene's multijointed forelimbs reached out, unfolding like twin construction cranes. The Tholian gathered two clawfuls of Burgess's gown. Akaar's left hand twitched. Sulu was glad he'd forbidden him to wear his *kligat*—a traditional triple-bladed Capellan throwing knife—as one of his dress-uniform adornments.

Still following your lead, Ambassador.

Burgess remained apparently unfazed. With the utmost calm, she straightened from her bow and looked directly into the creature's inscrutable, faceplate-obscured eyespots. With a rock-steady hand, Burgess touched the silver brooch she wore at her neck. When she spoke, a chorus of distorted, alien sounds that no human throat could have produced rolled from her pale lips.

Vocoder, Sulu realized, wishing he had taken the time to stage a complete dress rehearsal of this meeting beforehand. *She probably knows the Tholian language well enough, but she wouldn't be able to make their speech-sounds without some technological help.*

Kasrene froze, though her claws remained entangled in the front of Burgess's gown. Akaar and Chekov both appeared ready to ride to the rescue. Sulu placed a finger against his lips, and both men relaxed somewhat.

"Twice you have honored us already this day," Kasrene said at length, withdrawing her claws and returning a quadruple-jointed approximation of the human ambassador's bow. Although the Tholian's speech made a cacophony similar to that of Burgess, the universal translator rendered it into intelligible Federation Standard. "You greet us with our own voice—and have fashioned garb from our own secretions."

The gown is made of Tholian silk, Sulu thought, finally understanding the real urgency behind Burgess's sartorial demands. *Why couldn't she have just* explained *herself?* He fumed in silence as Burgess and Kasrene commenced an exchange of highly ritualized Tholian greetings, almost as though they were performing a sort of interspecies opera-cum-ballet.

Sulu felt a gnawing suspicion that an even more complicated job now lay ahead of him than simply observing, monitoring, and cataloguing the Tholian Assembly's new weapons programs.

Looks like I'd better keep a pretty close eye on Ambassador Burgess, too.

Chapter 3

After less than an hour of the required exchange of diplomatic pleasantries, Burgess, Chekov, and Akaar had shown the visiting Tholians to their specially modified quarters on Deck Eight. Satisfied that Kasrene's diplomatic team was settling in satisfactorily—they were evidently preparing to meet again in earnest with Burgess and her party later in the day, now that the bare preliminaries were out of the way—Sulu proceeded to the bridge.

As he stepped out of the turbolift, he looked toward the main viewer, which showed Admiral Yilskene's long, dagger-like flagship hanging in space. Like its wedge-shaped predecessors of thirty years earlier, the vessel looked sleek and deadly, and possessed no discernible external engine nacelles. The dim illumination of its running lights revealed a hull that bore a mix of mottled hues: red, orange, yellow, and green.

Studying the other vessel, Sulu felt as though the watchful eyes of the entire Tholian warrior caste were trained squarely upon him. Though the continued presence of the *Jeb'v Tholis* was no doubt comforting to the Tholian diplomats now temporarily ensconced aboard *Excelsior*, it was having quite the opposite effect on Sulu. He didn't relish the thought of Yilskene's reaction should the Tholians become aware of *Excelsior*'s clandestine surveillance on the far reaches of Assembly space.

Chekov rose from the captain's chair at Sulu's approach. Rather than take his seat, Sulu gestured toward the situation-room door at the rear of the bridge. "Pavel, I need a tactical update." He looked up toward the science station and caught Tuvok's eye. "I want your input, too, Lieutenant. Commander Rand, please have Lieutenant Akaar join us."

"Aye, sir," Rand said.

Followed by Chekov and Tuvok, Sulu entered the room and headed toward his customary chair, at one side of the octagonal table. The situation room was a relatively new addition to *Excelsior*, part of a redesign that Starfleet had begun introducing to many of Starfleet's ships of the line in recent years. Sulu had to admit that for quick bridge-officer meetings, the small chamber was certainly handier than the full-size conference room on Deck Two. Of course, the senior staff still used the larger conference room for more formal meetings, such as the diplomatic proceedings involving Burgess's party and the Tholian contingent; the big room had recently been outfitted with colors and decor calculated by Lieutenant Hopman to calm the Tholian delegates. The violent red-and-ocher color scheme down there made Sulu more grateful than ever to have an alternative space in which to conduct his staff meetings.

"What is the status of our probes?" Sulu asked once Chekov and Tuvok had taken seats that placed the three men at approximately equidistant positions around the table.

Chekov tapped some buttons on the multisided computer console that dominated the table's center. Operating in tandem, the viewscreens immediately displayed star charts overlaid with colored graphics. "The four probe drones we launched last night have been continuously sending subspace telemetry back from deep inside Tholian space. We're using a low-gain channel that our sensors can lock onto and the Tholians' likely can't. Combined with the data gathered by our long-range sensors, we've been able to detect and triangulate on several sectors containing energy signatures from Tholian military operations."

"Anything conclusive on what sort of military operations?" Sulu asked.

"Most of the energy signatures we detected are consistent with starship construction on a massive scale. We have also detected residual readings that could only have been produced by extremely powerful directed-energy weapons."

Sulu nodded. The science officer had confirmed the intelligence report that Sulu had received from Admiral Nogura. But he hadn't yet explained *why* the Tholians were stepping up their military production.

"The most significant fact, in my opinion," Chekov said, "is that almost all of this activity is taking place deep inside Tholian space. Perhaps along their far frontier, away from the Federation border."

"I concur," Tuvok said. "Although the Tholians are clearly developing new weaponry, it is equally evident that the Federation is not their current target."

Sulu leaned forward in his chair and spread his hands across the smooth tabletop. "Is there any evidence that the Tholians have deployed their new weapons in battle as yet?"

Tuvok's eyes widened slightly in the Vulcan equivalent of a shrug. "It is still difficult to know conclusively whether the Tholians have used these weapons in actual firefights, or if we have merely detected evidence of their field tests. However, the profile of the radioactive debris the probes have thus far analyzed suggests that the former explanation is the correct one."

Sulu's finger traced one of the on-screen graphics. "It appears that these sectors are barely mapped."

"Yes, sir," Tuvok said. "And as you can see, they are all concentrated along what may be the far border of Tholian territory, judging from the total absence of Tholian activity evident in the space beyond. No Federation ship has ever visited these regions to confirm this, however. What little information we have about the region is over seventy years old, and may therefore be somewhat unreliable," Tuvok said. "It was recovered from the databanks of an Orion slaveship that was impounded by an Andorian vessel."

"So we're not even certain if these charts are accurate?" Sulu asked.

"We're as certain as we can be at this point, Captain," Chekov said, his pronunciation of Sulu's title—"Keptin"—was still as heavily accented now as it had been for the more than three decades Sulu had known him. "So far, the sensors and probes have confirmed the Orion ship's stellar cartographic information. But there is something else." He tapped the buttons on the table before the screen, causing its images to shift and magnify. He pointed toward a previously unmapped volume of space. "See this region? We've been getting some very strange readings from here."

"Strange in what way?" Sulu wanted to know.

Tuvok spoke up. "The closest analog we've found are the energy signatures characteristic of wormholes. But instead of being a point in space like most wormholes, this phenomenon appears to run laterally through several dozen parsecs of Tholian space, and even extends half a light-year into Federation territory. It is almost as if it were a fissure, or 'rip' in space, rather than a hole."

Sulu and Chekov exchanged a wordless glance. A look of mutual recognition passed between them.

"Interspace," Chekov said, an expression of distaste crossing his saturnine features. Sulu guessed that he was recalling how this same distorted region of space had driven a starship's entire crew into a murderous frenzy. Or perhaps he was remembering how he had briefly been caught in the grip of that very madness himself.

The door chimed, then slid open. Lieutenant Akaar

stepped into the room and at Sulu's gesture took the largest chair, which Sulu had had specially customized for the security chief's tall, broad physique. "Lieutenant Akaar," the captain said. "We were just discussing the strange readings we've recovered from deep inside Tholian space."

Akaar nodded, his expression serious, as it nearly always was. "Commander Chekov and Lieutenant Tuvok have kept me apprised of the situation, Captain. I have been trying to isolate the various energy signatures and debris patterns shown in the telemetry, to ascertain for certain whether they originated from weapons tests, ship-to-ship combat, or from something else. But I have yet to reach any firm conclusion."

"Since you can't offer a conclusion, I'd like your opinion," Sulu said as he leaned back in his chair. He put his hands near his chin, steepling his fingers together.

As uncompromisingly formal as usual, Akaar drew a deep, thoughtful breath before speaking. "The residual energies and debris would seem to point to a conflict. But since some of the readings cannot be matched to known weaponry, my thinking is that the Tholians are facing an adversary unknown to our databanks. Perhaps it is some hostile species from further out in uncharted Tholian space. Or from beyond the Tholian Assembly entirely."

"Maybe they emerged from beyond the interspatial fissure Tuvok was describing," Sulu said. *Creatures from interspace would almost have to be insane by definition,* Sulu thought with an inward shudder.

"That sounds to me like a reasonable assumption," Akaar said. "The hostiles do appear to be associated with the extradimensional rift."

"Regardless of their hypothetical origin point," Tuvok said, arching an eyebrow at Akaar, "we should not immediately conclude that this new species is hostile merely because the Tholians have engaged them in battle. After all, until very recently the Tholians have been adversarial and aggressive during virtually every recorded contact with Federation nationals."

If Akaar was offended by Tuvok's brusque manner, he didn't show it. He merely nodded. Sulu had known Leonard James Akaar since he was a child, and had been partly responsible for getting the physically and mentally precocious Capellan into Starfleet Academy during the lad's hot-headed early teens. Sulu knew well how hard the exiled High Teer of the Ten Tribes of Capella had worked over the years to keep his volatile temper in check.

Akaar's response to Tuvok was slow and deliberate. "The reason it seems logical to think that the aggressors might be someone other than the Tholians," Akaar said, "is that the energy traces are all in *Tholian* territory, as is almost all of the detectable debris. If the Tholians were chasing someone out of the region, most of the debris and energy residue would likely lie beyond their known borders. If these traces are evidence of conflict, it seems very likely that the Tholians received the worst of it."

"Perhaps that's the entire reason they're courting the Federation now," Chekov said. "If the Tholians are facing a foe with more firepower than they have, they may want to strike a military alliance with us. After all, who else can help them now? The Romulans and the Klingons are both too far away for the Tholians to turn to."

Sulu nodded, agreeing that this was certainly a likely scenario. "And even if the Klingons were the Tholians' next-door neighbors, they're still rebuilding their homeworld after the Praxis explosion. They wouldn't be able to spare the resources for a military pact with the Tholians."

"Exactly," Chekov said. "Who besides us might have the strength to help the Tholians drive off a powerful new foe?"

"There is another possibility," Tuvok said, cocking an eyebrow upward. "We know that the Tholian Assembly's technology has not matured at the same rate as has that of many cultures within the Federation."

"Maybe that's the price they pay for being aggressive and xenophobic," Chekov said, almost interrupting. "They're not sharing technology or much of anything else with other societies. Why should anyone share with them?"

Looking almost annoyed by the interjection, Tuvok continued. "Despite the offensive capabilities of the Tholians—including their renowned energy-snares—it seems likely that they may merely want to gain access to more powerful weapons technology than they currently possess. That way, they might fortify their defenses without having to place their trust in an ally. It would certainly fit the overall pattern of xenophobic behavior the Tholians have always exhibited toward humanoid species."

Sulu had already considered that possibility, but had decided he didn't like the direction in which it led him. "Are you suggesting that the Tholian delegation is actually here to *steal* our technology, Mr. Tuvok?"

"Not necessarily, Captain. But it might be prudent to have security watch the delegates extremely closely. They may hope to be . . . 'inspired' by technology they see on the ship."

Sulu looked over at Chekov and Akaar, who seemed to agree. Perhaps Tuvok wasn't merely being paranoid. "All right. Let's postpone the scheduled tour of the engineering section. And I want security to keep the Tholians under close watch."

Tuvok seemed taken aback. "Captain, I trust you're not suggesting that we violate their privileged status as visiting diplomats."

Save me from Vulcan literalism, Sulu thought, watching the horrified expressions on the faces of both Chekov and Akaar. Had any member of his crew other than Tuvok questioned him in this manner, Sulu would have put him on report.

"I didn't say I wanted their rooms bugged, Lieutenant,"

Sulu said. "But I also don't want them scanning our ship's systems, even passively."

"Technology transfer protocols will be in full force, Captain," Chekov said.

"My people will watch them," Akaar said. "Without offending them or interfering with their diplomatic duties, of course. With your permission, I would like to post security crews at or near the diplomatic meetings with the Tholians."

"It would also be a good idea to keep an eye out for incoming Tholian ships," Chekov said. "We don't want to find ourselves suddenly outnumbered out here."

"I agree," said Akaar. "If the Tholian military really does intend to misappropriate our technology, then it might attempt to do so by hijacking *Excelsior.* And what better way to accomplish that than to place its agents aboard in the guise of diplomats?"

Chekov made a sour face. "If that's the case, then the Tholians could easily manufacture some slight in protocol on our part, or even claim we took aggressive action against them. That would give them their pretext to attack us. Starfleet Command would want to retaliate, but the Federation Council might be a lot more cautious if a Tholian attack could somehow be blamed on us."

Sulu nodded gravely. Overcautious though he might be, his old friend was entirely right. "I hate to give so much credence to negative speculation, but it's true that we have no reason to trust the Tholians yet. So let's be on our guard. Implement Class Four security measures, but be *discreet* about them. Only those with an operational need to know should be given the details. And we certainly don't want to involve Ambassador Burgess in any fashion until we absolutely have to."

"Captain, if I may make an observation?" Tuvok asked, though he barely waited for Sulu to blink before forging ahead. "We still have no solid evidence that the Tholians are harboring any hidden agenda against us. And if they are being attacked by an outside force—and are attempting to forge an alliance with the Federation because of that—it would hardly be the first time that such actions have been taken."

"So you're saying that we should keep an open mind toward the Tholians," Sulu said. "I agree. But we have to take all reasonable precautions as well. We have no reason to trust them, and every reason to think that something may be going on out on their frontier that they're trying to conceal from us."

"Yes, sir," Tuvok said, nodding. "Just as we are keeping secret the fact that we have deployed probes into their sovereign space. If they discover this, then they will have no reason to trust us either. In fact, our launch of those drones may give them a legitimate reason to attack us, should they be seeking one."

Though Sulu found Vulcan logic and brainpower an indispensable resource, he had to admit that they could sometimes be annoying. "I'm well aware of that, Lieutenant." Sulu cast a steely glance around the room, then rose to signal that the meeting was now at an end. "Again, gentlemen, all information about *Excelsior*'s surveillance activities is to be distributed strictly on a need-to-know basis. Dismissed."

He wished his orders from Nogura would permit him to explain and justify his actions further. Unfortunately, they didn't.

Alone in her quarters, Burgess was annoyed when one of her aides interrupted her in the midst of recording her journal. Then she saw the message disk in his hand and heard his explanation that it had just been received via subspace burst, directly from the highest levels of the Diplomatic Directorate in the Hague, on Earth.

The message, the aide had said, was for her eyes only.

After settling into a chair, she decrypted and played the message on her terminal. Afterward, she merely stared in numb disbelief at the screen, which had gone blank except for the Federation's Earth-and-olive-branch symbol. It took her several minutes to regain her composure enough to trust her voice not to break. But anger still burned intensely within her.

She rose, crossed to the companel, and pressed the button. "Captain Sulu, this is Aidan Burgess. I need to speak with you. Immediately."

Lieutenant Commander Lojur looked up from his meal of steamed vegetables when he heard the mess hall door open. He smiled as Tuvok and Akaar entered and approached the table.

"I see something's kept you both busy," Lojur said.

Lojur watched as his two laconic friends exchanged blank looks that might have meant anything.

"We were . . . detained," Akaar said finally before moving toward one of the food slots.

Tuvok merely took a seat directly across the table from Lojur, without bothering to get any food for himself. Although the Vulcan always consumed sparingly at lunch, he usually ate or drank *something*.

"Is anything wrong?" Lojur said.

Tuvok raised an eyebrow. "Not at all, Commander." He glanced around the room. Other than Akaar, who stood at the food slot, and the few other officers and other personnel eating and milling about on the other side of the room, they were essentially alone.

"It is unusual for you to have lunch by yourself, is it not?" Tuvok asked.

Lojur smiled. "I'm *not* alone." *My two closest friends are here with me.* A moment later, Akaar took a seat beside Tuvok, his tray weighed down with some sort of gravy-covered pastry.

"Where is Shandra?" Akaar said, speaking carefully before taking a bite of his meal.

"You know my Shandra," Lojur said. "She probably became enmeshed in a conversation on her way down here."

"Let us hope she does not also keep you waiting on the appointed day," Akaar said, allowing a small smile to cross his broad face.

Lojur returned the smile. "I don't think that's a danger. Our wedding is all she talks about."

"Indeed," Tuvok said dryly. "I have noted that your coming nuptials seem to be the primary topic of conversation for both of you."

Before Lojur could reply, the mess hall doors opened again. Lieutenant Shandra Docksey, *Excelsior's* principal helmsman and the love of Lojur's life, strode in. She was followed by Scott Russell, the ship's dapper young head cook. Russell carried a tureen topped by a silver cover.

"Sorry I'm late," Shandra said, kissing Lojur briefly before taking the seat beside him. "But I think you'll forgive me, considering what day it is."

"Day?" Lojur said. Tuvok and Akaar both stared at her blankly, then looked at one another.

"Come *on,* Tuvok. I looked it up, and triple-checked the calendar conversions. There's no mistake."

Lojur felt as confused as Tuvok looked. Then Russell set the bowl down on the table in front of the science officer and removed its gleaming lid. The aroma of steaming orange *plomeek* soup immediately began wafting through the room.

"What a delight to get away from Tholian food," Russell said. "*Plomeek* soup isn't my personal favorite, but at least I don't have to handle it with waldoes."

"Scott made it from my own private stash of *plomeeks,*" Shandra said, grinning at Tuvok, who looked nonplussed, at least for a Vulcan. "It's the real deal, I promise."

"Where did you get fresh *plomeeks,* Lieutenant?" Tuvok asked. "We haven't been to Vulcan in over two years."

"No, but we *did* meet some Vulcan traders on Sigma

Ceti about eight months back. And Dr. Chapel lent me some space in one of the medical stasis chambers. Happy birthday, Tuvok."

What a beautiful soul, Lojur thought, marveling at how the woman he loved never ceased thinking of others. As ever, her smile illuminated his own soul's darkest corners in a way he had never dared hope for.

Rand took a seat at Chapel's table just as Tuvok and Lojur had finished bussing their own table. Rand watched as Lojur and Docksey walked away arm in arm, clearly lost in each other.

"Ah, young love," Chapel said after the four younger officers had departed from the mess hall. The doctor sipped carefully from a mug of black coffee; rumor had it that this particular variety was grown on the Klingon Homeworld, yet another benefit of the Khitomer Accords. "Romance sort of puts a spring in your step, doesn't it, Janice?"

Rand chuckled, regarding her infinitely blander cup of Altair water. "Maybe. But I'll bet it can't compare to your coffee."

Chapel's smile made deep furrows around her eyes, reminding Rand of just how long she had known *Excelsior*'s chief medical officer, and just how far both had come in their respective careers since those early days. "Come on, Janice. Romance is always exhilarating. Even when it's somebody else's."

"Hey, if I weren't so impressed by those two, I wouldn't have agreed to be Shandra's Slave of Honor," Rand said.

Chapel almost did a spit-take with her coffee. "Isn't that *Matron* of Honor?"

"You obviously haven't been dragooned into as many wedding parties as I have, Christine. It's funny, though. I can remember a time when shipboard romances were discouraged."

Chapel shook her head. "Wrong. *Shipboard romances* weren't discouraged. *Our* shipboard romances were discouraged."

Rand laughed and raised her cup. The two old friends clinked their drinking vessels together as though in a toast to the paths best not taken, but only fantasized about.

I just hope Lojur and Docksey have better luck than the kids who tried to get married on the Enterprise, Rand thought after their laughter had subsided. Angela Martine and Robert Tomlinson had barely made it to the altar when a Romulan attack separated them forever. Ever since the Tholians had come aboard, Rand hadn't been able to get either of their young, hopeful faces out of her mind.

Rand set her cup down. "I think I'm going to need something stronger before the diplomatic business starts up again."

The door to Sulu's quarters had just barely closed behind her before Burgess asked, "Just how badly do you want this mission to fail, Captain?"

Sulu took a seat on the sofa and gestured toward a chair. "I'm not sure I know what you mean, Ambassador. Please have a seat and tell me what's on your mind."

Burgess didn't sit, but instead grasped the back of a chair, her knuckles white. It was obvious that she was in a highly agitated state.

"I think you already know what I'm talking about, Captain. What do you think will happen if the Tholians find out that you've sent probe-drones deep inside their territory?"

Sulu attempted to mask his surprise at her question, but wasn't sure he'd done it very well. She had very nearly caught him flat-footed. "What exactly are you talking about, Ambassador?"

Her fingers dug deeper into the upholstery. "Please, Captain. Don't try to be coy about this. You know as well as I do that there are diplomats who know Starfleet business just as there are Starfleet officers who work my side of the street. So I have it on very reliable authority that you have been ordered to spy on the Tholians at the same time I'm trying to negotiate with them."

Sulu knew that she might not really know anything of the sort. It was possible that she was only fishing. On the other hand, it wasn't inconceivable that someone close to Admiral Nogura had intentionally leaked word of Sulu's covert surveillance mission to some member of the diplomatic corps. Especially if the tension between Starfleet's brass and the Federation Council was really getting to be as bad as Sulu feared.

"All right, Ambassador. Please sit down." Still seated on the sofa, he stared at her until she complied. He considered offering her something to drink, but her serious demeanor made it clear that creature comforts were not uppermost on her mind at the moment.

"I'd appreciate it if you'd share with me *exactly* what you've been told about *Excelsior*'s mission vis à vis the Tholians," Sulu said.

She eyed him with evident suspicion. "That hardly seems fair, Captain. After all, I have no reason to expect that you'd be as forthcoming with me about any covert assignment you might have. Especially if Starfleet Command wants it kept secret."

Sulu chuckled. Until this moment, he had entertained the faint hope that Burgess might provide him with new intelligence about the Tholians, information that might help him interpret the data still coming aboard via *Excelsior*'s long-range sensors and probe drones. "Fair enough, Ambassador. So where does that leave us?"

"Still on the same side, I would hope. On the side of peace."

"I'm relieved to hear you say that," Sulu said. "But I'd say that peace depends largely upon what the Tholians decide to do. After all, it takes two sides to fight a war."

"Just as it takes two sides to wage peace," she said, nodding.

"You'll get no argument from me there. But you know how difficult it can be to create a lasting peace. Especially when there's already so much suspicion on both sides." *Unfortunately, Ambassador, that's as candid as I can afford to be with you right now,* he thought with a twinge of genuine regret. He didn't enjoy having to spy on a potential ally any better than she evidently did. But he also wasn't sanguine about giving a species whose warrior caste had once tried to kill him a potential opportunity to attack the Federation. Starfleet simply *had* to discover the reasons behind the Tholian military buildup. It was, at least potentially, a matter of survival.

Burgess rose, evidently sensing that he wouldn't—or couldn't—take her any further into his confidence than he had already. But she seemed anything but defeated. Her green eyes flashed like a pair of warp cores.

"Granted, Captain. Suspicion *is* a difficult beast to tame. You may have more of a gift for diplomacy than I'd given you credit for."

"Thank you," he said, surprised by the compliment.

Burgess continued. "So I'm sure you'll bear in mind that the Tholians' next actions will no doubt be greatly influenced by whatever they may discover about *your* activities here, in their sovereign space. If you *are* spying on them, Captain—and if they catch you at it—you could very well touch off a war."

Sulu bristled at that. "That's a lot of 'ifs,' Ambassador."

"Good diplomacy is largely about managing contingencies," she said, her emotions now seeming to be under far better control than they had been when she'd first come in. "And one of the contingencies I now must plan for is the possibility of a tragic error on Starfleet's part. A mistake that may frighten the Tholians back into belligerency and isolation."

Sulu was growing weary of the ambassador's Starfleet-as-the-villain perspective. He considered pointing out that some of the most accomplished diplomats in Federation history had begun their careers in Starfleet. Then he decided that his life's work, and the ideals it embodied, needed no defense. It was time to turn the tables.

"The outbreak of war is often seen as a failure of diplomacy, Ambassador," Sulu said.

She paused as if to consider his words. If they roused her anger, she concealed it well. Finally, she said, "If diplomacy fails because of the actions of the warriors, Captain, then whose failure is it, really?"

And with that, she crossed to the door and departed, leaving Sulu alone with his growing misgivings about the prospects for peace with the Tholians—and with Burgess.

She's on the same side I am, he reminded himself. *But the Tholians are definitely hiding something, whether she wants to face that or not.*

Chapter 4

Aidan Burgess carefully unlocked the purple bicycle which was chained to a post in the cramped alleyway between the townhouses. She made sure that it didn't clink as she laid it on the ground in the darkness. Since it was summer, the windows to her parent's bedroom were open, and she knew that Mama Maére and Mama Diana would punish her if they knew she was sneaking out this late.

But Aidan was ten years old, and there were lots of things she did that were secret. She had been coming out at night for two weeks now, pushing her bicycle up the steep incline of San Francisco's Lombard Street, and coasting on it all the way back down the other side. The first time, she had just wanted to see what the city looked like after everyone else had gone to bed.

The second night, she had ventured all the way out westward to Golden Gate Park, and had seen two people sleeping there, in bedrolls, under the stars. She watched them from a distance for a while, then crept closer. Eventually, one of them, a girl in her late teens, spoke to her.

Ever since then, Aidan had returned to the park nightly to have conversations with her new friends, Lynna and Cal. They were traveling across the country, seeing the sights, exploring the world around them. They had little that they took with them, but people took care of them along the way. Sometimes their benefactors were fellow travelers, sometimes they were locals.

Lynna and Cal told Aidan all about their adventures, good and bad. A few spots in North America, they'd said, still hadn't been put quite right after World War III, and that had happened over two hundred years ago. And while some areas had rebuilt their sprawl of cities, other sections of the country—just like here in the San Francisco Bay Area—had reverted to a greener, more natural state as portions of Earth's population traveled to the stars.

Aidan wanted to accompany them as they explored the country, but they told her it wasn't right, it wasn't her time. When she was older, she could make such decisions about her life. She could explore the world, meet people, perhaps even join Starfleet and see the galaxy. But for now, she had to be content with listening to her new friends' stories of life on the road.

One warm summer night, Aidan rode up to the usual meeting spot, but found that the sleeping bags and packs were gone. Lynna and Cal were missing as well. Aidan called for them, but no one answered. She sat in the grass where they had always sat together, and waited. Eventually, she decided she had to go home. But as she turned to go back to her bike, something at the base of a nearby tree caught her eye.

The small package had a piece of paper with her name on it, and the words "fellow traveler" written underneath. She opened the package to find a bracelet inside. Holding it up in the moonlight, she saw that it wasn't a fancy one made of metal, but was instead constructed of multicolored strings. None of the stones—which were strung like beads on the bracelet—matched. But Aidan knew that each one came with a story. Lynna and Cal had picked up the rocks on their travels—turquoise in Montana, an agate from somewhere in the Southwest, polished conch shell from the Florida Gulf

Coast, an Oregon sunstone—and Lynna had carried them with her in a sack.

Aidan came back to the park the following night, and the night after that, and the night after that. Each time, she wore the bracelet left for her by Lynna and Cal.

One day, Aidan's mothers took her to the beach, and she found some small seashells in the wet sand. Mama Diana went swimming in the ocean, and emerged with some seaweed or kelp draped atop her head. Aidan threaded two of the small shells onto her bracelet that evening, and vowed to remember the story about her day at the beach when she saw Lynna and Cal again.

Ten years later, Aidan Burgess had more stories to tell if she ever ran into her friends from the park again. She knew it wasn't likely, but stranger things had happened. Her explorations of the world had shown her that.

She and her fiancé, Ramon Escovarre, had come to the rainforests of the Amazon a few weeks earlier. Those forests had flourished during the two centuries following World War III. Now that the miners, factory farmers, and loggers were gone, most of the land was green again. There was little to explore here that technology had not laid bare in some fashion, though; sensor sweeps and mapping had shown exactly how many neo-hunter-gatherer tribes now lived within the jungles.

Although most of the tribes had frequent visitors from the outside world, many of them lived in relative isolation. The concept fascinated both Aidan and Ramon, the notion that there were humans living, loving, and thriving on Earth who had deliberately absented themselves from modern culture and technology.

So they had embarked on this journey of exploration, bringing with them as little of the outside world as possible. They had communicators and transponder tags, just in case of emergency; should they need medical aid, they could quickly be beamed or shuttled to safety. But they had debated whether or not to bring a universal translator and a hand-phaser. Finally, they had agreed to bring both, but remained determined to use them only in the direst of emergencies.

On the tenth day, Aidan could feel other presences in the trees and shadows around them. They were being watched, studied, measured, scrutinized . . . She called out to them numerous times, but an answer did not immediately come.

That night a response came, as shadowy forms approached from outside their encampment. Ramon saw them first, past the flickering flames of their small campfire. And then Aidan saw them, too. They were nearly naked, with dark skin and even darker hair. Aidan motioned them closer slowly, proffering the hand signs she had learned from explorers who had visited other indigenous tribes.

The tribespeople left later that night, but were back again in the morning. They led Aidan and Ramon to a village, where more of the natives viewed them with wide, curious eyes. Aidan allowed them to prod and touch her, feeling her clothing and her skin and her hair.

The natives maintained a communal house in the middle of the village, which Ramon identified as a *shabono*, of the type used by the Yanomami tribe. Whether or not these people were part of that tribe was unclear, but the geographical location of the village made it distinctly possible.

Over the following days, Aidan grew extraordinarily close to the aboriginal tribe. She never needed to use the universal translator, since she was quickly picking up bits and pieces of the tribe's language and customs. She listened to their stories, to their history, to their gossip, to their hopes, and to their fears. They knew of the world beyond them, and some had even departed to explore it, but most chose to stay safely within the bosom of their tribe.

One day, as Aidan was at the river with the other women, a great outcry came from the village. Two of the men—and

Ramon—had been mauled by a pair of jaguars who were intent on stealing the red brocket deer the men had brought down for food. By the time Aidan and the others reached the village, one of the wounded hunters had died.

Ramon and the other man were stable, but by nightfall, they were feverish. Although the decision caused her almost physical pain, Aidan used her communicator and activated an emergency beacon. She explained to the tribespeople that she had to get medical attention for Ramon, but they argued that their ancestral medicines were adequate to heal him.

Aidan wasn't willing to take the chance. She offered to help get the other injured man to safety, but he refused, staying with his family and his tribe. Weeping, Aidan gathered up all the things which she and Ramon had brought into the village and repacked them. Moments before the Federation Forest Service shuttle beamed them to safety, she took the bracelet off her wrist and untied a knot.

Removing one of the two timeworn seashells she had gathered as a child, Aidan knelt and gave it to Omëbe, the sturdily built little girl who had always paid the most attention to Aidan's stories of exploration. Aidan smiled as she closed the little girl's hand over the tiny shell, then hugged her. As she stepped away, she saw tears in Omëbe's dark eyes. Then the golden beam of the transporter took Aidan away.

She never found out if the villager had died from his wounds, or if the ancient tribal remedies had saved him. She never learned what became of Omëbe, but she hoped that the girl might one day explore the world herself.

Over the next thirty years, Aidan had changed. Her marriage to Ramon hadn't lasted long, and she had found a new calling, working her way up the ladder through the Federation's diplomatic service, discovering as she did so that the exploration of new cultures and new civilizations always brought her back to the things she loved.

She eventually remarried, but Shinzei, her beloved husband, was by now a decade dead, and she had been alone ever since his passing. Her parents were now both long gone. She had no forebears and no children. Her legacy was her work, and of late, even that was wanting.

During her college years, she had come to despise the militarism that Starfleet represented. Now, as the century counted down ponderously toward its end, she wondered if too many years spent working alongside that blunt military instrument had hardened her, turned her bitter. She wondered how any diplomat could accomplish anything of lasting value in Starfleet's heavily armed shadow.

Am I just marking time until the end of history, when the Federation—in all its well-intentioned beneficence—finally engulfs and devours every other technological society in the galaxy?

In her guest quarters aboard *Excelsior*, Aidan Burgess unpacked a special box. There, atop a velvet lining of deep indigo, lay the bracelet she had gotten as a child. Beneath the top layer of cloth was a collection of dozens of stones, bones, and shells, representing every planet she had visited.

Burgess held the bracelet up and moved to the mirror. Looking through her beloved keepsake, she stared at her reflection. She looked at her image and tried to find a glimmer of the girl from the park, or the woman from the rainforest, or the accomplished diplomat who had brokered momentous peace agreements on Epsilon Canaris III and Dreyzen.

But she could see no sign of them.

All she saw was a tired, bitter woman who had lost her dreams of exploration to a system of rules and regulations that too often seemed to value conflict over peace.

She closed her eyes, wishing she could break the rules and ride her purple bicycle off to adventure once again.

Then she came to a decision.

* * *

A low-pitched chime announced her arrival at the door to the special reception area on Deck Eight that was still human-compatible. A narrow walkway, kept separate from the adjacent Tholian-friendly environment by a complex series of interleaved forcefields—their boundaries tinted orange so as to be easily visible—ringed a portion of the room. Although the gravity and atmosphere within this walkway were kept to M-class specifications, the oppressive heat from the artificially maintained Tholian atmosphere was stifling. Burgess hadn't been anywhere this hot since the rainforest.

The Tholians were, of course, out of the environment suits they had worn when they'd first beamed aboard. Their scant clothing—chiefly flowing, bannerlike triangles of Tholian silk or some similarly tough fiber—seemed to exist purely for adornment's sake. Their large, polygonal heads were composed of numerous triangular and pentagonal shapes. Their six-limbed, moist-but-hard-looking bodies were all planes and angles, colored in every shade of gold, red, green, and white. However, the light refraction caused by the hot, high-pressure Tholian atmosphere and the surrounding containment forcefields made their actual hues difficult to determine.

Just like humans, Burgess thought, *these people can be judged only in terms of their own environment and experiences.*

She touched the small vocoder she wore around her neck and called out to a Tholian who was diligently engaging three of his insectoid limbs in some repetitive task over a blocky, crystalline machine; Burgess surmised that he was typing up a report. "Junior Ambassador Mosrene. I greet you in friendship."

"As I receive you," Mosrene said, clambering toward her on his lower four appendages. "What purpose does your visit serve?"

"I wish to speak to Admiral Yilskene. Please contact him for me."

Mosrene cocked his polyhedral head to one side, rotating it oddly. "You cannot contact him yourself?"

"I don't believe it is wise for me to do so," Burgess said. If Sulu's crew intercepted her message, they might cut her off before she'd had her say. The captain might even have her arrested. *He might do that anyway.*

Moments later, an apparently bewildered Mosrene had dragged a large viewscreen-communication device—apparently hewn from some sort of stone—closer to the forcefield, and keyed in the codes for contacting Yilskene's flagship. The screen quickly produced an image of both Yilskene—whom she had not yet met face to face—and Ambassador Kasrene, who had evidently returned to the flagship to confer with the admiral for some reason or other.

Swallowing hard, Burgess cleared her throat and said, "Admiral Yilskene, Ambassador Kasrene, I believe that only an honest and truthful exchange will help our peoples reach an accord."

Because of their lack of easily readable facial expressions, Burgess had trouble fathoming the emotions of the pair. Still, she thought their body language suggested intense interest.

"We concur on this," Kasrene chorused in reply.

Burgess took a deep breath. "Then in the interests of honesty, truth, and peace, I must tell you something that I know you will find greatly disturbing. . . ."

Chapter 5

In the near-darkness, Lieutenant Tuvok could feel the calm that had been slipping away from him ever more frequently over the past several days. The ritual candles that burned before him—the room's only illumination—gave his spartan quarters a warm glow.

Tuvok sat cross-legged on his meditation mat on the floor, his tunic and high-collared turtleneck laid carefully on his bed. His boots lay beside the bed. Shirtless and shoeless, he could feel even the slightest whisper of air in his room. Wriggling his toes, unfettered by footwear, was an indulgence for him, one of the few he allowed himself.

On the low table in front of him was a *keethara,* with many of its component blocks laying about nearby. He had begun assembling this particular "structure of harmony" two weeks prior, and had worked on it during each of his daily meditation sessions. Today it still remained unfinished. Each new block he added seemed unharmonious.

The purpose of the blocks was to focus his thoughts and help him to hone his mental control. Instead, they were causing him anxiety and frustration. *No. The* keethara *blocks are not the cause of my concern.*

His emotions had been building in intensity for some time now. More and more he felt tainted by the emotions of his crewmates. It had always been so, even from his first day at Starfleet Academy. With cold, dispassionate logic, he could fathom the most complex scientific questions; he had excelled in his studies, most especially the tactical sciences. But he could never understand—or perhaps allow himself to comprehend—the emotional attitudes of his teachers and fellow classmates.

Upon graduation, Tuvok had been assigned to the *U.S.S. Excelsior*, just four years after entering Starfleet Academy. Prior to embarking on this posting, Tuvok had consulted with his most trusted teacher and advisor, a middle-aged Vulcan named Xon. Professor Xon had confided to him that life aboard a starship full of emotional beings could be extremely difficult, especially if one was the only Vulcan among them.

Tuvok had had no problem believing Xon's words then. After all these years, he was still inclined to agree with them.

Though five years had passed since he had lodged his protest against Captain Sulu's ill-advised attempt to rescue a pair of colleagues during the Khitomer crisis, Tuvok remained bothered by the capricious emotions that so often seemed to guide the conduct of *Excelsior*'s captain and crew. Even with the current mission, Tuvok sensed that both Captain Sulu and Ambassador Burgess were basing their decisions regarding the Tholians mostly on what humans liked to refer to as their "gut instincts." The dispassionate logic that so often provided the key to survival in a chaotic universe was, as usual, being given short shrift by humans.

Tuvok carefully picked up a *keethara* block and held it over a section of the small structure on the table. He knew he could not blame his difficulties with human emotions entirely on his crewmates; it had been a part of him since his earliest days. Though he had been called brilliant as a child, his penchant for constantly questioning his teachers had exceeded the expected norms. More than once, his instructors had tried to impress upon him the importance of occasionally simply accepting their experience, erudition, and authority. Instead, he had responded with volleys of interrogatives that had bordered on insubordinate. And yet, despite his alleged deficiencies in tact, Tuvok had remained convinced that his questioning spirit was logical. How could the teachers have allowed themselves to react so emotionally to it?

Then, at the age of nine, Tuvok first grappled with his own emotional demons. And they had almost destroyed him.

Returning home from the primary seminary, young Tuvok was faced with bad news from his father, Sunak. The family *sehlat*, Wari, had stumbled into the path of a ground car. "Her injuries were too severe to be repaired," Sunak had told him in measured tones. "She had to be euthanized."

Tuvok felt pain stab into him, an agony unlike any he had ever felt before. Wari had been his pet all his life; she was older than he was, and had treated him like one of her own cubs as far back as he could remember. He used to hold onto her fangs and she would shake him gently from side to side. Sometimes, he had slept curled up next to her, warmed on desert winter nights by her thick covering of russet-colored fur.

Now, she was gone. His parents had already made plans to dispose of her body, but he had screamed until they allowed him to see his pet's corpse. T'Meni, his mother, had stood nearby as Tuvok ruffled Wari's fur and stroked her ears, unmindful of the verdant blood that matted it in spots.

Tuvok had squatted low, on the same level with Wari's lifeless head, and pried open her eyelids. The eyes were dark and glassy. "It's not here," he said, sobbing.

"What are you looking for?" his mother asked, her voice steady and emotionless.

"Wari's *katra*."

Sunak had come into the yard, and spoke then. "Wari did not have a *katra*. Animals are without *katra*."

Tuvok heard his father's words as a betrayal. He knew what he felt from Wari. She had loved him without reservation, in a way that he had never felt even from his own parents. She had protected him, played with him, touched him, cared for him.

"If Wari does not have a *katra*, then neither do either of *you!*" Tuvok screamed, tears scalding his cheeks. He hugged the *sehlat*'s head tightly.

T'Meni crouched, lowering one knee to the ground so that she could look Tuvok in the eye. "That isn't logical, Tuvok." She folded her arms and looked at him serenely, as if the truth of her statement was obvious.

Irrationally, Tuvok wanted her to hold him, to feel his mother and father embrace him the same way his pet so often had, to protect him and soothe away his pain. But she wouldn't. That was not the Vulcan way.

His hand clutching a few long hairs from Wari's coat, Tuvok ran out of the yard, pushing past his father. That night, with Vulcan's co-orbital world of T'Khut dominating the sky, he stole out of their home with a pack full of provisions and a thin, curved knife. The ritual blade—a *sessilent*—was his father's.

Tuvok had gone on a ten-day-long *Kahs-wan* ordeal when he was seven, but as he departed through the ceremonial grounds of ShiKahr and eastward toward the punishing heat of the Plains of Gol, he knew that ten days would not be enough to heal him. Now he was embarking on the ritual of *tal'oth*, making his way over the desiccated wasteland of Vulcan's Forge, across the jagged mountains that marked its eastern boundary. And back, if the gods willed it so.

Four months later, Tuvok returned to his home, slightly taller and much thinner than when he had departed. He spoke to no one of his journeys, except to tell his mother that he had learned to grow orchids in the parched desert, where no flowering plant should have been able to thrive.

But during his ordeal, Tuvok had forced himself to purge

the emotions he had felt. By ridding his mind of the need for affection, of the pride in his accomplishments, and of the sense of loss that had come with Wari's passing, Tuvok believed that he had come to feel nothing at all, other than the spiritual exultation of dispassionate, affect-free logic.

Over the following years, his path toward *Kolinahr* was interrupted again. At sixteen, he fell in love with a visiting Terellian girl named Jara, and his infatuation had almost consumed him. Another trip across the desert wastes—and months spent under the tutelage of a Vulcan Master—helped Tuvok to extirpate his emotions yet again.

Since that time, as he'd left adolescence and entered adulthood, Tuvok became better able to master and suppress his emotions, to channel his mind's energies into the pursuit of knowledge and the exploration of logic. He had entered Starfleet only at the urging of his parents, and his decision to bow to their will had led him inexorably here, now, to this ship so filled with self-contradictory emotion.

In a few weeks, his original five-year assignment aboard the *Excelsior* would be completed. If not for the persuasion of T'Meni and Sunak, who had believed that exposing their son to non-Vulcan cultures would prove beneficial to him, Tuvok would have resigned his commission and returned to Vulcan immediately after the Praxis-Khitomer affair had concluded. But now that he had fulfilled his promise to his parents to finish out his *Excelsior* posting, he saw that things weren't quite so simple. Now that he was a valued senior officer, loyal to his captain and his shipmates, he truly didn't know if he wanted to stay aboard the ship, accept another assignment with Starfleet—or perhaps pursue an altogether different path.

Staring at the *keethara* block he still held in his hand, Tuvok wondered idly if the meditation aid was attempting to tell him something. A *keethara* structure was supposed to reflect the state of its creator's mind. *I have been unable to build a cohesive structure from these blocks. Does this then mean that I cannot guide my life in a cohesive fashion either? Have the emotions so rampant aboard this ship* infected *me to such an extent?*

A computer chime interrupted his reverie, signaling that it was nearly time for him to attend another Tholian diplomatic function. As he put the block down on the table amongst a jumble of others, he knew only one thing with certainty: *If I remain aboard this ship, whatever serenity I have worked to acquire could be lost.*

And if that occurs, I will *fall prey to emotions.*

The voices of the diplomats droned on across the red-hued conference room under the watchful eyes of Lieutenant Akaar and his discreet security contingent. Sulu sat in the back of the room, studying the Tholians closely. Back when he had first encountered them, Sulu had only seen Commander Loskene on the bridge viewer. There had been much debate afterward about whether the multifaceted image they had seen had been a helmet, or the Tholian's actual head. Because their features were obscured by their bulky environment suits, Sulu still wasn't completely sure.

But from the conversations and negotiations that had unfolded so far today, Sulu had come to understand a number of things about the alien race. Biologically, they were almost living mineral formations. Their cells were mostly crystalline, although they must also have contained fluid media in order to carry out metabolic processes. Their skins appeared to be faceted, and each Tholian he had seen so far—whether through the faceplate of an enviro-suit or from behind an environmental forcefield—seemed to bear a unique color scheme. Like humans and their almost infinitely varying colorations of hair, eye, and skin, so too did the Tholians possess an apparently endlessly variegated array of tones.

For a fleeting moment, Sulu managed to forget that the

Tholians might represent a potential threat. Watching their utterly inhuman shapes and movements, he recalled the wonder and anticipation with which he had anticipated such encounters during his childhood. It felt wonderful to be free of fear and suspicion, if only for an instant. *They're so different,* he thought, exultant. *So exotic. Meeting creatures like this is what being in Starfleet is supposed to be about.*

The Tholians all wore their protective amber-colored enviro-suits, garments fashioned from the same Tholian silk from which Ambassador Burgess's special gown had been made. The Tholians' suits were cool to the touch on the outside, but Ambassador Kasrene had explained that they were broilingly hot internally. The atmosphere on their home world was caustic and superheated, almost like that of Venus. Since nitrogen, oxygen, and the cool temperatures characteristic of class-M environments were deadly to the Tholians, the suits were an absolute necessity on occasions in which humans and Tholians needed to mill about together in the same environment.

Even more peculiar than their biology, though, was Kasrene's explanation of the social structure on Tholia. The lifespan of a Tholian was generally six to eight months from birth to maturation to natural death. Their knowledge could be shared from one to another, and from generation to generation, in a process which seemed roughly analogous to a "crystal memory upload." This allowed the newly matured Tholians to continue the work and lives of their predecessors, with only a minimal amount of learning having to be accomplished by means of the old-fashioned trial-and-error method.

Maybe their short lives explain why they're such clockwatchers, Sulu thought, recalling Spock's observations about the Tholians' famed punctuality.

Responding to a question from Dr. Chapel, Kasrene explained that although memories were shared between generations or familial structures, the process did not quite create a "hive mind," since each Tholian chose the individuals with whom he would share his memories. There was a kind of shared memory archive for their species known as "the Lattice," but it contained more general, species-specific knowledge and history, and operated on an almost instinctual level.

According to Kasrene, the Tholians were not the only intelligent species on their world, though they were the dominant one. Their starfaring capabilities, though decades less advanced than those of the Federation by some accounts, still made them the only major interstellar player for several sectors in every direction.

Except, of course, for whomever they're fighting with near that interspatial fissure, Sulu thought.

His attention was drawn away from his reverie by the fidgeting of Mosrene, a Tholian junior ambassador. Something was clearly bothering him, and his body language was betraying it. Sulu noted that none of the other three diplomatic-caste Tholians appeared similarly twitchy; they seemed calm enough that for all Sulu knew, they might have been lulled to sleep by the proceedings. But Mosrene's tail switched, and his forelegs tapped intermittently against the tabletop. *He's never going to make it past junior ambassador if he doesn't learn some self-control,* Sulu thought, mentally smiling while his face showed only rapt attention.

Sulu noticed that next to Burgess, Tuvok was displaying the most intense interest in the proceedings. Doubtless his Vulcan nature—and his curiosity as a science officer—were keeping him enthralled. Kasrene began talking about the rigid caste systems on her planet. Most castes were generationally mandated, though rare intercaste unions allowed for some crossovers in the offspring. Among the more prominent castes were the warriors, like Yilskene, who had yet to leave his flagship; the politicals, who ran the machinery of government back on Tholia and throughout her subject territories; and the diplomats, like Kasrene and Mosrene, whose mission seemed to be to keep the warriors, politicals, other castes, and neighboring species sufficiently mollified to prevent the sectors bordering the Tholian Assembly from plunging headlong into war.

Sulu was surprised to hear that scientists, engineers, and mathematicians numbered among the lower castes. He wondered if this might at least partially explain why the development of Tholian technology was so slow in comparison with the Federation.

The door chimed, and Sulu saw Akaar move toward it. It opened, revealing Chekov and Rand standing in the threshold. Chekov, looking as though he'd just seen a ghost, stood in silence while Rand whispered in low tones to Akaar. Sulu saw Akaar stiffen slightly, and watched a frown cross his features. Akaar let out a quick breath, then moved swiftly in Sulu's direction. In a few terse, whispered syllables, the huge Capellan relayed Rand's message to him.

Sulu stood, feeling numb. Though the news shocked him, he did his best to reveal nothing with his facial expression or body language, though he doubted the Tholians could interpret either. As he moved toward the door, he noticed Ambassador Burgess turning her head toward him.

"Is something wrong, Captain?" she said, an expectant look on her face.

His eyes narrowed as he tried to read her neutral expression. *You know damned well that something's wrong. Because you're more than likely the cause of it.*

Noting that Kasrene and Mosrene were also apparently looking toward him, Sulu said, "I'm afraid that a rather urgent matter has come up that requires my immediate attention. Please excuse me."

He had taken another three steps toward Chekov and Rand before Ambassador Kasrene spoke up, stopping him in his tracks. "Captain, I believe I understand the nature of this 'urgent matter.' It is the fact that Admiral Yilskene has intercepted and destroyed all four of your probes. Is this not so?"

Sulu stood near the door, glancing significantly at Chekov. *Burgess* did *tell them,* he thought. At least, she must have told them of her suspicions. Looking around the room, he took in Akaar's slightly bulging eyes, Tuvok's raised eyebrow, and the blanched features of Chapel, Chekov, and Rand.

"We did indeed launch sensor drones deep into your territory," Sulu said to Kasrene, staying as close to the truth as he deemed prudent. "We've observed some fascinating interspatial phenomena out here."

"No doubt, Captain. And perhaps you're also concerned about what this revelation may mean to our negotiations here," Kasrene said. "Truthfully, after we were informed of the probes last cycle by Ambassador Burgess, we had many discussions as to the proper course of action to take."

Sulu strained not to give Burgess a withering glance. *She and I are going to go 'round and 'round over this later.*

Kasrene tilted her ungainly head slightly to one side. "Doubtless you'll justify these actions based upon your previous encounter with our species, even though that was twenty-four of our generations ago."

"Starfleet has had almost no contact with Tholians since that time," Sulu said. "We're trying to keep our minds open."

Finally, Kasrene spoke again. "Very good, Captain. Though you had no reason to expect that we would react well to your actions, you risked your well-being in the pursuit of pure knowledge. You've shown wonderful initiative. I admire that. *We* admire that. Doubtless your probes showed—"

Kasrene was interrupted by a tap on the forearm by Mosrene, and she ceased speaking. The group of Tholians all reached out and touched for a moment, and went silent.

Sulu realized that they were communicating using their limited telepathic abilities; therefore there was no way to determine what they were saying to one another. As he looked around the room, he saw tension etched onto everyone's faces. Even Tuvok's normally placid expression showed some concern. They were all standing on the precipice of war, and their potential enemies sat in front of them, silent but for the gentle rustling of their enviro-suits. Kasrene was moving the most, apparently agitated.

Sulu shot a quick glance at Rand, who was still standing near the door, awaiting orders. Flicking his eyes to one side, he signaled for her to return to the bridge. He knew that she would put the ship on a silent yellow alert, calling all personnel to their stations. She wouldn't raise shields or charge weapons yet, but she would be ready to do so at a moment's notice if Yilskene's flagship were to power up its weaponry.

Returning his gaze to those still in the room, Sulu caught Burgess looking at him for a moment. But she averted her gaze before he could sustain the eye contact. *If we survive this, I will make* certain *you're cashiered out of the diplomatic service.*

Finally, the Tholians broke their huddle, three of them settling back into their outsize chairs. Mosrene still seemed agitated as Kasrene swiveled her multifaceted head back to face both Sulu and Burgess.

"As I was saying, Captain—"

Mosrene touched Kasrene's arm again, but she brushed him aside and ignored him. "Doubtless your probes showed that there has been conflict along the far boundaries of our territory. I suspect that while your past dealings with us give you little reason to trust my word, your actions at this time give us little reason to trust *you*. However, we feel it is—"

Mosrene interrupted her again with another touch. Kasrene swiveled her head toward him, her eyespots glowing slightly brighter. She uttered a multisyllable word that the universal translator didn't quite parse. *No need*. Sulu could recognize an exclamation of "shut up!" in any language.

Kasrene spoke again, addressing the rest of the room. "The outer reaches of Tholian Assembly space have been under relatively sustained attack for the last seven of your months. This is one of the reasons why we chose this time to approach the Federation, despite the dissension this matter has caused within the chambers of our Castemoot. However, we recently captured one of the aggressor's ships. Members of our medical caste subsequently discovered that—"

Mosrene again moved forward, but this time he was more aggressive with his interruption. Rather than grabbing Kasrene's arm, he reached around her, grabbing at the area which would have been equivalent to a humanoid's upper chest.

Kasrene let out a slight squawk as Mosrene moved his gloved limb away from the ambassador's chest. A hair-thin, crystalline-hafted blade was now visible protruding from the front of Kasrene's enviro-suit. Instantly, the noxious fumes from within the compromised suit began to hiss outward into the surrounding air. Dark smoke began to roll outward from the incision.

It took Sulu about half a second to realize that Mosrene had just assaulted Kasrene, perhaps fatally.

PART 2

CASTAWAYS

Chapter 6

Thursday, 1 May 2053

Even with the computers enhancing every incoming signal, chaos and static ruled the entire radio spectrum, from the long wavelengths all the way up into the near microwave band.

There's no way this can be good, Zafirah al-Arif thought, brushing a hank of jet black hair away from her eyes.

The sounds of radio static receded into the background, like the eternal presence of a distant ocean. Zafirah's throat went dry as she watched the blue world on the small monitor she had tied into the Vanguard colony's largest optical telescope.

"Please tell me this isn't what it looks like," she said, turning toward Kerwin McNolan.

The russet-haired Irishman crossed Zafirah's cramped office to get a better look at the small monitor that sat on her jumbled desktop. He abruptly turned two shades whiter than usual, his unlined face a mask of disbelief.

Disbelief, Zafirah realized, but not surprise. She knew that a goodly plurality of Vanguard's 844 permanent residents were fairly apolitical types, mostly engineers, EV construction jockeys, and science-oriented academics.

But she also knew that almost everyone living inside the

massive O'Neill colony—nestled beneath the skin of a near-Earth stone-and-nickel-iron asteroid—had seen today's events coming for years. Nobody who had so much as glanced at the recent headlines beamed from Earth could be surprised by the drama now unfolding far below.

McNolan's thoughts seemed to echo her own. "My God," he said, his rough voice choked with uncharacteristic emotion. "They've finally done it. Those crazy bastards have finally done it." Looking revolted, the diminutive engineer shoved the slender monitor up against the wall as though it harbored a deadly bacillus. He looked away when the image on the screen persisted.

Zafirah wanted to look away as well. But she found it difficult to tear her gaze from the almost stately procession of city-sized white blossoms that was lighting up the Earth's night side. Absurdly, it reminded her of a garish electrical parade she had seen at an amusement park in the European Union during her childhood. Particularly arresting were the towering orange mushroom clouds and columns of gray ash that had begun to rise and spread themselves along the planet's terminator.

Dawn was breaking across India, Pakistan, and the Gulf of Oman. Soon daylight would fall upon the remaining Eastern Coalition nations—and would reveal how much or how little was left of Zafirah's native Arabian Peninsula. Tears came when she thought of Sabih and his huge, dark eyes. And little Kalil, who was always so curious, so trusting. She hoped that death would not linger when it came for them.

This may be the last new day the human race ever sees.

Along with its deadly freight of thermal energy, neutrons, X rays, gamma rays, and an irresistible blast wave, the detonation of a high-yield nuclear device unleashes something else: a fierce electromagnetic pulse that can scramble every electronic device—from radio transceivers to computers to the electronic ignition systems of automobiles, planes, and hovercars—within dozens of kilometers of Ground Zero.

Detonate scores of such devices simultaneously across every inhabited continent and the effects quickly engulf the planet. Hundreds of spots on the Earth's surface briefly become hotter than the Sun's photosphere, and the world-girdling electronic noosphere that comprises twenty-first-century global civilization abruptly crashes. Like a human being whose head is suddenly perforated by a high-powered rifle round, a world can die without even knowing what had hit it.

But Zafirah was also grimly aware that such a neat, tidy death would come only to a relative few. *The lucky ones*, she thought. *Kalil and Sabih are among those blessed few,* Inshallah.

If Allah wills.

Certainty was steadily growing within Zafirah that she had just witnessed the suicide of humanity's emerging global culture. But even if every human being on Earth had been instantly exterminated—an unlikely eventuality, even in a full-scale nuclear exchange—she knew that Vanguard was home to 844 of the best and brightest individuals that *H. sapiens* had ever produced. And there were five other L-5 colonies whose people and resources could also be brought to bear on the problem of saving whatever remained of Earth's civilization. After all, Earth's industries had for years depended upon the L-5 colonies' labs and factories for a good number of modern necessities, from genetically engineered pharmaceuticals and crops to ultrastrong nanotube construction materials that could be created only in microgravity environments, to the exotic subatomic particles that promised mankind the eventual conquest of the stars.

Fortunately, the electromagnetic blast that had silenced Earth was confined to the planet's atmosphere. Here in space—inside an asteroid orbiting a Lagrange point that stayed perpetually some 383,000 kilometers from both the Earth and the Moon—the pulse could not reach.

Simultaneously haunted and buoyed by these thoughts, Zafirah ran alongside McNolan into the lift, which swiftly rose forty-six levels. She felt their weight decline to nearly nothing as the lift progressed toward the asteroid colony's core, the region least affected by the spin that created the nearly Earth-normal gravity experienced by those who worked and lived on the outermost levels.

The lift soon deposited them on a catwalk overlooking the cavernous central chamber, a great, yawning abyss that stretched across the vaguely carrot-shaped asteroid's entire fourteen kilometer-long axis. Illuminated by sunlight brought through the colony's enormous transparent aluminum end-caps and reflected deep into the great rock's interior by a series of internal and external mirrors, the passage formed a rough cylinder some fifty meters in diameter. Deep gouges and striations were visible in the nickel-iron walls, marks left by the automated, diamond-tipped diggers that had scraped the radioactive layers away after Vanguard's builders had hollowed the asteroid out using shaped nuclear charges.

How easy it was to forget the true purpose of such devices, Zafirah thought. She wondered if the Kaaba, the ancient, cubical shrine at the sacred heart of Mecca, a place that had been holy since before the time of the Prophet, had survived.

Grasping the catwalk's handholds as though her very life depended on them, Zafirah closed her eyes tightly. Visiting this shaft of vast emptiness—essentially a giant straight cylinder whose ends vanished to pinpoints in two directions, neither of which seemed to be up or down—always gave her an intense feeling of vertigo. She preferred to stay nearer to the asteroid's crust, the direction that the great rock's spin—and her inner ear—told her was "down."

"You all right, Zaf?" McNolan asked, recovering some of

his customary singsong lilt. "You look like you're about to send your lunch out on an EVA."

When she felt his hand on her arm she opened her eyes. She assayed a weak smile. "If I do, I'll try to warn you first. But I'm afraid we'll have to take the express route regardless. I don't want to waste any time getting to the Director's office."

McNolan looked like he was considering carrying her back into the lift, then calling a groundcar to take them across one of the higher-gravity levels instead. That would have been quite a detour, however, since the Director's office lay some eight kilometers away, near the asteroid's south pole.

But when the director had called, she'd told all the senior staff to assemble around her as quickly as possible. Zafirah knew as well as McNolan did that flying along the freefall axis was by far the quickest way to get where they needed to go. Besides, she could already see several other raptorlike shapes in the distance, their broad, amber-colored wings pushing near-weightless human forms swiftly southward along the wide tunnel's seemingly infinite length.

Still feeling green, Zafirah nodded toward the emergency locker beside the lift, where several sets of three-meter-long wings hung.

"Pry it open, Mack. We're going flying."

Zafirah often thought that Kuniko Mizuki, Vanguard's director, might be the most ancient human being she had ever encountered. Because the director spent most of her time in the colony's light-gee, coreward levels, her sallow skin was no doubt far smoother than it would have been had she lived on Earth. But the slight woman's eyes held depths of wisdom and memory that Zafirah had never seen in anyone else. Zafirah wasn't sure of Mizuki's precise age, but guessed that she might have watched Neil Armstrong on live television as he left humanity's first bootprints in the lunar dust.

Today, it seemed to Zafirah that the director's years wore heavily on her.

The department heads and their staffs were still filing in, arriving from points all over the asteroid, having dropped whatever business or pleasure they'd been occupied with when the nuclear hammer had fallen upon Earth. At least twenty people were crowded into the director's spacious office-cum-conference-room thus far, and all eyes were riveted to the huge flatscreen monitor that dominated an entire wall.

Thanks to a satellite relay linking Vanguard to one of the orbiting Earth-science telescopes, the planet's entire day side was now in view. No new explosions were evident, though hundreds of surface fires were visible, even in the waning daylight. Huge gray plumes of dust and detritus—particulate material thrown aloft by the nuclear conflagrations—had spread out greatly, obscuring giant swaths of what had to be the Pacific Ocean and the western coastlines of the Americas.

It was immediately clear to Zafirah that very little sunlight was reaching the ground, and that it would probably take months for that situation to change.

"We seem to be witnessing Doctor Sagan's nightmare," said Director Mizuki, now looking and sounding even older than Allah Himself. "A full-scale nuclear exchange. A cloud-generated icehouse effect is starting right before our eyes. That will be followed by massive crop failures and world famine."

"Nuclear winter," Zafirah said, the words sounding surreal. *This cannot be happening.*

"Then it's 'Game Over,'" said Avram Baruch, the tall, lanky Israeli who oversaw the particle accelerator project. His eyes were sunken, hollow. "Humanity is finished. *Mekhule.*"

Zafirah knew a little Hebrew. *Mekhule* meant "exterminated."

"That's a lot of frog-hair," said Claudia Hakidonmuya, the sun-baked Hopi woman who ran the colony's genetics and life-science research units. "Humans are a pretty tough lot. Besides, the first thing a nuclear war wipes out is the ability to make more nuclear war. We just need to get a better handle on how much actual damage has been done down there."

"Why not just lob a few kilograms of that antimatter the particle folks have been synthesizing down there?" said Norman Arce, the huge Fijian construction foreman. "Put the goddamn place out of its misery."

"Stow that talk," Hakidonmuya snapped. Arce immediately went silent. But he still looked miserable, apparently on the verge of tears he didn't know how to shed.

"Fine," Baruch said, his eyes wild, nearly manic. "So mercy killing's out. How about I just say a long, patient *Kaddish* for the whole planet instead?"

Dr. Mizuki put up an aged hand and silence engulfed the room like a shroud. "Let's not do this, people. I know things look bad at the moment. But the human species is anything but finished."

That was true enough in a literal sense, Zafirah thought. After all, probably fewer than 100,000,000 souls perished in the actual explosions. Even the deaths from cancer, radiation burns, and famine that were sure to follow over the next few months might not come close to extinguishing all of the world's ten billion people.

But Baruch was still right in every way that really mattered. Humanity's nascent global civilization, still trapped in its cradle—the species's single inhabited world—now spasmed in its death throes. The dog packs of the nation-states and the multinational megacorps had finally unbottled the nuclear *djinn*, and human culture had reaped the whirlwind. Perhaps the various stockpiles of biological and chemical agents secreted around the world had also been unleashed, making further havoc, pain, and death inevitable. How many centuries might it take for the survivors to rebuild that civilization into some semblance of what it once had been?

Zafirah suddenly felt an unaccustomed kinship to Baruch, and only belatedly understood the reason for it: if the Kaaba of Mecca had been razed, then just as surely nothing remained of Baruch's native Tel Aviv but radioactive ash. Jerusalem, sacred to Jews and Muslims alike, was no doubt likewise destroyed.

"The human species will endure," Mizuki continued, her usually rock-steady voice slightly shaky. "Twenty-two years ago, a half-dozen Earth-crossing asteroids nearly sent us the way of the dinosaurs. But the Americans, the Europeans, and even the ECON decided to put aside their differences, at least for a while. That decision allowed them to develop the technology it took to land on those big rocks and nudge us all out of harm's way." She gestured broadly about the room.

"That's old news, Kuniko," Baruch said, flailing an arm toward the planetary charnel house still being displayed on the wall-screen. "What's your point?"

Mizuki seemed unperturbed by the physicist's outburst. "Just this, Avi: None of us would be here, living and working inside one of those hollowed-out rocks, if human beings lacked the capacity to cooperate. We're supposed to be humanity's best and brightest. Therefore we ought to have that cooperative quality in spades. We also have a lot of technology that nobody dirtside has. I'd say a great deal of Earth's recovery is going to be up to us."

"Ducking the 'Thirty-One asteroids was mostly dumb luck," Arce interjected, almost snarling his rage and pain. "We dodged a bullet back then because we happened to bend down to tie our shoes at the exact right time. Today we blew our own brains out deliberately."

The ironic truth of the orbital construction engineer's words was not lost on Zafirah, nor did anybody else seem to miss it either. Zafirah felt something gradually loosening, something deep within her soul. *It's hope,* she thought. *I'm simply letting go of hope.*

"What about the rest of the El Fivers?" said Hakidonmuya, still sounding aggressively upbeat. No one had to be told that she referred to the permanent denizens of the other five O'Neill colonies that orbited the Earth-Moon system's Lagrange Five point along with Vanguard.

Mizuki smiled, a pale, unconvincing gesture. "You mean do they see themselves as Earth's last, best hope as well?" The director shrugged. "I can't speak for anybody but Vanguard. But I've already checked in with the directors of the other colonies. Believe me, they're as stunned as any of us. But the NicholCorp colony has just given me news that gives me some real hope that human race will pull out of this. It's from a report they received on their microwave transmitter. Apparently, at least one of the Project *Phoenix* ground facilities has survived both the firestorms and the E-M pulse."

The director paused, her eyes meeting Zafirah's for a moment. Cautiously, Zafirah recovered her grip on the very faintest of hopes.

With all eyes upon her, Mizuki said, "Zefram Cochrane and a few key members of his staff are still alive."

Perhaps the world had not ended after all. Maybe the human adventure was really only beginning.

Inshallah, Zafirah thought, clinging stubbornly to a hope she'd nearly given up for dead. *If Allah wills it. If Allah wills it.*

Chapter 7

In the autumn of 2031, technology, money, and politics converged fortuitously. Had this not happened, the human species would very likely have come to an ignominious end, casually extinguished by an uncaring universe that had already created and destroyed so many other forms of life. Lieutenant John Mark Kelly, already aboard the *Ares IV* spacecraft on his solitary, year-long voyage to Mars, might suddenly have found himself the only Earth-born intelligent creature left alive in the entirety of the cosmos.

But such was not to be humanity's fate. The determined effort of many thousands of people around the world—from the United States, to the European Union, to the Pan-African Alliance, to the Eastern Coalition, to the emerging democracies of the Muslim Bloc nations—narrowly prevented Earth's destruction by a group of killer asteroids. The great rocks had apparently once been a single body, a mix of stony and metallic materials, until it had been ripped asunder by Jupiter's prodigious gravitational field, the same fate as had befallen comet Shoemaker-Levy 9 late in the previous century. But unlike the comet, which had plunged into the gas-giant planet's metallic-hydrogen heart, several of this new object's largest and heaviest fragments were flung elsewhere.

Directly toward the Earth.

After humanity's most powerful heavy-thrust nuclear-electric rockets had nudged the fragments from their original trajectory, six of these stone-and-nickel-iron hulks—each one measuring more than ten kilometers in length, with masses comparable to the bolide that slammed into Yucatan some sixty-five million years ago, putting paid to the reign of the dinosaurs—had taken up long-period orbits around the entire Earth-Moon system.

But this arrangement wasn't gravitationally stable. The great rocks would have to be moved again, within a very few years, lest the sky fall once again. Seeing as much opportunity as danger in this looming crisis, humankind acted in concert once again, this time employing the new technologies that had been developed to nudge the worldlets out of Earth's path in the first place, as well as a goodly number of Cold War–era nuclear weapons, devices that had never before found a constructive purpose.

So were born the O'Neill Colonies, forged in the very same nuclear fires that would one day consume much of mankind.

A generation later—and more than five years after the May Day Horror of Fifty-Three—Lidia Song Wu clung to a glistening steel handhold built into the external surface of one of the very same rock-and-metal bodies that had once threatened humanity's continued existence. Marking the time by the rhythmic hissing of her p-suit's respirator, Wu crept slowly and cautiously along the long axis of the asteroid shell that housed the Vanguard colony.

In Wu's eyes, the ironies of the world's current circumstances were as profound as its tragedies. The people who lived and worked within Vanguard and a handful of other tamed, nuke-bored rocks might be the Earth's only chance of emerging from the darkness that had shrouded it—both literally and figuratively—since the outbreak of the Third World War.

After the first nuclear bombs had exploded over London

and New York, Tel Aviv and Riyadh, Karachi and New Delhi, nearly half a billion people had died. The postatomic horror that followed the blasts made the Bell Riots of 2024 look like a Boy Scout jamboree. Terrorists and rogue states exploded so-called suitcase-nukes and released toxins and biological warfare agents, everything from sarin to ebola. Legions of battle-suited, drug-addled soldiers had been sacrificed in scores of dubious "conventional" battles on the ground after the computers necessary to guide the bigger tactical nukes had failed. Millions more civilians, including those responsible for maintaining even the pretense of law and order, continued even now to be slaughtered by the thousands in various conflicts around the world, as the remnants of the world's great powers and genocidal warlords like Colonel Green fought over the scraps.

Only up above it all, in the artificially created O'Neill habitats, did human civilization, technology, and culture stand an even chance of survival, the hostile environment of deep space notwithstanding. Only here, beyond the brown-and-orange haze of the still-fading remnants of the nuclear winter of Fifty-Three, could a traumatized humanity lift its eyes from the banal horrors of day-to-day survival.

Only here could a person find solace in the hope that better things lay ahead.

Even back in 2031—still referred to by most who had experienced it as the Year We Dodged the Bullet—the idea of constructing O'Neill-type space habitats was not a new one. Rafts of books had been written over the past century or so about the concept, its benefits, and its theoretical problems. In fact, it had been some of the works of the earliest space-age science writers—luminaries such as Asimov, Sagan, Ferris, and Zubrin—that had fired Wu's young imagination, spurring her to flee Hong Kong's inflexible social stratification to pursue an engineering degree at Cambridge. The twentieth-century scientific essayist Gerard K. O'Neill, another of Wu's favorites, had been among the first to champion the idea of constructing large-scale, permanent human habitats in space.

Now, clinging precariously to the hide of the Vanguard asteroid as she inched cautiously along its length, Wu understood viscerally that she and her colleagues were living out O'Neill's wildest dreams.

Wu felt a sudden, violent tug on the toolkit she had strapped to her thigh. Instinctively, her gloved hand grabbed for the small box. It took a moment for her to realize that the kit itself was secure; she had merely forgotten to close the cloth flap that covered it, leaving it vulnerable to the outward centrifugal pull of the asteroid's spin-generated artificial gravity.

Sloppy, she thought, chiding herself. Wu was all too aware that such accidents could easily get people killed. She quickly sealed the flap, pausing just long enough to recheck her suit for any other loose objects. Satisfied, she resumed her careful hand-over-hand motion toward photovoltaic array gamma-six.

Wu understood well that performing even basic maintenance work on the outer shell of a spinning O'Neill colony could be even more difficult and dangerous than the first spacewalks of the earliest Soviet cosmonauts and U.S. astronauts. True, her pressure suit was tremendously more advanced than the one that had kept Aleksei Leonov's blood from boiling as he stepped into the airless void that lay beyond the skin of his *Voskhod* capsule. Wu didn't have to contend, as Leonov had, with a garment that grew so distended that it had to be almost completely depressurized before she could go back inside. Wu's Kevlar-laced suit resisted the stiff-limbed "balloon" effect so prevalent during those ancient EVAs of nearly a century ago. It responded easily to the motions of her limbs, with joints assisted by small but powerful electrical servomotors. The internal fans and heat exchangers kept her helmet's faceplate almost entirely fog-free, no matter how much she exerted herself. And the paper-thin insulators of which her gauntlets were composed allowed her to work with the smallest of tools with almost a jeweler's precision. Wu sometimes imagined that Buzz Aldrin, the U.S. Gemini program's extravehicular-activity pioneer, would have been awed by the pressure suits that so many O'Neill-colony dwellers now took utterly for granted.

No, dealing with a p-suit wasn't the most challenging aspect of her job. The real difficulties lay in staying connected to the surface of a hollow asteroid that spun rapidly enough to create a feeling of almost Earth-normal gravity in the habitat's outermost levels. Because of this unending centrifugal motion, those inside the asteroid thought of its exterior layers, all the way around the roughly cylinder-shaped asteroid, as "down." One became progressively heavier as one moved "down" toward the asteroid's skin. At the moment, Wu was as far "down" as it was possible to be on Vanguard.

For Leonov and Aldrin, coming untethered from their respective spacecraft while in orbit had been a real worry. Had that happened to either man, the result would have been a slow drift away from the capsule. With nothing to push against, the lost person never could have been recovered.

Wu knew that if she were to come untethered from fast-twirling Vanguard, her own inertia would launch her, projectilelike, into space with better than a one-gee acceleration. Rescue might be possible before the suit's resources exhausted themselves, but using a powered skiff to locate and match velocity with her would be no mean feat.

She therefore had to hang on for dear life as she worked, like a supine window washer working on a skyscraper that had been pitched onto its side. A multiply redundant safety net of diamond-composite tethers held her suit to the asteroid's rough, metal-rich surface, which was still being pitted even now by exposure to the L-5 region's high concentrations of dust particles.

Years ago, Wu had learned to avoid vertigo by ignoring

the noticeable movements of the Earth and the Moon, both of which steadily wheeled over and past the asteroid's extremely short horizon, only to reappear less than a minute later from the opposite direction.

Wu finally came to a stop when she reached the edge of a football-field-sized cluster of space-black photovoltaic collectors, one of the habitat's principal sources of electrical power. Using a key strapped to her leg, she opened a small junction box mounted beside the array. Replacing the burned-out relay took only a few moments. Once she had finished and run a quick diagnostic test on the relay's keypad, she tapped a control near her suit's neck ring, engaging the radio transmitter.

"Wu to al-Arif."

"I read you, Liddie," came Zafirah al-Arif's smooth voice in response. There was very little static on the connection, probably because sunspot activity was currently in its low but slowly rising phase. Wu chose to regard this as a good omen.

"How do the power relays look?" Zafirah wanted to know.

"They're all operational now," Wu said. "You can power them back up. And you can tell the other habitats that we're finally ready to fire up all six accelerators in tandem."

"Good work, Liddie. I'll give the others the go-ahead signal as soon as you're back inside."

"If it's all the same to you, I'd like to stay out here and watch the fireworks," Wu said. "I have the best seat in the house."

"I'm not sure that's such a good idea," Zafirah said.

Wu scowled. She'd expected this. "Come on, Zaf. It's not like I'm standing in the path of the beam. And just being outside the rock exposes me to a hundred times more stray radiation than the experiment is going to give off. Besides, you're not gonna order me to miss witnessing history are you?"

After an elastic moment of silence, Wu heard her colleague sigh resignedly. *"All right, Liddie. You win. Just take some nice pictures for me, all right?"*

"For all of us," Wu said, patting her toolkit, where the camera remained stowed. *And for all the generations who are going to follow us.*

Wu cast her eyes toward the asteroid's western horizon. The Earth and the Moon, respectively at their slender crescent and nearly full phases as seen from the L-5 point, had just disappeared behind the colony's sunlit side. In their absence it was far easier to see the outlines of the potato-shaped asteroid that housed the Roykirk colony, which loomed a mere 150 kilometers away. The remaining four asteroid colonies, though out of Wu's immediate line of sight at the moment, were spaced at similar intervals along an ellipse centered on the Earth-Moon system's gravitationally balanced L-5 point.

Wu shivered with exhilarated anticipation. The time for the test firing had finally arrived, a tangible justification for hope. Barring some last-minute equipment foul-up either here or on one of the other colonies, the six O'Neill habitats, working in concert, would soon offer the world a limitless supply of cheap energy. Shortly the O'Neill colonies would furnish heat, light, and transportation for ordinary people all over the Earth, instead of merely supplying exotic antiparticles to Earthbound researchers like Zefram Cochrane.

Within the next few moments, they would create the first completely functional subspace warp field.

The Earth and the Moon reappeared in the east, moving inexorably across the star-dappled night. Turning sideways, Wu looked at the cloud-fleeced magnificence of the Earth, its dark side lit sporadically by the lamps and hearths of a much-reduced human civilization. What little she could see along the planet's narrow sunlit crescent now seemed pristine, its cerulean hue evoking a time before anyone had heard of nuclear winter.

It was as though Gaia herself were holding her breath, eagerly anticipating whatever was to come next.

Wu touched the radio controls at her neck ring once again, tuning in the channel being shared by Zafirah and the other five particle-accelerator managers. She wanted to remember every word spoken on this historic occasion. Perhaps Zafirah had prepared a brief but profound comment, some immortal turn of phrase that would forever after be identified with Friday, 9 August 2058. *One giant leap for mankind, indeed,* Wu thought, ruefully aware that in many parts of the world stone axes and the bow once again represented the apex of technological progress.

One by one, the spokespeople for each O'Neill colony checked in over the open channel, forming a bouillabaisse of accents from every corner of the Earth.

"All systems show green on the Moss-Offenhouse colony."

"The NicholCorp facility is green for go."

"Starling habitat here. We're looking good."

"Brynner asteroid is all set."

"Colony Roykirk here. We're ready and standing by for a full-up warp-field test."

Wu heard Zafirah's voice next, utterly serious and businesslike. *"Particle flow shows green on Vanguard. Magnetic bottles are stable. Antimatter containment is positive."*

A couple of heartbeats later another voice came over the channel. Its rough, world-weary quality, along with its noticeable lightspeed delay, told Wu that she was listening to Christopher Brynner himself. Too enfeebled by age and illness to leave Earth for the O'Neills, Brynner was the founder of Brynner Information Systems as well as the chairman emeritus of the Gerald Moss-Ralph Offenhouse Conglomerate. Despite reversals of fortune during the war, Brynner's pockets remained deep enough to bankroll today's experiment.

"This is Ground Station Bozeman," Brynner said. *"I want*

to thank and congratulate you all for the extraordinary forward stride you're about to make on behalf of the entire human race. Now let me hand the microphone over to someone who speaks your language far better than I ever could."

Another voice spoke up a beat later. *"Uh, hello, everybody,"* it said. Wu instantly recognized the bourbon-roughened voice of the man whose warp-field theories Dr. O'Neill's spiritual children were about to test.

"I can't offer you anything to top what Mr. Brynner just said," Cochrane continued, sounding uncomfortable. *"Except to tell you that if the sustained warp-field experiment ends up looking as good up there as it does on paper down here, then Project* Phoenix *could have a prototype warp-capable vessel ready for launch as early as next Spring."*

Wu hoped Zafirah and the key players on the other O'Neills weren't prone to flop-sweats.

"So I'll finish by wishing all of you good luck," Cochrane said. *"And godspeed."*

Except for the hiss of her respirator, the universe went utterly quiet around Wu for several moments after Dr. Cochrane signed off. Zafirah's much nearer-sounding voice finally broke the silence.

"You heard the man, people. Initiate the activation sequence."

Reconfiguring her suit tethers so that she faced "down"—straight out into space—she reached into her toolkit to free the miniature digital Hasselblad camera from its restraining strap. The nearly full Moon now stood directly above her like a glowing sentinel, its image preternaturally crisp in the vacuum.

She pointed the camera toward the eastern horizon, where Vanguard's portion of the warp field would soon begin forming before it connected up with its counterparts on the Roykirk asteroid and the habitats beyond.

Wu felt a slow pulsation beginning to radiate from beneath the asteroid's skin. It quickly increased in amplitude, jarring her. Surprised, she lost her grip on the camera, which launched itself into space as though shot from a rifle.

Then the universe exploded around her, and she saw and heard nothing more.

Were it not for the fading effects of the nuclear winter, this August evening on the outskirts of Bozeman, Montana, might have been pleasantly warm. Against the gradually intensifying cold, Lily Sloane drew her coat tightly about herself, her arms crawling with gooseflesh. She stood on a hill just out of sight of the dilapidated Quonset hut Cochrane had grandly dubbed "Ground Station Bozeman."

Lily heard Cochrane's boots grinding against the gravel path as he approached from a nearby stand of trees. She didn't bother looking up from the eyepiece of the tall prewar telescope that had occupied her attention for the past ten minutes.

"Hey, Zee," she said, still squinting through the eyepiece, Cyclops-like. The telescope was pointed at about a forty-five-degree angle upward into the night sky. "I must have bumped this damned thing. You had it pointed straight at the O'Neills. I saw a flash a while back, but now I can't make out anything."

Lily was beginning to suspect that considerably more was wrong here than merely a maladjusted telescope. Straightening up from the eyepiece, she met Cochrane's gaze.

She thought she had already observed the full spectrum of his emotional extremes, all the way from hyperproductively manic to nearly suicidal. But she hadn't seen him look so stricken, so blasted—so *old*—since just after the war had broken out.

"What's happened, Zee?" Lily prompted, her voice catching in her throat.

Cochrane pulled a beat-up metal flask from his jacket pocket and took a huge quaff before replying. "The colonies aren't up there anymore, Lily. There's been . . . an accident."

Lily's heart sank. Old vids of *Ares IV* and *Columbia* and

Challenger inscribed arcs of fire across her memory. The realization hit her like a punch in the stomach—some five thousand of the Earth's best and brightest were gone, probably vaporized, just like that. The flight of the *Phoenix* would surely be held up for years, the antimatter fuel stocks the O'Neill particle accelerators had created for the project lying unused in a rusty Titan V missile silo. The project might even be canceled altogether, now that Team *Phoenix* could no longer count on exotic materials or replacement parts from the orbital factories. Sure, Lily knew she could cobble together a serviceable cockpit out of scrap titanium, given enough time. But Zee couldn't just whip up the really weird engine-related stuff—say plasma coolants, or crystallized dilithium, or unobtanium-plated warp-field frammistats—in his garage.

Project *Phoenix* was effectively grounded. And a lot of good people were gone.

Lily reached for Cochrane's flask. *Maybe we humans just don't have the right stuff to reach for the stars,* she thought, then emptied the battle-scarred container in one long, bitter swallow.

Chapter 8

Friday, 9 August 2058

"What the hell just happened to us?" Zafirah said, pulling herself unsteadily to her feet in Vanguard's darkened central control room. A confused moan was the only response she heard. Unseen broken things crunched beneath the springy soles of her sneakers.

The emergency circuits restored the lighting a few seconds later. The place seemed to have been turned completely upside-down, then abruptly righted.

Avram Baruch lay stunned on the floor, a heavy desk pinning him there. Kerwin McNolan, the small Irish engineer, strained against the asteroid's spin-generated gravity to free the dour Israeli. Zafirah wasted no time helping McNolan shove the desk aside.

"What happened?" she repeated, her eyes on a trio of shell-shocked-looking junior technicians who were returning upended pieces of equipment to their proper places. A few other technical people milled about, looking disoriented. But no one seemed grievously injured.

McNolan was helping the disoriented Baruch to his feet. Apparently satisfied that the physicist was all right, he turned to Zafirah. "This is just an educated guess, Zaf, but I'd say something must have gone very wrong with the warp-field experiment."

Lidia! Zafirah thought with a start. Lidia had been working outside the shell when all six O'Neills had linked to form the continuous toroidal warp field. And moments after that—

Zafirah rushed to the communications console, which displayed a green "power-on" light. "Al-Arif to Wu," she shouted into the microphone. "Wu, do you copy? Wu, come in!"

The only response was a wash of static.

Zafirah bolted toward the array of consoles that monitored the asteroid's surface, and the space beyond. Three of the half-dozen monitors there had toppled onto the decking, and now were so much scrap. Though the remaining screens didn't look damaged, they displayed only snow.

She noticed that Director Mizuki was already busy at one of the consoles, obviously trying to bring in a view of the outside. The darkness of deep space slowly coalesced across two of the still-functional screens, with numerous fixed stars shining invariantly in the distance. Zafirah stood beside the director before the large, flat screens, with Baruch and McNolan flanking them.

Zafirah's stomach suddenly became buoyant. Something wasn't right with the image before her.

Baruch seemed to notice the same thing. "This is as wrong as a Russian rock band. What's happened to the Roykirk colony?"

The nearest other O'Neill habitat was nowhere to be seen. And none of the other four hollow-asteroid colonies was visible either. If debris from any of them remained, there wasn't sufficient light present to make any of it visible. The infinite abyss seemed to have swallowed them all whole.

Zafirah felt sick at heart. *I hope you died quickly, Lidia. Like Sabih, and little Kalil.* Inshallah.

"Gone," McNolan said, his voice a rasp. "All of them are gone. Probably blown to hell when the warp field collapsed."

A terrible silence descended. It was the director who broke it. "I'm not so sure the other colonies went anywhere—unless everything else did, too."

It was only then that Zafirah noticed that both the Earth and the Moon were also missing. And that Bellatrix and Rigel, the left shoulder and legs of Orion the Hunter, were visibly out of position relative to giant Betelgeuse, as though the constellation had been distorted by a funhouse mirror of time, distance, or perhaps both.

The next half hour was a blur, as the survivors checked in with the director's office and began a frantic checkout of the habitat's status. Zafirah was surprised by how little serious damage the Vanguard facility had actually sustained, at least in terms of its physical plant. Especially considering how far the entire asteroid had evidently traveled after the torus-shaped warp field had collapsed against it.

More than sixty-one parsecs. Approximately two hundred light-years.

No one had believed that figure at first. It wasn't until after Director Mizuki and Zafirah had both taken separate measurements of several of the most readily identifiable first-magnitude stars—compiling a three-dimensional model that the computers could compare with the constellations as seen from home—that the truth at last began to settle upon the 827 asteroid dwellers who had survived Vanguard's unprecedented transit.

They were now stranded two hundred light-years from Earth. Sol was a distant ember, lost among countless others in the infinite night.

We've gone farther than anyone has ever gone before, Zafirah thought, looking back at tiny, dim Sol through one of Vanguard's surviving optical telescopes. *Trouble is, nobody back home knows about it. They must think the collapsing warp field destroyed us.*

And what of the other five O'Neills? Were they, too, dispersed through the void? Or had the failed experiment blasted them all to rubble?

There was simply no way to know.

Zafirah felt a bizarre exhilaration, a feeling she thought might be an amalgam of wonder and dread. On one hand, seventeen of her Vanguard colleagues were either dead or missing, the dead apparently killed by the sudden inertial effects of the asteroid's breakneck passage. On the other, the collapse of the warp-field bubble had proved one thing conclusively—that travel via subspace over interstellar distances was indeed possible.

The director had given everyone aboard a couple of hours to consider Vanguard's weirdly altered circumstances before summoning the senior staff to her office for an extremely tense meeting.

She must have spent the last two hours picking everything up in here, Zafirah thought as she entered the large, immaculate chamber alongside several of her colleagues. She found herself grateful for the feeling of normalcy and order fostered by the room's tidiness, and realized that such must have been Dr. Mizuki's intention. Zafirah had always thought that Mizuki's keen understanding of crew morale was one of the talents that made her so well suited to her job. Zafirah had once entertained the notion of eventually becoming director herself.

Now she was delighted and relieved not to be the one in charge.

The director sat behind her desk, her aged eyes sweeping the room as she displayed a smile which Zafirah found enormously reassuring. "The good news is this: We were a self-sufficient colony before the accident. And self-sufficient we will remain."

McNolan shook his head. "This far from a star? Our solar arrays aren't going to get too much business way out here."

"That might not matter," Zafirah said, chiming in almost

before she realized it. When she noticed that everyone in the room had turned to look in her direction, she nearly lost her train of thought, then swiftly recovered. "I mean I think we can generate considerable power from what's left of our warp generators. Probably not enough to create a warp field capable of getting us back home. But the output certainly ought to make up for our lack of nearby solar power." Her gaze lit upon Avram Baruch. "What do you think, Avi?"

Baruch's smile was wan and unconvincing. "Maybe. If nothing else fails. I've already examined the generators up close, and they're a real mess. Three of them overloaded, and four others are melted to slag."

"What about the nuclear reactor?" Mizuki asked.

"The autosafety programs kicked in during the accident and jettisoned it," McNolan said. "They would've done the same to the warp generators, too, if the computers hadn't glitched somewhere."

"I think we can get by with what's left of the warp generators," Zafirah said, trying to sound hopeful. "Antimatter containment is still positive."

Baruch scowled. "If it wasn't, we wouldn't be having this conversation, Zaf. And even if the antimatter storage fields don't go south, it could still be a real trick coaxing everything we need out of the remaining generators without blowing ourselves out of the sky again."

"Well, we can't afford to go *too* easy on the throttle," said Claudia Hakidonmuya, Vanguard's head geneticist. "We'll need to convert a good deal of that power into the equivalent of sunlight. That is, if we want the hydroponics units to keep feeding everybody on board."

The director smiled again. "As I said," she repeated, "we are self-sufficient. Or at least we *can* be, if we're very careful, and very clever."

"Not to mention incredibly lucky," Baruch said.

"We weren't vaporized when the warp field collapsed,"

Zafirah said. She was beginning to tire of the Israeli's relentless negativity. "That would seem to bode well for our continued survival." Inshallah, she thought silently.

"Then I'll consider that issue settled for the moment," the director said, her confident smile never wavering. "Now we must look beyond mere matters of survival."

That surprised Zafirah, even coming from Dr. Mizuki. What, other than the fate of one's immortal soul in the next world, could take on a higher priority than the colony's survival?

Baruch looked suspicious, his shaggy salt-and-pepper eyebrows raised. "What do you mean?"

"Earth is still choking on the ashes of the Third World War," the director said, evidently unfazed by Baruch's reaction. "We've just demonstrated that we can tap a power source that could pull the rest of humanity out of that morass. We can offer the world hope."

"We'd have to learn to stabilize the warp field," McNolan said, "before we'd be able to offer anyone anything."

The director nodded. "If we'd thought that was an impossibility, we never would have undertaken the experiment in the first place."

"We'd also have to tell somebody on Earth about it," McNolan countered. "And that we survived in the first place."

"There are two tiny things wrong with that," said Baruch. "One, a radio signal will take two centuries just to reach Earth. And two, all the external radio dishes were sheared off during the accident."

Sheared off, Zafirah thought, wincing slightly. *Along with Lidia.*

Mizuki rose from behind her desk, signaling that the meeting was coming to a conclusion. She appeared undaunted by the difficulties that lay ahead. "Then the sooner we get started, the better. How soon can we get one of the radio transmitters operating?"

Monday, 2 September 2058

At first, Zafirah thought the blip on the telescope's viewer was a comet. But as it approached in a long, leisurely ellipse, she realized that the object possessed one particular feature that she'd never seen before on a comet.

It has running lights.

Less than an hour later, the viewers in the main control room displayed the spindle-shaped object—now clearly a sophisticated spacecraft of nonhuman origin—making a close approach to the asteroid's exterior, and extending mooring grapnels to secure itself to the surface.

Holding herself even more erect than usual, Director Mizuki stood in the room's center and addressed everyone present. "We obviously have a first contact situation here, people," she said, smoothing a wrinkle on the front of her dark blue jumpsuit.

The human race's very first *first contact situation,* Zafirah thought, trying and failing to prevent her hands from trembling. She wasn't certain whether fear or joy was the cause.

All she knew was that she could see no trace of fear or hesitation in the director's eyes.

"Let's go and greet them, Zafirah," Mizuki said. Turning toward Hakidonmuya and McNolan, she added, "I'd also like Claudia and Kerwin to join the welcoming committee."

The Hopi geneticist crossed to the director immediately. Zafirah, feeling overwhelmed by the enormity of the moment, walked over to Mizuki a few seconds later.

But hard-eyed McNolan, seated at a console beside the apprehensive-looking Baruch, didn't move.

Mizuki frowned. "You have objections?"

Baruch spoke up when McNolan hesitated. "In a word . . . *yes.*"

"Fear is what plunged mankind back into the Stone

Age," the director said, extending her arms as if to embrace the entire universe. "We ought not repeat that mistake out here."

McNolan finally broke his silence. "Why haven't they hailed us?"

"They may have been sending us friendship messages for the past hour," Mizuki pointed out, referring to the balky high-gain antennas which remained in disrepair. During the past several weeks, simple survival had taken precedence over trying to send messages that Earth couldn't possibly receive for a score of decades. "We have no way of being sure."

"That's precisely my point," McNolan said. "Their intentions are a mystery."

"Any civilization capable of traversing interstellar space has to be peaceful by definition," said the director, adopting the didactic classroom-lecturer tone she preferred over confrontation.

"Assuming that they think in a way we can even understand," Baruch said, casting a glance toward Zafirah. "Remember, most human cultures have always had a hell of a time understanding how *other* human cultures think. Never mind aliens."

Baruch's glance reminded Zafirah of frightened young Israeli soldiers with quivering trigger fingers. And her own desperate, demoralized cousins who had for decades counterattacked indiscriminately by strapping bombs to their bodies. Justifiable fear had motivated both sides. Those recollections made her wonder whether Baruch and McNolan might not be equally justified in their wariness.

"And that's what's kept our species trapped on Earth for so long," Hakidonmuya told Baruch. She gestured toward the image of the just-landed alien vessel. "Less enlightened beings are almost certain to destroy themselves before they figure out how to handle the energy sources interstellar travel requires."

The director walked toward the door, followed by Hakidonmuya. Zafirah fell into step behind the geneticist.

"Are you coming, Kerwin?" Mizuki said, pausing in the open hatchway.

McNolan rose slowly. "All right. But at least let me take a few simple precautions."

"Precautions?"

"We need to have some weapons handy. Just in case our visitors turn out *not* to be friendly."

"*What* weapons?" Zafirah asked. Vanguard wasn't exactly a military installation, after all.

"Some of the rock-boring and digging equipment will do in a pinch," McNolan said. "And a few of the construction beamjacks even have target pistols. It'll only take a few minutes to get them ready."

Zafirah got the distinct impression that this was because McNolan had already made a few surreptitious calls; he'd probably gotten started the moment the alien ship had been identified as an alien ship.

The director's mouth became a grim slash. "Absolutely not."

McNolan approached her. "Director, a smile and a few kilos of mining explosives will always get you a lot farther than just the smile."

He was *not* smiling, however. His eyes remained hard, his resolve clearly immovable.

"Amen," said Baruch.

After a seeming eternity, the director averted her gaze from Baruch. She looked about the room to measure the opinions of everyone present. The dozen people in the room seemed split down the middle on the issue.

Then Mizuki trained her probing gaze squarely on Zafirah. "And where do *you* stand, Zaf?"

Zafirah swallowed hard. Visions of rock-hurling teens and suicide bombers flashed across her mind's eye. She knew in her heart that distrust was not a productive path to follow. But as she tried to tame her own mounting fear, she found it nearly irresistible. *Allah forgive me. Did you not create these alien visitors as well as us?*

"I think Kerwin and Avi have a point," she said finally. "Maybe we should consider keeping some armed people behind the welcoming party. Discreetly."

" 'Trust, but with verification,' " Baruch said, no doubt quoting some ancient Cold Warrior from the previous century.

Norman Arce, the construction foreman, was studying the image of the alien ship displayed on the monitor. Bright lights flashed intermittently between the vessel's hull and the asteroid's nickel-iron-marbled surface. "Better make a decision soon. They're cutting a doorway."

Dr. Mizuki sighed, then nodded her grudging consent to McNolan's proposal. As she followed Claudia and the director into the corridor, Zafirah felt relief that pragmatic *realpolitik* was evidently as important to the director's job as was raw idealism.

But her fear remained, to her enormous shame.

The alien boarding party consisted of four creatures whose robust-looking sidearms and long, sheathed knives were immediately apparent. Zafirah's heart pounded; she hoped that the visitors' open display of weaponry signaled mere caution rather than naked aggression.

Zafirah stood beside Mizuki, Hakidonmuya, and McNolan on the rough metal surface of Vanguard's lowest, highest-gravity level. The members of the welcoming committee were empty-handed, with the exception of McNolan, who carried a small, unobtrusive radio transceiver that he'd left patched into the main control center.

All of their eyes were trained on the aliens who strode purposefully toward them. The hole through which the visitors had gained ingress was visible some twenty meters behind them. The lack of so much as a breeze indicated that they had done Vanguard's residents the courtesy of installing an airlock of some kind on their way in.

They're not monsters, Zafirah told herself silently and repeatedly. Just like the Israeli soldiers, they were merely the products of a different culture.

As well as, obviously, a different biology. Although the quartet of creatures provided living proof that the general humaniform template was not unique—each of the newcomers possessed two arms, two legs, and a head that harbored something roughly analogous to a face—they were clearly like nothing human beings had ever before encountered. They were all large, broad across the shoulders, and perhaps two-and-a-half meters in height. Their hair was shaggy and black, and hung past their bulky shoulders in untidy mullets that were adorned with bushy topknots and uneven, dreadlocklike braids. Their garments were motley and loose-fitting, predominantly blousy shirts, baggy jackets, and pantaloonlike leg coverings that brought to mind the pirates of the Barbary Coast, or her own people's legends of *djinn*.

But it was the aliens' faces that Zafirah found to be their most arresting feature. Their skin was dusky, their eyes obscured by multiple folds of wrinkled flesh. Nose and mouth converged in a single, snoutlike projection, bordered by a sharp chaos of sharp tusks and fangs.

They're not monsters, inshallah.

When only a handful of meters lay between the two groups of sentients, the visitors came to a halt.

The being at the front of the group raised a single meaty hand. *"Be'huh laku fraken Nausicaa,"* it said, its voice deep and booming. Zafirah wondered if it was identifying itself, or its species, or its intentions.

We'll find a way to speak to them, Zafirah told herself. *These creatures have had to contend with the same laws of physics we do just to get so far out into space. We have at least that much in common already.*

The lead alien tipped its head, apparently expecting a response. Zafirah recalled the sixteenth-century Spanish explorers who had read proclamations to the indigenous people of the Americas, then slaughtered them when they failed to make a satisfactory reply.

But they're not humans, Zafirah thought, hoping that the director's instincts would win out over McNolan's. *They won't necessarily behave the way we humans have always behaved.*

Director Mizuki spread her hands in a gesture of peace. She stepped forward, and away from the rest of the group, closing the distance between herself and the alien leader to a gap of about a meter.

Zafirah suddenly realized she was holding her breath.

"I am Kuniko Mizuki," the director said. "I am in charge of this facility. It is my honor to welcome you to the Vanguard colony."

The director bowed respectfully.

The alien before her bellowed, "*Kak Nausicaa!*" In a blur of motion, it unsheathed a long, evil-looking serrated blade.

Almost too quickly to see, the blade rose, then swept across the back of the director's still-bowed head.

A scream escaped from Zafirah before she could find the will to squelch it.

"No!" Hakidonmuya shouted.

McNolan cursed, then barked a single terse order into his handheld transceiver unit.

The director's head fell from her body, landing on the rough-hewn rock-and-metal floor with a sickening wet crunch. Frozen across her broad features was an expression of pure, unadulterated surprise.

PART 3

SECRETS

Chapter 9

Damn it! Sulu thought, instantly on his feet and moving toward the wounded Tholian ambassador. The pungent odor of sulfur permeated the conference room, as did a gabble of shouting human voices.

None of the Tholians uttered a sound.

Smoke and other superheated gases quickly roiled through the room, making the air uncomfortably hot. The sounds of coughing filled the air as an alarm shrilled. His eyes already stinging, Sulu drew and held a deep breath of what he hoped was clear air; it was already redolent with the acrid stench of rotten eggs. He heard the roar of the emergency fans as the environmental system struggled to get the room's atmosphere back into class-M equilibrium. The smoke and vapor swiftly began to recede.

Kasrene's aide, Mosrene, had already backed away from the evidence of his dirty work—he had apparently applied some sort of crude patch to the rent in Kasrene's enviro-suit, no doubt for the benefit of the humans present—and made no further threatening moves toward his superior. The remaining three members of the Tholian diplomatic party took up similar poses at Mosrene's side, all of them behaving as though they had just witnessed a genteel debate rather than an act of possibly mortal violence.

Why aren't any of them trying to help Kasrene?

Looking through the faceplate of Ambassador Kasrene's suit, Sulu tried to interpret the emotions on the Tholian diplomat's rigid, unreadable crystalline features. Was she surprised? The burnished red-and-gold planes of her countenance revealed nothing he understood.

Though the moment seemed frozen in time, Sulu and Chekov both arrived at Kasrene's side almost immediately. They simultaneously caught her heavy body as it began collapsing deckward, the haft of Mosrene's whisker-thin blade still protruding from the front of her suit. Taking care not to let the blade touch him—the weapon had just cut through the heavy, durable fabric as though it were whipped butter—Sulu strained against Kasrene's great weight, which felt like a tumbling neutronium wall.

"Clear the room!" Sulu roared as he struggled. "Security!"

"I need a trauma team in conference room four!" Chapel was shouting into a communicator. "And get me some help from that Tholian ship."

Chekov was already frantically patching into *Excelsior*'s communications system to alert Yilskene's nearby flagship that a Tholian doctor was needed urgently.

Where's Akaar? Sulu thought. The giant Capellan could probably have lifted Kasrene with a single steel-muscled arm. But a glance over his shoulder confirmed that the security chief was busy fulfilling his primary duty—maintaining order among both the Tholian and Federation delegations. He was directing two small teams of lightly armed security guards as they escorted both groups out of the conference room and into the corridor. Sulu presumed they were being ushered back to their respective quarters until things settled down, but at the moment he didn't much care.

Aidan Burgess, however, wasn't going quietly. Clearly determined to reach the fallen Tholian's side, she all but dared an owl-eyed young security guard to either stand aside or shoot her. She instantly ran afoul of Akaar, who draped a heavy arm across her shoulder. Sulu might have enjoyed the sight of the Federation special envoy being lifted and carried away like a sack of quadrotriticale were he not still in danger of becoming pinned beneath an enormous heap of living—or perhaps dying—crystal.

Two more pairs of hands grabbed at the wounded alien's suit, making Kasrene's mass suddenly far more manageable. With the help of Tuvok and Chapel, Sulu and Chekov carefully lowered Kasrene into what appeared to be a sitting position, balancing her on her long, wide tail. The rotten-egg aromas evidently still issuing from Kasrene's suit were becoming almost overpowering.

Dr. Chapel was already running her medical tricorder over the Tholian's wounds, her face pinched in concentration.

Sulu eyed the weapon that remained lodged in Kasrene's thorax. *Monomolecular blade,* he thought with an inward shudder, glad he'd never faced anything like it in the fencing lanes. *Very nasty piece of work, that.*

"How bad?" he asked.

"Looks about as bad as it can get," Chapel said, kneeling beside Kasrene and coughing because of the effluvium escaping from the Tholian's compromised and imperfectly patched suit. Improvising with a protoplaser, she sealed the breach, thereby preventing the fumes from overcoming every oxygen-breather in the room.

Chapel looked up and gazed significantly at Sulu. "I'm really going to need a Tholian doctor."

Sulu turned to Chekov, who shook his head. "When I explained to Yilskene's watch officer that this was Mosrene's doing, he said 'the castes must look after their own.' Then he cut off the channel."

"Why doesn't that surprise me?" Chapel said. "Then I'm going to need to get her to sickbay, so I can cut off this suit and work on her through an environment forcefield."

"Where's that trauma team?" Chekov wanted to know.

At that moment, a trio of med techs rushed into the conference room, a large antigrav stretcher floating between them. Tuvok assisted the medics in hoisting the Tholian's still form onto the hovering platform, which bobbed and oscillated momentarily as it adjusted to the ambassador's considerable mass. Kasrene was placed awkwardly on her side, to prevent the still dangerous blade from causing any further injury, either to the ambassador or to the medical personnel.

Akaar and a pair of security guards returned to the conference room then, and the security chief ordered his people to clear a "fast crash-cart route" to sickbay. Holding a phaser, the Capellan looked ready to vaporize anything that got in the trauma team's way. Sulu guessed that it must have been difficult for Akaar to restrain himself from shooting Mosrene down in his tracks. Aware that the father Akaar had never met had been murdered during a political coup, Sulu knew that the young officer had little love for would-be assassins.

Just as the med techs began moving Kasrene toward the door, one of the ambassador's gauntlet-clad hands shot out. Before anyone could react, she seized Tuvok's right wrist in an iron grip.

"Vulcan," Kasrene said, the chorus of layered voices that formed her translated words now sounding jangled and discordant. "Vulcan. Mind-toucher. Think to you. Touch. Touch."

Tuvok froze, his expression even more blank and unreadable than usual.

"Save your strength, Ambassador," Chapel said.

The Tholian's grip appeared to tighten. Tuvok suddenly looked pained.

"Let him go, Ambassador," Sulu said. "We can't help you if you fight us."

"Dying," she said. "Vulcan. Is. Only. Help."

The Tholian's grip suddenly relaxed.

His face blank once again, Tuvok collapsed, prompting Sulu to dive to catch him before his head hit the deck.

"Bring him along, too," Chapel said, indicating Tuvok.

Sulu nodded, hoisting the young Vulcan to his feet. Tuvok remained limp as Sulu and Chekov each took one of his arms and bore him quickly through the corridor behind Kasrene's swiftly-moving stretcher.

"What's happened to him?" Chekov asked as the group rushed into a wide turbolift.

"Sickbay," Chapel told the computer before turning to face Chekov. "I don't know. Maybe he inhaled too much of the leakage from Kasrene's suit."

Sulu knew that Chapel was making a purely off-the-cuff guess, since she was preoccupied with her struggle—apparently a losing one—to keep the Tholian ambassador alive.

Still helping Chekov hold Tuvok's slack form, Sulu listened to the Vulcan's breathing. It didn't sound labored, though it was slightly shallow. It seemed unlikely that the hot gases from Kasrene's suit had seared his lungs.

And yet Tuvok's open eyes were vacant and glassy, staring off into infinity as though they'd been exposed to something no humanoid had ever seen before.

"Circulatory pressure is crashing, Doctor," one of the med techs laboring over Kasrene said. "She's flat-lining."

"I can read the tricorder, Ensign," Chapel snapped as the turbolift deposited them across the corridor from sickbay. Everyone dashed through the main doors and into a corner in which the medics quickly improvised a Tholian-compatible isolation chamber. Reaching through the forcefield boundary with a pair of medical waldoes, Chapel wasted no time using a laser scalpel to slice open Kasrene's suit.

Even to Sulu's untrained eye, Kasrene's seeping chest wound appeared mortal. The blood—if indeed that word could be used to describe the escaping viscous fluid—appeared to be a brilliant, shimmering turquoise in color, at least as seen through the dimness and distortion of the isolation forcefield and the class-N atmosphere that lay behind it.

Mosrene obviously didn't want Kasrene to tell us whatever it was she was about to tell us. What is he trying to hide? Sulu recalled some of Kasrene's last words before she had fallen unconscious. *Vulcan,* she had said. *Mind-toucher.*

Had Kasrene known that Vulcans were touch-telepaths? It seemed as likely as not; it wasn't as though the Federation kept that information classified.

As he and Chekov carefully laid Tuvok on an unoccupied biobed away from the corner where trauma team worked, Sulu looked once again straight into Tuvok's glassy, staring eyes.

Perhaps those eyes had glimpsed whatever it was that had moved Mosrene to attempt murder.

After slicing away most of Kasrene's suit, Chapel and the trauma team employed an artificial respirator, a pair of cardiostimulators, and even a forcefield-mediated open-thoracic surgical procedure. Using waldoes to cross the isolation field, they continued working on the ambassador's still form for another forty-two minutes before Chapel finally pronounced her patient dead.

Chapel turned away from the waldoes and the gore-spattered trauma table, cursing. She had lost patients before, many times. She had learned to live with that long ago, though it was still extraordinarily painful whenever it happened. She knew that some percentage of those who required her help would arrive too injured, too ill—or just plain *too late*—to be saved.

But she found it hard to accept such a loss when she understood so little about the dying patient's physiology. For all she knew, a first-year Tholian medical student might have been able to keep Kasrene alive. Now that she could never know the truth of it, all she had was self-recrimination.

"You did everything you could, Doctor," said Chekov,

who seemed to have no trouble guessing the drift of her thoughts. He had dropped by the sickbay every fifteen minutes or so since the trauma team had begun its futile effort to save Kasrene.

Chapel shook her head. "What I did was precious little. Maybe the Tholians ought to consider training some of their junior diplomats in emergency surgery. Or do they have a separate goddamned medical caste, too?"

"Chris, I'm sorry," Chekov said, putting a hand on her shoulder.

She gently brushed the hand away. "I'm all right, Pavel. I just wish these people had at least shared a little of their medical data with us. I was flying blind."

"Admiral Yilskene's people didn't seem overly concerned about what happened to Kasrene," Chekov said. "Yilskene doesn't even seem in much of a hurry to debrief Mosrene about what happened. I just don't get it."

"I think you explained it pretty well earlier. 'The castes must look after their own.' Well, they did a pretty miserable job. And so did I."

"Doctor, Kasrene was run through with a monomolecular blade. You *do* understand that this patient was beyond saving, don't you?"

"Certainly beyond *my* abilities."

"When you consider the internal injuries a weapon like that can inflict, I don't think a Tholian medic could have done any better."

That's why monoblades are illegal on most Federation worlds, Chapel thought. *But then, we're a long way from the heart of the Federation, aren't we?*

"I'm not sure I understand your point, Pavel," she said aloud, doffing her surgical smock and tossing it into a nearby clothing 'cycler.

He sat on the end of an empty biobed and ran a hand through his gray-streaked hair, apparently gathering his thoughts. *Oh, please. Not another story about growing up in Novy Riga, Russia.* Chapel controlled a wince.

Chekov looked around as though making sure none of the sickbay staff were close enough to overhear him, then studied her with a serious expression. "Did I ever tell you what it was like to be forced to watch while Khan cut the throats of everybody on the Regula I research station?"

Chapel nodded, though she was surprised that he would mention this. From her medical database, she knew that Chekov had suffered intense posttraumatic stress as a result of that experience, which had later sidelined him from serving as Captain Sulu's exec for several years. She was also aware that he generally took great pains not to discuss that particular chapter of his career, even with *Excelsior*'s chief medical officer.

"Khan stuck these . . . alien slugs into my ear, and into Captain Terrell's," Chekov continued, staring off into his memories. "Once those creatures had entwined themselves into our brains, we had no other choice but to follow Khan's orders. No matter how hard we tried to resist, we couldn't stop ourselves. At least, when Khan ordered him to kill Jim Kirk, Clark Terrell found the courage to point the phaser at himself instead."

Watching his hands slowly turn white as they gripped the sides of the biobed, Chapel felt she had to stop him from going any further. She simply didn't want to see her old friend trot out his pain, particularly for her benefit.

"Me, I just stood there until I couldn't stand the pain from that damned eel anymore," Chekov continued. "I discovered that I just wasn't strong enough to—"

"Why are you telling me this, Pavel?" she interrupted.

"Because even though you did everything you could, Christine, sometimes that simply isn't good enough."

Chapel favored him with a wan smile. "Thanks, Pavel. Maybe you should consider hanging out a shingle for psych-counseling services."

"That would be too much like evaluating crew morale reports, Doctor," he said, returning her smile before nodding toward a nearby biobed. "How's Tuvok?"

Chapel led the way to the bed where Tuvok lay, far from the mess and clamor of the trauma team, whose members were still packing up their instruments and discreetly covering up the Tholian ambassador's sliced-open corpse with a light blue tarp.

Chapel looked up at the readings on the biobed monitor above Tuvok's head. "Not good. He's suffering from some sort of neural shock. I haven't seen a Vulcan brain exhibit trauma of this type since Spock tried to mind-meld with V'Ger."

"Spock got better," Chekov pointed out.

"He was also extremely lucky." Chapel recalled, not without a little melancholy, the unrequited infatuation she had felt toward Spock when they had served together on the original *Enterprise*. With the benefit of many years of hindsight, she realized now that her nonrelationship with Spock probably stemmed from her feelings of loss after her separation from Dr. Roger Korby, her late fiancé; Korby had proved to be even more remote from love—to say nothing of simple humanity—than even the most stoic of Vulcans.

Still, she occasionally wondered whether Spock ever thought about her after all these years.

"So what's Tuvok's prognosis?" Chekov wanted to know, concern striating his forehead.

"It's too soon to lay odds, but I do have an initial treatment idea," Chapel said as she crossed to the companel on the wall and punched a button. "Chapel to Dr. T'Lavik."

"T'Lavik here, Doctor," came the Vulcan physician's response, her voice a calm, even contralto. Though her shift had ended several hours earlier, she didn't sound like someone who'd been roused from slumber. *"What can I do for you?"*

Vulcans, heal thyselves, Chapel thought. "Please report to sickbay immediately, Doctor. I need a consultation for treating psionic trauma. The patient is Lieutenant Tuvok."

There was a slight but noticeable delay in T'Lavik's response. Chapel imagined that, like most Vulcans, T'Lavik would be somewhat sensitive about discussing Vulcan touch-telepathy with a non-Vulcan. *"I will be there presently. T'Lavik out."*

Chapel turned from the companel and faced Chekov. "Don't worry, Pavel. I've already lost one patient today. I'll be damned if I'm going to let another one slip through my fingers."

A huge weight had settled upon Sulu's shoulders after Christine called to inform him of Kasrene's death. *So Mosrene's plan succeeded, whatever the reasons behind it.*

Sulu stood between Aidan Burgess and Janice Rand in the dimly lit VIP quarters that had been assigned to Tholian Ambassador Mosrene. Mosrene, now out of his cumbersome enviro-suit, sat on the floor behind the orange-tinted forcefield barrier that contained the hot, high-pressure sulfurous atmosphere he required. Outside the barrier, the air was uncomfortably warm, though breathable for class-M life.

Sulu found himself wishing that the forcefield separating him from Mosrene were attached to the entrance to the ship's brig. The only problem with that, as Burgess had already pointed out, was that Mosrene may not have done anything wrong in the eyes of Tholian law.

Kasrene's erstwhile assistant betrayed no emotion that Sulu could construe as either guilt or remorse; to the contrary, the Tholian's demeanor seemed as unfathomable as ever, his face and body an enigmatic congeries of fractured-looking gold-and-ruby crystal formations. Mosrene's limbs were folded beneath him, his tail outstretched to the rear, sphinxlike.

Sulu decided that the direct approach would be best.

"Mosrene, I need to know why you killed the ambassador. Can you explain yourself?"

Mosrene's voice, mediated by the universal translator, rose in a chorus that sounded somewhat nettled. "I am Ambassador Kasrene's lawful successor, Captain Sulu. Please address me as *Ambassador* Mosrene."

Sulu closed his eyes to tamp down his frustration. He took a long, deep breath before opening them and speaking again. "There must be far more discreet methods of rising in the Tholian hierarchy, *Ambassador* Mosrene, than killing your superior in the middle of a diplomatic meeting. So I have to conclude that you had reasons to act that go beyond simple career enhancement." He glanced significantly at Burgess, hoping she would pick up on his wordless message: *Let me handle the interrogation. You've already said more than enough to these people.*

Mosrene turned his head so that his white, emerald-rimmed eyespots seemed to widen very slightly. "That is so. Ambassador Kasrene was about to divulge . . . sensitive information, which I deemed best contained. I owe no further explanation to anyone, save my superiors in the diplomatic caste. They will understand the necessity of my actions, just as the other members of our delegation did."

"I'm sure he's right about that," Burgess said.

Rand nodded. "I have to agree, too, Captain. Either all three of Kasrene's other aides were Mosrene's confederates in an assassination conspiracy, or else they're all absolutely confident that Mosrene will be vindicated."

Reluctantly, Sulu was forced to concur. Since none of the surviving Tholians aboard *Excelsior* had so far implied that anyone besides Mosrene was responsible for Kasrene's death, he tended to trust Rand's latter hypothesis.

Still, the fact that a cold-blooded killing had occurred aboard his ship—one apparently sanctioned by Tholian law, no less—bothered him intensely. On top of that, he was irked by Mosrene's dismissive tone, which he was convinced wasn't a product of his imagination or a maladjusted translator. Though Federation law and Starfleet protocol prevented him from taking any action against Mosrene, Sulu found himself tempted to give this newly promoted Tholian ambassador over to the tender mercies of Security Chief Akaar, at least for an hour or two.

"What sort of information might have been worth Kasrene's life?" Sulu asked.

Mosrene made a sound like a choir hiccuping in six-part harmony. Sulu interpreted the noise as an involuntary chuckle. "It is the sort of information that requires containment—at *any* cost," the Tholian said. "Therefore it is the sort of information which I will discuss with you no further."

Mosrene's eyespots narrowed and vanished, as though he had suddenly fallen asleep or entered a deep meditational trance. He seemed almost literally to turn to stone, and did not respond when Sulu called his name.

The companel on the wall sounded. "*Chapel to Captain Sulu.*"

Sulu stepped to the wall and punched a button, his eyes still fixed on the immobile Tholian. "Sulu here."

"*It's about Lieutenant Tuvok, Captain.*"

"Please don't tell me you have more bad news, Doctor."

"*Why don't you come back to sickbay, and let Tuvok give you the news himself?*"

For the first time, it seemed, since the attack on Kasrene, Sulu allowed himself a sigh of relief. "I'm on my way."

"What do you remember, Lieutenant?" Sulu asked, anxious to learn everything that had passed between Tuvok and Ambassador Kasrene. Besides himself and Tuvok, Dr. Chapel and Dr. T'Lavik were also present in the sickbay, along with Chekov.

Sitting up on the biobed, Tuvok appeared alert and energetic, if somewhat pale. "I remember one of the ambassador's hands reaching toward me. Next, I experienced a lancing pain through my skull. And then I felt . . ." The young Vulcan trailed off, an uncharacteristic look of confusion crossing his face.

"You felt what?" Sulu said, leaning forward.

Frowning, Tuvok turned toward Dr. T'Lavik, who was watching him attentively. "What is wrong with me, Doctor?"

T'Lavik, a centenarian Vulcan female with large ears and iron-gray hair, raised a placating hand. "Your memories of this experience may remain disorganized for some time, Lieutenant. You must be patient while your ability to recall them returns."

Tuvok appeared to mull that over for a moment before nodding in apparent resignation. But to Sulu's experienced eye, the young science officer was positively refulgent with impatience.

Sulu had to admit that he was beginning to feel that way himself. "What else do you remember, Mr. Tuvok?" he asked, trying his best to sound soothing rather than badgering.

After a moment's apparent consideration, Tuvok said, "I believe that the ambassador initiated telepathic contact with me. I cannot recall the specifics as yet, but I do remember her consciousness reaching out toward mine. I remember our minds . . . touching."

"Is that even possible?" Chekov asked no one in particular. He sounded skeptical. "I know that Vulcans are touch-telepaths, but I thought there always had to be skin-to-skin physical contact."

T'Lavik looked as doubtful as Chekov did. Speaking to Tuvok, she said, "It is unlikely that you experienced a genuine mind-touch with the Tholian ambassador, Lieutenant."

"I *know* what I experienced," Tuvok replied. Sulu was impressed by the bedrock certainty he heard in the lieutenant's voice. That certainty was something he had learned to trust implicitly over the past five years. Perhaps . . .

"Ambassador Burgess briefed us about Tholian telepathy," Sulu said, his words staying just ahead of the hypothesis that was forming in his mind. "She said that Tholians possess a sort of . . . networked intelligence, in addition to their sentience as individuals. Almost a hive intellect."

Dr. T'Lavik nodded. "You are referring to the Tholian Lattice, Captain."

"You're familiar with it, Doctor?" Sulu asked.

"I studied the Tholian culture extensively during my Starfleet Academy training. Although there are significant gaps in the Federation's knowledge, we do know that Tholians of the political, diplomatic, warrior, and worker castes spend a significant percentage of their short lives immersed in the Lattice. However, the brainwave frequencies of the Lattice are entirely incompatible with those required to initiate a Vulcan mind-meld."

So that's that, Sulu thought, dejected. *Kasrene probably* did *try to send Tuvok whatever information provoked Mosrene into killing her. But she never had a serious chance of success.*

"And yet I distinctly recall Ambassador Kasrene's mind touching mine," Tuvok said, still insistent. "The contact did not last long, but I am convinced that it was genuine."

"Yet you say you cannot recall any details from this encounter," T'Lavik said.

Tuvok glared at her, his uncharacteristic emotions making his features look even more alien than usual. "You yourself counseled patience, Doctor. Perhaps the details will return to me with time."

"Maybe Tuvok is right," Chapel said.

T'Lavik looked askance at the chief medical officer. "Again, the Vulcan-Tholian brainwave incompatibility cannot be ignored," she said, shaking her head slightly.

"But brainwave frequencies tend to change during the

dying process," Chapel said. "When Kasrene's brain began shutting down, her neural patterns might have become momentarily compatible with Tuvok's. Long enough to establish a very brief mental link."

Tuvok raised an eyebrow. "That is a very logical explanation, Doctor Chapel."

"Don't look so surprised," Chapel said with a wry smile.

"Lieutenant Tuvok's experience may merely be a delusion induced by simple neurological trauma," T'Lavik said, ignoring the banter and still speaking directly to Chapel. "That scenario is the most basic application of T'plana-Hath's Razor—the idea that the simplest explanation is also likely to be the most logical one."

The science officer's eyes suddenly became unfocused, as though he were looking inward.

"What is it?" Sulu asked.

"I believe I'm beginning to recall more of the experience, Captain. Kasrene wanted me to know something." A sweat broke out on Tuvok's brow as he concentrated in protracted silence. At length, he said, "I cannot yet reconstruct Kasrene's message in its entirety. But I do recall certain . . . emotional subtexts." This came out sounding almost like an admission of unseemly behavior.

" 'Emotional subtexts,' " T'Lavik repeated, an ever-so-slight tinge of scorn coloring her words. Sulu wondered, and not for the first time, whether he would ever encounter an intelligent species that was *more* emotional than Vulcans. At times they seemed uncannily proficient in the fine art of sarcasm.

"Yes," Tuvok continued, a vaguely confessional shame still shading his words. "I experienced her . . . belief that the knowledge she wished to impart was essential to the welfare of both the Federation and the Tholian Assembly. She was convinced that whatever it was she knew—whatever it was that Mosrene wanted suppressed—had to be brought to light quickly. It seemed to concern some calamity that both Kasrene and Mosrene believed to be imminent. I regret that I cannot visualize the coming disaster itself. Perhaps if our telepathic contact had lasted longer . . ." He trailed off, scowling.

"Did Kasrene give you any idea why Mosrene might have wanted to stop her?" Chekov asked.

"Perhaps, Commander," Tuvok said. "But I am not certain. I do, however, know that Kasrene wanted *us*—that is, representatives of the Federation—to be the only recipients of the information she carried. And strangely, she also seemed to share Mosrene's reticence about allowing the information to circulate generally with the Tholian Assembly. To do so would have precipitated the very disaster she envisioned."

"If the information really is that sensitive, then keeping it out of the Tholian Lattice will be a neat trick," Chapel said.

Chekov shrugged. "Not if only a few Tholians know about it, and then keep themselves sequestered from the Lattice. Maybe that's the reason Mosrene doesn't seem to be in any hurry to return to Yilskene's ship."

But Sulu noticed a huge problem with Mosrene's apparent need for concealment. "There's a very wise old proverb about secrets, Pavel. 'Three can keep a conspiracy a secret—but only if two of them are dead.' "

"What are you saying?" Chapel wanted to know. "That I can expect more Tholians to take up space in my morgue?"

"Not necessarily. I'm saying that we might not have the luxury of waiting around until Lieutenant Tuvok's memories return more fully before we're forced to act."

Aware that everyone's eyes were upon him, Sulu came to a decision. He had served in Starfleet for far too long to believe in coincidences. Whatever it was that Kasrene had wanted the Federation to know—but had also wanted hidden from her own countrymen—had to be related to the Tholian military buildup that so concerned Starfleet Command. And to whatever alien adversary menaced the Tholians on their far frontier.

So perhaps the solution to one mystery would help to solve the others.

Sulu crossed to the companel on the wall and pressed a button. "Captain Sulu to bridge."

"Lojur here, sir."

"Commander, how far are we from the nearest volume of interspatially unstable space?"

"Captain, are you referring to the region where the Defiant *disappeared thirty years ago?"*

"The very same."

"There's a filament of unstable space running through much of the territory claimed by the Tholians. The near end of it lies less than a parsec from our present position."

Sulu smiled a fencer's calculating smile. "Good. After Yilskene's ship picks up the Tholian diplomatic party and sets out for Tholia, Mr. Lojur, I want you to lay in a course parallel to that interspatial filament. And I want you to follow it all the way to the far end of Tholian space."

"Won't we show up on Yilskene's sensors if we take that heading?" Lojur asked.

"Not if we cover our tracks."

"Sir?"

"We can create a sensor ghost by bouncing a deflector beam off the edge of the filament. That will make it appear that we're headed back the way we came. Keep us a few dozen klicks from the filament's edge, but don't let us actually slip over into interspace. We're not looking to join the *Defiant*, after all."

"Aye, sir." Lojur sounded apprehensive. Some three decades after her disappearance, the *Defiant*—whose personnel had slain one another while in the grip of a berserker rage caused by this region's interspatial distortions—had quickly become the stuff of some fairly hair-raising ghost stories among Starfleet Academy's midshipmen.

After Sulu had signed off to allow Lojur to prepare for *Ex-*

celsior's course adjustment, he noticed that Chekov and Chapel appeared to be having reservations similar to Lojur's; they looked nearly as stony-faced as the Vulcans.

"That's a pretty dangerous course, Captain," Chekov said. "And I'm not only talking about the chance of running into Tholian patrols."

"*Defiant*," Chapel said, almost whispering.

Sulu nodded, acknowledging his old friends' reticence. "We're just going to have to trust that *Excelsior*'s shields—and the skills of her helmsman—will keep us from sharing *Defiant*'s fate."

Both Chekov and Chapel seemed satisfied with that. "I'd better whip up a theragen compound to be on the safe side," Chapel said. "Just in case interspace starts affecting us the way it did *Defiant*'s crew."

Sulu nodded yet again. He wasn't keen on administering what was essentially a Klingon nerve agent to his crew, but he couldn't forget how a cocktail of theragen derivative had prevented the crew of the *Enterprise* from plunging irretrievably into interspace-caused madness.

Addressing everyone present, he said, "Whatever dangers might await us out there, the far side of Tholian space is where we'll find our answers. Such as exactly what the Tholians are willing to spill their own blood to keep hidden from us."

Chapter 10

Earlier . . .

Do we have proof? The question reverberated through the Diplomatic Castemoot SubLink. Fekrene [The Gold] had posed the interrogative.

We have their ship and have examined their bodies, answered Benrene [The Gray], her inter-voice bright and tinkling. *Fulskene's ship captured the invader vessel after three of our other warcraft were destroyed. But even as their defeat arose to shatter them, our warriors inflicted great damage upon the enemy.*

Tosrene [The Violet] chimed before projecting into the SubLink. *I have the memories of the late Fulskene and his crew from the battle. Allow me to share them.*

Then they all saw it, from twelve different points of view, all similar but slightly different. The multifaceted image was of a space battle. One Tholian ship was gutted nearby, wreckage and flotsam tumbling randomly in freefall, while another was on fire, with green spikes of energy crackling across its wedge-shaped hull.

The memory played in reverse, showing four Tholian craft as they engaged the enemy ship, energy bursts and charged missiles reentering the weapons banks from which they had come. The quartet's energy web flickered and broke apart, was disrupted by blasts which now returned to the aggressor's tubular ship, then recovered, suddenly becoming strong and cohesive. The Tholians unwove the web around the enemy ship, then faced energy blasts which answered their own volleys of firepower.

Eventually, the memories rewound to the point at which the enemy ship had entered Tholian space, apparently tumbling out of the very same OtherVoid that the sentinel ships had begun to explore in earnest during recent times.

They come intent on invasion, as have so many others before them, Fekrene [The Gold] projected.

What of their ship now? asked Elkrene [The Ruby].

Benrene's mind-line brightened a bit. *The craft of the invaders is being brought to Tholia. The invaders are being destructured and dissected, their components analyzed and catalogued.*

Could the speculations of the physicians be correct? Kasrene asked. As multiple thoughts affirmed it, Kasrene's mind took on a darker hue. *We must not allow this information into the Lattice-at-large. Halt transport of the ship and confine the thoughts of those who know the truth of this matter.*

Dinrene's alarm was almost palpable. *Why should we hide such information about the aggressors? The truth will empower both defense and unity among the castes.*

Such a truth will not bring a wholeness to the Lattice, Mosrene said, his response glowing turquoise in the Sub-Link. *It will more likely solidify the distrust so many already feel toward the Federation.*

Conflict with the Federation while we are beset by formidable adversaries from the OtherVoid will deplete the energies of the Tholian Assembly, Tosrene [The Violet] chimed.

Kasrene spoke. *If we make allies of the Federation first, and bring the Assembly into harmony with its greater power, we will then have aid rather than conflict. Such an arrangement may be our only chance.*

But the castes will not unite to ally with the Federation if they know the truth, Mosrene's dark thoughts rang.

Energy from Fekrene [The Gold] washed in, and the Diplomatic Castemoot SubLink fell silent. *The worlds of outside are coming to us, and we can choose to grow stronger thereby, or be shattered. I believe/know the time is now for an appeal to the Federation. Kasrene is correct.*

Benrene echoed the earlier thoughts of many others. *Mosrene is correct as well. And if we are to keep the truth from the Lattice-at-large, we must be aware that its implications increase the potential for conflict with the Federation. Particularly from the warrior caste.*

Revelation may also breed trust, Kasrene offered serenely. *The lower echelons of the warrior caste are accustomed to the Diplomatic Castemoot keeping its decisions and strategies concealed from them. But potential allies may not be so forgiving/understanding.*

So do we fracture the facets of the Great Castemoot Assembly in favor of outsiders? The tones and colors that underlay Mosrene's question were threatening.

The SubLink again went silent for a time as excerpts of the conversation—if not its most salient and sensitive facts—filtered down, out, and laterally across the complex webwork of the Tholian Lattice.

Sulu settled back into his chair just as the turbolift doors whisked open to deposit Chekov and Akaar onto the bridge.

Turning his chair to face them both, Sulu said, "Everything go smoothly?"

Chekov stepped down toward the captain's chair, near the bridge's center. "As well as can be expected after transporting a group of alien diplomats who see no need to speak to us any further until after they take care of their leader's funerary rites and consult with their superiors."

"Did Mosrene agree to speak with Burgess privately?" Sulu asked.

"If he did, she's keeping it to herself. I get the distinct impression that she's pinned the blame for Kasrene's death on *us*."

"Shocking," Sulu said, deadpan. *She blames me, because of my assignment to monitor the Tholian war machine,* he thought with more than a little rancor. *As though her own loose lips had nothing to do with Mosrene's attack on Kasrene.*

Akaar had taken his post at the main tactical station, which was located to the right of Sulu's chair. "Security crews are doing a thorough sweep of all areas that the Tholians have occupied while aboard *Excelsior*, in search of listening devices or signs of sabotage."

"Good," Sulu said, nodding. Given the clandestine nature of his own mission here, Sulu thought Akaar's actions were appropriate and prudent.

Turning to communications, Sulu caught Rand's eye. "Please hail Yilskene's vessel, Janice."

"Aye, sir."

Moments later, the multifaceted visage of Yilskene appeared on the main viewer. Sulu began to address him. "Admiral Yilskene, I trust that your diplomatic team and their belongings have made it back to your ship safely?"

"They have. Your transmission is breaking up, Captain. Please boost your signal if you have anything further to discuss."

"I'm terribly sorry," Sulu said, rising from his chair and looking to his left. "We seem to be having difficulty with some of our systems. I believe it may have to do with the local interphasic radiation. We're not far from the region of interspace where our starship *Defiant* was lost, after all."

"Captain, your transmission is very garbled." Yilskene's eyespots seemed to glow brighter, but Sulu thought this

might have been his own imagination at work. Did the Tholian suspect subterfuge?

"I am withdrawing *Excelsior* from the 15 Lyncis system to effect repairs on our systems. Please hail us when your diplomats are ready to resume their discussions with us."

It seemed to take Yilskene a beat longer than necessary to respond. *"I understand that you are withdrawing for repairs. We will contact you within a few of your diurnal cycles to discuss further diplomatic matters."*

Sulu dipped his head in a nod. "Very good, Admiral. Until then."

The viewscreen replaced Yilskene's image with that of his sleek flagship, cast against the star-bedecked backdrop of space. Sulu took his seat and glanced over at Rand. "Looks like your 'interference' worked like a charm."

She flashed him a grin. "Piece of cake, sir. He heard just enough of what he needed to. I think those high-pitched subspace 'whistlers' I threw in over our transmission convinced him that he was dealing with a force of nature rather than an incredibly gifted Starfleet communications officer."

Sulu smiled, then turned back to the center of the bridge where his helm and navigation officers awaited his orders. "Take us out, Lieutenant Asher," he said. "And let's make sure that everything's coordinated with engineering, Commander Lojur."

"Aye, sir," the Halkan navigator said as he touched the control surfaces on his console.

Thirteen minutes later, Asher announced, "We're out of range of Yilskene's sensors, sir."

Lojur tapped his console. "I detect no other ships in the area, and confirm no active sensor contact."

Sulu toggled the comm button built into his armrest. "Chief Azleya, are we ready to switch over?"

"*Affirmative, sir,*" came the smooth, gregarious voice of the Denobulan chief engineer. "*You need only to give the word.*"

"Then let's become a Tholian ship," Sulu said. Aside from a subtle, nearly imperceptible change in the vibration of the deck plates, nothing on the bridge was altered. But Sulu knew that Azleya and her crew had made some critical modifications to *Excelsior*'s warp generators. Now, anybody actively scanning the ship—or even passively examining her warp trail—would encounter only the telltale traces of a Tholian military vessel. The disguise Azleya had concocted was calculated to withstand all but the closest scrutiny.

"Take her right up to the far edge of the interspatial filament, Mr. Lojur. *Don't* let us dip into it, but make best speed alongside it until we reach the region of conflict at the far edge of Tholian space." *And let's hope this region of space doesn't force Christine to shoot us all up with theragen just to keep us from going insane and murdering each other.* A chill ascended his spine as he recalled the horrible way *Defiant*'s crew had died.

Enough worrying about the questions I can't answer, Sulu told himself. *It's time to concentrate on the ones I can.*

Sulu rose again and turned to Chekov. "You have the bridge, Commander. I'll be in sickbay, checking on Tuvok."

"Aye, sir."

"Then I'll look in on Ambassador Burgess," Sulu added as he stepped into the turbolift.

The doors closed on Chekov's silent, sympathetic, *Go-with-God* expression.

Tuvok sat on the biobed, doing his best to meditate in the bustle of sickbay. One orderly was still cleaning up the trauma area where Chapel and her crew had tried to save the Tholian ambassador, and being none too quiet about it.

Turning inward, he tried to find the thoughts and memories which Ambassador Kasrene had placed there. *Could she have transferred part of her* katra *to me?* He rejected the stray thought almost as quickly as it had come. *No, that is not log-*

ical. The concept of katra *is a myth. Kasrene merely transferred some of her memory engrams to me, nothing more. I must find a way to access them.*

He closed both sets of eyelids tightly. As he dug more deeply into his subconscious, the darkness was broken by flashes of color mixed with long, steady bursts of light. The discharges were random and chaotic, and Tuvok knew on some instinctive level that these were the messages from Kasrene. *But how do I decipher them?*

Tuvok envisioned himself as an immaterial form within the spaces of his own mind, and reached out with an imaginary hand toward the ever-changing displays of multicolored, fractally complex lights. At first, they passed through his hand, but then one stuck, as if glued there. Moments later, more colors swirled about his hand, wending their way down his arm. Then he began to see other flashes . . .

. . . warm orange between trapezoidal structures . . .

. . . a Tholian, still and unmoving, suddenly shattered by a blow from another Tholian, its thousands of shards commingling with crystals of every imaginable color in rolling hills constructed of great heaps of multiplanar gemstones . . .

. . . Captain Sulu introducing his crew to the Tholians in the transporter room, amidst a glowing green hue . . .

. . . vaguely humanoid figures lying on dull brown pedestals, their rough, gray skin peeled back from elongated chest cavities as Tholian doctors dissected them . . .

. . . cool crimson fluid washing down the side of a metal wall . . .

"Tuvok?"

And then, the lights fled from him, splintering into ever-tinier shards, as he felt himself being pulled out of his meditative state. With a shudder that might have been imperceptible to any but the most highly attuned Vulcan Master, Tuvok awoke. Opening his eyes, he saw Captain Sulu and Dr. Chapel regarding him with apparent concern.

"Sorry to wake you, Mr. Tuvok," Sulu said.

"I was not asleep, Captain. I was in a deep meditative state, attempting to discern what Ambassador Kasrene was trying to tell us just prior to her death."

Sulu nodded. "Did you find anything new?"

"I found many color-intensive visual elements that were unfamiliar to me," Tuvok said. "And when I attempted to examine them, I saw other images nested within them. I still have yet to make sense of them. However, I believe it is safe to assume that these are the specific memories the Tholian ambassador implanted in my mind."

Chapel leaned forward and pried open Tuvok's outer eyelids, peering intently into his pupils. Apparently not satisfied, she then began scanning him with a handheld tricorder. "Go ahead, Tuvok," she said without looking up. "I'm just double-checking your neurological readings. Relax."

But Tuvok felt anything but relaxed. His inability to completely access the memories Kasrene had placed into his mind had left him feeling restless and frustrated.

"What do you make of the images so far, Lieutenant?" Sulu asked quietly.

"I have yet to find any imagery that seemed specific to our current situation," Tuvok said. "But I remain convinced that the reason behind Kasrene's murder—and the explanation for the Tholian military buildup—remains locked within me. And I am equally certain that some tangible danger threatens both the Tholian Assembly and the Federation, and that Kasrene wanted to warn us of this."

Tuvok was surprised by the harsh voice he heard directly behind him, from the sickbay's opposite entrance. "Perhaps it's the threat of imminent war that had Kasrene worried," Burgess said.

Tuvok watched as Sulu and Chapel turned to face the ambassador, whose arms were folded across her chest. She appeared to be almost livid with restrained anger.

"Ambassador, I had planned to speak with you alone when I was done with Mr. Tuvok," Sulu said.

"I see," Burgess said, speaking with the exaggerated politeness humans often used to signal that they were actually quite angry. "I suppose that was when you intended to inform me that my outgoing communications capabilities have been disabled. And perhaps you were also going to explain why this ship is now headed *deeper* into Tholian Assembly space, risking the lives of everyone aboard. Not to mention jeopardizing any chance for a Tholian-Federation peace agreement."

Sulu stared at her for a protracted moment, as though carefully weighing how best to handle this volatile personality. Tuvok found it odd that she should accuse the captain of jeopardizing lives, when she had already done that herself by revealing *Excelsior*'s surveillance activities to the Tholians.

"Since you've saved me the trouble of scheduling a private meeting with you, Ambassador," Sulu said at length, "I'll brief you and my science officer at the same time."

Chapel moved away from Burgess and closer to Tuvok, holding her tricorder up again. But Tuvok noted that the doctor seemed to be paying the device scant attention, evidently repeating the same scans she had just completed. She was clearly uncomfortable with Burgess, and Tuvok could understand why. The diplomat was highly emotional, more so than most other humans he had encountered so far. She seemed unhappy not just with the way her diplomatic mission to the Tholians was unfolding, but also with something more fundamental. *She seems discontent with her very life.*

"Outgoing communications have been disabled for all but command-level Starfleet officers because we are currently on yellow alert status," Sulu explained to the ambassador. To Tuvok's ears, the captain's politeness sounded every bit as forced as the ambassador's. "We are now engaged in a highly sensitive mission that could easily be compromised by accidental—or intentional—communications leaks."

Burgess's eyes widened. Tuvok surmised that she had taken the captain's last statement as a reprimand for her earlier unauthorized revelations to the Tholians.

"All right," she said. "But that doesn't explain our current heading. Can't you see that moving deeper into Tholian territory is likely to spark a conflict with them?"

Sulu spread his hands. "Believe me, Ambassador, a conflict with the Tholians is the *last* thing I want. But the Tholians are already in the midst of hostilities with *somebody*, and the future stability of the Federation-Tholian border may well depend on our learning everything we can about their new adversary. And I strongly suspect that Ambassador Kasrene was murdered because Mosrene caught her trying to help us do just that."

"You can't know that for sure."

"Of course not," Sulu said. "But that's why I've put us on our present course. To find out for sure. In fact, I think that by being out here, we may actually stave off a conflict rather than ignite one. We might even find a way to help the Tholians defend themselves from whomever is attacking them."

"This all sounds pretty far-fetched to me, Captain. And I don't think Admiral Yilskene will buy it either, once he discovers what you've done."

"With a little luck, he won't. Not until after we're in a position to evaluate the tactical situation on the far Tholian border well enough for Starfleet to draft a practical plan to assist the Tholians. But the longer it takes us to do that, the more Tholian lives will be lost. Believe me, Ambassador, this is for the best."

Burgess suddenly grew more intense, her icy politeness melted away by a fumarole of outrage. "Don't you understand? The Tholian Assembly has an extremely rules-oriented culture. You have no business entering their space without their express permission. Even if your stated intention is to aid the Tholians against some new foe, your actions still risk destroying *any* hope of creating trust between their government and the Federation."

"Only if we're caught," Sulu said, holding up his index finger as if making a point. "And we're doing our best to make sure that doesn't happen."

Burgess paused, then sighed in frustration. "I should have expected something like this from you, Captain."

"Why?" Sulu asked.

"Because I researched your participation in the Khitomer affair of five years ago. You broke more than a few rules then, too, and only a happy outcome saved you from getting severely dressed down by Starfleet's brass hats."

Tuvok recalled that occasion with crystal clarity. He had been on *Excelsior*'s bridge when Captain Sulu, intent on rescuing Captain James Kirk and Dr. Leonard McCoy, had violated Starfleet orders by attempting to rescue them from the Klingon prison world of Rura Penthe. That day, Tuvok had protested the captain's apparently reckless disregard for the official chain of command. Though the crisis had ultimately turned out well for all concerned, the science officer still sometimes rankled at the capacity of human Starfleet officers to set aside propriety when it appeared to suit the circumstances. *Is this another one of those times?* Tuvok thought.

He wondered if such questions could ever be answered save in retrospect.

Tuvok watched Sulu grin at Burgess. "Yes, Ambassador. Like you, I've been known to break a rule or two from time to time."

"*Unlike* you, Captain, I've never played dice with galactic peace," she said.

"Really, Ambassador? What do you call revealing the presence of our probe drones to the Tholians?"

"I call it trying to make the best of yet another Starfleet-initiated alien-relations cockup," she said, almost snarling. "Frankly, I'm amazed that you haven't been sentenced to a nice long stretch mining dilithium somewhere yourself."

"I must live right," Sulu said, his grin only broadening. If Tuvok didn't know better, he'd think the captain was actually provoking the ambassador for the sheer perverse joy of it.

Burgess shook her head, now seeming more mystified than angry. "I really don't understand this, Captain. What is it you hope to gain?"

Immediately adopting a more serious demeanor, Sulu said, "What I hope to gain, Ambassador, is a more complete understanding of exactly what it is that the Tholians are trying so hard to keep us from discovering. I think even *you* would have to agree that it's not in the Federation's best interests to ally itself blindly with a people who are not only already engaged in an interstellar conflict, but are also trying their damnedest to cover it up."

Burgess's mouth opened and closed several times, but she said nothing. Tuvok was momentarily reminded of the Antedean with whom he had shared an apartment briefly during his Starfleet Academy years.

Tuvok decided then to voice his thoughts regarding the matter at hand; although they might have been taken as overly subjective—perhaps even illogical—he was certain that they were correct and deserved to be heard.

"Ambassador Burgess, while I share your concerns and apprehension regarding our apparent breach of Tholian law, I have found that Captain Sulu is an entirely capable and trustworthy Starfleet commander. I myself have expressed doubt as to the advisability of his actions in the past, but have most often found that they *are* appropriate to the situation. Despite his possessing the all-too-common human penchant for excessive emotionalism, Captain Sulu's command decisions are, in the main, eminently logical."

Sulu's face twitched almost imperceptibly, but his overall expression didn't change. Tuvok momentarily wondered what emotions had just gone through his captain's mind before continuing. "Additionally, although I have not yet been able to ascertain the meaning of the information Ambassador Kasrene planted in my mind, I remain firmly convinced of two things: first, that she did indeed pass some of her memory engrams to me, and second, that any future peace we may achieve with the Tholians depends largely upon our taking decisive action at this time."

Burgess stared at him for a lengthy interval, and Tuvok thought much of her rage had begun to dissipate. *Perhaps she recognizes the logic of my words,* he thought.

Nodding curtly to Tuvok and Sulu, Burgess turned to leave. Pausing in the doorway, she said, "I can see that your mind is made up, whether I agree with you or not, Captain."

Sulu nodded. "That's right, Ambassador."

"Then would you do me a small favor?"

"By all means."

"When my diplomatic meetings with the Tholians resume, I won't be able to operate in the dark, Captain. Please keep me apprised of all further developments on the Tholian military front."

"Of course, Ambassador," Sulu said. "As long as I can rely on your discretion." Tuvok sensed that the captain had only barely avoided appending the words "this time" to the end of that sentence.

Burgess laughed bitterly. "It looks like you'll have to. After all, the lives of everyone aboard *Excelsior* depend upon yours." And with that, she strode out of sickbay.

Afterward, Tuvok noted that Dr. Chapel was shaking her head, a look of frustration evident on her face. "Maybe it's just me, Hikaru, but that woman could drive an El-Aurian 'listener' to grab a set of ear-plugs," she said. Like Tuvok himself, Christine Chapel obviously placed a great deal of faith in Captain Sulu's discretion and judgment.

As Sulu chuckled in response to the doctor's quip, Tuvok wondered fleetingly just how deep the captain's belief in his own judgment went.

Chekov was beginning to breathe a bit easier, though only a bit. *Excelsior* had managed to escape being identified not only by Yilskene's ship, but also by three other Tholian patrol vessels whose rounds had taken them within a light-year of *Excelsior*'s route of travel along the length of the interspatial filament. Each time a Tholian craft appeared on the Starfleet vessel's passive scanners—equipment honed to exquisite sensitivity-levels during *Excelsior*'s lengthy survey of Beta Quadrant gaseous anomalies several years earlier—Lojur and Asher edged the starship just out of Tholian sensor range.

One of these encounters had been an extremely close call. Probably after making a faint sensor contact with *Excelsior*, the Tholian patrol vessel had altered course. Asher had moved the ship counter to the path of the Tholian vessel, spiraling about the boundary of the interphase filament like thread on a spool. Each time they were directly opposite the Tholian ship, *Excelsior* put on a slight burst of speed, drawing them further and further out of the other vessel's sensor range. Eventually, they had placed enough distance between *Excelsior* and the patrol ship to sustain a higher speed without creating undue risk of the Tholians penetrating the starship's disguised warp signature.

Now *Excelsior* was rapidly nearing what the charts indicated was the far border of Tholian space, the very region where their probes had been sent—and destroyed—earlier.

"Commander, sensors have just detected a warp signature from another ship," said Ensign Fenlenn, one of the junior science officers.

"Tholian?"

"No, sir."

"Range?" Chekov asked, eyebrows raised. *Are we finally about to meet the enemy?*

"Only light-days away, Commander. They're in close proximity to a small planet orbiting an F-type star."

"Where did it come from, Ensign?" Chekov wanted to know. A ship that close should have been visible much earlier, even via passive long-range scans.

"The sensors are picking up some very strange interspatial readings emanating from not far outside that system," Fenlenn said. "It's as though the interspatial filament has widened into some sort of terminus. Like a colossal rip leading straight into interspace."

And maybe straight into wherever that ship came from.

"Mr. Akaar," Chekov said. "Give me a tactical appraisal, please."

"Aye, Commander," came the Capellan's rumbling response. "The vessel does not appear to be scanning us at the moment, but . . . sir, they have just deployed their weapons."

"Against whom? Scan for other vessels. There's no way we could be within range of their weapons." Chekov leaned forward in the command chair, even as Akaar's fingers danced across his own console.

"They appear to be firing on the planet," Fenlenn said. "It's inhabited. Given the harsh class-N atmospheric conditions, I suspect that it's a Tholian border settlement."

"I confirm that," said Rand, raising a hand to her earpiece. "I'm receiving several Tholian distress signals from the surface."

"Maintain yellow alert status," Chekov said. "Lieutenant Asher, bring us in closer. Let the attackers know we're here."

He turned his head slightly. "Commander Rand, hail them."

Rand looked quizzical. "Are we dropping our disguise, sir?"

Chekov shook his head. "Let them think we're the biggest, meanest Tholian ship they ever saw." He punched the comm button on the chair's armrest. "Captain Sulu, please come to the bridge. We've got a situation here."

"Hailing frequencies open, Commander," Rand said. "Making challenge."

Akaar spoke before Chekov could, his voice raised somewhat. "Sir, they have just begun strafing the planet with a volley of ionic blasts. They appear to have hit some structures on the surface. But I cannot ascertain casualties as yet."

Chekov's mind raced. "Keep hailing the attacker, Jan—"

Rand interrupted him. "They're hailing *us*, sir."

The viewscreen dissolved into static, then gradually regained a measure of coherency. The creature who stared out of the viewer was humanoid, though clearly not human. It's skin was a mottled gray, with a rough texture that resembled thick tree-bark. The ropy black hair atop its head was shaved into dozens of slender, even rows.

"*Weki kwen jun belaï stofre winá Neyel daod joela.*"

"Sounds like the universal translator is still trying to sort out their language," Fenlenn said.

The alien continued speaking, its rigid brow crumpling into furrows, apparently moved by incredibly powerful facial muscles. "*Tia foti örwek zam dis de'evl woos émim Neyel,*" it said just before the screen went blank.

"Find out what they're saying," Chekov said. "Run the recording of that transmission through every exolinguistics protocol we have. And hail them again as soon as we can communicate."

As the doors to the turbolift opened and Sulu stepped out, Akaar spoke again. "Sir, the alien vessel has just fired on the planet again. This time our sensors have confirmed casualties. *Hundreds* of them."

Chekov glanced toward Sulu, who wasted no time saying, "Let's go put a stop to this, Pavel."

And so it begins, Chekov thought. Relinquishing the command chair with an efficient nod, he set about filling his old friend's simple order. He raised his voice so that everyone on the bridge could hear him clearly. "Red Alert. Raise shields. All hands to battle stations . . ."

Chapter 11

Sulu felt energized as he took back the captain's chair from Chekov. He ordered Janice to disable the red warning lights and alarm klaxons, and Pavel quickly brought him up to speed on the events of the last few minutes. Lieutenant Hopman—once again in her male form—arrived on the bridge as they were speaking, and positioned herself near the science station, where Ensign Fenlenn was working.

"Captain, I believe the universal translator has finally cracked the aliens' language," Rand announced suddenly.

Sulu took this as an encouraging sign. Talking was always the most desirable starting point in any first contact situation. Without a mutually intelligible language, combat with these obviously aggressive beings would shortly prove inevitable.

"Good work, Rand," Sulu said. "Let's start by replaying their hail in Standard."

On the viewer, the long-range image of a tapered, cylindrical alien ship orbiting the yellow-tinged planet was replaced by a recording of the alien hail. *"Incoming vessel, the Neyel Hegemony has no record of a ship matching your configuration. State your purpose here."*

"Neyel," Sulu said. "So, now we at least have a name for them." Turning to Rand and Fenlenn, he asked, "Can you confirm that the U.T. is up for a full, real-time conversation?"

"Yes, sir," Rand nodded, one hand lifted to the communications receiver in her ear.

"Then open a channel, please." Sulu stood as the screen briefly went black. A moment later, the rough-skinned humanoid—presumably the same one from the earlier transmission—appeared on the viewer.

"Commander of the Neyel vessel, I am Captain Hikaru Sulu of the Federation starship *U.S.S. Excelsior.* We were on a diplomatic mission to negotiate with the Tholians—the species which claims the world you have attacked—when we learned of their conflict with your people. We would like an opportunity to discuss your side of this matter in a peaceful, neutral setting if—"

The screen went black again, prompting Sulu to smile crookedly. "Was it something I said?"

"I'm sorry, Captain," Rand said, hurriedly touching panels on the communications display in front of her. "They've broken off communication."

"Reestablish," Sulu said, scowling.

Moments later, the Neyel leader was back on the viewscreen, but before Sulu could manage to say anything, the Neyel interrupted. *"These crystalline Devils are an opportunistic infestation, a scourge to be exterminated,"* the alien spat. *"Nothing more, nothing less. Anyone who would treat with them is most assuredly an enemy of the Neyel."*

"Captain, they are locking their weapons on us," Akkar said.

Two seconds later, *Excelsior* was rocked by a blast of directed energy, and the bridge shimmied as the inertial dampers worked to even out the impact. Sulu grabbed onto his chair to stay steady as the deck righted itself.

"Shields at ninety-three percent and holding," Akaar said.

"They're using what seem to be multiphasic ion beams," Fenlenn said from the science station.

Sulu turned to face Akaar, who looked up from his station. "They appear to have weapons ports installed along the entire length and girth of their hull, sir. It is unclear whether all of their weapons employ directed ionic energy or not."

"How strong are their shields?" Sulu asked.

"Hard to say, Captain," Fenlenn said. "Our initial scans haven't penetrated very far into the alien vessel. Its hull seems to contain a high percentage of some kind of refractory metal alloy."

"They've only fired once, so I'd take that as a warning shot," Chekov said.

"You may be right," Sulu said, nodding, "but just because they aren't firing at *us* right now doesn't mean I'm going to stand by while they massacre this colony."

"Unless they're jamming outgoing signals from the settlers," Rand said, "it's likely that Tholian warships are already on their way, Captain."

"Good point," Sulu said. "Mr. Akaar, keep a sharp eye out. We may have some more company soon."

"Aye, sir."

Looking nervous, Lieutenant Hopman approached Sulu's chair. "Captain, if we do get identified by Tholian patrols out here, not only will our presence here be known to the Assembly almost immediately, but it could even look as if we're *helping* the Neyel. On the other hand, if we try to *stop* the Neyel, the Tholian warrior caste is just as likely to take offense."

"That doesn't make any sense."

"Captain, by rescuing them without carefully negotiating with them in advance for the privilege, we're all but telling their warriors that we think they're incompetent. And, of course, just about every caste in the Assembly will be frustrated by our, ah, unauthorized incursion into their space."

"Damned if we do, and damned if we don't," Sulu said, feeling grim. But he took heart in the fact that no Tholian warships had arrived as yet.

"The aliens are firing on the Tholian outpost world again," Akaar announced loudly, and the viewscreen showed the evidence of his words. Multiple ion rays lanced out from the Neyel ship and into the planet's atmosphere.

"Asher," Sulu said. "Take us into the path of those blasts, between the Neyel ship and the Tholian settlement. We're putting a stop to this. Now."

Chekov moved toward his chair and leaned in. "Please tell me you a have a plan," he said quietly.

"If we lost only seven percent of our shield capacity from the previous attack, then we ought to be able to sustain another few direct hits without serious damage. And that may buy some time for the Tholians down there."

"You hope," Chekov finished for him. "If that first volley they fired at us really was only a warning shot . . ."

"I can't just allow the wanton slaughter of those people down there, Pavel. And if we can stop the attack without having to open fire ourselves . . ."

"Big gamble," Chekov said.

"I know," Sulu told him.

Punching the comm button on the arm of his chair, Sulu said, "Chief Azleya, we're going to take some heavy flak in a few seconds. Make sure our shields hold, however much power it takes."

"You'll have power to spare for the shields, Captain," the chief engineer said in the mock-chiding tone to which Sulu had grown long accustomed. *"So long as you don't ask me to draft any new laws of physics, that is."*

Sulu grinned. "No promises, Chief. Sulu out."

"We do not know what other weapons they may possess, sir," Akaar said. "They may be able to shoot us out of the sky with something even more potent than what we have seen so far."

"Or, they may listen to reason and stop shooting long

enough to hear us out," Sulu said. "Let's not assume the worst about them until they give us a reason."

He saw the veins in Akaar's neck throb visibly. Clearly, his security chief wasn't happy with the situation. *But it* is *his job to expect the worst,* Sulu reminded himself.

"I haven't given an order to stand down weapons in the meantime, have I, Lieutenant?" he asked, fixing the much taller man with his gaze.

"No, sir." Akaar seemed to try, unsuccessfully, to restrain his enthusiasm.

"Good," Sulu said. "I want to bring this affair to a peaceful conclusion if I can. But the Neyel *did* fire on the Tholians—and on us—first. And without any apparent provocation. Make sure all weapons batteries are ready."

Akaar nodded. Without glancing at his tactical readout, he said, "Already done, sir. All phaser banks are fully charged, and all torpedo tubes are loaded and ready."

Let's hope we can greet them eventually with open hearts and hands, Sulu thought, quoting the well-known Capellan greeting. *Rather than with our security chief's closed fist.*

He turned his attention toward Rand. "Janice, please keep trying to hail the Neyel ship. If you get through to them, put me on immediately."

"Yes, sir."

Sulu studied the viewer as the Neyel ship, with its long, weapons-festooned hull, loomed steadily larger in *Excelsior*'s flight path. He wondered for a moment if any sort of parlay or peace was even possible with such apparently hate-filled people. After all, the Neyel with whom he had spoken had referred to the Tholians as an "infestation."

I just hope I'm not placing my ship and my crew in jeopardy over a lost cause, he thought.

In the torpedo bay on the starboard side of Deck Twenty, Chief Julia Pitcher's crew scrambled to prep the complement of photon torpedoes. She knew that the portside crew was simultaneously doing the very same job, under the command of Lieutenant Curry, one of the junior tactical officers.

Each torpedo had to be checked and double-checked before being loaded into the torpedo bays. Even though the equipment was scanned at least twice a day—mainly to check on the magnetic containment of each weapon's internal supply of matter and antimatter—a red alert called for even more stringent quality-control measures.

"Julia, we've got a red light on the M/A fuel cell for Torp37A," said Petty Officer Tagame.

Pitcher moved over to that particular torpedo quickly, her tricorder in one hand to double-check whatever she diagnosed with her eyes. She afforded a quick grin to the young Japanese man. "Since when do we use first names during red alerts, *Mister* Tagame?"

He blushed and stammered an apology as she crouched to check on the miniature warp fuel cell. "It's okay, Gen," Pitcher said good-naturedly. "If we have to be all spit-and-polish with our duties during battle, at least we can be informal with our use of names."

A wisp of hair fell across Pitcher's face as she leaned in to study the mechanism; she blew the hair upward with a gust of breath. Prodding the control panel on the device, she ran the scanner over the surface. As expected, it told her the same thing she already knew. "Pull this one, Gen. We're going to have to replace the cell."

As she stood, the room jolted violently, knocking several of her crew onto the floor. Pitcher had barely recovered her balance before another blow to *Excelsior* knocked her off her feet entirely. She heard a sharp cry from her left, simultaneous with a sickening, wet crunch.

Looking across the room, Pitcher saw that one of the torpedoes had gotten off track from its antigrav carrier and had pinned Win Lemkopf. He was struggling to move the heavy casing, and something was clearly wrong with him.

Pitcher and two other crew members got on their feet to help him, even as the feminine computer voice droned out *"Shields at seventy-four point eight percent. Minor damage to Decks Three, Four, and Five."*

Lemkopf screamed in pain as Pitcher, Bell, and Rolquin lifted the massive torpedo off of him. As they moved it, Pitcher could see why. His leg was crushed, probably broken in several places, and a large shard of bone protruded from just above his knee.

"Sickbay, we've got a medical emergency coming your way," Pitcher yelled. "We need a trauma team, Deck Twenty, Torpedo Bay Two." The communicator channel on their consoles in the torpedo bay were locked on to allow for hands-free communication.

"Acknowledged," came a female voice. Pitcher didn't immediately recognize it, but figured it probably belonged to one of the new nurses. *"We'll dispatch a team immediately."*

"Need any help down here?"

Pitcher turned to see Lieutenant Shandra Docksey standing in the open doorway. The pretty East Indian officer generally worked the helm on the beta shift, but if she was here now, Pitcher wasn't about to refuse her help. She knew that Shandra had had a good deal of previous experience working both in the photon torpedo bays and the phaser stations. Besides, Pitcher genuinely liked working alongside anyone whose disposition was as positive as Docksey's.

"Stay here with Lemkopf until the medics arrive," the weapons exec said. "We've got to prep these torpedoes."

Docksey knelt beside Lemkopf, who was moaning in pain. She immediately removed her belt and cinched it around Lemkopf's leg at mid-thigh. Pitcher turned back to the others and ordered them to get back to loading, then moved to double-check the viability of the torpedo that had fallen on Lemkopf.

She heard a familiar hissing, followed by a thump, and a quick glance to the wall-mounted computer screens confirmed that the port torpedoes had just been deployed. Curry and his crew were no doubt readying their second salvo. *We'd better finish getting our* first *salvo ready.*

"Torpedo Bay Two, is your complement ready?" That was Lojur's voice from the bridge over the comm channel. Pitcher knew that Lojur and Docksey had been an item for several years now, and that the day of their wedding was fast approaching.

She wondered if Lojur even knew that his sweetheart was down here.

The ship shuddered again as Pitcher prepared to reply. Pushing the torpedo that had fallen on Lemkopf onto the floor-mounted tracks that led into its launching bay, she yelled, "Two more to load, Commander Lojur. Give me five seconds."

"Acknowledged."

Bell and Rolquin slammed their own bay doors closed and gave her the thumbs-up sign. "Clear to launch," Pitcher yelled to Lojur.

An instant later, the hissing sound became much louder and the coordinated thumps grew as sonorous as a gong as the torpedoes launched toward their target. Pitcher turned to see two white-suited medics rush into the room, and then—

A deafening roar filled the chamber, and Pitcher could hear metal tearing and an explosive decompression, directly below. *"Warning. Hull breach on Decks Twenty-One and Twenty-Two,"* the computer said. A beat later, it added, *"Emergency forcefields now in place."*

One deck below us. One deck is all that separated life from death. Pitcher saw the same shocked look on her staff's faces, and realized that they all were having the same chilling thought.

"Torpedo Bay Two, are you all right?" Chekov's concerned voice came over the comm system this time.

"We're steady. What happened?" Pitcher watched the medics injecting Lemkopf with a hypospray. He passed out beside their antigrav stretcher.

"Weapons fire from the Neyel ship hit two of the torpedoes as they exited the ship," Chekov explained. *"The torps had already been armed."*

The Neyel. That must be who's firing at us. Never even heard of them before. Pitcher looked to Tagame, Bell, and Rolquin. They all appeared scared but steady. As the medics carefully loaded Lemkopf onto the stretcher, Docksey stood. Pitcher saw Lemkopf's blood spattered all over the woman's tunic.

"They must have figured out where our torpedo launch bays are, Commander," Pitcher said, projecting her words toward the communicator. "Is it safe to prep any more torpedoes?"

"They're having more effect on the enemy vessel than our phasers are," Chekov said, pronouncing one word as "wessel." *"We're distributing more shield power across your decks."*

"Very good, sir," Pitcher said, swallowing. "We'll have another set prepped and ready in two minutes." She allowed herself a gratified smile as she watched her crew, busy at their tasks.

"Anything else I can do here?" Docksey asked after checking and loading another pair of torpedoes. Behind her, the medics were gently carrying Lemkopf's stretcher out toward the corridor.

Pitcher was about to respond when the communicator of one of the medics beeped. *"Medical aid needed on Deck Five. Three members of the forward phaser crew are injured."*

"I think they could probably use some help there, Lieutenant," Pitcher told Docksey. "They sound even more short-handed than we are. As long as we don't get breached, I think we'll be able to hold the fort up here. Thanks for your help."

Docksey gave Pitcher a quick smile before dashing off down the hall. Pitcher had rarely seen Docksey *not* smiling; maybe that was part of the reason she was so well liked among *Excelsior*'s crew.

The ship shuddered to one side again as Pitcher turned back to the torpedoes that still needed to be loaded.

Sulu gripped the armrests of his chair as the battle raged, and the two ships exchanged salvo after salvo.

The plan to block the Neyel from firing on the Tholian settlement had gone sour almost immediately, as the Neyel ship instead began to try to hit both *Excelsior* and the colony. However, *Excelsior* had finally been successful in drawing most of the Neyel vessel's attention away from the planet by circling around the aggressor and firing successive volleys at its tough, refractory-metal hull.

And *Excelsior* had indeed inflicted *some* damage on the Neyel ship, enough for scans of some of the breached areas to reveal that the ship's internal design was very different from that of Federation starships—rather than consisting of stacks of horizontally oriented decks, it was effectively a collection of nested curves, cylinders stacked within cylinders. This made the main power systems, which were presumably located in the relative safety of the Neyel ship's core, extremely difficult to target.

Sulu could only hope that he wouldn't be forced to destroy the Neyel vessel in order to disable it. And that it wouldn't finish off *Excelsior* first.

"There," Sulu said, rising and pointing to a particular spot on the main viewer, where Akaar had mounted a tactical diagram of what their scans had so far revealed of the Neyel ship's internal layout. "If we direct a combined phaser and torpedo bombardment *there,* I'm betting it'll take down their propulsion system."

"I agree," Fenlenn said, and Chekov and Akaar nodded as well.

Lojur spoke into the companel on his console as he touched several lighted keys. "Phaser Array Three, we're sending a spread to the coordinate sets on Lieutenant Akaar's tactical display. Torpedo Bays One and Two, prep a set of torpedoes to coordinate set twelve, then another to set thirteen."

Sulu watched the progress of his weapons teams on the computer, then gave the command, "Fire."

Turning toward the forward viewscreen, Sulu saw thirty-odd phaser blasts strafing the hull of the Neyel ship, while several light bursts from the torpedos zoomed toward their target. Seconds later, a conflagration erupted in the intended portion of the enemy vessel, almost directly amidships. Suddenly, much of the cylindrical craft seemed to lose power, whole sections of its hull going as dark as the surrounding space.

Several people on the bridge let out small cheers.

"They're not yet disabled," reported Fenlenn, quickly damping the sense of triumph. "But there appear to have been significant casualties."

Sulu felt a twinge of real regret, but he pushed it aside. After all, what choice had the Neyel left him?

He turned to Rand. "Hail them again. Maybe now they'll talk to us. And listen to reason."

Docksey and two other off-duty crew members had arrived on Deck Five at approximately the same time. They made their way to Phaser Array One, located just behind the registry numbers on the forward dorsal side of *Excelsior*'s primary hull.

The damage that had caused the injuries to the three technicians was obvious. One of the blasts *Excelsior* had taken sent an arc of power into the computer banks there, and two of them had exploded, their ODN relays and scorched duotronic circuits spilling out like viscera from a slain animal. Those unhurt by the blast were now operating the phaser banks manually, since most of the control systems were off-line.

Quickly assessing the situation, Docksey was reminded of ancient Earth history, when powder-and-lead-crammed cannons had been manned by artillery crewmen who had rolled the ungainly weapons about on creaking wooden decks.

"Over here, Shandra," a familiar voice called. It was Dennis Beauvois, another beta-shifter with whom she often had lunch in the mess hall. The dark-haired man had recently received some very good news; his wife, back on Starbase 35, had just given birth to a new baby boy, their third child. He had seen only holograms of his son so far, but he was quite excited to have a boy to join his two little girls.

Docksey hurried over to help him. "Quite a mess up here, isn't it?" she said, her smile faltering.

"Yeah, two of the guys got burned pretty badly, and Fri'lin got skewered in the leg with some shrapnel when one of the consoles overloaded," Beauvois said. He shook his head and added, "Nasty."

"So, what's the deal here?" Docksey asked. "You want me to take the target-lock or the trigger?" She was joking. The phaser cannons didn't have triggers *per se*; but when run manually, they had to be triggered by a code sequence relayed down from the bridge on a display panel.

"You seem more like a trigger person to me than a *squint-through-the-crosshairs-at-the-target* type," Beauvois said, grinning.

"They're still refusing our hails, Captain," Rand said.

Sulu shook his head and let out a heavy sigh. *Some people just don't know when to quit.*

"Phaser Array One and Two are targeted and ready,"

Akaar said, looking at Sulu expectantly. "We have detected functional weaponry near the vessel's core. But if we destroy those weapons, a great many Neyel may find themselves floating home without a vessel around them."

Sulu turned back toward Rand. "Send one more hai—"

Lojur interrupted. "Captain, the Neyel are firing at us again. Looks like a missile of some kind."

Sulu turned back toward the viewscreen and in less time than it took him to blink, saw a bright streak headed directly at *Excelsior.*

"Coordinates are locked in," Beauvois said.

"I'm all set here." Docksey looked over at him. "So, how's the new boy doing? You thought of a name yet?"

Beauvois shook his head. "No, we're still mulling names over. How are the wedding preparations go—"

Docksey saw a bright light shining through the windows of the phaser bay, illuminating Beauvois and herself and all the others present so brilliantly that they seemed to be ashen bas-reliefs set into a gray stone wall.

The shield in front of the hull sparkled and cracked for a heartbeat, and then the hull itself blew inward as the Neyel missile suddenly expended its destructive energies.

No longer able to breathe, her lungs afire, Docksey surmised that the oxygen in the bay was igniting along with the Neyel incendiary device. But she could still see the gaping rent in the bulkhead, beyond which lay darkness and toward which the remaining air was blowing with gale intensity. She sensed dimly that her body was in motion, a straw in a hurricane.

Docksey tumbled in the endless dark for a cold eternity, her tears sublimating in the vacuum, along with her blood. Knowing she was dying, she thought of Lojur, and wished her intended happiness and peace. And she wondered if the emergency forcefields had clicked on in time to save Beauvois, so that he might have an opportunity to see his newborn son.

Then the eternal night enfolded her.

"Shields are now at forty percent and holding, Captain," Lojur said, still blinking from the brilliant explosion that had blanked out the main viewer.

"The forward sections of Deck Five were badly hit," an ensign at the aft tactical station called out. "We lost some personnel along with the phaser power."

No more, Sulu thought, gripping the sides of his chair nearly hard enough to snap something off. "Fire all weapons," he said, his voice a low rumble.

Moments later, the surface of the Neyel ship was dotted with explosions. A gout of flame and debris shot out into space from a hull breach near the vessel's midsection.

Then the Neyel ship went completely dark and silent.

PART 4

SURVIVAL

Chapter 12

Thursday, 5 April 2063, 2:42 am

Zefram Cochrane found the bearded man's story incredible. After all, he and his two companions just claimed they'd voyaged backward more than three centuries to save humankind from ravening hordes of cybernetic zombies.

On the other hand, they carried impressive tools and tech with them. Or at least it *looked* impressive.

And they said they wanted to help make the *Phoenix* fly.

The man who called himself La Forge was bent over the eyepiece to Cochrane's telescope, peering into the clear night sky. He snapped shut an instrument of some sort, then straightened to face Cochrane.

"All right," La Forge said, grinning. "Take a look."

As if this is going to prove anything, Cochrane thought. He laughed as he approached the 'scope, a reaction no doubt fueled by the copious quantities of liquor he'd absorbed at the Crash & Burn alongside the beautiful Deena, or Deanna, or whatever the hell her name was.

"Well, well, well, what have we here?" he said as he bent his head toward the eyepiece. "Ah, I love a good peep show."

The telescope displayed a crystal-clear image of a long,

sleek, graceful spacecraft, obviously the product of a culture whose technology far surpassed anything Cochrane had ever seen.

Now he felt fear. If he allowed himself to hope that this apparition was real, he knew he would be devastated beyond recovery when he finally discovered he'd been had.

Cochrane stood erect, facing the bearded man, who had identified himself only as "Commander Riker." Like Deanna and La Forge, Riker watched him with an air of almost reverent anticipation.

"That's a trick," Cochrane said, before returning to the 'scope for another quick peek. The image, illusory or not, persisted. *Maybe it's real after all. Maybe their story about being from the future really* is *true.*

He faced them again, still not entirely ready to let go of the armor of conservative skepticism that had sustained him through so many experimental setbacks and outright calamities. "How'd you do that?"

"It's your telescope," La Forge said.

Deanna finally spoke up, the effects of the alcohol she'd imbibed earlier evidently having worn off already. "That's our ship. The *Enterprise*."

Cochrane decided to allow for the possibility that their tale *might* be true. "And, uh . . . Lily's up there right now?"

"That's right," Deanna said, smiling.

"Can I talk to her?"

"We've lost contact with the *Enterprise*," said Riker. "We don't know why yet."

How convenient. "So . . . what is it you want *me* to do?"

"Simple," Riker said without hesitation, his blue eyes flashing. "Conduct your warp flight tomorrow morning, as you planned."

Apparently, they only wanted him to do what he'd already spent years—not to mention countless lives—trying to accomplish. Had they wanted to stop him, they could have done so easily. Still, their exacting requirements—and the nervous glances thrown toward Riker by Deanna and La Forge—roused his suspicions.

"Why tomorrow morning?" Cochrane wanted to know.

Riker paused thoughtfully before answering, as though he'd just made some irrevocable decision. *If he really is from the future, and has to decide just how much he can afford to tell me without screwing up the timeline, then maybe he has.*

"Because," Riker said at length, "at eleven o'clock an alien ship will begin passing through this solar system."

That was the last thing Cochrane wanted to hear. "Alien. You mean extraterrestrials. More bad guys?" The effects of the alcohol he'd consumed earlier seemed all at once to multiply. With some effort, he took a seat on a flattened tree stump. He found himself hoping that it had been either these new E.T.s or the zombie cyborgs Riker had spoken of earlier who had been responsible for the destruction of the O'Neill habitats.

Otherwise the blame has to land squarely on me and my goddamned egomaniacal warp-drive project.

"Good guys," Deanna said. "They're on a survey mission. They have no interest in Earth. Too primitive."

"Oh," Cochrane said. It made sense, given how little remained of human civilization, even though the war itself already lay a decade in the past. *Hell, if I were an alien, I wouldn't even stop off here to take a leak.*

Riker approached him, a fervor in his eyes that was both frightening and exhilarating. "Doctor, tomorrow morning when they detect the warp signature from your ship and realize that humans have discovered how to travel faster than light, they decide to alter their course—and make first contact with Earth, right here."

Cochrane considered the patch of perfectly ordinary ground that surrounded the stump on which he sat. "Here?"

"Actually, over there," La Forge said, gesturing a short distance to his left.

"It is one of the pivotal moments in human history, Doctor," Riker continued, pacing as he spoke, moving behind Cochrane. "You get to make first contact with an alien race. And after you do, everything begins to change."

La Forge approached more closely, looking almost worshipful. "Your theories on warp drive allow fleets of starships to be built, and mankind to start exploring the galaxy."

"It unites humanity in a way that no one ever thought possible, when they realize they're not alone in the universe," said Deanna. "Poverty, disease, war—they'll all be gone within the next fifty years."

Riker spoke again. "But unless you make that warp flight tomorrow morning—before eleven-fifteen—none of it will happen."

They were treating him as though he were the savior of mankind, and it was making him distinctly uncomfortable. And yet . . . their story made a bizarre sort of sense. After all, if they really were saboteurs from ECON or some other faction, they could simply have killed him and ended Project *Phoenix* without having to resort to subterfuge. But they seemed sincere in their stated desire to see him succeed.

Cochrane's eyes lit from face to face before he spoke again. "And you people—you're all astronauts, on some kind of star trek."

La Forge's expression became grave. For the first time, Cochrane noticed the unnatural-looking blue tint of his irises. "Look, Doc, I know this is a lot for you to take in, but we're running out of time here. We need your help."

Zefram Cochrane turned, leaving the future-people standing behind him. He gazed heavenward, his eyes seeking the lightless Trojan point around which the destroyed space habitats had orbited, now a silent graveyard in space. The people who'd lived and worked in those colonies had died trying to make his dream of warp flight a reality.

Perhaps now he could redeem those deaths, as well as

those pieces of his own soul that had died along with the O'Neills. For the first time since that horrible day, he felt eager to greet the future.

"What do you say?" Riker asked.

"Why not?" Cochrane whispered to the waxing half-moon.

"I'll *tell* you why not," Baruch said. "Because we have no idea who else might be listening in on us."

Zafirah could hardly believe what she was hearing. Now, after more than four and a half years, Vanguard had finally achieved self-sufficiency, despite having been stranded two-hundred light-years from home.

And in defiance of the brutal reduction of its population by two-hundred and fifty-two souls when those snaggle-tusked aliens had tried to plunder the asteroid's resources.

Zafirah had to admit that it had not been humanity's better angels that had won the day then. Rather, it had been the suspicious natures of current Director Avram Baruch and the late engineer Kerwin McNolan—along with their hastily improvised explosive projectile weapons—that had convinced the tusk people to depart in search of easier prey.

But the raiders had never returned, and Zafirah and others—including head geneticist Claudia Hakidonmuya, the only other survivor from the initial first-contact party—reasoned that Vanguard had turned inward to lick its wounds long enough. After having lost nearly a third of the habitat's population to the raid, after having worked so hard subsequently to survive and adapt to the harsh conditions of trackless interstellar space, it made sense finally to make restoring contact with Earth a priority. Even if the effort was destined to take centuries to come to fruition.

Surely Earth and its teeming, war-ravaged billions would still need help, even if that help took centuries to come to fruition. And the advanced technologies that sustained Vanguard in the interstellar dark could provide that help.

"We're not sending any signals toward Earth or anywhere else," Director Baruch repeated, rising from behind the great desk he'd inherited from the slain Dr. Mizuki after Vanguard's conservative, ultracautious majority had swept him into office. "The risk of calling attention to ourselves is simply too great. We're still way too vulnerable out here."

Zafirah threw up her left arm in frustration, a gesture which made her empty right sleeve flap like a banner being carried into battle. The missing limb, lost to the injuries she'd sustained during the alien raid, served as a constant reminder that a little distrust could be a very positive thing. *Unless*, she thought, *it's allowed to be taken to extremes.*

Aloud, she said, "Using *your* logic, Avi, Earth should have been invaded a hundred years ago, when those old *I Love Lucy* broadcasts first started reaching the stars."

"There's always a first time for everything," the morose Israeli said, shrugging. "We've already suffered one attack that nearly crippled us. We'd be fools to invite more of the same." His unapologetic use of the word "cripple" prompted a phantom pain to shoot through her right sleeve.

Zafirah felt her anger at last beginning to boil over. "I'm so sorry to burden you with these radical ideas, Avi. But I thought we were supposed to be Earth's last, best hope. After we got stuck out here, Director Mizuki made it fairly clear she considered that her life's work."

"And we all saw how short the rest of that life was."

Zafirah regarded Baruch in silence. Only now did she really perceive how haggard and drawn he'd become over the past few years. His salt-and-pepper beard had gone almost white. The weight of responsibility for every human life inside this asteroid had rounded his shoulders, which reminded her of pebbles worn smooth in a riverbed.

Glowering, he gestured toward his office door. "I've got a lot of work to do, Zaf. And I'd appreciate it if *you* would get back to work dealing with the first order of business—this colony's continued survival."

Zafirah left the director's office in a daze, wandering aimlessly through the stone-floored corridors of the lower levels. She felt desolate, isolated. When had mere survival become life's sole purpose? There had to be more. A line of Robert Browning, a ghost from her undergraduate days, sprang to mind unbidden: *"If a man's reach does not exceed his grasp, then what's a heaven for?"*

After perhaps an hour, her meanderings took her coreward, to the vast cylinder of zero-gee space that ran down Vanguard's entire long axis. Her spirits were buoyed slightly by what she saw there.

A dozen or more children were flying, wheeling gracefully on their gossamer wings. Some of them seemed to be playing a water polo-inspired game with a ball. All were extraordinarily long of limb. Most of them were born after Vanguard had been cut loose from the rest of humanity. And thanks to their gene-mods, these children and their offspring would reach maturity far faster than their ungenengineered cousins back on Earth, speeding up the propagation of subsequent generations.

As the group drew nearer to the railing where Zafirah stood, she could see that some of the very youngest ones bore the unmistakable marks of futurity. As these children—scarcely more than toddlers—tossed an oblong airbladder to and fro, Zafirah noticed that they, too, were not only long-limbed, but also had opposable thumbs on their bare feet, a genetic trait that Claudia's labs had lately made available to Vanguard's newest parents, along with increased genetic variability—an absolute necessity with such a small breeding population—and enhanced resistance to disease, radiation, and temperature extremes.

A generation of humanity, one that had never lived on Earth, was already becoming uniquely adapted to the high-stress, variable-gravity environment of a spinning asteroid. As always, Zafirah was both chilled and exhilarated by the sight of beings capable of using all their limbs for grasping with equal facility.

She remained certain of only one thing: These children would survive and prosper out here, and would no doubt carry Claudia's genetic improvements even further in their own progeny, regardless of the scars the rest of the human species had borne since the Eugenics Wars of the previous century. Humanity would continue out here in some form or other, whatever adaptations the random, uncaring universe forced upon them. Even if its light were to be extinguished on Earth, mankind would spread its seed across the deeps of space. *Homo sapiens celestis,* the children of O'Neill, would survive.

But life aboard Vanguard has to be about more than mere survival, she thought as she watched the children arc and turn in graceful flight. *It also has to be about creating a future that's worth surviving for.*

Were the bedtime stories these children heard each night, and the prayers they offered to whatever gods they revered, to be filled with delighted anticipation of the unexplored wonders that the universe held in store for them?

Or would they instead be reared on tales of ravening, bloodthirsty tusk-men?

The difference between truly living and merely enduring could very well come down to nothing more than that.

Chapter 13

Saturday, 9 August 2155

Sayyid al-Adnan assumed that the alarm was just another drill. After all, what were the chances of encountering a second alien raider ship during the ninety-seventh official Commemoration of the First Contact Massacre?

Of course, the reason the Dread Event should be memorialized so arbitrarily—once every approximately three-hundred-sixty-five-point-two-five twenty-four-hour intervals—made about as much sense to Sayyid as the bizarre, biped-oriented furniture some of the Oldsters still kept around in the high-grav Museum Levels.

Sayyid grasped the railings with his feet, thrusting his long prehensile tail behind him to provide a counterbalance as he swung himself down the tube—his grandfather had told him that the tube had housed an automated lifting-and-lowering device during the Age of Two-Handedness—toward the asteroid's outermost high-grav layers.

It was unfortunate that so many of the colony's key apparatus were still located at such uncomfortably intense grav-levels, but moving them coreward into the spinning asteroid's null-grav regions would have required the installation of a prohibitive number of power relays. It also would have run the risk of causing mass null-grav wasting among the Citizenry, as well as sealing the People off completely from the Outside, an eventuality that could prove as dangerous as welcoming into the colony more of the Tuskers who had slain the First Director and so many others.

Sayyid recalled his recent Midschool days, when he had heard an audio recording of a very old story—quite a rarity these days, considering how much of the digital library had been lost to radiation exposure during the Passage—that one of the Oldsters had described as a "skiffy." In the tale, a tribe of People ventured from Earth and voyaged into the infinitude of space inside a vast Ship. Within a few generations, mutineers had tried unsuccessfully to seize control of the great vessel. The descendants of both the legitimate crew and the mutineers were no longer even aware that they dwelled within the giant Ship's belly. To them, the notion that the extent of the Ship's interior comprised the totality of the universe was merely common sense.

Fools, Sayyid thought, every time he thought of that ancient skiffy story. *To be ignorant is to be vulnerable.*

No, the scions of 'Neal had no desire to cut themselves off completely from the universe, whatever undiscovered terrors it held. One had to keep oneself apprised of what was out there, lest the unknown bare its tusks again and resume the lopping off of heads.

Sayyid swung himself down onto the Control Level, where the blaring of the alarm Klaxons was loudest.

"What took you so long?" Graben demanded the moment Sayyid pulled himself laboriously through the Instrument Room hatch. Sayyid hated high-grav.

Graben was older—old enough, at least, not to carry much of the genework that had made null-grav the preferred environment for the newest 'Neal generation to come of age—and Sayyid assumed that this was why he always complained so much about the performance of the Youngsters in his crew. Many of these were still arriving in response to the alarm, literally right behind Sayyid's tail.

"What's happening?" Sayyid asked, ignoring Graben's gruff query. Grinning, he added, "More Tuskers?"

Graben scowled. "Not Tuskers. The bogey doesn't appear to be a ship this time."

"What then?" Sayyid asked as he draped his long form across one of the instrument couches and donned his gloves and visor.

"You tell me, boy genius," Graben said as the virtual display activated, immersing Sayyid in the unknown.

Thanks to the virt, Sayyid was suddenly floating outside in the void. The illusion would have been perfect save for the insistent pull of the asteroid's spin-generated gravity, which inexorably pushed his body into the unyielding couch. But the velvet depths of trackless space and the bright stellar baubles that punctuated it made the high-grav sensation a manageable annoyance. When he turned his field of vision 180 degrees, the Large and Small Magellanic Clouds—a pair of relatively small globular galaxies that lay well beyond the familiar confines of the Milky Way—stared at him like a pair of baleful eyes.

Ahead of him, perhaps pars'x away, or maybe only a few hundred klomters distant, lay a silver, shimmering *ripple* in space, moving in undulating, sinuous waves. Sayyid could not determine what was producing the effect, nor how it was being illuminated so far out in interstellar space.

"Whatever it is," Sayyid said, "it seems to be moving *fast.*" Of course, that was relative. Although Vangarde wasn't moving at anywhere near relativistic speeds, the Great Rock still retained a fair amount of momentum from the days of the Passage.

Sayyid recalled a story that Great-Grandmother Zafirah had shared with him when he was little. She had spoken of an energetic wave or disturbance of some sort that had swept through the Earth's solar system more than a century earlier. One of the planet's space-based telescopes had observed the phenomenon's unexplained superluminal passage across the plane of the ecliptic. The anomaly had apparently destroyed the *Ares IV*, the first manned ship bound for Mars.

As a small child, Sayyid had always wondered if the Mars ship had actually somehow survived its encounter with the unexplained on that fateful day. Might Loot Kelly's little vessel have simply been kicked out among the stars, arriving at some impossibly far destination intact, the way the Vangarde colony had been dislocated a generation later? Because of his own life circumstances, Sayyid could never discount such possibilities out of hand.

Maybe this is another weird energy anomaly like the one that took the Ares. *And maybe* this *one is going to punt us* back *to Earth.*

Earth. He wondered if the place could be anything like the Earth of his dreams, the Earth conjured by the many stories Greatgran Zafirah had shared with him before entropy and her old Tusker wounds had finally taken her—

"Enough dustgathering," Graben snapped, startling Sayyid from his peaceful torpor. "I need an analysis of this thing. Could it be hiding another aggressor ship?"

Sayyid shrugged. "Can't rule it out, Boss." He was old enough to remember the asteroid miners who had landed several craft on the Vangarde's skin, only to be "persuaded" to leave by a complete fusillade from the colony's Baruch pulse cannons. Afterward, he'd sneaked into the pathology lab where one of the recovered alien corpses lay on a slab, evidently dead from exposure. He'd never forget how much like a Vangarde Oldster the thing had looked.

Except for its sickly green bodily fluids and those sinister-looking pointed ears.

Still floating in space and watching the images coming in

from the external telescopes, Sayyid heard Graben begin barking orders to the others. He heard the echoing clatter of the big Baruch tubes being locked and loaded again. Sayyid felt a cold sweat trickling between his shoulders, as though an enraged Tusker were breathing down his back.

Suddenly, the glistening silver band of spatial distortion greatly increased in size. Before a scream could escape Sayyid's lips, the effect seemed to have entirely engulfed Vangarde, which lurched and shuddered, tossing him from the couch onto the cold, rigid deckplating. The universe was plunged into utter darkness.

Sayyid didn't realize that he'd blacked out until he noticed that Graben and Keller were lifting him bodily back onto the virt couch. The lights were dim, as though whatever had struck the asteroid had also knocked out the main power circuits.

The scene reminded him eerily of Greatgran Zafirah's story about How Vangarde Got Way Out Here.

"What happened to my virt-helmet?" Sayyid said, searching around on the floor in the semidarkness until his feet came into contact with the helmet's curved surface. He wrapped his footthumbs around its edge and donned it using both feet while his hands and tail sought out the emergency power controls.

Almost at once, he was back Out There.

He saw right away that everything was . . . *different.* The stars were far more densely packed now than they had been mere moments before. Neither of the Magellanic Clouds was anywhere to be seen.

Beyond the main mass of stars lay a vast, multiarmed pinwheel of light that reminded Sayyid of the tri-dee maps of the Milky Way he'd made in school.

It took several days of painstaking comparative positional analysis of every known pulsar and black hole in the astronomical database before Sayyid was able to account for the presence of the additional stars, the gigantic spiral galaxy that dominated the stellar backdrop, and the complete and utter disappearance of both Magellanic Clouds.

The result was both unbelievable and undeniable. In a twinkling, the anomaly had tossed Vangarde almost dead-center *inside* the smaller of the two Magellanic Clouds, some 210,000 light-years from the asteroid's previous position.

Slowly, very slowly, Sayyid allowed the truth of his discovery to sink in. *Compared to the distance we just covered, those first two-hundred light-years the Oldsters crossed when they made the Passage from Earth look like a rounding error.*

Gazing at the pearlescent brilliance of the Milky Way, Sayyid began to understand that the Earth of his fantasies, the Earth of Greatgran Zafirah's stories, hopes, and dreams, was now forever beyond the reach of the 'Neal People and their descendants. He wondered if the Tuskers had ever ventured out this far.

Or if something even worse might dwell here.

PART 5

GRIEF

Chapter 14

Though several minutes had passed since the battle's abrupt end, the anticipated phalanx of Tholian vessels still had yet to arrive. However, Ensign Fenlenn had detected the approach of four Tholian warships, evidently rushing toward the colony world in response to its distress calls. With the warships still nearly an hour away, *Excelsior* remained on yellow alert. The damaged Neyel vessel—the cause of the entire situation—merely hung silently in space, apparently refusing to acknowledge all hails and offers of assistance.

To Lojur, it almost seemed as though the alien ship was mocking him.

Standing alone on *Excelsior*'s aft observation lounge, the Halkan navigator wondered what could be going on inside the Neyel vessel's thick, refractory metal hull. As the minutes passed, he could feel the increased vigilance and nervousness of the crew emanating from the bulkheads, like some strange new form of radiation.

But he didn't care about any of that just now. His shift on the bridge finished, Lojur now looked out of the enormous curved transparent aluminum window that ringed most of the lounge. Located one level below and slightly behind the bridge, the room overlooked the flat dorsal section of the primary hull. Although neither the equally vast lower engineering section nor the saucer's two gigantic impulse engines were visible from this vantage point, the faint blue glow of the twin warp nacelles seemed to stretch out to infinity behind the mighty starship. Beyond that lay the eternal, boundless dark.

It was also about the farthest point across *Excelsior*'s saucer section away from the ruined phaser bay where Shandra had died, defending a colony of inscrutable aliens whose military caste was likely to arrive at any moment, weapons blazing. Lojur hoped they would forgive *Excelsior*'s intrusion into Tholian territory once the captain explained that they had come in answer to distress signals from the Tholian colony world. But from what he'd seen of the Tholians so far, he wasn't too sure about that.

To *Excelsior*'s starboard side lay the slender yellow crescent of the Tholian colony world the Neyel had attacked. To port, the apparently crippled Neyel warship made a slow, unpowered circuit about the planet, still evidently unable either to change its trajectory or to mount any further hostilities.

Lojur was distracted from the alien ship by a reflection in the window. He almost failed to recognize the drawn and worn face he saw there as his own. Set beneath thick, pale brows, his eyes seemed absent, their hollow shadows far darker than his russet-colored goatee. Clearly visible in the middle of his ashen forehead was the red crest of his family, tattooed there nearly two decades earlier, after the village Elders had declared him an adult, a True Man of Halka.

He reached up and touched the intricate, thumbnail-sized design. The marking was all the Halkan Council had permitted him to take with him into his permanent, irrevocable state of exile. *Had the Orions attacked Kotha Village just a few weeks earlier, I would have been denied even this.*

Lojur heard the doors hiss open behind him. He saw the huge reflection of the approaching Akaar an instant later.

"Computer, lower room illumination by seventy-five percent." At once, the lights dimmed and the reflections abruptly vanished, replaced by the endless vista of space. Lojur did not wish to allow anyone, even a close friend like Akaar, to watch him pining over things that could not be changed.

He turned and faced Akaar, who towered over him. The giant Capellan maintained his distance, his large hands clasped behind his back as though he didn't know what else to do with them.

"I thought I might find you here," Akaar said, his voice deep and resonant despite its muted volume.

Lojur offered his friend a wan smile. "You could have asked the computer to locate me."

"A hunter should rely upon his wits," Akaar replied. Despite their Starfleet training and their respective homeworlds' diametrically opposite philosophies—Akaar was the product of a warrior society, while Lojur's Halkan culture had inculcated total pacifism—Lojur knew that they both preferred not to use technology gratuitously. This shared eccentricity, as well as the mentoring they had both received over the years from Captain Sulu and Commander Chekov, had provided the initial impetus for their unlikely friendship.

"True enough," Lojur said. Though Halkans did not hunt for game animals, they did gather wild plants as well as cultivate tame ones. Neither pursuit was very kind to idiots.

Lojur studied Akaar, who had adopted an even more stoic demeanor than usual. It brought to mind the grave-faced village Elders who had banished him eighteen years ago.

"You should know that Lieutenant Docksey died bravely," the Capellan said at length.

Lojur nodded, feeling numb and blasted inside as he revisited, yet again, the brutal fact of Shandra's death. He had already known that she was off duty during the battle with the Neyel; immediately afterward, photon torpedo specialist Pitcher told him most of the rest. Shandra had stepped into the breach, first assisting in one of the torpedo bays, then taking over for an injured member of one of the forward phaser crews.

Then she'd been blown out into space when the final Neyel salvo tore through both the shields and the hull plating directly outside her temporary post.

"Chief Pitcher told me that Shandra died instantly, L.J.," Lojur said. "She probably didn't have time to become frightened." *At least I hope that's so.*

Tears of rage and shame stung Lojur's eyes, prompting him to turn again toward the window. He stared at the Neyel ship, placing his hands behind his back, where they clasped one another as tightly as airlock seals.

Akaar could hardly have missed his roiling emotions. "You wish to punish them," he said. It did not sound like a question.

Lojur shook his head. "Violence is not in the Halkan character. It has no place in the Halkan heart." He turned to face his friend, fixing him with his most withering *don't-forget-that-I-outrank-you* glare.

Akaar was undeterred. "And yet violence is the very reason you have no place on Halka."

Lojur wanted to roar at the Capellan, but restrained himself. Barely. "That's enough, *Lieutenant*. Dismissed."

Akaar nodded, then walked back to the door. He paused a moment near the threshold after it opened. "I understand. I know I cannot compel you to discuss your loss, or what it might drive you to do."

Why wouldn't Akaar leave it alone? "That's exactly right, L.J.," Lojur said with an exasperated sigh.

"That is why I have asked Commander Chekov to do so," Akaar said, placing his hand over his heart and extending his open hand. Then he departed, leaving Lojur alone with his fiercely churning thoughts.

A moment later, the intercom sounded. Lojur sighed, resigned to what was to come. He pushed the button. "I'm on my way, Commander Chekov."

"What are you bringing me now, battle trophies?" Chapel said as the med techs antigravved the corpse into the pathology lab adjacent to the main sickbay.

"Ensign Fenlenn beamed this body aboard after the sensors picked it up drifting in space right after the battle," said one of the medics, a well-muscled human woman named Caitlin Bersentes. Chapel was pleased to see that she and her colleague, a human male named Beck, were treating the dead alien with apparent respect. "Evidently a few of the Neyel were blown out into space, like poor Shandra and the others."

The body the med techs deposited onto the examination table was large, gray, and unlike anything Chapel had encountered before. Though essentially humanoid in shape and size, its unclothed form was adorned with a muscular tail nearly as long as its body. Its torso was long and slender, and each of its four equally graceful limbs was equipped with opposable thumbs, recalling the hands and feet of a nonhuman Earth primate. The top of its head sported short, bristly black hair; its dark gray, coarse-textured epidermis had the approximate consistency of tree bark, though she noted that it was gracefully arranged in articulated, interleaved sections that Chapel guessed were as tough as the hide of a Vulcan dunewalker. Even the eyelids, closed in the repose of death, suggested apertures in the battlements of some impregnable wooden fortress.

"These folks are obviously built to last," Chapel said, her researcher's natural curiosity now fully roused. She reached for a medical tricorder and made a few cursory scans, noting that most of the vital organs—none of which showed more than the residual activity of the very recently deceased—didn't seem overly mysterious. That wasn't a surprise, since the humanoid body plan, including most of the internal biological architecture it required, seemed to have arisen independently in so many disparate parts of the galaxy.

Next, she directed the med techs to set up the portable deep-tissue probe, which she carefully calibrated to focus on the creature's unique biomolecular and DNA features. She tapped a few commands into the device's keypad, instructing it to feed the results to her tricorder.

While the scanner worked and the results of the scans were being collated through the main sickbay computer and routed back to her tricorder, Chapel walked to the food slot in her office and ordered a cup of hot, black coffee. She sipped from her cup as she returned to the alien corpse. A green light on the portable probe reported that the first scans were finally complete. Still holding her cup, she thumbed the tricorder one-handed to see the results.

When she saw the initial readings, Chapel gagged on her coffee, almost dropping both cup and tricorder. She set them down on a nearby instrument tray while she coughed and sputtered, gently waving away Bersentes and Beck as they offered to help her. *Those readings aren't possible.* After recovering her breath, she rechecked the settings on every piece of equipment involved in the scan, including the tricorder, which she replaced just in case it was malfunctioning.

This time accepting some assistance from her staff, Chapel ran the test four more times to eliminate any possibility of error. Nothing changed. Her two assistants looked stunned, obviously having worked out the implications for themselves.

Chapel crossed to her office, where she tapped the intercom on her desk. "Chapel to Captain Sulu."

"Sulu here."

"I've just finished my initial examination of the Neyel corpse Fenlenn found. I haven't even started the invasive autopsy yet, but I've already learned something rather . . . startling about our alien friends."

"And what's that, Doctor?"

Chapel nearly blurted out what she'd learned, then thought better of it. "Let's just say that you and Ambassador Burgess are going to want to see this for yourself. Immediately."

"I'll be right down."

"I really don't think you have any reason for concern," Lojur said.

"I certainly hope that's so," Chekov said, sitting behind the desk in his quarters. He gestured toward a guest chair, where Lojur took a seat. "But as executive officer, crew morale is my special area of responsibility."

"Even when we might be under attack soon by some extremely territorial Tholians?" Lojur said quietly.

"*Especially* then. I have to make sure the captain and I can count on you in a crisis, Commander. And I would be remiss if I pretended I didn't know certain things about you."

Lojur thought that *Excelsior*'s exec looked, as usual, far more comfortable dispensing photon torpedoes than advice. But he knew Pavel Chekov better than that. With Captain Sulu in charge *Excelsior*'s overall operations, the welfare of the ship's crew fell squarely on Chekov's shoulders.

"Granted, sir," Lojur said. "But I think Lieutenant Akaar overreacted when he asked you to . . . psychoanalyze me." Lojur felt tremendous gratitude toward Chekov, whose mentorship had been invaluable to him. Still, there were certain areas of Lojur's life that he wasn't eager to talk about, even with the man who had sponsored his entry into Starfleet Academy.

"Possibly," Chekov said. "But you've just suffered a tremendous, sudden loss. And don't forget, I know Akaar's background about as well as I know yours. He's been able to smell pent-up violence ever since he was a little kid."

Lojur smiled in spite of himself. "I find it hard to believe that L.J. was ever a 'little' *anything*."

"He was cute as a bug. But not even your lieutenant commander's bars will save you if you ever say that to his face. Don't forget, Akaar was born to rule the Ten Tribes of Capella. That's why his mother is still financing the ongoing construction of a huge tomb and monument for him on their homeworld, to let everyone know that he's the one who has the rightful claim to the title of Teer."

Lojur had first heard of the Tomb of Leonard James Akaar back in Starfleet Academy. He had been appalled then at the Capellan obsession with death.

But a lot had changed since those carefree days.

"Akaar was only five when the coup happened," Chekov continued. "And it was his warning that prevented a nasty Cossack named Keel from murdering him and his mother in their tent. You might ask him to tell you about that sometime."

Despite Akaar's renowned laconic manner—Lieutenant Tuvok must have envied it—Lojur already knew these details about his friend. It was no secret to anyone that Lojur, Tuvok, and Lieutenant Akaar had been close colleagues and friends for more than three years now. So Commander Chekov must have been well aware that he wasn't "telling tales out of school," as humans sometimes described the practice of repeating gossip.

Lojur merely nodded, contemplating the violence that had such an impact on Akaar's life, and his own.

He was halfway through his eighteenth summer, an adult on the cusp of becoming eligible to marry and establish his own Freehold, when the Federation rock-buyers first arrived in Kotha Village.

The first thing that impressed Lojur about the Starfleet negotiating team was their clothing. Maroon jackets and black trousers, very precisely assembled and tailored, looking nothing like the motley congeries of homespun robes and cloaks that adorned most of the people of Halka. The Halkans of Kotha Village favored slow, tranquil, farm-tethered lives, and that had not changed appreciably in several millennia. By contrast, the men and women who came to bargain for Halka's energy-saturated crystal formations dressed in a uniform fashion that spoke of progress, change, efficiency. They went to far places and brought back knowledge beyond any Halkan farmer's wildest dreams.

Lojur found it simultaneously exhilarating and terrifying.

He watched for days as the four Starfleeters moved about the village, whose people welcomed them with open arms and huts. The visitors repaid the village's generosity in kind during their stay, helping with an irrigation project, and providing medical aid to some of the outlying families whose fortunes had been ruined by the recent unseasonable floods and the grainblight that had caused so much devastation during the last Harvest.

Judging from the long faces the Starfleet people wore toward the end of their stay, they—like the handful of other Federation negotiating teams that had preceded them in earlier decades—had ultimately failed to persuade the Council to allow them to mine the rocks they sought.

On the night before the Terrans' vessel was to return to Halka to retrieve them, Kotha Village threw a great feast for its honored visitors, replete with song, dance, and the traditional tribal story pantomimes. Lojur exchanged shy glances with Kereleth, a girl two summers his junior. She was as yet betrothed to no one, as far as he knew. The future stretched before them both, promising anything and everything.

It was a joyous, hopeful time to till the soil and breathe the air.

Then the green men came, with their rifles and pistols. They shot at everything that moved. Lojur wasn't certain how many of them there were. But they made it clear that they wanted the rocks as well. And they employed a very different bargaining style from that of the Starfleeters.

"Orions!" one of the Starfleet people, a woman, had

shouted just before one of the invaders' dreadful weapons vaporized her. The remaining three Terrans raised weapons of their own in defense of Kotha Village, despite the protestations of Iathen, the Village Elder, who deplored the notion of using violence in order to curb violence.

Lojur hated the idea as well, was sickened by it. Peace was all he knew.

And yet, people are dying right in front of me.

The rest of the afternoon was a blur. Two dozen villagers, vaporized, blown apart, or maimed. Kereleth gone, her fate never discovered. Two more Terrans dead, and another lying injured, pierced through the shoulder by fragments of a hut blown asunder by an Orion explosive device.

The injured Terran's weapon, lying discarded in the dirt. People continuing to die, everywhere Lojur looked.

No more. No more of my people will die.

Lojur remembered crawling through the dirt, grasping the cold weapon with shaking hands. Hiding behind a charred stump as he aimed the hideous deathtool at a cluster of brutally laughing Orions, coarse, evil men who had expected no protest from the Halkans and thus had not made the slightest preparation for it.

And then Lojur was firing and running, running and firing, tumbling into a blood-red haze. His heart burned, ached, exulted, wept.

More people died, many more. But none of these were residents of Kotha Village.

Afterward, Lojur remembered little of the horror, at least consciously. He still thanked Halka's gods every night for that gift of forgetfulness. But there were also the other nights. The nights when the awful truth of what he had done exhumed itself from its shallow grave and visited him in his dreams.

After the bodies were interred—Halkan, Terran, and Orion—Kotha Village turned its entire attention toward rebuilding itself. Though injured, the sole surviving Terran, along with a few others from his newly returned vessel, assisted with the physical reconstruction. Winter was descending quickly, so every remaining Kothan was grateful for the help.

The injured Terran, tended by his own medical people as well as by a Kothan Healer, never asked for so much as a single crystal in return.

But he could not help the village repair the damage that had been done to its spirit. Only the Elders could do that.

Gray, sad-eyed Iathen still led Kotha Village, despite the loss of his right arm during the Orion attack. And though most of the people stood by listening, Iathen's harsh words on that cold, long-ago morning were clearly intended for Lojur alone: "The violence you have done does not belong in the Halkan heart. We repudiate it. We banish it. We send it into exile.

"And the same we do with you."

"But I helped save your lives," Lojur said. No one responded. *Of course not. It doesn't matter. Halka would rather embrace its own death than soil its hands with the blood of others. Even the blood of those who would kill us without a second thought.*

The Elder's pronouncement settled upon Lojur like a millstone tied about his neck. Bleakly, he stared across the village square as Elders and rank-and-file villagers alike waited for him to say something in his own defense. He didn't bother. What was the point? *They're right: I have raised my hand in violence. I have taken lives.*

Then, in a solemn ritual, the Elders began turning their robed backs on him. Looking on from farther down the main dirt thoroughfare, women, young men, and even the children followed suit. Lojur called out to them, his voice thick and heavy as though he were caught in the grip of some horrible dream.

"I *saved* you! You would all be dead now if I had not acted!"

But no one would acknowledge him. No one would tell him whether Kereleth had died, or if she yet lived and was merely avoiding him. He was now a cipher. A non-person. A ghost.

Where will I go now? How will I stay alive?

Nothing moved in Kotha Village, save the gathering chill wind and the door of the Healer's hut. The injured Terran emerged, the rest of his colleagues evidently having returned to the skies. How much had he seen and heard of what had just transpired?

The shorter man's eyes were dark and piercing. Angry. But Lojur sensed that he was not the target of that anger. The Starfleeter extended a hand in Lojur's direction. Lojur approached the Terran silently, and no one in the village made a move to block his path.

The wind was kicking up leaves and dust, its icy fingers cutting right through Lojur's thin robe, making him shiver. He had never felt so cold and alone before in his young life.

The Terran was glaring at the crowd, which regarded him with wide-eyed curiosity. Then he slowly and deliberately removed his maroon uniform jacket, placing it gently around Lojur's narrow shoulders. The Elders remained standing statuelike in the square, their faces impassive.

The human removed a small device from his belt and spoke into it. As long as he lived, Lojur would never forget the peculiar lilt and inflection of the man's speech.

"Chekov to *Reliant*. Two to beam up."

Lojur noticed that Chekov was staring at him inquisitively. "Commander, are you listening to me?"

"Violence has no place in the Halkan heart," Lojur repeated, startled out of his reverie.

"Violence is often the way of the universe, Commander," Chekov said, leaning forward. "And that universe is inhabited by many who are considerably less gentle than the people of Halka."

His earlier anger at Lieutenant Akaar now largely spent, Lojur found himself nodding. "I think there are few who understand that better than I do, sir." *Especially now.*

Chekov's eyes reflected concern. "I don't doubt it. If you need some time off to help you through this—"

Lojur interrupted. "No, sir. Staying busy is the way to healing. As are the writings of Tharn the Wise."

"Such as?"

" 'When one sheds the blood of others,' " Lojur quoted, " 'the stains are indelible. In war, even the victor can never come home again.' "

Rising from behind his desk, Chekov said, "That's a good principle to live by. When the universe lets you get away with it, that is. If you need to discuss this further later on, Lieutenant, my door is open. Now I'd better get to the bridge, in case either those territorial Tholians arrive early, or the Neyel finally decide they want to talk to us."

"Yes, sir," Lojur said, also rising.

After Chekov had dismissed him, Lojur wandered the corridors aimlessly, his next duty shift not due to begin until early the next morning.

Shandra was dead.

A familiar, though long-absent, burning sensation welled up from somewhere deep within him. He had not known it since the day the Orions had descended upon Kotha Village. It was a demon that he'd hoped his transgression—raising Chekov's dropped phaser in anger—had exorcised forever.

Shandra is dead.

Despite all that his people had taught him, in defiance of a lifetime of faith in the ways of peace, he now wished only suffering and death upon the aliens who had consigned the woman he loved to the abyss. *We should destroy them. Crack their hull open like a ripe* h'eka *nut. Those animals would surely do the same to us were we to let them. And they won't even deign to speak to us.*

No one on Halka, or even in Starfleet, could sanction such thoughts. Probably not even a man like Akaar, who had been born to blood and violence.

As Lojur continued toward his quarters, hot tears seared his cheeks. *Maybe Tharn the Wise was more right than he knew. Not only can I never go home, I can't even seem to find or make one of my own.*

As Sulu, Lieutenant Hopman, and Ambassador Burgess simultaneously descended upon the sickbay pathology lab, Chapel desperately wished she had a way to account for the test results. Unfortunately, the results themselves would have to serve, at least until more data arrived to explain the inexplicable.

"What you're saying is impossible, Doctor," Sulu said in answer to her terse announcement, his eyes riveted to the Neyel corpse that lay on the table.

"I'm forced to agree with the captain, Doctor," Hopman said, her voice deeper than it had been the last time Chapel had seen her. She was in her male phase. "I mean . . . *look* at him."

"I know," Chapel said, nodding. "But you can examine the DNA patterns for yourselves. The electrophoretic graphs don't lie. Say 'hello' to your cousin. This creature's DNA is as human as yours or mine."

Hopman wrinkled her nose. "I think you can count me out of this family reunion, Doctor. The only thing human about me is something entirely vestigial."

Chapel wasn't sure she wanted to follow Hopman wherever she was going with this. Being around someone who could be a man one day and a woman the next took some getting used to. "Your appendix?"

"My married name," Hopman said with a chuckle.

Chapel smiled back. "Well, Lieutenant, that's one bit of surgery I'm not qualified to perform."

Looking impatient, Aidan Burgess moved silently along the length of the table, bending down as she studied the motionless, supine creature. Her eyes followed the curve of its club-tipped tail, which extended to the floor.

"How could a long-lost population of humans have gotten so far from Earth?" Sulu asked, his eyes alight with curiosity, clearly in his element.

Chapel shrugged, feeling genuinely at a loss. "Maybe they were blown here somehow by the weird winds of interspace." She wasn't at all certain that the bizarre interdimensional phenomenon that had swallowed up the *Defiant* could really account for the dislocation of these strangely altered humans. But it was an explanation that could serve as a scientific placeholder until something better came along. Perhaps Lieutenant Tuvok could find some definitive answers, once she certified that he was ready to leave sickbay.

Burgess straightened and met Chapel's gaze. "If this creature is human, then how do you explain these . . . features?"

Chapel folded her arms before her. "In the absence of any other information, my best guess is some sort of crash genetic engineering program. Recombinant DNA. Note the opposable thumbs on the feet. That wouldn't be a difficult tweak to make to the human genome, and the extra hands would be useful to people who spend most of their lives in variable gravity environments."

"And the tree-bark skin?" Sulu said, laying a hand against the gray being's rough thorax.

Chapel shrugged again. "It's not impossible. Other species have similar, naturally occurring traits. Nasats, for example, are equipped with plates of biologically generated armor. They can withstand even hard vacuum for quite a long time."

"A trick like that would certainly have come in handy

today," the captain said in a low tone. Chapel wondered if he was thinking of the dead alien, or Lieutenant Docksey and the phaser specialists who had been blown out into space when the Neyel attack breached the hull.

"This is crazy," Burgess said, shaking her head. "Human genetic engineering has been forbidden ever since Khan Singh was banished at the end of the Eugenics Wars."

"Surely you're aware that not everybody always follows the rules, Ambassador," Chapel said. She was convinced that Burgess's unauthorized revelations to the Tholians had not only led to Kasrene's death, but also endangered *Excelsior.* She was gratified to see a spark of anger—mixed, perhaps, with guilt—appear in the ambassador's green eyes.

Sulu seemed to be studying the dead being's face. "Human, yet not human," he murmured thoughtfully. "We can guess the 'how.' The real question is . . . why? And what are they doing out here?"

"Great Bird," Hopman said, looking stunned.

"Lieutenant?" Sulu said. All eyes turned to Hopman.

She recovered her composure a moment later. Pointing to the still form on the table, she said, "*This* is the reason Ambassador Kasrene was killed. She must have already known that the Neyel were a variant of the human species."

To Chapel, that sounded like quite a leap.

"So you think that *this* is Mosrene's 'sensitive information,' " Sulu said, his brow furrowed as he considered Hopman's idea. "That might explain Tuvok's insistence that Kasrene wanted us to receive her information just as much as she wanted it kept hidden from the other Tholian castes."

"I'm not really sanguine about placing my trust in a Vulcan metaphysical experience," Burgess said.

"Then you obviously haven't spent enough time around Vulcans," Sulu said dryly.

Touché, Chapel thought, suppressing a grin.

Burgess held up a hand in a gesture of surrender. "All

right. Assuming for a moment that your science officer is correct, then why would Kasrene want us to know that the Neyel are human while simultaneously trying to hide that fact from her own people?"

Sulu smiled. "Isn't it obvious? Tholians are about as peaceful as piranha, Ambassador, their current efforts at détente notwithstanding. If their warrior caste got wind of what we've just discovered, they'd likely be swarming across the Federation border in a heartbeat."

My God, Chapel thought. She'd been so caught up in the labyrinth of the Neyel's genengineered DNA that she hadn't spared a moment to consider the galactic geopolitical chessboard. *The Tholians have had thirty years to refine the weapons that once nearly destroyed the* Enterprise. *Now they might discover they have a legitimate reason to use them in anger against Earth.*

The group exchanged sober looks, and even Burgess was beginning to appear convinced. Turning his back on the inert Neyel so that he could address Chapel, Hopman, and Burgess all at once, Sulu said, "So how do we prevent the Tholian warrior caste from making the same discovery we just did?"

"We may have a more immediate problem," Hopman said, pointing.

Seeing movement out of the corner of her eye, Chapel snapped her head toward the table. The Neyel's heavily shuttered eyes were open now, and he was rising to his rough-skinned, prehensile feet.

Before anyone could react, the creature charged straight for Chapel, its powerful, clawed fingers seeking her throat.

Chapter 15

Sulu bellowed loudly as he leapt toward the Neyel, hoping to distract it.

The gambit worked, at least well enough to allow Dr. Chapel to dive for cover behind a rack of shelves stacked with instruments. She narrowly evaded the rough-skinned humanoid, who came within centimeters of grabbing her neck, apparently intent on twisting her head off. Using one of the lab tables to brace himself, Sulu launched a brutal two-legged kick straight into the Neyel's tree-like solar plexus.

He might as well have attacked one of the bulkheads. Sulu landed hard on his left shoulder, upending the cart that supported Chapel's portable scanning equipment. As quickly as he could manage, he rolled to his feet, nearly tripping over a tricorder as he did.

"Clear the lab!" he shouted, trying to focus past the starburst of pain in his shoulder. "Hopman, call security."

Snarling, the creature advanced on Sulu, even as Hopman hustled Burgess out the door, speaking into a handheld communicator as she did so. From the corner of his eye, Sulu noticed that Dr. Chapel hadn't yet left the lab; instead, she was moving toward the creature's rear, a hypospray in her hand. *Christine, you and I are going to have a talk later.*

Sulu jumped over a table, trying both to evade the Neyel

and prevent it from noticing the doctor's approach. At the same time, Chapel dived at the Neyel, throwing an arm around the middle of its back while trying to administer the hypo with her free hand. The Neyel turned its head quickly, swatting her with its tail. She fell heavily to the deck, where she lay in a dazed heap.

Taking advantage of Chapel's momentary diversion, Sulu kicked at the creature again, this time connecting solidly with one of its knees, which gave way with a satisfying crunch. Evidently the Neyel had yet to engineer away every weakness inherent to human anatomy. The Neyel howled in agony, throwing roundhouse punches that Sulu saw coming in plenty of time to evade them.

But what he failed to see coming was the end of the creature's prehensile tail, which struck him like a club across the back of the head. Sulu sagged to his knees, his head swimming, darkness threatening to engulf him. Behind him, he heard the hiss of the sickbay doors opening, then closing again.

Some inestimable interval later he noticed Chapel standing beside him, a shiny purple bruise beginning to blossom across her face. She helped him to his feet.

"Doctor, was there anything ambiguous about my 'clear the sickbay' order?" he said, rubbing his aching shoulder. His head was pounding.

He saw no contrition in her cool blue eyes. "In my medical judgment you needed help more than you needed blind obedience. Besides, Hikaru, this is *my* sickbay, not yours."

He considered a biting retort, but held his tongue. Chain-of-command discipline was not a hill he wanted either of them to die on at the moment. "Granted. But what the hell happened? I thought you said your 'patient' was dead."

"So did I. Evidently he got better. So much so that he just checked himself out."

"But he was *dead*, Chris. You scanned him down to the cellular level."

"I scanned him all the way down to the *molecular* level."

"And you didn't happen to notice that he was still *alive?*"

Her blue eyes flashed with an irritation she didn't bother to conceal. Sulu knew they'd known one another too long to have to hold such things back. "I didn't expect to find a humanoid capable of surviving prolonged anoxia and vacuum exposure. As far as I know, it's unprecedented."

"All right, Chris," Sulu said, raising a placating hand. "I didn't mean to second guess your medical judgment."

Her expression softened immediately. "I *did* notice some residual metabolic activity in his cells, but you always expect to see some of that immediately after the body's major systems suffer a fatal crash. The cells don't suddenly commit mass suicide the moment the heart and lungs stop functioning. Looks like our Neyel friends have more in common with the Nasats than any of us thought."

Sulu nodded, shuddering inwardly. The idea of humans being genetically engineered to survive even a limited exposure to hard vacuum—the way a naturally armored, insectile Nasat could—was hard to accept. *If the Neyel really* are *of human stock, then they must never have learned the lessons of the Eugenics Wars. Or is it possible they simply chose to ignore them?*

"Our guest is damned lucky I hadn't got around to laser-cutting into that thick hide of his yet," Chapel said. "He just missed the messy part of his autopsy."

Sulu followed the trail of wrecked and upset shelves, tables, and instrument carts that stood between him and the lab's exit. A moment before he reached it, the doors opened again, admitting Lieutenant Akaar and six armed security officers.

"Put *Excelsior* on full security alert, Lieutenant," Sulu told Akaar. "A member of the Neyel ship's crew is loose aboardship. He's extremely dangerous, but he's to be taken alive. We need to communicate with him."

"Understood, sir," Akaar said. Turning smartly on his huge heel, he led his people back out into the corridor.

There has to be a reason that our . . . cousins would attack an apparently harmless Tholian colony world.

Sulu crossed to the bulkhead, where he thumbed the companel. "Bridge, this is the captain."

"Bridge. Chekov here."

"Pavel, we have a huge problem."

Lojur was in his quarters trying to relax enough to take a restorative nap when he heard the intruder alert. The initial report said that a Neyel had escaped from sickbay. Shocked to discover that one of the aliens had been taken aboard—alive—he sprang from his bunk and ran into the corridor. When the turbolift deposited him near sickbay, he collided with a bulkhead, then fell unceremoniously onto his posterior.

The bulkhead turned out to be Akaar.

The security chief scarcely broke his stride as he ran past Lojur, at the head of an armed security team. The group was moving away from sickbay, fanning out through the corridors in various directions.

"You should not get involved in this, Commander," Akaar rumbled, phaser pistol in hand. Then he moved down the corridor with an alacrity that belied his great size.

Rubbing his backside and feeling humiliated, Lojur picked himself up off the deck, unable to think of anything other than the horrid presence that had invaded *Excelsior.* Would the Neyel bastards who killed Shandra resemble the bile-green Orions who had razed Kotha Village? He had to find out.

Don't get involved, L.J.? Just try to stop me.

Chekov looked at the chronometer on the arm of the command chair. His body was tense as he considered how little time remained until the Tholian ships were due to arrive.

Turning toward the center seat from the bridge's main

science station, Lieutenant Tuvok—who had insisted on returning to active duty the moment Dr. Chapel had pronounced him fit—looked as composed as if he were about to recite the mess hall menu. "Commander Chekov, the four Tholian vessels are entering the system, on a direct heading for the colony."

Chekov fixed his gaze on the main viewer, which stubbornly displayed only the crippled Neyel ship, the limb of the planet, and the stars beyond. "Have they detected us yet?"

"I am not certain, sir," Tuvok said.

Chekov watched as Tuvok stared into the scanner built into the science-station console. "One of the four approaching vessels is Admiral Yilskene's flagship, the *Jeb'v Tholis.* They have just dropped out of warp approximately thirty thousand kilometers off our port stern. They appear to be conducting intensive sensor sweeps of the Neyel vessel. Judging from energy-signature readings, Yilskene's ship also appears to be using a transporter beam to collect debris samples from the vicinity of the ship."

Damn, Chekov thought. *Yilskene's going to be absolutely delighted if he finds us here, in the middle of a Neyel attack on a Tholian outpost.*

As Chekov was preparing to alert Sulu, the companel on the command chair beeped, heralding a familiar bass voice. *"Bridge, this is the captain."*

Chekov stabbed a button with his thumb. "Bridge. Chekov here."

"Pavel, we have a huge problem. The dead Neyel in sickbay isn't *dead. He's loose somewhere on the ship, and he's violent. Akaar's trying to capture him."*

"Understood, Captain," Chekov said, looking toward Commander Rand, who was seated at the tactical station, starboard aft. She was apparently intent on information coming through her earpiece, and her hands moved quickly across her console; Chekov suspected that Security Chief

Akaar had called in moments ahead of the captain. The intruder alert klaxon immediately began to sound, and Chekov gestured to Rand to mute the volume.

Turning his attention back to the main viewer, Chekov could now clearly see the image of the four approaching Tholian warships. Addressing Sulu, he said, "We have another problem, sir. Yilskene's flagship has arrived, with three escorts."

"Has he detected us yet?" Sulu wanted to know.

"The Tholians are scanning *Excelsior* now," Tuvok said.

Rand turned toward Chekov. "Yilskene is hailing us, Commander. He doesn't sound happy."

Chekov sighed. "Make that an affirmative, Captain."

"I'm on my way. Sulu out."

Sulu entered the bridge almost at a full run.

Yilskene was already glowering down from the main viewer, his crystal-plane face an unfathomable mask.

"Greetings, Admiral," Sulu said, taking the command chair as Chekov vacated it to stand at attention beside him.

From the jangling dissonances in the Tholian's chorus of voices, Yilskene was clearly not in the mood to exchange pleasantries. *"Captain Sulu, why have you entered Tholian space without my government's authorization?"*

That is an excellent question, Admiral. But it's one I can't afford to answer with complete candor.

"We received a distress call from the outpost on this planet, Admiral. We came to assist as quickly as we could."

"The Tholian vessels are closing," Tuvok reported. "They appear to be taking up equidistant positions around *Excelsior.*"

Chekov leaned toward the command chair. "I could do without getting caught in another Tholian web," the exec said, *sotto voce.*

"We're not caught in anything yet," Sulu whispered, rising from his chair.

"My people are not fond of alien incursions, Captain Sulu. Even well-intentioned ones," Yilskene said, then turned his polygonal head to the side to bark a series of unintelligible orders before facing Sulu again. *"Nor can we allow you to leave as yet. We see evidence of a savage attack upon our outpost."*

"An attack carried out by the other vessel," Sulu said evenly. "Your own scans ought to bear that out."

"Perhaps. Perhaps not. Regardless, your vessel is to remain where it is until we can fully determine the truth behind your presence here. When we are satisfied that you intended no aggression against us, we will escort you directly back to the Federation border."

"Very well," Sulu said, hopeful that Yilskene would give *Excelsior* the benefit of the doubt.

"As you have no doubt observed, Captain," Yilskene continued, *"the outpost planet you now orbit is extremely vulnerable."*

Sulu nodded. "We noticed that as well, Admiral. Our intervention in the other vessel's attack saved many Tholian lives."

"Perhaps. Perhaps not," Yilskene repeated.

"Surely you can't believe *we* had anything to do with this attack," Sulu said. "The Federation Council has a great deal invested in normalizing diplomatic relations with the Tholian Assembly. Talks initiated by *your* people."

"Undisputed. But we are long accustomed to treachery and deceit from humanoid species such as yours."

Sulu ruefully considered his covert surveillance mission, as well as the undeniable kinship between the Neyel and humanity. The latter fact, if revealed, would no doubt make matters far worse. *You don't know the half of it, Admiral. And let's make sure we keep it that way.*

Chekov stepped forward. "You've scanned both our vessel and the Neyel ship, Admiral. Surely you can see that their vessel and ours have recently exchanged fire."

A second Tholian officer stepped into the viewscreen's

field of vision, apparently to whisper something into whatever Yilskene used as an auditory organ.

After listening for a few seconds, the Tholian admiral shoved his underling aside, throwing his head back to release a cacophonous noise that Sulu could interpret only as a thunderclap of pure rage. The external view of Yilskene's vessel returned as the channel was interrupted, no doubt on Yilskene's end.

"The Tholian flagship appears to be powering up its weapons systems," Tuvok said. "And I am detecting similar energy signatures emanating from the other three vessels."

"Evasive maneuvers, Captain?" asked Lieutenant Asher. "What if they deploy their energy web?"

"Steady, Lieutenant," Sulu said quietly, a practiced calm borne of countless similar crises descending upon him. "I've seen the Tholian energy web in operation, and it took hours to deploy. So we're going to sit tight. If we try to run before Yilskene does anything aggressive, then we're sure to have a firefight on our hands. But we'll keep our shields up. Just in case."

"Aye, sir," said Asher, apparently reassured.

On the viewer, Sulu saw a blinding shaft of golden energy lance out from the *Jeb'v Tholis.* He raised a hand to shield his eyes, as did everyone else on the bridge, before the computer automatically muted the intensity of the light.

The bridge shook and jumped, as though *Excelsior* had collided with something.

"Tactical!" Sulu shouted, grabbing the arm of his chair to steady himself. Rand tapped in a quick series of commands, and the image of Yilskene's flagship was replaced by a small wire-frame representation of *Excelsior* and the damaged Neyel vessel, both of which were surrounded by four orange, wedge-shaped icons that stood in for the Tholian ships. Bright lines linked each of the Tholian craft, trapping *Excelsior* and the Neyel ship within a large tetrahedral volume of space.

Not again, Sulu thought, taken aback at how quickly the Tholians had deployed their energy web. Being on the *Enterprise* when Tholian Commander Loskene had unleashed a similar but much more slowly woven weapon had been a nerve-wracking experience. The Tholians' energy webs had obviously become far more effective over the past three decades.

Sulu rose and walked to the railing behind Rand's station. She was ashen-faced as she watched the tactical display. "Raise Yilskene again," Sulu said.

The captain turned back toward the viewer, from which Yilskene radiated hostility. "This attack is not necessary, Admiral," Sulu said, trying to keep the anger out of his voice, but without complete success. "We have demonstrated no hostile intentions toward you."

"Really, Captain Sulu? Need I remind you that your own envoy has already implicated you as a spy? And can you explain the discoveries my knowledge-caste subordinates have just made?"

Sulu kept his expression impassive. "What discoveries?"

"My specialists have just examined several human and invader bodies we discovered drifting in the space near your two vessels."

"That should help prove to you that we fought the Neyel—the invaders—on behalf of your colonists."

"It might, Captain, except for one salient fact: the invader and human genomes, when compared, are identical. My specialists have assured me that this would not be possible unless Terrans and these aliens both belonged to the same species. Can you explain this?" As he spoke, Yilskene's chorused voices rose steadily in intensity, and his crystalline skin became progressively more red.

"We've noted those same genetic similarities ourselves," Sulu said, keeping his voice carefully even. "But we haven't yet been able to explain them. We're not that familiar with these beings yet."

Yilskene did not seem mollified in the least. "*And can you account for the presence of a live invader aboard your vessel?*"

Sulu decided he'd best stick to the truth as closely as possible. "Admiral, we've never encountered the Neyel—the ones you refer to as 'invaders'—before today. When we brought this individual aboard, we believed him to be dead. If you're beaming their bodies aboard, you might want to double-check their condition."

"*Your story strains my credulity, Captain. Nothing living survives in a vacuum—even hardy beings such as ourselves quickly explode under such conditions. I believe that our diplomatic and political castes may have seriously misjudged the trustworthiness of your species. And that your apparent clash with the invaders is a mere ruse intended to conceal your true intentions.*"

Frustrating as it was, Sulu had to admit to himself that Yilskene was at least partly right. *Excelsior*'s imbroglio with the Neyel had been entirely incidental to Starfleet's clandestine order that he reconnoiter the Tholian Assembly's recent military buildup. In spite of that, Sulu somehow had to convince the admiral of the simple truth of the Federation's overall benevolent intent.

"Please speak plainly, Admiral," Sulu said. "What do you believe our 'true intentions' are?"

"*I believe that you and the invaders are secret allies, Captain Sulu. And that your vessel's unauthorized incursion on Tholian Assembly territory may be part of a joint invader-Terran plan to conquer my people and annex our worlds.*"

Still staying as close as he dared to the real truth, Sulu replied, "Prior to today, no Federation species—*including* humans—has had contact of any sort with the 'invaders.' I assure you, Admiral, their genetic similarities to humans are a complete mystery to us."

"*Again, I find that assertion difficult to believe.*"

He's hesitating, Sulu thought, continuing to keep his expression blank. *If he truly believes everything he's saying, he ought to open fire. Or snap his energy web shut. There has to be a good reason why he's holding back.*

Aloud, he said, "If what you're saying were true, Admiral, then you would be justified in simply destroying us here and now."

The Tholian regarded him silently, and Sulu felt the level of tension on the bridge steadily escalating. To his crew's credit, no one so much as murmured.

"Indeed, I would be more than justified," Yilskene said at length, evidently still contemplating his next move.

Recalling Burgess's earlier briefings on the Tholian social structure, Sulu pressed what he hoped would prove to be an advantage. "But that would require unilateral action on the part of the warrior caste, wouldn't it? I think your counterparts in the political and diplomatic castes would have something to say about not being consulted before you did anything . . . precipitous. Tell me, Admiral, is Ambassador Mosrene still aboard your vessel?"

"Regrettably, we were unable to return him to Tholia prior to the advent of the current crisis."

"Then perhaps you should include the ambassador in this conversation. I am convinced that he knows far more about the Neyel—the 'invaders'—than either of us do." Sulu considered mentioning his belief that it was Neyel-related information that had motivated Mosrene to assassinate Kasrene, but decided against it.

After another brief pause, Yilskene said, *"I will confer with the diplomat presently, Captain. But if you attempt either to escape or attack us in the meantime, we will not hesitate to destroy you."*

The screen abruptly went dark as Yilskene interrupted the transmission. His image was replaced by that of his aggressive-looking warship and the energy web that radiated from it.

Sulu considered the deadly grid of energy that surrounded both his ship and the Neyel vessel. If necessary, *Ex-*

celsior's shields might withstand a direct attempt to run the energy gauntlet. Then again, they might not, considering the beating they'd just taken; he sincerely hoped he wouldn't have to find out the hard way.

"What now?" Chekov asked.

Sulu returned to the command chair and sat. "Now that the warriors have gotten the preliminaries out of the way, maybe it's time to bring *our* diplomatic caste back into the proceedings."

Chekov shrugged. "Ambassador Burgess? I suppose crazier ideas have worked before."

"You don't think she can make Yilskene see reason?"

"I might be biased, but I don't think she's exactly the easiest person to get along with."

Sulu smiled grimly. "Maybe that's why she was picked for this mission in the first place—she already has something in common with the Tholians."

By the time the two semi-anthropoid security guards finally agreed to conduct Aidan Burgess to the bridge to see the captain—an armed escort being necessary because the escaped Neyel still had yet to be recaptured—the Federation ambassador was in a stomping, crimson fury. Ever since the incident in the pathology lab, she had been under virtual house arrest in her quarters, ostensibly for the sake of her safety. When the ship went on red alert again, the security guard posted outside her quarters had evidently received orders not only to protect her from the unexpectedly resurrected Neyel, but also to keep her safely out of Captain Sulu's hair for the duration of whatever new crisis had arisen.

"What the hell is going on?" she demanded of Sulu before the bridge turbolift doors had even finished opening.

"And a good afternoon to you, Ambassador," Captain Sulu said, smiling as he turned his chair toward her and rose to his feet.

She fumed at his lighthearted manner. *You're only going to make it harder on yourself, Captain.*

"I need your help, Ambassador," Sulu said.

Burgess stopped in her tracks. She couldn't have been more surprised if he had suddenly dropped to one knee and made an earnest proposal of marriage. *Things must really be getting desperate up here.*

"What's happened?" Burgess wanted to know.

Chekov stepped away from the console at which Commander Rand was seated and approached Burgess. "Here's the short version, Ambassador: Admiral Yilskene thinks we're in league with the Neyel."

"And he's seriously considering destroying us," Sulu added with no discernible emotion. "We're currently snared in a Tholian energy web, along with the Neyel ship."

She swallowed. "Oh. I thought for a minute something really serious might have come up."

The glowering young Vulcan rose from an upper-level console to address Sulu. "Captain, I have conferred with Commander Azleya. She and her senior engineers concur with my opinion that we can disable the Tholian energy web by channeling warp power through the deflector grid. If, as our sensor scans indicate, Yilskene's ships cannot match our maximum speed, we can effect an escape before they can bring any of their weapons to bear."

"Are you *insane?*" Burgess roared. "We don't want to provoke them any further."

"The Tholians have already initiated hostilities by deploying their energy web," the Vulcan replied evenly. "Provocation is hardly an issue now."

"Since *we're* the ones who are guilty of espionage and trespassing, Lieutenant, it seems to me that we've already given them more than enough reason to distrust us." Burgess whirled on Sulu, her hands balled into fists. "Surely you can't actually be considering running away like a band of pirates."

The captain held up both hands, as if to placate both Burgess and his aggressive young officer simultaneously. "Stand down, Mr. Tuvok. We're going to have to play our hand the ambassador's way."

Tuvok focused his steely gaze on the captain. "Breaking the Tholian web and running may be our best and only hope of survival."

"Maybe," Sulu said, apparently not angered in the least at Tuvok's near insubordination. "But it would be pretty shoddy diplomacy, Tuvok. We're not here to start a war. Besides, I have no intention of leaving the crew of that Neyel ship to Yilskene's tender mercies. I won't simply abandon these human offshoots before we've even found out how they got out here and what they want. So we're staying put."

Burgess stared at Sulu, her eyes wide with surprise. All this time, she had pegged him as an old-guard officer of the *shoot-first-and-ask-questions-later* school. *The universe certainly contains no end of wonders.*

Then she reminded herself that this was the same man who had tried to conceal his military espionage mission from her while she had been trying to negotiate in good faith with the Tholians.

Sulu lowered his hands and approached her. "Ambassador Mosrene is still aboard the *Jeb'v Tholis.* We were hoping that the two of you might be able to buy us some time to find a peaceful way out of this crisis."

Burgess nodded. "All right. Let's do it." *No pressure.*

Sulu smiled. "Hail them, Commander Rand."

"Aye, sir."

As Rand set about her work, Burgess turned to face the viewer. Sulu and Chekov stood on either side of her. A moment later, a pair of larger-than-life Tholians were regarding them with their unfathomable crystalline expressions.

"Ambassador Mosrene," Burgess said, addressing the figure on the left. "I must speak with you. It is imperative that you understand that our mission here is a peaceful one—and that we are not allied with your colony's . . . antagonists."

Mosrene's white eyespots were twin geodes set inside a face like that of a stone cobra. *"You have always dealt honestly with us, Ambassador. I believe you. However, my belief is not the decisive factor in this situation. The preponderance of the evidence—your illegal presence in our space, Captain Sulu's espionage activities, and your apparent genetic oneness with our foes—supports Admiral Yilskene's contention that you harbor ulterior motives inimical to the security of the Tholian Assembly."*

Burgess found that it took a supreme effort of will not to scowl at Sulu, whose Starfleet-issue subterfuge was largely responsible for this mess.

Keeping her eyes on Mosrene, she said, "With your permission, we would like an opportunity to gather evidence of our innocence."

"I would welcome any such evidence," said Mosrene.

"We'll need time," Sulu interjected.

Yilskene finally broke his silence. *"Very well, Captain Sulu. In the interests of the nascent peace between our two civilizations, I will grant you twelve of your hours to persuade me that you are not allied with the invaders.*

"Should you fail to do so by that time, I will destroy both your vessel and that of your invader confederates."

The Tholians abruptly vanished from the screen.

Chekov interrupted the long wordless interval that followed. "Twelve hours will give Yilskene plenty of time to call up reinforcements."

Looking pensive, Sulu nodded. "No doubt."

"And the commanders of *those* ships won't necessarily be bound by Yilskene's bargain with us."

"Maybe," Sulu said. "But at least we've bought a little time for ourselves. And for the Neyel."

"Do we really want to concern ourselves about what happens to the Neyel?" Chekov said. "We might not have the luxury of saving our hides and theirs both."

Burgess scowled. "We can't just *abandon* them out here, Commander. They're *us*."

Sulu nodded again, though with apparent reluctance. "Again, Ambassador Burgess is right, Pavel. Like it or not, the Neyel are human. Or at least they used to be, once upon a time. And that makes whatever they do—and whatever the Tholians may do to them—our responsibility."

In spite of herself, Burgess felt a smile slowly spreading across her face—even as she watched the frown forming on Chekov's. "Captain Sulu, perhaps we actually *are* playing on the same team after all," she said.

Sulu chuckled, though the sound conveyed little mirth. "Welcome aboard, Ambassador. Now we just have to figure out how to prove our good intentions to the Tholians."

"We should begin by questioning the Neyel who rose from the dead today," Burgess said.

Sulu nodded. "I agree. But first we need to find him and contain him. My chief of security is seeing to that as we speak."

"If we didn't have a working relationship with the Neyel before, Yilskene has certainly given us a good reason to forge one now," Chekov said.

As backward as that sounded, it made a certain amount of sense to Burgess. Why *not* try to make peace both with the Neyel *and* with the Tholians?

Tuvok paced from his station on the upper bridge and entered the lower, central area. He came to a stop beside Sulu's chair, pointedly ignoring Burgess.

"Something on your mind, Mr. Tuvok?" said Sulu.

"Any effort to exculpate us in the eyes of Admiral Yilskene and Ambassador Mosrene may be doomed to failure from the outset, Captain."

"Why?" Sulu asked. "True, we've violated their space,

and that doesn't look good in their eyes. But our overall intent as well as our actions have been benevolent."

"But you are proposing to convince the Tholians that we have never been allies of the Neyel," Tuvok said.

"That's about the size of it," Sulu said, nodding. "And it's the truth."

"Nevertheless, I am constrained to point out that this plan is built upon a fundamentally illogical premise."

Burgess, Sulu, and Chekov all looked questioningly at the science officer.

"And that is?" Sulu asked.

Tuvok lifted an eyebrow in evident surprise, as though his observation should have been intuitively obvious. "Whether one has twelve hours or twelve centuries in which to attempt it, Captain, it is logically impossible to prove a negative."

Then let's hope that the impossible, Burgess thought, *only takes a bit longer than the merely difficult.*

"Captain," Chekov said suddenly. "May I have a word?"

Burgess saw Sulu meet his first officer's eyes, then nod. "In the situation room. Excuse us, Ambassador. Commander Rand, you have the bridge."

"All right, Pavel," Sulu said as soon as the door slid closed behind them, ensuring their privacy. He sat at the head of the conference table and gestured for Chekov to take his usual place at Sulu's right hand. "Tell me what's on your mind."

Sulu knew that his old friend would never question his orders in front of the bridge crew. But he'd known Pavel Chekov long enough to be able to see at a glance that he had grave reservations about some aspect of the current situation.

"It's about the Neyel," Chekov said after a moment of pensive silence. His dark eyes bored straight into Sulu's from just above the tips of his steepled fingers. "We stayed here partly to protect them from the Tholians. I'm not sure that was such a good idea."

"Because we're trapped here with them now?" Sulu asked.

Chekov shook his head. "No. I'm confident that Azleya and Tuvok can get us out of this if we have to leave in a hurry."

Sulu found that reassuring. "As am I."

"But you're not eager to do that if it means leaving the Neyel ship behind."

That nettled Sulu. Hadn't he put paid to this issue a few minutes ago on the bridge? "All right, Pavel. Let's take off the gold braid for a while and just talk. What's your point?"

"Just this. You may have a very tough decision ahead of you soon. Of course, you can count on me to support it, whichever way it goes. Because I know you're going to make the *right* decision."

Sulu sighed. "To what decision are you referring?"

"The decision to admit that you can't save both *Excelsior* and the Neyel ship."

"That's not a decision I'm even close to having to make."

"Right. You might have up to twelve hours. But after that, you may have to stop trying to protect the Neyel."

Sulu had known Chekov long enough to understand that neither of them needed to fear having an argument. So he didn't bother shrinking away from his rising pique. "God damn it, Pavel, we *have* to protect them. Burgess was right about the Neyel. They're *us*."

"No, they're not," Chekov said, raising his voice as well. "But that's exactly my point! They're *not* us. It's pretty clear that they've done some horrible things to the Tholians, and, for all we know, to other species as well."

"They split off from humanity during some pretty bloody times," Sulu pointed out. "Since then, our species has come a long way ethically, politically, and along just about any other dimension you can measure."

Chekov nodded. "But the poor, benighted backwater of the human gene pool known as the Neyel missed out on all that."

"I never said that. But if everything humanity has achieved

since the launch of *Sputnik* means anything at all—if it represents a sort of human birthright—then it's their birthright too. It's up to us to share it, to guide them back home."

Chekov wouldn't relent. "Are you *sure* that's all you're after, Hikaru?"

"Of course. What else is there?"

Chekov leaned forward as if to punctuate his next point. "How about absolution for humanity?"

His anger now thoroughly ignited, Sulu had to remind himself that he had asked Pavel to speak freely. He couldn't very well shut him down now. "That's absurd," was all he could think of to say.

"Is it? I've known you for a lot of years, Hikaru. You've got a conscience that's strong enough to jump-start a cold warp core. But this time it may be getting in the way of your judgment."

"Really?" Sulu said, fuming.

Chekov remained relentless. "Really. You're thinking that if the Neyel really have committed atrocities against the Tholians, then we bear major responsibility for their actions."

Sulu stood, fists clenched at his sides. "Well, don't we?"

Chekov rose as well, unintimidated. Sulu reminded himself that his exec wouldn't be much use to him if he were easily cowed, even by the ship's captain.

"That's the real question, isn't it? That's the root of it all. When the Romulans went to war with Earth, and later started blowing up Federation outposts along the Neutral Zone, was Vulcan responsible? When Khan almost succeeded in getting control of the Genesis Device, would all of humanity have been responsible for the consequences? After all, Khan was human, too. But we ended up having to take him out the hard way."

Sulu saw the emotion in Chekov's eyes, no doubt brought upon him by the memories of what he personally had endured at Khan's hands, and the certainty of the greater horrors that had been only narrowly averted all those years ago. Sulu's anger suddenly fled as he reminded himself that his old friend understood responsibility and guilt very well indeed.

Sulu took his seat again, emotionally deflated. "What do you think I should do, Pavel?" he said, keenly aware of the enormous responsibilities that both he and his old friend now shouldered. Unlike those long-ago days when they'd served literally side by side aboard the *Enterprise*, no senior officers were behind them, ready to make the hard decisions. Whatever was to come next, success or failure, plaudits or blame, life or death, depended on them.

On me, Sulu thought, feeling desolate inside.

Chekov's anger appeared to soften as well, and a reassuring smile replaced his scowl. "You see the Neyel as sundered members of the human family, so you feel responsible for what they do, and for whatever happens to them. It's understandable that you might think you owe them something. Save them if you can."

Sulu nodded. "That's exactly what I intend to do."

"I know, Hikaru. But just remember that taking responsibility for a family member sometimes means having to decide against them when they go astray."

Then Chekov turned and exited, leaving Sulu alone to wrestle with his conscience.

Chapter 16

"Watch out for the tail!" Akaar shouted.

Boyer managed to roll to the side just ahead of the angry whipcrack of the Neyel's rear appendage. Rogers, who was a split-second slower, went sprawling across the corridor, where he lay unconscious beside his phaser.

Akaar leveled his own weapon at the creature's midsection and fired. The Neyel recoiled slightly, but continued running away down the corridor and straight into an open Jefferies tube. Though the tube was extremely narrow by Capellan standards, Akaar threw himself into the upward-sloping crawl space without hesitation. Glancing upward, he saw the Neyel's tail disappear around a corner as the creature hastened away.

Still following, Akaar pulled out his communicator. "Akaar to Gold Team. Fugitive has gone to ground in Jefferies Tube Eight-Eleven on deck Twelve, just beneath the port-side impulse engine housing. I am right behind him. Seal off sections K and L, and you will corner him."

"Acknowledged, Lieutenant," said Ensign Cahill, one of the security officers Akaar had assigned to the Gold Team.

Pocketing the communicator, Akaar clambered quickly upward, following the Neyel. Around the corner, the well-illuminated Jefferies tube leveled out and widened. Power relays and EPS conduits ran behind metal grillworks set along the floor, walls, and ceiling. Though the space was now considerably wider than the tube's entryway, Akaar still had to stoop to avoid smacking his head on the ceiling.

Moving forward, he looked up and saw that a meter-wide section of the overhead grating had been pulled aside. The Neyel was obviously trying to slip out undetected, possibly by doubling back the way it had come, only this time concealing itself by crawling along the top of the ceiling grate.

Something clanked behind Akaar, and he turned toward the sound, phaser at the ready. No one was visible.

An object struck him in the back, hard and painfully. Akaar stumbled forward, his head bouncing off the grillwork of one of the walls. His massive body landed on the floor, and he found himself without enough room to reorient himself. His phaser skittered away, falling through a gap in a deck grating. Akaar turned his head and saw the snarling Neyel advancing on him. It shouted something that he thought he almost recognized.

Then a phaser beam sliced the air, striking the Neyel full in the chest and filling the air in the cramped chamber with the acrid stench of ozone. The creature jumped back a meter before it came to rest on the floor and lay still, a smoking scorch-mark inscribed diagonally across its rough gray thorax. Akaar turned his head toward the origin-point of the beam.

Lojur stood in the Jefferies tube, a phaser clenched in his bone-white fingers. *He must have picked up the weapon Rogers dropped,* Akaar realized.

With considerable effort, Akaar pushed himself into a crouch and slowly regained his feet. With a brief sidelong glance, he verified that the Neyel remained immobile. However, a slight oscillation of its chest revealed that the creature was still alive. *That is a relief,* Akaar thought. *The captain needs him interrogated, not executed.*

"I saw what happened when you fired on it," Lojur said. "Heavy stun didn't even slow it down. It seems to take the kill setting just to knock it unconscious. And that makes me think that the disrupt or dematerialize settings should be able to send this horror back to whatever hell it crawled out of."

Akaar looked into Lojur's eyes, which remained fixed on the insensate Neyel. The Halkan's face was a study in pain and grief, bordering on madness.

"Lojur, what you are doing mocks everything your world stands for. You cannot take part in such an act."

Lojur laughed, an unpleasant sound in Akaar's ears. "I already did 'take part' during the battle, didn't I?"

"That is different. You and everyone else who manned a battle station acted to save the ship, as well as the lives of the people the Neyel were attacking. What you are contemplating now is vengeance."

"The Elders of my village never appreciated such fine distinctions, L.J." Lojur raised his weapon. "Maybe they were right about me all along."

"Please, Commander," Akaar said, extending a large hand. "Give me the phaser."

"I will, L.J. After I'm finished with it." With a flick of his thumb, Lojur changed the setting on the weapon. Akaar could see from the weapon's flashing red telltale light that he'd turned it all the way up to its maximum energy output.

"The captain wants to question this creature," Akaar said, keeping his deep voice level and calm. "If you fire that weapon, you will vaporize him."

"That's the idea, L.J. He's part of what took Shandra from me. And for that, he's going to die." Lojur's hand trembled noticeably.

Akaar walked slowly toward his friend. His large frame made him impossible for the weapon to miss should Lojur attempt to make good his threat.

"Stop right there, L.J. That's an order."

Akaar paused, then continued moving forward slowly.

"No, Lojur. You cannot pull rank on me when I am acting on the captain's direct orders."

"I'm going to rid us of that thing." Lojur's voice sounded brittle, like a rotten tree limb about to snap in a stiff wind.

"Then you will have to kill me, too." Akaar continued his advance, slowly but relentlessly. He recalled the stories his mother had told him of his late father's killer and first successor, Maab, who had also once challenged a phaser-wielding man. That man, a treacherous Klingon soldier named Kras, had burned Maab down where he stood. Akaar felt that to show less courage than the usurper Maab would dishonor his father's memory.

Lojur's hand and voice both shook visibly. But the phaser remained aloft and deadly. "I don't want to hurt you, L.J. I don't—"

"Neither my birthworld nor yours are Federation members as yet," Akaar said as he came to a stop less than a meter from his friend. "Capella remains unready to enter the fold largely because of vendettas such as this. Your people, however, do not wish to join because they cannot condone the Federation's willingness to defend its interests." He paused and smiled before continuing. "I think our respective peoples would agree that we have both assimilated very well to this culture's extremes of war and peace."

The quaking in Lojur's gun-hand grew steadily more pronounced. "Stop trying to save this . . . *monster.*"

"Except for my duty to follow the captain's orders, this creature's existence is incidental to me," Akaar said, shaking his head. "The only one I am trying to save right now is *you.* What would Commander Chekov say if he could see you now? Or Shandra? Look me in the eye and tell me that she would have wanted this."

Tears streaming down his face, Lojur lowered his arm and allowed his fingers to go limp. The phaser clattered to the floor grating, and the grief-stricken Halkan collapsed sobbing into Akaar's arms. The Gold Team arrived a few moments later and prepared to bring the unconscious Neyel to a security cell, where members of the medical staff had already been summoned to see to his injuries.

After informing his people that Lojur had been knocked unconscious by the alien, Akaar gently carried his traumatized friend to sickbay.

"Apparently, our genes aren't the only things we share with our tough-skinned friend here," Lieutenant Hopman said, turning away from the shimmering blue forcefield that prevented the agitated Neyel from leaving the security cell.

"Explain," Sulu said, flanked by Hopman, Commander Rand, and Ambassador Burgess. He stepped away from them, toward the barrier, and studied the creature, which in turn regarded him. The Neyel, which wore a heavy, sashlike bandage diagonally across its chest, seemed to be utterly without emotion and looked almost completely inhuman. The sole exception was its eyes. Sulu hoped those eyes might provide a window to a soul not terribly unlike his own.

"His speech appears to be based on one of Federation Standard's root languages," Hopman said. "But that's hard to see until you get past the strange syntax, the extreme vowel drift, and all the highly unusual constructions. The changes are so radical, in fact, that it's no surprise that the universal translator had trouble parsing it. Working backward along the common linguistic tree, I'd venture a guess that their ancestral primary language has absorbed at least two centuries of cultural isolation and memetic drift. So now it's about as different from Standard as, say, Basque is from Spanish."

Rand, who was standing at Sulu's side, looked impressed. "You figured all of that out just by conversing with our . . . guest?"

"No, unfortunately," Hopman said. "The recordings of our earlier interactions with the Neyel ship's commander were actually far more helpful. Our guest is only just now becoming talkative."

"Maybe he's starting to realize that he's out of options unless he voluntarily talks to us," Rand said, nodding. "He may have decided to cooperate, at least a little."

"Let's find out," Sulu said, motioning to the two security officers who flanked the brig entrance. One of them lowered the cell's forcefields, while the other kept his phaser trained on the prisoner.

Good thing Pavel's up on the bridge, Sulu thought. *He'd have tribbles if he saw this.* Then he stepped into the spacious cell, followed by Rand, Burgess, Hopman, and a single phaser-carrying guard.

The Neyel remained crouched in a corner, from which he regarded Sulu with obvious suspicion. However, the creature's tail was coiled limply at its side, convincing Sulu that it wasn't preparing to attack. Trying to appear both nonaggressive and confident, Sulu moved to within a meter of the Neyel. Though it was sitting on the floor, the tall being scarcely had to look up to meet Sulu's gaze.

"My name is Hikaru Sulu, commander of the *U.S.S. Excelsior.*"

The Neyel hesitated for a moment, as though trying to decide just how much or how little to say. "My clade-given desig is Jerdahn," it finally said in sepulchral tones. Sulu wondered if exposure to vacuum had damaged the creature's ability to speak.

"Welcome aboard, Jerdahn," Sulu said. "You are my guest."

Jerdahn snorted in apparent derision. "Usually do you shoot and cage your guests, Hikarusulu?"

Sulu spread his hands. "Please forgive us. Before you woke up in our sickbay, we thought you were dead."

"Neyel are not so easy to kill," Jerdahn said, chortling and exposing two even rows of white, quite human-looking teeth.

Burgess stepped forward, the security guard hovering at

her side. "I'm Aidan Burgess, a special envoy from the United Federation of Planets. We're relieved to see that you survived being blown out of your ship, Jerdahn."

"Hah. I was blown out into space because of *your* weapons."

"You were attacking innocent Tholian civilians," Sulu said. "Not to mention firing on *us.* We couldn't permit either action to continue."

"You acted to protect your allies. The crystalline Devils."

Here we go again, Sulu thought, barely resisting an urge to roll his eyes. "The Tholians—the 'Devils'—think you're *our* allies, Jerdahn. Soon, they'll try to kill us all if we can't persuade them that they're wrong about that."

"We are neutral parties in whatever dispute exists between your people and the Tholian Assembly," Burgess said. "We favor neither you nor the Tholians."

"Yet you attacked us," Jerdahn said. "You killed many of us."

Sulu shook his head. "We acted to preserve as many lives as possible. Both Neyel *and* Tholian lives."

"The Devils' lives are not for preserving. Even the greatest Neyel minds understand that these creatures cannot be reasoned with. They are a scourge, fit only for eradication."

Sulu shuddered inwardly, as though he'd glimpsed a ravening monster leering back at him from his shaving mirror. This *is my cousin?*

Burgess answered the Neyel with a wolfen grin of her own. "There was a time when my people thought the same thing, about many races in the galaxy. We've been proved wrong. Many times."

"If you've spoken truly to me," Jerdahn said, "then the Devils intend to prove that my people have judged them aright."

"For the moment, we seem to share a common adversary," Burgess conceded.

Sulu reflected that *Excelsior*'s human crew members had

a great deal more than Yilskene's enmity in common with the Neyel.

Neyel. Something about the name sounded familiar. Sulu tried to recall what it was, but failed to retrieve it. *Neyel.*

"You seem to need my trust," Jerdahn said, his thick eyelids narrowing his gaze to twin slits. "But I will be a challenging winover while I remain caged. And while your soldier stands here, ready to burn my hide again."

Burgess nodded. "You're right, Jerdahn." Turning to Sulu, she said, "I want everyone out of this cell except for you, me, and Jerdahn."

Hopman, Rand, and the security guard looked toward Sulu, all nonplussed. The Neyel wore a guarded expression.

Sulu considered it for a protracted moment before deciding that Burgess was right. Playing it safe wasn't going to get them anywhere. There wasn't enough time left for anything but bold strokes. *Pavel is* really *going to have tribbles when he hears about this,* he thought, and nodded his assent to the guard.

A moment later, he and the ambassador stood unaccompanied and weaponless before the Neyel. *Neyel.* The almost-familiar name echoed frustratingly through his mind yet again.

Jerdahn's gray-rimmed eyes widened. "I did not truly think you had the bolides to face me gunless. You have at least some courage."

"We're not your enemies, Jerdahn," Burgess said. "It's vital that you and your leaders understand that."

"A pity it is you still cannot prove it." Jerdahn gestured toward the cell door, across which the forcefield continued to ripple. Rand, Hopman, and the security guards watched anxiously from the other side. "I remain your prisoner."

"Don't forget, Jerdahn," Sulu said. "So far you've given us precious little reason to trust *you.*"

"We've arrived at an impasse, then," Jerdahn replied, folding his arms.

"Not necessarily," Burgess turned toward Sulu, adding, "Could you give him a look at what his ship and ours are facing together out there?"

Sulu nodded. *Good plan,* he thought as he crossed to a far wall. After he placed his hand on the dermal recognition interface, a large hidden panel slid aside, revealing a recessed viewscreen and companel.

"Sulu to bridge."

"Chekov here, Captain."

"Pavel, I'm in the main brig with our . . . guest. I'd appreciate it if you could pipe down an exterior view of our current dilemma."

"Understood, sir. Right away."

Seconds later, the viewer displayed full views of both *Excelsior* and the crippled Neyel vessel, undoubtedly provided by the new sensor drones Tuvok had recently launched to analyze the Tholian energy web. The potent, crackling energies of that web were visible, forming an apparently impassable, lethal-looking cage about both ships.

Burgess gestured toward the viewer. "Whatever you may suspect about us, Jerdahn, the Tholians obviously regard us as enemies at the moment. Just as they do the Neyel."

"Your images might be false," Jerdahn rumbled. "Treachery and hydrogen are the two most abundant things in this universe. That's why Neyel always think it safest to regard all Outsiders as enemies, until proved either harmless or useful."

"That's a pretty bleak philosophy," Sulu said.

Jerdahn shrugged. "It is reality. It has kept us alive ever since the sojourn into the Outer Darks first began. Such has been the Neyel way since the times of our helpless, soft-bellied Oh-Neyel ancestors."

Neyel, Sulu thought. *Oh-Neyel?*

Sulu felt a sensation of *déjà vu* suddenly descend upon him. And just as abruptly, a memory, a very old memory, clicked into place. And the seemingly impossible—yet undeniable—shared genetic heritage of humans and Neyel suddenly began making sense, albeit sense of a far-fetched sort.

Oh-Neyel.

"O'Neill," Sulu whispered, stunned by the implications of those two mythology-encrusted syllables.

He noticed that both Jerdahn and Burgess were regarding him with obvious curiosity.

Facing Jerdahn, Sulu said, "It's clear to me, Jerdahn, that your people and ours are bound to one another. We really do have a great deal in common—besides being trapped by the Tholians."

Jerdahn still appeared skeptical. "What could our two species have in common, truly? You do not even *look* like us."

Sulu smiled. "For one thing, there was an asteroid colony, long ago. A great rock in space known as . . . Vanguard. Perhaps you've heard of it."

Burgess scowled, as though Sulu had just tried to pass off a fairy story about Trevis the Talking Tree as peer-reviewed science. After all, the destruction of at least five of the O'Neill Colonies during the tumultuous postatomic horror years was well documented, despite the often fragmentary nature of many mid-twenty-first-century historical records.

Jerdahn's face, however, bore a look of startled recognition. Sulu also thought he might have noticed a trace of fear there as well.

He realized now that he stood at the threshold of reconnecting with a long-lost branch of the human species. And at the same moment, he began to understand his earlier feeling of *déjà vu.*

Chapter 17

Stardate 1709.2 (2266)

A year after transferring from the physics department of the *U.S.S. Enterprise* to take the starship's helm, Lieutenant Hikaru Sulu was already no stranger to untimely death. He had first been touched by the random hand of violence as a preteen living with his parents in the village of Ishikawa on Ganjitsu, a wild border world which was frequently the target of Klingon raids. It had been unimaginably different from the safety and sophistication of San Francisco, his birthplace on Earth.

But today was the first time he had witnessed another human being's demise as it happened, right before his eyes. When Commander Hansen's image appeared on the bridge viewer, the man already looked dead on his feet. Obviously suffering from grave injuries, Hansen was smeared liberally with soot from the electrical fires that were consuming what remained of Neutral Zone Outpost 4's wrecked command center. At Captain Kirk's request, the commander had linked the outpost's external viewer system into that of the *Enterprise*, allowing everyone on the bridge to glimpse whatever had delivered so much devastation through the more than one and a half kilometers of iron asteroid that sheltered the outpost.

The Romulan ship that appeared across the placid starscape seemed literally to come out of nowhere. It swooped straight toward the rapidly approaching *Enterprise*—or rather toward the still-distant outpost, Sulu reminded himself—like the savage bird of prey it resembled.

Despite Captain Kirk's efforts to warn the aggressor off, the hostile vessel continued on its course, still too far away to be concerned about any challenges coming from the *Enterprise*. Even hurtling toward the outpost at warp 8, the Federation starship was still some five minutes out of weapons range.

Sulu watched helplessly as the alien ship opened fire, sending a large, greenish cloud of plasma straight toward its hapless target.

As the outpost's communications circuitry was scrambled by the impact, Sulu caught another glimpse of Hansen's battered control center. He watched the blast throw the commander about like a rag doll before the communications link between the *Enterprise* and the outpost was destroyed, returning the screen to its view of the local starscape.

Sulu knew that the raider would be long gone by the time the *Enterprise* reached whatever remained of Romulan Neutral-Zone Outpost 4. *I hope Hansen and his people died as quickly as everyone on outposts* 2, 3, *and* 8 *did*, he thought, feeling desolate as he stared out at the indifferent, uncaring stars.

A short time later, Sulu quietly took a seat at the corner of the conference room table. To his right sat Chief Engineer Montgomery Scott and Lieutenant Stiles, the alpha-shift navigator. Glancing to his left, Sulu watched a grim-faced Captain Kirk seat himself at the table's opposite corner, where he was flanked by Dr. Leonard McCoy and the half-Vulcan science officer, Commander Spock.

A little earlier on the bridge, Spock had succeeded in tapping into the cloaked Romulan ship's communications as it made its leisurely way back toward the Neutral Zone; he had displayed a visual of the Romulan control center—and of the vessel's decidedly Vulcan-looking commanding officer. It was hard not to conclude from that image that Vulcans and Romulans were virtually the same species, though so far only Stiles had used the incident to impugn Spock's loyalty.

Spock must be going through hell right now, Sulu thought. He could only imagine how he would feel were he to suddenly discover that a hostile alien race actually belonged to humanity's family tree. But he also knew that Spock, being half-Vulcan, wasn't likely to let any of his shipmates observe whatever emotional turmoil he might be experiencing.

Holding a jagged fragment of curved metal in both hands, Spock took a seat beside the captain. Moving the piece of debris to his right hand, he spoke with the equanimity so characteristic of Vulcans. "From the outpost's protective shield. Cast rodinium. This is the hardest substance known to our science."

The science officer flexed his right hand slightly, and the metal fragment shattered, showering dozens of smaller pieces across the table.

So who says Vulcans don't have a flair for the dramatic? Sulu thought.

"The lab theorizes an enveloping energy plasma, forcing an implosion," Spock said.

Kirk looked expectantly toward the entire group. "Comments?"

Everyone sat in silence, staring at the rodinium shards. Sulu wondered what a weapon like that would do to the *Enterprise*, despite its superior screens and shields. He looked toward Stiles, who seemed to be seething with barely controlled anger. *That makes sense,* Sulu thought. He knew that Stiles was very knowledgeable about his family's history, particularly where it intersected with the Earth-Romulan wars of more than a century ago. Several of Stiles's ancestors had died serving Starfleet on the front lines of those bloody conflicts, including at least one command-level officer. What Sulu had trouble understanding was why the navigator seemed to work so hard to keep those century-old wounds from healing.

Spock broke the silence, addressing the room. "Obviously, their weaponry is superior to ours. And they have a practical invisibility screen."

Dr. McCoy fixed his piercing blue eyes on Spock. "You're discussing tactics. Do you realize what this *really* comes down to? Millions and millions of lives hanging on what this vessel does next."

"Or on what this vessel fails to do, Doctor," the science officer said.

Kirk stroked his chin thoughtfully. "Yes, well, gentlemen, the question still remains: Can we engage them with a reasonable possibility of victory?"

"No question," Scott said, a grim almost-smile crossing his face. "Their power is simple impulse."

Sulu supposed that had to mean that the Romulan vessel intended to rendezvous with a nearby warp-driven mothership, then decided that the notion was so obvious it was hardly worth mentioning.

"Meaning we can outrun them," Kirk observed.

Stiles's fury seemed about to boil over. "To be used in chasing them or retreating . . . sir."

Kirk paused for a beat, evidently unsure how to take the lieutenant's almost insolent tone. "Go ahead, Mr. Stiles. I called this session for opinions."

Stiles leaned forward, his gaze sharp as a lancet. "We have to attack immediately."

Is he crazy? Sulu thought. *Everyone saw that Romulan ship turn itself invisible. And we still don't know the extent of their abilities.*

"Explain," Kirk said.

"They're still on our side of the Neutral Zone. There would be no doubt that *they* broke the treaty."

Sulu could no longer restrain himself from leaping into the fray. "Attack? Without a visible target? How do we *aim* our phasers?"

"Aim with sensors," Stiles said, undeterred. "Not accurate, but if we blanket them, we could—"

Sulu interrupted him. "And hope for a lucky shot before they zero in on *us*."

"And if we don't?" Stiles persisted. "Once back, they'll report that we saw their weapons and ran."

"And if they could report that they destroyed us?" Sulu countered.

Stiles rose to his feet, his anger and frustration palpable. He leaned forward, his hands splayed across the table. "These are *Romulans!* You run away from them and you *guarantee* war. They'll be back. Not just one ship, but with everything they've got." The navigator turned his venom upon Spock. "You know that, Mr. Science Officer. You're the expert on these people, but you've always left out that one point. *Why?* I'm very interested in why."

Silence descended upon the room again as everyone present scrutinized Spock, whose expression remained as distant and unreadable as always.

"Sit down, Mister," Kirk said to Stiles in a tone that clearly brooked no questioning. Stiles complied sullenly.

A moment later, Spock looked up and spoke. "I agree. Attack."

Dropping his left hand from his chin to the tabletop, Sulu saw his own surprise and alarm mirrored in the faces of most of the other humans in the room, especially Stiles, who'd clearly expected Spock to take the side of his Vulcanoid "cousins."

Does Spock feel responsible for what the Romulans have done to the Neutral Zone outposts? Sulu wondered.

Sulu watched McCoy, whose craggy features bore an expression of tightly bridled outrage. Spock and the captain seemed to be the only islands of calm in the emotionally stormy room.

Speaking to Spock, Kirk asked quietly, "Are you suggesting we fight to prevent a fight?"

"Based on what?" McCoy thundered. "Memories of a war over a century ago? On theories about a people we've never even met face to face?"

"We know what they look like," Stiles said, his emotions now seeming as tightly reined as Spock's.

Spock nodded, his eyes upon Stiles. He spoke with uncharacteristic urgency. "Yes, indeed we do, Mr. Stiles. And if the Romulans are an offshoot of my Vulcan blood—and I think this likely—then attack becomes even more imperative."

"War is never imperative, Mr. Spock," McCoy said, disgust tingeing his words.

"It is for them, Doctor. Vulcan, like Earth, had its aggressive colonizing period. Savage, even by Earth standards. And if the Romulans retained this martial philosophy, then weakness is something we dare not show."

McCoy's blue eyes, as bright as fully charged phaser banks, were locked onto Spock. "Do you want a *galactic war* on your conscience?"

Spock merely stared at the doctor in response, and Sulu wondered for a horrifying moment whether the science officer even understood McCoy's question.

Standing in the brig, Captain Sulu saw that the Neyel was now regarding him with an expression bordering on reverence. Burgess studied him as well, though she looked perplexed.

"The O'Neill colonies?" she said. "The Hapless Half-Dozen? Don't they teach history at Starfleet Academy? The old L-5 asteroid habitats were all destroyed over two centuries ago. Some sort of space-industrial accident."

"That's debatable," Sulu said. "A lot of O'Neill debris turned up after the accident."

She shrugged. "Sure. I've read that a lot of rocks and dust tend to clump together in Earth's L-4 and L-5 points. What's your point?"

"Just that none of the O'Neill habitat debris was ever positively identified as being from the Vanguard colony."

"That's the stuff of cheap romantic holovids, Captain," she said, obviously working to suppress a grin. "It's a pretty unlikely hypothesis."

Sulu gestured toward Jerdahn. "Is it really any more unlikely than encountering *him?* All the evidence so far suggests that the Neyel split off from humanity at around the time the O'Neills were all supposedly destroyed. So if the Neyel aren't descended from the Vanguard colonists, then where do you suppose they came from?"

Clearly still awed, Jerdahn craned his head toward Sulu and said, "You know of the Oh-Neyel, the words and worlds of the Eldest. Perhaps that proves that some of my progenitors came from the same clade from which some of yours sprang."

In other words, Sulu thought, *Jerdahn's finally starting to wonder if both humans and Neyel are indeed the fruit of the same vine.* He hoped that this particular Neyel's reaction was a lever he could use to open a dialogue with the Neyel leadership—and to avoid having to make the same fateful decision that had faced Spock more than three decades ago.

"Yes, there's evidence that my people and yours are genetically related," Sulu told Jerdahn, meeting his now extraordinarily human-looking eyes. "And it's an issue I need to explore with the captain of your vessel." *Otherwise, Yilskene will end up destroying at least one of our ships. Other than escaping with* Excelsior, *there won't be a damned thing I can do about it without at least* some *Neyel cooperation. And this may be our only chance to resolve the Tholian-Neyel conflict before the Tholians blame us for starting it and drag the Federation into war over it.*

Given the relatively recent ancestral relationship between humanity and the Neyel, Sulu wondered if Yilskene and the rest of the Tholian warrior caste would be truly wrong in blaming Earth for the depredations of the Neyel. Thinking again of Spock and the Romulans, Sulu hoped he wouldn't be forced to participate, either actively or passively, in the destruction of beings who were essentially his own people. *People who've been separated from our common humanity for so long that there may simply be no reconnecting with them.*

Leaning close to Jerdahn, Burgess said, "We also need to ask your captain why your people attacked the Tholian colony."

Jerdahn blinked in evident surprise. "Why do we fight the Devils?" The ambassador might as well have asked him why water was wet.

"I propose a truce between your people and ours," Sulu added, growing tired of plumbing the Neyel's obscure motivations. "Otherwise, the Tholians will destroy both our ships in a little under nine hours." Sulu did a quick calculation in his head. "That's about how long it will take our vessels to orbit the Tholian colony world six times."

Jerdahn took a deep breath as he considered Sulu's proposal. A long moment later, he appeared to have reached a decision.

"I will guide you to our drech'tor," he said. "But only if the two of you have bolides enough to accompany me back to my ship."

Sulu took Burgess aside. "There's no way I'm letting you beam onto Jerdahn's ship, Ambassador. You're under my protection for the duration of this mission."

"With all due respect, Captain, I don't think the decision is entirely up to you this time." Her face was stone. "Trust me, you're going to have enough explaining to do in front of your superiors as it is. You can't afford to get sideways with mine as well."

Sulu had to admit that she had just made an excellent point.

A scowling Chekov paced around the transporter console, almost joggling the transporter chief's elbows as he walked back and forth behind her.

"I don't like this one little bit, Captain. I wish we could contact the Neyel before simply sending you onto their ship uninvited."

"That would just confirm the suspicions Yilskene already has about us, Pavel," Sulu said. "We can't afford to provoke him."

"I know, Hikaru. But if the Tholians notice your beam-in, we'll end up just as destroyed as if we'd called ahead."

"The resonances of the energy web surrounding *Excelsior* should make our transporter beam difficult for the Tholians to detect," said Tuvok.

"But not impossible," Chekov countered.

"That's an unavoidable risk," Sulu said. "We don't have a lot of time left. Or options." Standing in front of the console, he checked the charge on his phaser and tucked it into one of the pockets of his field jacket.

Aidan Burgess, now dressed in a utilitarian civilian jumpsuit, slung a tricorder across her shoulder as she stepped onto the transporter stage, beside Jerdahn, who was now wearing an engineering jumpsuit, modified to accommodate his long limbs and tail. The Neyel now seemed fully recovered from the injuries he'd sustained during his capture, and had even dubiously accepted Sulu's explanation of the transporter system.

Dr. Chapel, Tuvok, and Akaar took the transporter pads adjacent to the Neyel, each of them checking their phasers, tricorders, and communicators.

"You bear weapons," Jerdahn noted.

"Do you object?" Akaar said to the Neyel. He was obviously watching Jerdahn very carefully.

Jerdahn chuckled. "I have no objection to your weapons, Lieutenant. You would be fools to come among my people without ways to protect yourselves."

"You said you'd vouch for us to your leader, Jerdahn," Sulu said, his brow crumpling. Could Jerdahn really be trusted after all?

"And I shall. But I cannot guarantee that either the drech'tor or his crew will want to listen."

"As I was saying," Chekov said. "I don't like this one little bit."

"I'm afraid that entering the lion's den is both our best and only option, Commander," Burgess said.

The executive officer threw his hands in the air. "One of the things I like least about this is sending a civilian into a nest of unknown aliens."

"It's part of the deal I struck with Jerdahn, Pavel," Sulu said as he and Burgess joined the other members of the boarding party on the transporter stage. "Besides, the Neyel are neither unknown nor alien. Try to think of them as our long-lost cousins."

"Remind me sometime to tell you just how well I get along with my cousin Oleg from Krakow."

Sulu smiled, trying to convey more confidence than he actually felt. "If all goes well here, Commander, then maybe there's hope to reunite the warring clans of Tribe Chekov as well."

"Let's worry about one miracle at a time," Chekov said, shaking his head. But at least he'd stopped his pacing. He'd come to a stop beside the transporter chief, who was double-checking the coordinates of the Neyel ship's interior. "Having trouble locking onto a section that wasn't exposed to vacuum?" Chekov asked.

The transporter operator shook his head. "No, sir. But I am getting some anomalous gravitational readings from the ship's interior."

"*Dangerous* anomalous gravitational readings?" Chekov wanted to know.

"Just a peculiar gravitational orientation. I've already compensated for it."

"Then energize," Sulu said. A moment later, the transporter's golden, shimmering light swept over him and the rest of the boarding party.

Chapel hated materializing in the darkness, but she knew that there were times when it was unavoidable. As the transporter's confinement beam released her inside the Neyel ship, she knew that this was just such an occasion. She inhaled deeply, reassured by the cold-yet-breathable air that the party hadn't materialized too close to a hull breach.

"Tricorders and lights," Captain Sulu said almost at the same time as Tuvok began scanning the immediate area. Chapel saw that Akaar was in hyperalert mode, his phaser already out and at the ready, held parallel with the bright beam of his palmlight. The Capellan's breath steamed like that of a dragon in the small light's cold glare.

Jerdahn was looking around with eyes as big as deflector dishes. He had obviously been unnerved by the transporter, but didn't seem anywhere close to panic. Chapel wondered if he was an atypical Neyel, or if they were all so adaptable.

"It takes some getting used to, Jerdahn," Chapel said in an effort to comfort the Neyel. He nodded mutely in response, and seemed to calm, evidently noticing the businesslike demeanor of the other members of the boarding party.

Chapel activated her tricorder. According to her initial scans, no one besides the boarding party was in the immediate vicinity, though the decks just above them—other cylindrically configured levels, which lay closer to the vessel's core region—teemed with Neyel life-signs.

As her eyes adjusted to the dim lighting, Chapel saw that the party had beamed into a long, tube-shaped corridor. It was strewn with debris clearly left over from a series of recent, extensive, and apparently hasty hull repairs. *Now we know what the Neyel crew has been doing ever since* Excelsior *crippled their ship.*

The corridor's form was obviously dictated at least in part by the exterior curvature of the Neyel ship's hull. Her weight felt about Earth normal, almost indistinguishable from *Excelsior*'s gravity-plating. But the decking beneath his feet curved gently away to the right and left, as though the "downward" direction was actually "outward"—the direction that led through the hull and into space.

Chapel saw that Tuvok was also examining the unusual shape of the deck. "Curious," the science officer said. "This vessel's internal arrangement is highly unusual. It is composed of a series of nested cylinders, with the decks curved so that the downward direction radiates outward from the ship's central axis."

"That's what Ensign Fenlenn's initial scans indicated," Sulu said. "What's your point?"

"Merely that it seems an odd arrangement of interior space," Tuvok said.

Chapel nodded. "It would make sense if they had to spin the ship to create artificial gravity. They've laid the decks out like they're on a colossal centrifuge."

"Indeed," Tuvok said. "However, this vessel is not spinning, nor was it at any time during our initial encounter with it. And my tricorder scans show that the decks beneath our feet are outfitted with artificial-gravity plating. The redundancy of this design makes little sense."

"It might make perfect sense," Sulu said, leading the team forward into the darkness, which he cut through with his own palmlight. "That is, it might if your ancestors had hollowed out an asteroid and rebuilt its interior along lines similar to this, settled inside it, and then spun it to simulate a planet's gravitational field. Later on, they must have discovered gravity plating, but clung to the familiarity of this arrangement."

"And later still they found themselves lost in the galactic wilderness," Burgess said, walking alongside Sulu. "The Neyel engineers evidently have quite a sense of tradition."

"It would appear so," Sulu said.

"That gives me some real hope that we can find a way to reconnect with them," said Burgess.

As if on cue, a moving blip suddenly appeared on Chapel's tricorder. Then two more bogeys resolved themselves, and those were joined a moment later by several more. They were quickly converging on the boarding party's position from opposite directions.

Nearby, Tuvok started, apparently having noticed the same thing. "A large number of Neyel life-signs are now heading toward our position," he reported calmly. The science officer gestured upward, shining his palmlight on the three-meter-high metal gridwork of the ceiling. "They seem to be moving along the next deck inward from this one."

"Phasers," growled Akaar, raising his weapon. Chapel saw the captain and Tuvok do likewise, then followed suit herself. The weapon felt alien in hands far more accustomed to medical instruments. She desperately hoped she wouldn't have to fire.

Jerdahn turned toward the ambassador. "I think my people are about to grant your wish for 'reconnection.' "

"Captain, your people are only going to provoke the Neyel," Burgess snapped.

"Our simply being here might be provocation enough for them," Sulu replied. To the rest of the team, he said, "Circle formation. Keep your weapons low, but ready. Nobody fires until my order, or until the Neyel do. Remember, we didn't come here to fight."

Chapel heard an echoing, painfully loud clatter along the ceiling grid. The sound surrounded her. Looking up, she saw metal panels falling from overhead, landing deafeningly a few meters ahead and behind. Lithe, dark-complexioned Neyel bodies leapt to the deck from the newly exposed ceiling portals.

In the dim light, Chapel couldn't easily determine how many black-clad Neyel figures now swarmed about the boarding party. But she could tell immediately that the team was surrounded.

The illumination levels suddenly rose at least tenfold in intensity, prompting Chapel to shield her eyes with her free hand.

"Please let's don't do anything stupid, people." The hissing voice belonged to Ambassador Burgess.

"Orders, Captain?" Akaar's voice was unmistakable.

"Stand by, Lieutenant," the captain said. "That goes for everyone."

Spots swam before Chapel's eyes. She clung to her sweat-slicked phaser, pointing it toward one of the indistinct dark forms that stood before her. It approached, carrying something small but unfriendly-looking in one of its long-fingered hands.

"Lower your weapons," the shape said, in a rough and commanding voice. "All of you."

"Captain?" Akaar repeated. As Chapel's vision slowly returned, she felt the level of tension all around her increasing exponentially, almost as though someone was tampering with the ship's climate controls.

She could see now that the nearest Neyel figure wore the same simple black coverall as the rest of the dozen or so troops who had surrounded them. The foremost creature's imperious manner and gray uniform sash implied that he was in charge. Each Neyel was armed, bearing either small pistols, or long, evil-looking blades with serrated edges. A few carried both. Their collective breath threw a shroud around them in the chill air, reminding Chapel of gathering storm clouds.

"Lower your weapons," the sandpaper-voiced Neyel squad leader repeated as a half-meter-long blade found its way into his free hand. Chapel wondered if he could throw the weapon as accurately as Akaar could hurl one of those lethal, triple-bladed Capellan *kligats*.

Her vision now more or less clear, Chapel looked toward Sulu. The captain was nodding to Akaar as he complied with the Neyel's orders. Then the huge Capellan slowly brought his weapon down, as did Tuvok.

Chapel felt relieved to be able to lower her own weapon. *Except for the fact that we've been captured again,* Chapel thought, recalling the crackling energy filaments that already hemmed in both *Excelsior* and the Neyel ship.

A *trap within a trap.*

PART 6

RAGE

Chapter 18

2169, Auld Greg Aerth Calendar

Watching from the concealment of a space-black shadow on Vangar's rough-hewn exterior, Hanif Wafiyy took the point position at the head of the grapnel team. Securely tethered to the Rock by an impossibly slender cable—one of the more useful artifacts the People had taken from the pointy-eared raiders who had landed a generation or so back—he watched as the blocky, oblong ship approached, gradually matching its velocity to that of Vangar.

Hanif's nose itched, but the faceplate of his p-suit precluded his doing anything about it. He tried to focus instead on whatever new horrors the alien vessel promised to bring among the People of 'Neal. Would the newcomers turn out to be more of those green-blooded elves who'd once tried to chop the Rock into fragments for their ore ships?

Or maybe it's another gang of Tuskers. He shuddered, though the suit's e-controls maintained a constant comfortable temperature of eleven degrees see-grade.

Glancing over his shoulder, Hanif saw the great bejeweled dervish of the Milky Way Galaxy. The powerful centrifugal spin of the Vangar Rock spoke eloquently to his inner ear. He knew well that a snapped tether would send him falling forever toward that brilliant assemblage of distant stars. He fought down a momentary surge of vertigo, reminding himself that he—and the rest of the 'Neal People he was sworn to defend—were over 64,000 pars'x from the blazing Milky Way's closest spiral arm.

As were, more than likely, the nearest elves or Tuskers.

A quick, sharp jolt, transmitted along Vangar's rock-and-iron surface through his thick-soled boots, interrupted his musings. The alien ship had made contact with the Rock. The waiting had ended.

Good. Maybe we won't have to stay out here in the hard-rad rain until all of our internal organs shut down. One of the serious drawbacks of life in the Lesser M'jallanish Cloud was the intense and constant wind of X rays, gamma rays, and high-energy neutrons that streamed outward from the densely packed stars at the cloud's relatively nearby galactic core. Retrovirally delivered DNA recombinants had greatly ameliorated the problem since the 'Neal People's arrival out in this cosmic hinterland, but enough high-rad exposure could still cook an unshielded Person from the inside out, and with dismaying swiftness. With luck, after the mission nobody on the team would need more than a liver transplant, or perhaps a few minor endocrine replacements. *No sweat,* Hanif thought. *Now all we have to do is neutralize the invaders.*

Using his p-suit-enshrouded tail, he tugged on his secondary tether, giving the "move" signal to the rest of the boarding team. He wasn't going to risk breaking radio silence while the alien crew was in a position to intercept the team's communications.

Leading the group out of the shadows, Hanif looked behind him. Gavin, Moira, and Safa had all emerged from the darkness, crawling like spiders along the permanent exterior safety rails. Without those rugged hand-, foot-, and tailholds, they would all be catapulted away from the spinning asteroid's surface, a human meteor shower running in reverse.

The team got into position, not more than half a klomter away from where the vessel had moored itself. Thanks to the ship's running lights, the p-suit's night-vision enhancements, and his own genengineered visual acuity, Hanif could see the marauder ship in considerable detail. So far, he'd seen no sign that the invaders had observed the team's approach. Using a theo'lite built into his helmet display, Hanif carefully gauged how much safety tether they would have to pay out as he computed the distance that the boarders would have to leap, using the asteroid's spin to accelerate them toward the marauder vessel.

Recalling his training exercises, Hanif made the first jump, which was over almost before he realized it. His pneumatic crampons deployed flawlessly, retethering him to the rock before Vangar's spin had an opportunity to fling him into space. Now he was only scant meters from the marauder ship.

Before continuing toward the alien vessel, Hanif took a few seconds to evaluate his condition, and that of his p-suit. He thought he might have sprained his right ankle during his landing, or perhaps even fractured it. *The Genescience Heads need to build us better limbs,* he thought wryly. Fortunately, his tail had taken the brunt of the impact, without compromising the integrity of his p-suit.

When he took stock of the rest of the team, however, he immediately saw that Gavin had not been so fortunate. His explosively decompressed corpse drifted from its tether like an obscene parody of one of the balloons the 'Neal technicians lofted through the high-grav exterior levels when tracking down slow atmospheric leaks.

Poor bastard, Hanif thought. *Maybe someday the genengineers will make us Rock rats tough enough to survive even an accident like that. At least long enough to slap on a p-suit patch, or crawl into a Safety Hutch.*

With no small amount of difficulty, Hanif put all such thoughts out of his mind. There would be time to grieve later, once the threat posed by the aliens had been neutralized. Without ceremony, Hanif, Moira, and Safa each cut their tethers to their dead comrade, and Moira kicked the body loose. It quickly pinwheeled out of sight, slung away by Vangar's relentless spin. Perhaps someday, Gavin would fall all the way back to the Milky Way and Auld Aerth.

The remainder of the team swarmed quickly across the marauder's hull, holding themselves in place with magnetic grapnels. Hanif was sweating freely by the time they'd finished planting the shaped explosive charges into what appeared to be the vessel's most prominent hatches and key structural points.

When Safa started to sabotage what appeared to be an external engine strut, Hanif pulled on the tether that connected them.

He shook his head when she looked toward him. He was well aware that Director al-Adnan had ordered the alien vessel "completely crippled and neutralized." However, as leader of the boarding team, he also knew that it was up to him to interpret the director's orders. Out on the Rock, where death could and often did strike without warning, Hanif was the one in charge. And demolishing what might turn out to be a completely functional Efti'el spacedrive—especially after the 'Neal People had failed to develop one of their own after more than a century of albeit intermittent attempts—struck Hanif as an utterly unconscionable waste.

Al-Adnan wouldn't have put me in charge of this op if he didn't trust my judgment. He can always order me and the marauder's engines spaced if he's really unhappy about this acquisition. But if he tries that, the Science Heads just might slice his throat from ear to ear and hand the little mullah's job over to me.

Two tether-tugs from Moira told Hanif that all was in

readiness. Using his tail, he pulled on the line three times in response. *Go!*

The trio leapt clear of the hull again. After landing, Hanif was sure that his sprained ankle must now surely be broken. But there wasn't any time to think of that. The pain was intense, but manageable. He relied on the suit's servomotors to keep him walking as the final explosives were put into place and the remote-control keypad booted and ran through its initialization procedures.

The explosions were silent, though the ship's hull transmitted their vibrations through the asteroid's skin. Hanif felt the percussive rumbles in his hands and feet, as though Vangar had suddenly begun shivering in the icy, neverending M'jallanish night.

Hanif looked at the ship. whose hull now showed deep rents and gashes. Clouds of atmosphere were venting, swiftly transforming into tumbling ice crystals that moved away, projectilelike, following the same course that Gavin's corpse had taken.

He touched the sealed holster strapped to his thigh. The elfish energy weapon was still where he'd left it. With his other hand, he found his chest controls and keyed open the boarding team's preselected radio channel.

"Let's move, people," he said, finally breaking radio silence. "I'm taking point. We kill whatever still moves in there."

After entering the ship, Hanif was almost disappointed. They had found a total of thirteen of the squat, three-limbed creatures aboard the alien vessel, eleven of whom had already been finished off by the explosives-generated hull breaches before the team had even come aboard.

Stepping over the messily decompressed corpses, Hanif led Safa and Moira into a large aft chamber. Hanif surmised that this was the alien vessel's engine room, judging by the glowing central structure, a four-mitr-tall semitransparent cylinder which pulsated with mysterious, blue-tinted energies.

Here they also found the vessel's two survivors. They were small, cowering things dressed in yellow pressure suits, creatures whose faces sported a pair of fist-sized, golden eyes, bordered by tufts of luxuriant white fur.

Hanif saw their complicated mouthparts moving repeatedly, but evidently wasn't tuned to whatever comm frequency they were using. In the airless room, the creatures made no sound. They might have been trying to sue for peace, or beg for their lives, or even threaten the team.

Or they might have been trying to buy time, waiting for an opportunity to turn the tables on their victims-turned-captors. Hanif unholstered his weapon and shot one of the beings through the chest. Its thick orange blood flowed, sublimating immediately into vapor in the vacuum.

Safer to assume they're all Tuskers, Hanif thought. *Given half a chance, they'd do the same to us, and take everything we have. Including our lives.*

The second creature looked terrified, and tried to flee. Safa knocked it down with her tail before it had moved a handful of mitrs away. But she hesitated after that, as though wavering in her purpose.

Then Moira stepped forward and shot the thing dead with three bursts from a lead-projectile pistol.

Hanif found that he couldn't take his eyes off the blue-glowing cylinder at the room's center. He wondered if it was the power plant or engine core that enabled these aliens to reach Vangar. They would have needed a truly potent energy source to cross the great gulf of interstellar space that separated the Rock from even the nearest star.

Then he noticed Safa, staring down at the motionless bodies of the two aliens. Her tail lay limply across the floor, like a coil of discarded EV tether.

Hanif touched his radio controls. "What's wrong, Safa?"

"Did we . . ." she hesitated. "Did we do the right thing here, Han?"

He sighed. "What on the Rock are you talking about?"

"These . . . creatures," she said, pointing down at the body nearest to her. "They're not exactly Tuskers, are they?"

"No, Safa. But they could have turned out to be something far worse. Fortunately, that's no longer a problem."

"Unless their people start sending out rescue teams. Or war parties."

Tucking her weapon back into its holster, Moira approached Safa. "If that happens, we'll be ready for them."

Hanif resumed watching the roiling energies contained within the tall blue cylinder. "Our dead visitors may have already given us the solution to that problem. But if that thing really is an Efti'el spacedrive, I wonder how they survived the acceleration."

Moira shrugged. "Maybe they have some way to manipulate gravity and inertia locally."

Hanif nodded, and an idea came to him. Pointing to his booted feet, he said, "We're upside-down."

"Sorry?" Safa said.

"This ship's belly is moored to the Rock. And we're walking around *inside* the ship's belly. Because of Vangar's spin, that way," he pointed at the deck plating, "should be *up*."

Moira grinned, understanding. "And I thought I was just having an attack of vertigo when I came through the hatch." She knelt on one knee and carefully pried up a mitr-square deck plate with her gauntleted hands.

She placed the deck plate against a nearby bulkhead, holding it steady with one hand and her tail. With her free hand, she removed a small spanner from her suit's utility kit and held it parallel to the deck plate. Then she released the spanner.

The tool "fell" sideways, coming to rest against the deck plate.

Hanif felt his eyebrows launch themselves toward higher orbits. *Spinless artificial gravity!*

He touched his suit's radio controls again. "Wafiyy to Director al-Adnan."

After a beat, the director's voice crackled into Hanif's helmet. *"What's happening over there, Hanif? Are the hostiles neutralized?"*

"All dead, Director. We lost only Gavin."

The director hesitated another moment before responding. *"Gavin. That's . . . unfortunate."*

Hanif smiled, but without any humor. *Unfortunate, you mean, that the sole casualty on this mission wasn't* me. *Do you really fear that I'll take your job?* He could remember a time when al-Adnan had been more concerned with protecting the 'Neal People than with maintaining the trappings of authority.

Hanif decided then that what the director feared most was change in general. And that made al-Adnan a most dangerous man to follow, especially in an environment where survival depended upon the ability to adapt quickly to the universe's random exigencies.

"Is there anything else?" al-Adnan added, sounding impatient.

Get ready to adapt to the future, Director, Hanif thought. *Lead, follow, or get the hell out of its way.*

Aloud, Hanif said, "Tell the Science Heads we're bringing back some things that will keep everyone in Vangar busy for decades." Then he cut off the transmission without waiting for the director's reply.

Hanif stared once again into pulsating depths of the enigmatic blue cylinder. Standing quietly beside him, Safa and Moira were doing likewise.

Maybe we won't have to sit around waiting for the universe to come after us much longer. Perhaps the time has come for us to start pursuing it.

Chapter 19

2204, Auld Greg Aerth Calendar

"In composition, mass, and atmosphere, it looks very much like Aerth, sir," the control deck's officer of the watch said. "And that's a rare thing, with all the hard rads flying about in this corner of the cosmos."

Drech'tor Hanif Wafiyy nodded. He sat back in his padded chair, feeling every one of his eighty-four Aerth-years, as lifespans were still measured within Vangar. The plates of coarse flesh that interleaved across the small of his back ached. He reminded himself to adjust the gravity in his quarters yet again.

Eighty-four years, he thought, gazing at the great blue world displayed in the wide viewer. *We must still reckon time that way because even now our hearts hunger for a home like the one our Oh-Neyel fathers and mothers remembered.*

Hanif lost himself in the sunlit swirls of blue and white. Such a world could provide practically endless supplies of whatever Vangar needed, everything from food to the raw materials to build new Elfive worlds—or even entire navies of weapon-bristled star-vessels. During the generations since Hanif had acquired the machinery that had eventually given the People of Neyel mastery of both the stars and gravity, the fact that such a place lay at the bottom of a steep, Aerthlike gravity well now posed no serious difficulties.

Rather, their main problem had been exactly as the officer of the watch had framed it—the finding of such a world. Habitable planets were rare baubles indeed in the cauldron of violence that comprised the local stellar group, so far distant from the Great Pinwheel wherein Ancient Aerth lay forever lost.

"Prepare to dispatch survey expeditions," the drech'tor said. "I will require a complete inventory of this world's usable resources as soon as possible."

The officer of the watch nodded, his tough gray hide rasping against itself as he passed Hanif's order down to one of the sergeants, a female who had lost her tail to an EV accident a few months earlier. The new limb seemed to be growing back nicely.

The sergeant hesitated.

Hanif lofted his thick brows. "Is there a problem?"

She took another moment to find her voice. "The . . . the world beneath us seems already to be inhabited by sentients."

The drech'tor frowned. He suddenly realized that he hadn't given that possibility sufficient thought. It had been so long since any alien species had posed any serious challenge to the Neyel People as they used their Efti'el technology to move Vangar wherever they willed in M'jallanish Space . . .

"What level of attainment have these sentients reached?" Hanif wanted to know.

"The long-range probes showed evidence of cities, as well as heavy industries and their burnings. Iron foundries and the like. Apparently wet navies sail on their oceans."

"Have they space vessels? Orbital defenses?"

The sergeant shook her head. "No evidence of such. Nor have we detected any nukes, or even telecom activity."

Hanif recalled a descriptive term he'd encountered long ago in one of the Elder texts: *Iron Age.*

The officer of the watch bared his teeth in a war-grin that

would have done an older, more properly blooded officer proud. His tail switched back and forth as though in anticipation of the battle to come. "When do we attack?"

The drech'tor adjusted himself in his seat, relieving his aching back. He had been thinking the same thing himself, when a more subtle idea occurred to him.

"Not right away," Hanif said, returning the younger Neyel's grin.

"Are we not to send out the survey vessels then?" the injured sergeant said, looking confused.

"Send them," said Hanif. "Let us learn the hearts of these indigies first. We may be able to help them even as we enjoy their world's bounty. Such largesse from us could win considerable gratitude from them."

The officer of the watched looked stunned, as though he'd just borne witness to an unspeakable heresy. "Sir? I must respectfully remind the drech'tor that the makings of an empire are down there, awaiting us. We can put those resources to far better use than can the backward indigies."

Ah, impertinent, stupid youth.

Drech'tor Hanif Wafiyy leaned forward and spoke in a conspiratorial whisper. "Exactly so. And who better to construct such an empire for us than the multitudes who already populate its provinces?"

"How long has it been since the aliens landed on the lawn of the Deliberative Althing, Wataryn? Fifteen years?" g'Isen wanted to know.

Presider Wataryn considered his trusted advisor's question in silence. *Long enough for the Neyel to have raised great numbers of their ilk in their enclaves all around the planet.*

G'Isen, ever the apologist for the newcomers, was apparently just warming up. "Presider, when will you finally accept that the Neyel may be exactly what they seem to be?"

What special covert promises have the Neyel made to you, g'Isen? Wealth? Guarantees of star travel for your younglings?

Wataryn turned his back on g'Isen, moving toward the wide window that encircled his office. Glass, the Oghen people's Neyel benefactors had called the clear, thin, silicate stuff. The substance had been unknown on Oghen before the coming of the Neyel. Even now, the aliens continued teaching the people how to create still more exotic construction materials.

After the First Landings, the world had begun to change virtually overnight. And Wataryn had been uneasy ever since the day the ancient Neyel chief had come to Oghen bearing his so-called Proclamation of Friendship and Understanding.

Wataryn looked out at Mechulak City's ever-changing skyline. In the distance, great plumes of thick, black smoke rose in columns like the legs of mythical colossi.

"The Neyel foul our air and water far faster than ever we did before their coming," Wataryn said, casting several of his eyes skyward. "And they take much back with them into their Skyworld."

"It could be as they say," g'Isen said. "Merely the price of progress. But examine what we've gotten from them in return for what they ask of us, Presider. Before the Neyel, we could not even adequately feed ourselves. Nor could we do aught to ward off disease. The Neyel have not only put paid to those ills, but they also promise us the stars."

"But can they deliver on that promise?" Will *they deliver on that promise?*

"The Neyel *can* ply the space between the stars. Their starcraft demonstrate the truth of it."

Starcraft our foundries now manufacture for them in great numbers, Wataryn thought, his stomachs rumbling as his distress mounted. His dual-thumbed hooves clattered on the floor as he turned to regard his advisor.

"And haven't they also given you the office of Presider?" g'Isen continued before Wataryn could speak.

Wataryn chuckled at that as he chewed on the tough flap of skin that covered his lips. He had worried it and tugged on it so often during the last two years that it now hung down nearly as far as the dewlap that dangled beneath his neck. *What have I done to really question the Neyel and their oh-so-altruistic behavior? When have I ever publicly asked what* they *get out of their great munificence?*

"I suppose they did well to back such a compliant leader," Wataryn finally said aloud, despising himself for his weakness and timidity. "It would do no good to oppose beings so mighty and benevolent that the people treat them almost as gods."

The chamber's heavy door opened with a loud crash. In the threshold stood an office clerk, whose forehooves banged together nervously. Beside the clerk stood a tall, aggressive-looking Neyel who wore a simple black coverall which bore scores of military-looking decorations. The hard-skinned being's slate-gray tail clutched at the door's ornate bonetree handle, then slammed the door closed.

The clerk's dewlap quivered when he spoke. "One of our Neyel b-benefactors wishes to see you, Presider."

Wataryn nearly laughed aloud at the ridiculous obviousness of the clerk's comment. "Yes. Yes, I can see that," he said, trying to gather his dignity about him. He was surprised that he, too, wasn't shaking. Being in close proximity to Neyel had always made him nervous.

"Drech'tor Hanif Wafiyy is dead," the Neyel announced, his voice like thunder.

Wataryn had dreaded this moment ever since he'd first learned of the drech'tor's great age and fragility. "That is sad news, indeed," he said. It was no secret to Wataryn that many of the ancient drech'tor's underlings had far less beneficent intentions toward Oghen and its people.

"And who succeeds the august Wafiyy in ruling the Great Stone Skyworld?" Wataryn continued, already dreading the answer.

The Neyel drew a lethal-looking blade in one great, clawed hand and unholstered a massive pistol with the other.

"That need not concern either you or the rest of the Oghen cattle," the creature said, its hard face somehow contorting into a vicious sneer. "Your continued service to the Neyel is all that need occupy your attention from this moment forward."

At that, Wataryn finally did laugh aloud, while g'Isen and the clerk watched him with puzzlement written large across their faces. A perverse sense of relief flooded him, and the horrific tension in his stomachs abated somewhat.

At last, we are slaves in name as well as in fact.

Chapter 20

2265, Auld Greg Aerth Calendar

"The fleet reports ready, Sub-drech'tor Jonat," the helm officer reported.

Jonat's eyes were on the main viewer, where the Oghen homeworld slowly turned, the setting sun emphasizing the haze of orange and ocher that dominated its atmosphere. Several other Neyel vessels, all of them long, tapering cylinders that mimicked the noble lines of the Great Vangar Rock itself, were visible in lower orbits.

From nowhere else than high above Oghen was it clearer that this world, the nucleus of the Neyel Hegemony, was now all but used up. The time had finally arrived to annex some of the other worlds whose presence had been discovered since the consolidation of the historic conquest of this one. Their resources could be used in fairly short order to restore the Coreworld of Oghen to something approximating its former beauty and glory.

A *pity so few of the Oghen cattle now remain down there as witnesses to Oghen's coming rebirth*, Jonat thought, considering the expendable indigie workers whose mortal labors had built the bulk of the newly commissioned fleet. *Some of them were excellent stargazers and worldfinders. It's a pity for them that they were so ill-equipped to take and hold such worlds as their 'scopes could locate.*

There were times, usually in the dead of night when sleep refused to come, that Jonat wondered if the slaughter of the Oghen had been truly justified. After all, the cowfolk were hardly the Tuskers of Neyel children's bedtime tales. In fact, they were passive in the extreme, and had proved far easier to dominate than any other race the Neyel had encountered before or since. He sometimes secretly wondered what might have happened had the Neyel and the Oghen indigies gone out into the universe together as partners.

But it was self-evident that the Oghen were slaves by nature. And every Neyel knew that slaves could never be trusted as equals. Slaves, even seemingly passive ones, could only turn to treachery and rebellion in the end.

"Your orders, Sub-drech'tor?" the helm officer prompted, his club-headed tail twitching behind him. Jonat wondered how many times the young officer had had to repeat himself before capturing his attention.

"Acknowledge the fleet's readiness. Tell them we move out now, on a heading for the primary target."

Lirillia, Jonat thought, turning the name of the soon-to-be-subjugated world over and over in his mind. *An attractive name for such a harsh ball of dust.*

But a conquest was a conquest, and orders were orders. Of such small links were the mighty chains of empire forged.

"It will be done, Sub-drech'tor," the helm officer said. Using both hands and tail simultaneously, the youth quickly set about pressing buttons and moving vernier switches. A throb of eager, barely-constrained power vibrated through the deck plates beneath Jonat's feet.

All those decades we searched until we found Oghen, a world once so very like lush and fabled Aerth. And all the while we had forgotten that ever since leaving Aerth we Neyel have made ourselves capable of surviving and prospering on any *sort of world, so long as it is one we can wrest from whoever holds it. Now that we have sufficient ships and crews to take such worlds outright, let it at last be done.*

Jonat's gray lips peeled back from his rows of sharp, even, white teeth. "Engage," he said, punctuating the command with an authoritative slash of his tail. "It is time to teach the sky who truly owns it."

PART 7

VANGUARD

Chapter 21

Sulu stood in an iron-barred holding cell, along with the rest of the boarding party. After confiscating their equipment, their captors had ignored Sulu's initial request to be taken to the ship's commander. Now he listened, via the universal translators sewn unobtrusively into each of the team members' field jackets, to the Neyel troops as they debated how the mysterious intruders got aboard their vessel without cutting their way in, and without any evidence of having been deposited by another ship.

So they really don't know about transporters, Sulu thought, recalling Jerdahn's earlier confusion and incredulity at the prospect of being beamed back onto his ship. But Jerdahn appeared to have adapted to the situation quickly. If the commander of Jerdahn's ship proved equally adaptable, then there was real cause for hope.

Sulu listened with greater interest as the Neyel troops engaged Jerdahn in the conversation, and began arguing amongst themselves about just what to do with their prisoners.

"Surely they cannot be beings of reason, like us," said the gray-sashed commander of the guards.

"They are," Jerdahn said. "They had many chances to kill me. But each time they offered peace instead."

"*Bellstine!*" one of the guards exclaimed. "They are too

dangerous to be allowed further life. One of these may have been the *toktof* who killed my Gretsel."

Several of the Neyel began thumping their club-tipped tails onto the ground and walls, creating a discordant, metallic gonging sound. The rough-hewn hands of a few of them also began to twitch on or near their weapons.

Chapel was crouching near Sulu. "Now would be a good time for a plan, Captain," she said in a low voice. "Before they decide to escort us straight to the nearest airlock."

"Sit tight, Chris," Sulu said, sensing a great deal of uncertainty in their captors' body language. "Something tells me these soldiers won't want to take on that kind of responsibility."

"Let's hope you're right," said Chapel.

Glancing toward Akaar, Tuvok, and Burgess, Sulu saw the same calculated stillness in each of their gazes. He suspected it masked completely different mental preparations. Akaar was likely planning how best to tear the Neyel limb from elongated limb, should the need arise; Tuvok seemed to be carefully evaluating every word and gesture; Burgess was no doubt engineering a last-ditch plan to negotiate with them, should the situation deteriorate further.

But it was Jerdahn who spoke up first on their behalf. "Adjun-drech'tor Bannohn, in case you do not recall me, I am Subaltern Jerdahn from Level 47, Post 16. As you can see, I have spent some time among these *humans*, and believe them to be . . . different from most other species we have encountered before."

The leader of the Neyel forces snorted, his mouth twisted into a derisive grin. "Why should I care what a waste reclamation worker thinks? These humans fired upon our vessel, hulling it and killing many Neyel in the process."

Sulu felt his heart sink for a moment. Jerdahn was apparently only a lowly maintenance tech. Clearly, his opinion held little sway here.

But Jerdahn didn't flinch from the provocation. Instead

he puffed up his chest and squared his massive shoulders. "My *present* occupation has nothing to do with my old life, nor the knowledge I still retain, Adjun-drech'tor. It would be in your best interest to remember that."

Bannohn flinched almost imperceptibly. Sulu noticed it, however, and he suspected that others in his boarding party might have picked it up as well. *Clearly, Jerdahn is* more *than just a maintenance tech. That's good.*

"Although many facts remained to be confirmed, my belief grows that this group may indeed be OROM," Jerdahn continued.

As a noisy muttering began amongst the soldiers, Jerdahn addressed Sulu's group as well. "If they are indeed an Other Race of Men, they must command respect. Their actions have shown them to be gentle unless provoked, rather than a dangerous or hostile species fit only for killing or enslavement."

The angry guard who had earlier spoken of the loss of his Gretsel snarled and brandished a vicious-looking knife. "He speaks heresy. How many truly OROM aliens have the Nçyel met since the Long Fall from Far Aerth? He is clearly under their influence. Look! He even wears their garb."

Jerdahn held up his hand, and amazingly, the Neyel troopers quieted. "I think I'm well aware of what is heretical and what is not," he said with conviction. "I wear their garb because they clothed me. My garments were destroyed when I was blown into space. I would have been killed and gone, had they not recovered my body just before death embraced it."

"So what are you proposing we do with them?" the Neyel squad leader asked, clearly refusing to show Jerdahn respect by using his name.

"They must speak with the drech'tor and his visor," Jerdahn said. "*Oghen's Flame* is currently ensnared by the Devils, as is the humans' own ship. If our crew is to have hope of escaping this trap, then we must work with the humans."

Jerdahn stepped forward, staring directly into the leader's

eyes. The action might have seemed defiant, but Sulu didn't sense that any of the soldiers felt threatened.

"I believe that this is not just a matter of the survival of our persons and our vessel, Adjun-drech'tor Bannohn, nor of the *humans* and their *Excelsior*," Jerdahn said. "These people may represent the salvation of worlds, perhaps even of the entire Neyel people. You *must* allow us to speak of this to the drech'tor. Immediately."

The gray-hued leader stared intently into Jerdahn's eyes, and Sulu saw him flinch almost imperceptibly yet again.

What power does Jerdahn have over him? he asked himself. *And will it be enough to convince whoever commands this ship to cooperate with us?*

Minutes later, Sulu and the group had ascended through several levels of the Neyel vessel, *Oghen's Flame*. Sulu assumed that they were traveling toward the core. None of his team said anything, especially since their armed Neyel escorts still looked ready to shoot them dead or slice them into pieces if they stepped out of line, either verbally or physically.

Eventually, they were herded into a large rounded chamber that seemed both ceremonial and functional. Narrow tapestries festooned the walls, but between each of them were large monitors that showed various internal and external views of the ship, as well as the space surrounding it. On one of them, Sulu could see *Excelsior*, while another was focused on one of the wedge-shaped Tholian vessels and the energy web filaments that emanated from it.

A Neyel man was watching one of the monitors closely, as was a female Neyel who was seated nearby. Both were dressed in garments that were clearly of better quality than those worn by the soldiers, but still seem to retain a completely utilitarian function.

Ignoring the soldiers, Jerdahn approached the pair and began speaking to them. He kept his voice low enough so that the universal translator couldn't pick up what he was saying, but Sulu saw Jerdahn gesture toward them several times during the conversation.

Finally, the male approached Sulu's group, his tail switching languidly behind him. "You are Hikarusulu?" he asked. "You are the drech'tor of your ship?"

"I'm the captain of the *U.S.S. Excelsior,*" Sulu said, offering what he hoped was a nonthreatening smile. He gestured toward the others in the boarding party. "I bring with me Federation Ambassador Aidan Burg—"

"I am Joh'jym, the drech'tor of the Neyel Hegemony Fleet Cruiser, *Oghen's Flame,*" the Neyel man said, interrupting Sulu. He gestured toward the woman. "This is my visor, Oratok."

Since neither of them offered their hands to shake, Sulu didn't offer his. He noticed that Burgess was regarding him almost as intently as were the Neyel leaders.

Oratok spoke, her voice soothing, almost purring. "Jerdahn says that you have come to us with knowledge and offers of peace, although even today you have aided the Devil scourge and caused the deaths of many Neyel."

"I've taken no one's side in this conflict," Sulu said. "The actions I took were intended solely to prevent the slaughter of innocent civilians on the planet."

Oratok sniffed disdainfully, her tail switching back and forth behind her in agitation. "There are no 'innocent' Devils, Hikarusulu. Either we eradicate them, or they will us."

Sulu decided that the best way to persuade Joh'jym and his visor to make peace was to "humanize" their adversary. " 'Devil' is an interesting term," he said. "It implies an assumption of evil intent."

"They have attacked Neyel vessels every time a vessel of ours encounters one of theirs," Joh'jym said. "No other assumption is prudent."

"Perhaps, in the absence of more information about

them. Your adversaries may have a similar name for you in their own language," Sulu said, ignoring Burgess's warning scowl.

Both of the senior Neyel officers chuckled. "They are creatures of pure instinct," Oratok said. "The Devils have no language."

"Tholians," Burgess said, stepping forward. "They call themselves 'Tholians.' In their own language, of course."

"Ridiculous," Joh'jym said. "The Devils are as incapable of speech as is the hull of this ship."

Jerdahn approached the drech'tor and spoke. "The humans possess devices which can translate our speech into theirs, and back again."

"As we've also done with the Tholians," Burgess said, nodding. "With your permission, we would like to make your speech and that of the Tholians mutually comprehensible."

Neither Joh'jym nor Oratok appeared convinced in the slightest.

"You speak of *skiffy* things," the visor said, her purring voice becoming more of a growl. "Impossible things."

"We have no reason to lie to you," Sulu said. "And we have every reason to wish for a peaceful end to your conflict with the Tholians."

"And what reason have you to wish us well, after having traded fire with us?" Oratok asked.

Sulu drew a deep breath. *Here's where it gets even dicier,* he thought.

"Because your species and mine are closely related," he said. "If your doctors compare samples of our blood to yours, they can confirm this."

Joh'jym's eyes narrowed and his voice grew low and dangerous. "If we decide to exsanguinate you, Hikarusulu, it will not be for study." He gestured toward Bannohn and the other guards, who approached and made ready to take the prisoners away, including Jerdahn.

This is not good at all.

"Wait!" Jerdahn shouted. "Hikarusulu and his people *are* Neyel-kindred. I know it does not appear so, but it is true."

"I have heard enough," Joh'jym said with a wave of his tail. "Take them away. I will decide their disposition later. After we've freed ourselves from this cursed Devil-web."

"We should interrogate them," Oratok said. "We need to know everything they do about the Devils."

Rough hands grabbed Sulu's shoulders. The entire group was being hustled toward the door. If there was ever a time to pull a trump card, this was it.

Sulu raised his voice so everyone could hear him clearly above the tumult. "We know about Vanguard."

Utter silence swept the room.

"Release them," Joh'jym said after a seeming eternity. Sulu began breathing again. He glanced toward Burgess, whose eyes reminded him of the twin moons of Andor at full phase.

The drech'tor approached closely. Half a head taller than Sulu, the Neyel looked down to meet his gaze, and regarded him with obvious caution. But Sulu also glimpsed something else behind the hard coals of the drech'tor's eyes.

Curiosity.

"Say on, Hikarusulu," Joh'jym said. "What do you know of Holy Vangar?"

Here goes. "I know that your ancestors were once people very much like us. Centuries ago, they hollowed out an asteroid and made it their home. They called it Vanguard."

"The Great Rock," Oratok said reverently. She looked stunned.

Sulu continued, not wishing to lose his momentum. "Then an accident lost Vanguard among the stars. Your ancestors never again saw their birthworld."

"Auld Aerth," Joh'jym said in a surprisingly gentle tone. "Far Aerth."

Sulu nodded. However inhuman these people seemed

now, he could see that they attached mythic, perhaps even religious, significance to the now all but timelost story of their origins. He hoped he could use that to build a bridge between his crew and the Neyel.

"Far Earth," Sulu repeated, though he sensed that the universal translator was missing some subtle nuance of accent. "Far Earth. The homeworld of the Oh-Neyel, your forebears."

"We think of it often," Joh'jym said solemnly. "We know that we will find it again someday, and enfold it into the bosom of Neyelkind. Perhaps soon."

"Once the Devil menace that stands in our way has been extirpated," Oratok said, her eyes flinty.

Not for the first time, Sulu wondered whether Earth's culture would really be able to reabsorb the Neyel, or if it would be the other way around. *One problem at a time.*

"Then you have good reason to consider making peace with the Tholians," he said. "Perhaps they can be persuaded not to bar your path to Far Earth. We can help you achieve that." *And, while we're at it, stop an offshoot human species from waging a genocidal war that can only destroy us all.*

Though Sulu could see that the now-silent Joh'jym had, at least for now, succumbed to his curiosity, Oratok evidently hadn't abandoned her initial wariness.

"How can you know these things, Hikarusulu?" she asked, her hard face now giving nothing away. "How can creatures so unlike us recite our most sacred tales?"

"It's as I tried to explain before. My species and yours . . . are related."

Sulu noticed then that Burgess had sidled over to him. She was staring at him in horror, as though he were about to step on a rock that was actually a ravening Manarkan sand bat.

He recalled what she'd told him on the way to the transporter room. *"It's clear from our interviews with Jerdahn that these people have shrouded their origins in a complex body of mythology. They might even worship their ancestors as gods. So we should avoid mentioning being born on the same planet the O'Neill colonists came from."*

"*Why?*" Sulu had asked. After all, the Neyel were a warp-capable species, so there were no Prime Directive issues at play.

Burgess looked surprised at his question. "*We want to maintain our credibility, don't we?*"

"*Of course we do.*"

"*And if some alien who didn't look even remotely human landed among us and claimed to have been a college roommate of Muhammad or Jesus, well, how believable would* that *be?*"

Still considering how to expand on his answer to Oratok's question, Sulu recalled the chilly reception the Greek god Apollo had received from the crew of the *Enterprise*.

"Where we come from," Sulu said at length, "knowledge about Old Earth is almost commonplace. Much of its history and literature still exists, scattered around the galaxy."

"We've, ah, studied the literature extensively," Burgess said.

Oratok gestured toward the viewscreen on which a Tholian ship was visible. "If your words are truthful, Captain, then why did you attack us?"

"I must apologize if you interpreted our actions as an attack," Sulu said evenly. "We did not fire first against you. As I said, we were protecting the Tholian civilians upon whom *you* were firing. It was only after you attacked our ship that we returned fire."

"The order of things matters not so much as the intent," Adjun-drech'tor Bannohn said from nearby. "Had you not interceded, we never would have fired upon you."

"Our mission to this part of the galaxy is one of peace," Burgess replied. "We were attempting to negotiate a détente with the Tholians, after decades of misunderstanding and conflict."

"So you, too, consider the Devil scourge an adversary. Yet you defend them against your own blood?" Joh'jym asked, his eyes wide.

Sulu shook his head. "We weren't aware of our kinship with you at the time. In the course of our earlier discussions with the Tholians, we became . . . aware that they were in conflict with another force. It was only upon our investigation into that conflict that we discovered who and what the Neyel are. But what we still don't understand is why you attacked a weaponless colony world."

"Thanks to our attack, their weaponry is not currently operating," Joh'jym said. "But our own detection devices have traced its effects to this world. There can be no doubt."

Sulu found that answer confusing in the extreme. "I don't understand. There's very little technology evident on the planet, apart from some power stations and several environmental forcefield generators. In fact, we've found no evidence of military activity or weaponry of any sort down there—only the debris and radiation residue from a recent space battle in this system."

"Do not fall prey to Devil trickery, Captain. Because you halted our attack, they may succeed in reconstituting their weapon. When in use, the Devil machinery causes devastation in Neyel space as its effects are propagated across the Rift."

The drech'tor gestured for the group to follow as he walked over to one of the larger viewscreens. He touched several symbols on it, and an external starscape appeared, overlaid a moment later by a tactical grid that obviously represented an aperture leading into the nearby interspatial rift.

"The pathway toward our home lies through here," Joh'jym said. He touched another symbol and the screen changed yet again, depicting a graphic of the Milky Way Galaxy, which swiftly shrunk in size. A representation of a smaller globular star formation appeared beside the Milky Way graphic, and swiftly increased in diameter until many of its individual stars were visible. Another interspatial entrance appeared in the midst of the star cluster.

"Over forty-three worlds in this volume of space, the Neyel Hegemony rules," said Joh'jym, pride evident in his voice.

Tuvok leaned toward Sulu, speaking quietly. "Sir, he has identified the Small Magellanic Cloud as the far terminus of the interspatial rift located in this system."

It took a moment for Sulu to digest that. The Small Magellanic Cloud lay 210,000 light-years from Earth. Centuries before anyone aboard *Excelsior* had even been born, the human species had ventured further into the unknown than even Starfleet's fastest long-range exploration vessels. It was awe-inspiring.

Joh'jym either hadn't heard Tuvok's interjection, or had chosen to ignore it. "When active, the Devils' weapon threatens a number of key Neyel planets with destruction. The weapon is even capable of destabilizing several of the stars that lie near our side of the Rift."

Sulu's mind raced. From the beginning of this mission, he had distrusted the Tholians, but he had attempted to put his suspicions aside in the interest of peace. The Tholians had certainly done their best to hide the truth about their conflict with the Neyel from the Federation, and members of the Assembly's political and scientific castes had clearly conspired to keep secret the knowledge of the human genome that the Neyel carried.

But whether they had done this in pursuit of peace was still an open question.

On the other hand, Sulu was painfully aware that his own actions as captain of *Excelsior*—whether mandated by Starfleet or not—had stretched the limits of peaceful Tholian-Federation interaction, perhaps past the breaking point. He had trespassed upon their territory not only with sensor probes, but also with his own ship and crew.

Now, *Excelsior* was balanced on a razor's edge, caught between the two warring factions: the Tholians, who had actively sought a rapprochement with the Federation; and the Neyel, who were apparently completely unaware of the existence of either the Federation or of Starfleet, and yet were the descendants of humanity and heirs to its birthright of freedom and dignity.

Both groups are quick on the trigger, Sulu thought. *And each is prepared to destroy* Excelsior *for its cause.* He knew he had to decide soon which was the deadlier adversary. At this moment, it was the Tholians who posed the greater threat to *Excelsior*'s safety. If his crew was going to survive long enough to find a peaceful resolution to the Tholian-Neyel conflict, the Tholian energy web that had snared both *Excelsior* and *Oghen's Flame* had to be dealt with first.

"Drech'tor Joh'jym, how can I persuade your people to call a truce with the Tholians?" Sulu asked.

Joh'jym, Oratok, and Jerdahn all looked at him as if he had suddenly sprouted another head. After what seemed like an eternity of silence, Joh'jym spoke. "Why would we *want* peace with these . . . Tholians? They are beneath us, mere animals to be destroyed. After this war is finished, then there will be peace. One way or another."

It was worth a shot, Sulu thought. "I expected that to be your response. But we are faced with a dilemma, Drech'tor. Neither your ship nor mine is currently able to escape or defeat the Tholians. We don't have many choices: we can call for a truce between you and the Tholians; we can allow them to destroy us; we can fight until we are both destroyed; or we can work together to find a way to escape."

He paused for a moment. "For my crew, I would choose the last option. There is an ancient saying in the literature of Old Earth: '*For he who fights and runs away, May live to fight another day; but he who is in battle slain, Can never rise to fight again.*' "

Jerdahn and Oratok exchanged glances and nodded. Then Joh'jym grinned at Sulu. "I would agree. What do you propose?"

Sulu briefly looked at Akaar, Tuvok, Chapel, and Burgess, then turned back to Joh'jym and Jerdahn. "I have an idea."

Chapter 22

Sulu was feeling weary as he and other members of the boarding party stepped down from *Excelsior*'s wide transporter stage, then immediately scattered to attend to their various tasks. But he knew that he had to soldier on, fatigued or not. Too much was at stake.

Luckily, the next few hours went far more smoothly than he had imagined possible, which cheered him considerably. Though he still harbored no illusions that Drech'tor Joh'jym and his ever-vigilant visor Oratok were prepared as yet to embrace any initiative aimed at ending their war on the Tholians, the Neyel captain not only had decided to allow the boarding party to return to *Excelsior*, but he also had signed off on Sulu's idea of exchanging engineering personnel between the two vessels.

After all, so long as both *Excelsior* and the Neyel vessel remained trapped by the Tholian Assembly's potent energy webs, both ships, both crews, both *captains* had identical problems.

I just hope that Commander Azleya doesn't talk any of those Neyel techies' ears off, Sulu thought, sipping his still-warm tea as the turbolift deposited him on the bridge. He'd seen how distracted his gregarious chief engineer could become when guests descended upon the engine room in which she took so much justifiable pride. He wondered what it would be like to have a chief engineer who spent more of her time yelling, both at subordinates and visitors.

From all the reports he'd received so far—including a scrambled subspace message from Jerdahn, who had stayed aboard *Oghen's Flame* to assist the damage control parties working there—the two engineering teams seemed to be making excellent progress on a tandem escape tactic for both ships. It appeared that a modified version of Tuvok's contingency plan—a limited disabling of the Tholian energy web by means of warp power channeled through the deflector grid—was going to prove useful after all.

With any luck, *Excelsior* and the Neyel ship would both be safely across the interspatial rift before Yilskene's fleet could do anything to stop it—and well before the deadline the Tholian admiral had given Sulu to prove that the Federation and the Neyel Hegemony were not allied against the Tholian people. Dr. Chapel had already reported that she was ready with theragen-based inoculations against the madness that close exposure to interspace was known to cause. (The Neyel were apparently far more resistant to the mind-damaging aspects of the phenomenon.) Soon, both *Excelsior* and the Neyel ship would escape into territory that, according to Joh'jym, was patrolled by enough Neyel ships to make Yilskene think twice about mounting a pursuit.

But Sulu still found one thing troubling: *After we escape, how can I ever convince Yilskene and the rest of the Tholian power structure that the Federation can be trusted? He'll be more convinced than ever that we're in bed with his enemies.*

Unless, of course, a way could be found in the meantime to turn those enemies into something else entirely.

Seated at her communications console, Commander Rand responded to a silent, flashing alarm. Touching the earpiece that dangled at the right side of her head, she turned toward Sulu, a look of apprehension on her face.

He sighed. He knew that things couldn't go smoothly forever. Not with the clock steadily ticking toward Yilskene's deadline—and *Excelsior*'s destruction.

"Let me guess," he said as Chekov relinquished the command chair to him and he seated himself. "Yilskene needs another hug."

"Something like that, sir," Rand said, smiling a very small smile.

Yilskene's image appeared on the main viewer, rippled and distorted by his ship's intensely hot atmosphere. Sulu thought that the Tholian admiral's vaguely triangular, crystalline head looked like a sculpting student's abstract study of the concept of outrage.

"Good afternoon, Admiral Yilskene. What can I do for you?"

"We have detected material transmissions being directed from your ship to the invader vessel," Yilskene said without preamble.

Recalling Tuvok's earlier warning that their transporter activity might not go undetected, Sulu decided there was no point in denying it. "We have been supplying humanitarian assistance to the Neyel crew, Admiral."

"Then you admit to consorting with our foes?" Yilskene's multilayered vocal chorus grew discordant as his anger escalated.

"There were many injuries and casualties aboard the Neyel ship," Sulu said, hoping to calm the admiral with dispassionate reason. "Because of our biological similarities, we were far better equipped to render such assistance than you were."

The port side turbolift doors hissed open, and Sulu's eyes flicked momentarily toward the noise. He silently noted the arrival of Aidan Burgess and Lieutenant Akaar. With a grace that belied his size, Akaar silently crossed to the tactical station and began studying the displays there. The ambassador approached the railing that curved around the bridge's lower section, her eyes riveted to the main viewer.

"We are not in the habit of offering succor to those who would kill us," Yilskene thundered from the forward screen.

Sulu kept his manner polite, but not obsequious. "We would have done the same for you, Admiral."

"Your continued fraternization with our enemies does not inspire my confidence, Captain. I believe you are attempting a deception."

"We're still trapped in your energy web," Sulu said, "We can't go anywhere. What good would it do to try to deceive you?"

In actual fact, Sulu hadn't lied to Yilskene at all. Dr. Chapel and a medical team *had* gone aboard Joh'jym's vessel to treat the injured. Some of the most severely debilitated Neyel patients had been transported back to *Excelsior* for more intensive treatment than the medics could provide on-site.

He'd merely neglected to mention the Neyel engineers who had come aboard *Excelsior*, and vice versa, to work on their mutual escape plan.

Hoping to move on to a possibly more fruitful topic, Sulu said, "Other than the safety of my ship and my crew, all I want is to find a path to peace for each of the parties involved in this situation: the Federation, the Tholian Assembly, and the Neyel Hegemony."

"And peace is the sole reason why I am aboard this ship," Burgess said, descending to the lower section of the bridge, to stand beside the captain's chair. Though Sulu found her intrusion irritating, he knew he couldn't accuse her of meddling. He had just made a diplomatic gambit, and she was the ranking diplomat aboard; he had to remind himself that *he* was poaching in *her* territory.

"I have a proposal to make," she continued, still addressing Yilskene.

The Tholian regarded her in silence for a moment. Sulu wondered if the admiral was assessing how far he could trust the human diplomat who had already broken with her own people's protocols to give him beneficial information.

"*I am listening,*" Yilskene said.

Burgess stood ramrod straight, looking every inch the confident statesman. "I wish to set up a three-way discussion, to include you, me, and Drech'tor Joh'jym of the Neyel Hegemony Fleet Cruiser *Oghen's Flame.*"

"*We have attempted to initiate communication with these beings ever since our first encounter with them. They appear incapable.*"

"Members of your own science caste have concluded that we humans are closely related to the Neyel. Am I correct?"

"*Yes.*"

"Since you and I are now conversing, Admiral, I must assume that you do not think of *us* as mere brutes who lack the power of speech. So why would you make the same assumption about the Neyel? Why not suppose instead that their mode of communication is simply greatly different from your own?"

"*That is as may be, Ambassador. But whether they be dumb or articulate, our adversaries clearly lack the translation devices with which you communicate with us.*"

Burgess nodded. "Our universal translator has gone a long way toward bridging the gulf of mistrust that has for so long separated us. I believe it can do the same for you and the Neyel."

Yilskene moved forward, and his face grew even larger on the main viewer. "*Such devices may indeed prove useful. Principally in dictating the terms of their surrender after we annex their space, destroy their warfleets, and begin Tholia-forming their worlds for colonization. Yilskene out.*"

The admiral's image vanished.

"That went better than I expected," said Chekov, who was leaning on a railing to Sulu's right.

"Damn," Burgess said. "I thought I had him."

"It was a good try, Ambassador," Sulu said.

"Not nearly good enough. Yilskene's just as bad as Joh'jym. I'm beginning to think that the only way to get them talking is to lock the two of them in a room equipped with a universal translator."

"And a squad of armed guards," said Chekov. Turning to Rand, he asked, "How much time do we have left to make our case to Yilskene?"

"A little over three and a half hours," Rand said.

Yilskene made his ultimatum more than eight hours ago, Sulu realized, his fatigue catching up with him. *No wonder I feel so wiped out.*

Tuvok rose from the main science station and faced Burgess. "With respect, Ambassador, perhaps it was a tactical error to remind Yilskene that he will require our assistance if he wishes to speak with the Neyel."

She bristled. "Really?"

Tuvok seemed unaware of, or at least unfazed by, her evident anger. "Indeed. As a member of the warrior caste, his pride may be exceedingly vulnerable. I have witnessed similar reactions in numerous non-Vulcan spec—"

"I wasn't aware that you were a credentialed expert on exopsychology, Lieutenant," Burgess snapped, interrupting him.

He blinked at her, now seeming to comprehend the ambassador's nettled response. "Perhaps you have helped underscore my point, Ambassador."

"All right," Sulu said, stepping on Burgess's rejoinder. "Perhaps a consultation with an expert is just what we need right now." He pushed a button on the right arm of his command chair. "Captain Sulu to Lieutenant Hopman."

"*Hopman here, Captain.*" From the somewhat higher timbre of her voice, Sulu could tell that she was once again in her female phase. "*What can I do for you?*"

"I need to pick your brain about how to make nice with members of martial cultures."

"I gather that Yilskene still doesn't believe that we come in peace."

"No. And he's liable to believe it a whole lot less once we break out of his energy web. Any thoughts?"

"I've spent the last few hours poring through everything the library computer has on the Tholian warrior caste. Maybe 'making nice' isn't the right way to win him over. If logic won't persuade Yilskene of our benign intentions, then a little calculated violence might do the trick better."

"Explain."

"For centuries, members of the Tholian warrior caste have lawfully settled disputes with a ritual that translates roughly to truthcombat*."*

"Somehow I get the feeling that we're not talking about filibustering in the government chambers."

"That's right, Captain. It's an ancient form of Tholian dueling."

"Pistols at dawn?"

"Something you'll like even better: swords. *The* truthcombat *ritual reflects the warriors' belief that the right or wrong of any dispute can be ascertained most accurately through personal struggle. The fight is resolved when either one party yields, or when one is dead."*

That sounded pretty straightforward—and not necessarily lethal, provided Yilskene's desire to survive trumped his anger. *And provided I can beat him.*

"Do you think Yilskene might agree to make the release of *Excelsior* and the Neyel vessel contingent on the outcome of this . . . *truthcombat*?" Sulu asked.

Hopman hesitated, evidently already having surmised where his questions were headed. *"I can't say for certain, Captain. You're not a Tholian, after all, so he might not regard you as a 'peer' with whom he can do lawful combat. But if he* does *accept a* truthcombat *challenge, he'll be bound by both caste honor and Tholian law to abide by the results."*

Akaar moved toward the center of the bridge and spoke. "Captain, I respectfully request that I be allowed to represent *Excelsior* in this ritual."

"Request denied. *Excelsior* is my ship, and her safety is my responsibility."

An uncharacteristic look of concern crossed the huge Capellan's face, but he relented. "Aye, Captain." The words seemed to cause him physical pain, but he was too disciplined an officer to argue with direct orders.

"Captain, I can see no logic in dueling with Admiral Yilskene," Tuvok said, evidently not quite so concerned as Akaar with protocol. "The weapons would no doubt be some variant of the monoblade which Muskene used to assassinate Ambassador Kasrene. Even a glancing blow would be lethal. Logic suggests—"

"Opinion noted, science officer." Sulu rose from his chair and glared at the Tuvok. Though he appreciated his instincts, he did not enjoy having his orders questioned, especially right out on the bridge in front of everyone. "Now do I have to send you to Dr. Chapel to have your hearing checked?"

Tuvok's eyes bored into Sulu like mining lasers. "No, sir," he said, then returned to his station.

"Um, Captain?" It was Hopman's voice, coming from the intercom on Sulu's chair. *"Not that I'm questioning your judgment, but I think you might not want to rush into this."*

Taking his seat once again, Sulu massaged his temple, which was beginning to flare with an incipient headache. "Lieutenant, there's not much time left. My only other options are either to protect the Federation's honor by waiting around for Yilskene to destroy us, or to damage our reputation even further by escaping into Neyel territory through interspace.

"I like the idea of a straight fight a lot better than either of those choices. Report to the bridge immediately. Sulu out."

He punched a button, cutting off contact with Hopman. Then he turned his seat aftward, toward the communications station.

"Commander Rand, open a channel to the *Jeb'v Tholis.*"

"I accept, Captain," Yilskene said. *"I will be gratified to see this matter settled decisively."*

Exchanging a quick glance with Lieutenant Hopman, who had arrived on the bridge a few minutes earlier, Sulu tried to conceal his surprise at how little time the Tholian admiral had spent considering his challenge.

"As will I," Sulu said.

"My compliments, Captain, for your willingness to follow the precepts of Tholian law," Yilskene continued.

Under other circumstances, Sulu might have basked in the admiral's compliment. But considering that he and Yilskene would shortly become embroiled in a duel that could well leave them either maimed or dead, he decided that it was far too late to concern himself with diplomatic brownie points. The next few hours would be about survival, plain and simple.

"When in Tholian space, one does as the Tholians do," Sulu said.

"Well said, Captain. Then I trust you are aware of the privilege of the challenged. The choice of venue for our truthcombat *is mine."*

Looking to his side, Sulu saw Hopman's slight nod of affirmation. "I understand," he said. "When and where?" Sulu hoped that the scheduling of the truthcombat might buy *Excelsior* at least a little additional time.

"Where is here, aboard the Jeb'v Tholis. *When is at the expiration of my original twelve-hour deadline. Will that give you sufficient time to craft an environment suit capable of sustaining your life processes while you are aboard my flagship?"*

"Three and a half hours will be ample," Sulu said. He was grimly aware that his skill with a blade would at least be as crucial to maintaining his "life processes" as would his EV suit. He wondered how badly the suit would encumber his motions. Luckily, from what he'd observed of the Tholians, their own physiology didn't permit them to move very quickly. Though Yilskene wouldn't need to wear an EV suit in his own ship's environment, the high pressure there would doubtless slow the admiral's movements down even further.

Suddenly Chief Engineer Azleya's pleasant voice sounded from the intercom. *"Azleya to the captain."*

"Stand by, please, Commander," Sulu said, pressing the mute button. The last thing he needed was for Azleya to let Yilskene know about their escape contingency plans.

"Then let the record reflect that the truthcombat *challenge has been lawfully given and accepted,"* Yilskene said. *"My communications specialist will send you the precise coordinates to program into your transporter. I will see you at the appointed time, and will furnish the weapons.*

"You will be remembered long in the Tholian Assembly, Captain Sulu," he added. *"I shall see to that personally, following the destruction of your ship and the invader vessel."* And with that, he vanished from the screen, leaving a view of the Tholian colony world in his place.

"He sounds pretty confident about winning," Sulu said. "Maybe too confident."

Still standing at Sulu's side, Hopman nodded. Speaking barely above a whisper, she said, "He's not the only one, sir."

Doesn't anybody *on this ship think I can win this?* Sulu thought. Whispering also, he said, "You've sparred with me plenty of times, Pam. You know I can handle a blade. Why the pessimism?"

"I'm not questioning your skills, Captain. They're world-class, and I'm not just saying that to sweet-talk you into promoting me. It's just that you're about to compete in a very different 'world.' We're not talking about the Inner Planets championship here. And a monoblade is a whole lot less forgiving than an épée."

"*Touché*," he said. "But I still have to go ahead with this. I'm committed now."

Azleya's quizzical voice returned to the intercom, evidently over an alternate comm channel. "*Is everything all right up there, Captain?*"

He pressed another button. "Sulu here, Commander. Report."

"*We're all set down here, Captain. The tractor beam and deflector grid are powered up, and* Excelsior's *shields are ready to be extended around the Neyel vessel. Once you give the word, I'll have both ships out of the web and across the rift before Yilskene can react.*"

"Acknowledged, Commander," Sulu said, smiling. "Good work. Continue standing by, however. We're also working on an alternate plan." He clicked off the channel.

"Captain?" Chekov asked. "Now that we can get both *Excelsior* and *Oghen's Flame* to safety, there's no need to follow through with the duel."

"We must also consider the crew of the Neyel vessel," Tuvok said. "Leaving their fate to be decided by the outcome of a one-on-one physical altercation may needlessly cause their deaths."

"We can't run now, not after I've made a lawfully accepted *truthcombat* challenge," Sulu said, shaking his head. "If we do that, then Yilskene will only have further reason to think the worst of us."

"That's not necessarily so," Hopman said. "We won't be in violation of the laws governing *truthcombat* until and unless you fail to show up for the contest. I found nothing in Tholian law to suggest that we couldn't take a little side trip in the meantime."

"Well, then," Sulu said, heaving a sigh. "That calls for a

change of plans." He looked carefully around the bridge at Chekov, Rand, Akaar, Tuvok, Hopman, Burgess, and Lojur, who was silently running the forward navigator's station. All of them, save for Hopman, seemed visibly relieved.

That's because Pam understands that I haven't actually canceled *the match. I've only postponed it.*

Turning toward Rand, he said, "Inform Drech'tor Joh'jym that we're nearly ready to make for the rift."

"Aye, sir." Her hands moved across the console with the skill of a concert pianist.

Sulu punched one of his chair's comm buttons. "Sulu to Azleya."

"Azleya here, sir," the engineer said, sounding eager. *"Is the word given?"*

Sulu smiled at the chief engineer's can-do demeanor. "Affirmative, Commander. Coordinate with your counterpart on *Oghen's Flame,* and make for interspace as soon as you're both ready. Alert the bridge before you hit the switch."

We'll be fine, Sulu thought. *Just as long as* Excelsior *gets back here within three and a half hours.*

Chapter 23

"I think that about does it," said Lieutenant Commander Terim Azleya, grinning as she watched the flow of diagrams and numbers that scrolled continuously across her screens. Along with the data describing the output of *Excelsior*'s warp drive, tractor beam, and shield generators, as well as the deflector-grid throughput, she was monitoring corresponding telemetry coming via a subfrequency scramble directly from the engine room of *Oghen's Flame*.

Several junior and senior engineers, including a pair of awkward-looking but surprisingly graceful Neyel, looked on, the rhythmic switching of their tails the only evidence that they might be at all nervous about what was to come. Nodding to the assembled technical personnel, the chief engineer signaled that she was at last satisfied that all was in readiness.

"Bridge," Azleya said after touching a companel on the bulkhead. "Confirming that all is green for 'go.' "

"*Acknowledged, Commander,*" came Sulu's smooth bass voice in response.

A moment later, the ship lurched slightly.

Sections of one of the bulkhead suddenly looked transparent. She wondered whether the shot Chapel had given her was affecting her mind; either her eyes were playing tricks on her, or else *Excelsior* had just roared straight down into the gullet of interspace.

"Admiral! They've vanished!" exclaimed Ruskene [the Sallow], the Officer of the Watch in the main cryoneural cluster, the command center of the Tholian Assembly Flagship *Jeb'v Tholis.*

Yilskene found the discordant quality of Ruskene's voice-chorus alarming. It evoked cascades of fear colors, yet conveyed no more content than the barking of the gray savages the humans had dubbed Neyel.

"Speak intelligibly. *What* has vanished?"

The fear colors oscillated, brightening and darkening by turns. The emotional chiaroscuro was beginning to affect Yilskene's own equanimity.

Ruskene [the Sallow] began to regain some composure. "Both of the captive vessels, Admiral. They are gone. And their disappearance coincided with momentary gaps in the energy web. Perhaps they disrupted it in some manner, and then escaped."

Yilskene blazed in rage colors. *Human deceit. The Terrans and the Neyel are indeed alike.*

He decided that Captain Sulu should not have to wait any longer for his appointment with death.

"They must be heading for the rift into the OtherVoid at the system's edge, with their invader allies," Yilskene declared, his bodyplanes grinding against one another in outrage. "Inform the fleet. We shall mount pursuit."

Let's hope this works, Sulu thought.

The bridge lights dimmed as *Excelsior*'s deflector grid brought the output of the mighty starship's warp core, tractor beam, and shield generators to a sharp focus on four of the energy web's nearest vertices. With *Oghen's Flame* securely enfolded in both her shields and tractor beam, *Excelsior* surged forward at high warp, suffusing the bridge with a deafening whine of labored systems and the smell of ozone.

On the main viewer, the nearest portions of the Tholian web curled away and vanished, like leaves caught in a gale. At Sulu's order, Akaar changed the image to an aftward view, confirming that the oblate cylindrical shape of the partially repaired *Oghen's Flame* was following about ten kilometers behind *Excelsior*, riding on a slender beam of refulgent tractor-beam energy.

"We're coming up on the interspatial boundary in ten seconds, Captain," reported Lojur from the forward navigation console.

Precisely ten seconds later, Sulu experienced a brief sensation that was not unlike freefall—only the effect seemed to be confined primarily to his stomach. With merciful swiftness, the discomfort passed.

"Status report," Sulu said, leaning forward in his command chair.

In front of him, Lojur swiveled his seat backward and met Sulu's gaze. "Navigational monitors confirm we have entered interspace," the Halkan said impassively. "At this velocity, we should make contact with the far terminus of the interspatial rift in approximately seventy seconds."

From the Tholian back forty to the Small Magellanic Cloud in just over a minute, Sulu thought, sparing a moment to marvel at the feat his crew had just performed. *Not bad at all.*

From tactical, Akaar said, "I read positive tractor beam contact with *Oghen's Flame*. Shields are holding, though they are attenuated because of their coverage of both ships."

"Well done, people," Sulu said, speaking to the entire bridge. He felt a surge of pride, but put it aside. The ship was by no means out of danger.

Turning his chair toward starboard aft, he addressed Tuvok and Rand simultaneously. "I want an aft sensor sweep. Check for signs of pursuit. Monitor any Tholian comm traffic that might be spilling into the rift."

"Aye, sir," both officers said in tandem, reminding Sulu of the way the universal translator rendered Tholian speech.

Sulu pointed his chair once again toward the main viewer, which displayed an impressive hash of colorful static. He leaned forward again, resting his hand on his chin. "Clean that up for me, Rand. I want to get a good look at what's out there."

The static quickly rearranged itself, revealing a bland, gray expanse. They might have been flying through the interior of a storm cloud on Earth.

Then Sulu saw that the vista before him was not entirely devoid of detail. Randomly scattered dark shapes, no doubt visible only because of enhancement by *Excelsior*'s main computer, were becoming visible.

"Commander Lojur, increase magnification by a factor of ten," Sulu ordered. A moment later, the dark spots became easier still to resolve against the gray background. He thought he could make out an assortment of wedge shapes, juxtaposed against long, roughly cylindrical objects. He knew at once what it was.

"It's a graveyard of ships," Chekov said from a secondary science station. "I'm reading dozens of Tholian and Neyel vessels. Maybe hundreds."

"Increase viewer to full magnification," Sulu said.

"Full mag," said Lojur.

Almost at once, the drifting shapes of the fallen ships, a mass astrogational cemetery for two great cultures, grew even more distinct. It was a mute testament to the last several years of sustained Tholian-Neyel conflict, a war as old as the first contact between the two species.

Suddenly, amid the tumble of dead, forgotten vessels, Sulu found his eyes drawn to a still more distant, yet familiar, shape. It lay just on the ragged edge of his visual resolution, but for an instant he was utterly certain of what he'd seen.

A saucer, connected by a narrow pylon to a bulbous secondary hell, from which depended a pair of graceful outboard nacelles. It betrayed no sign of light or life. For it had been wandering here, a tomb within another tomb, for three decades.

"*Defiant*," he whispered, the pang of loss commingling with the exultation of discovery. For a fleeting moment, the Neyel and the Tholians were forgotten, lost in the desire to bring the long-dead starship home.

Two alarms blared almost simultaneously, from the main science and tactical stations respectively. The tumult prodded Tuvok, Chekov, and Akaar to frenetic activity.

"Two proximity alarms, Captain," said Tuvok evenly.

"I read four Tholian vessels approaching us aft," Akaar confirmed. "Yilskene must have decided to chase us."

"Then we'd better lose him," Sulu said. *Defiant*'s drifting corpse would have to wait for another day, another ship. "What's the other alarm about?"

Chekov hunched over a hooded scanner at the secondary science station. "It's about what's ahead of us. A large grouping of Neyel power signatures. More ships than I can count. Far bigger than the Tholian contingent."

Sulu grinned at his first officer. "Whatever else Yilskene may be, he isn't stupid. Once his sensors pick up what's ahead of us, I don't think he'll be bothering us for a while."

But he also knew that this begged a more important question: *How will the Neyel react to* us?

The thoughtcolors of Ruskene [the Sallow] had grown even more offensively shrill and strident. "Sensing Units have touched additional invader vessel signatures."

"Quantity?" Yilskene asked.

"More vessels than we possess. Many more. We are far overmatched."

Yilskene's righteous anger became viscous and fluid, like

the volcanic Underrock upon which Tholia's three great continents floated. He tried to force the colors of calm and equanimity upon himself, but had little success.

"Turn *Jeb'v Tholis* about," he said at length. "Inform the others that all vessels are to reverse course. And summon reinforcements. We will take up station once more at the rift aperture. Captain Sulu will not wish to live out his days in the remote places from which the invader infestation comes.

"*Excelsior* must return the way it came. And we will welcome it appropriately when it does."

"Reaching the far interspace terminus . . . *now*," Lojur said, bracing himself against his console.

Sulu felt *Excelsior* lurch again, just as during the initial passage into interspace. He watched as the gray nothingness on the screen vanished, to be replaced almost instantaneously by a far more familiar-looking starscape. But against the velvet backdrop of trackless space, the stars were more densely packed than any other region of space Sulu had ever visited.

Then he noticed that some of those stars weren't, in fact, stars at all.

"Ships. Neyel ships." Sulu turned to Tuvok and Chekov. "How many are there?"

"I am reading several dozen Neyel vessels, massed along the edges of interspace," Tuvok reported, crouching over his scanner. "Long-range sensors show hundreds more in a nearby system. There's a class-M planet there that appears to be the source of these vessels. The Neyel Hegemony must have established a substantial shipbuilding operation there."

"Right near their side of the interspatial rift," Chekov said, staring at the viewer's magnified images of row upon row of armed, cylindrical vessels built along the same general lines as *Oghen's Flame*.

"What better place is there for mounting a massive invasion than your mortal enemy's backyard?" Sulu said.

Akaar turned from his console. "Judging from the number of ships apparently still being assembled in orbit around the Class-M world, I would estimate this invasion to be mere weeks away. If not sooner."

"If any Tholians have seen this, the Neyel must have prevented them from reporting back," Chekov said. "Otherwise, the Tholians would have set up some fortifications on their side. And we'd have detected more than the occasional skirmish." Chekov shook his head. "I'm certainly glad you ducked out of that sword fight, Captain. This looks *much* safer."

Grinning at his exec, Sulu said, "Relax, Pavel. We're among friends. Janice, please open a channel to *Oghen's Flame.*"

"Aye, sir."

A moment later, the gray faces of Joh'jym, Oratok, and Jerdahn appeared on the viewer. Fortunately, it appeared that Jerdahn had succeeded in hanging onto some pretty highly placed friends. *Let's hope his luck continues,* Sulu thought. *I have a feeling we're all going to need it.*

"Fortune has favored us," Joh'jym said, a smile slightly bending his blunt features. *"We have defeated the Devils' snare. We owe you our thanks."*

"No more than we owe you, Drech'tor Joh'jym," Sulu said.

"Would you return through the Rift to your home space?" Jerdahn asked.

"I'm afraid we must, Jerdahn. We can only stay here long enough to check *Excelsior* for damage. Then we'll have to return the same way we came."

"To face the Devils," Oratok said.

"Alone," added Joh'jym. He sounded wistful, as though *Excelsior*'s destruction at the hands of the Tholians were a foregone conclusion. *Maybe it is.*

"Perhaps death cannot be outrun, Hikarusulu," Joh'jym said. "But there is no reason to rush into her grasp. Oghen, our Coreworld, lies only mennets away at Efti'el speeds. I would like you to see it—and the fleet that will avenge you shortly after you return to Devil space."

Sulu realized that he still had more than three hours before his honor would be forever tarnished in Yilskene's eyes. There would be time to visit, at least briefly, the planet the Neyel thought of as their homeworld.

"I would be honored, Drech'tor," Sulu said, then ordered Lojur to follow *Oghen's Flame* to its destination.

Excelsior settled into a standard orbit only a few kilometers away from *Oghen's Flame*. Standing before the bridge viewer beside Chekov and Burgess, Sulu finally found a quiet moment to simply admire the tainted, yet still beautiful world that turned slowly some six hundred kilometers below.

The blue class-M planet that Joh'jym had called Oghen was obviously a busy place. From the brownish-yellow haze that stippled the atmosphere, Sulu concluded that the planet had been one of the Neyel Hegemony's most heavily utilized industrial sites for at least a century.

And the scores of orbital factories and drydocks, and the thousands of partially-assembled warships he saw everywhere he looked made it abundantly clear to what use the planet's abundant resources had been put.

War.

Using filters, Tuvok trained *Excelsior*'s visual sensors on the planet's primary star, a hot F-type sun whose yellow-white surface rippled with frequent and violent flares and immense, horseshoe-shaped prominences.

Caused, Tuvok quickly theorized, by the close presence of a sizable aperture leading into interspace. Could the fact that this rift connected to the sectors of space controlled by the extremely suspicious, territorial Tholian Alliance be mere coincidence?

"No wonder the Neyel are so bent on destroying the Tholians," Burgess said. "Maybe they think that the interspatial rift itself is actually a Tholian plot to destabilize their stars and scour all life from their planets."

"If we were in their position, I wonder if we would have done the math any differently than they did," Sulu said. He felt a gnawing sadness as he considered the wide gulf of culture that separated this long-sundered branch of humanity from Earth's civilization. It was arguably a far broader chasm than the even physical distance that lay between Federation space and the Neyel Hegemony's territory.

"Given the hardships their ancestors had to overcome when they found themselves stranded out here, I doubt it," Burgess said.

"They're us and we're them," Sulu said quietly, looking to Chekov for a reaction. This time, the exec did not argue the point.

Facing forward, Sulu watched the viewer as a large, oblong shadow came up over the terminator from Oghen's nightside and continued to rise on its long orbital arc. A few lights and safety beacons lined the object's exterior, no doubt intended to prevent Neyel spacecraft from accidentally crashing into it.

It slowly emerged into the harsh glare of the sun, which revealed the great rock's kilometers-long shape and the near side of its rough, battered surface. The object seemed to be composed of both nickel-iron and stone, and bore little resemblance to the relatively smooth, modular orbiting factories and the utilitarian, cylindrical space vessels that Sulu saw just about everywhere else he looked in Oghen's skies. It reminded him more of one of the moons of Mars, or one of the innumerable rocks that studded Sol's asteroid belt.

Then he realized exactly what it was he was looking at. "Looks like the Neyel have kept it in pretty good shape," he said.

"It's a shrine," Burgess said. "Like Independence Hall. Or the Peace Dome on Axanar."

"I never thought I'd actually get to see it," Chekov said,

his eyes riveted to the rocky shape. "It's like a myth come to life."

"It's no myth, Pavel," Sulu said, shaking his head. "Any more than the Neyel are."

The sight of the great Vanguard asteroid colony filled his heart with awe and wonder. It was a symbol of both promise and catastrophe. A reminder that the horrors the Neyel intended to inflict upon the Tholians—and vice versa—were, in large part, humanity's responsibility.

My *responsibility*, he thought.

PART 8

WAR

Chapter 24

2268, Auld Greg Aerth Calendar

Life aboard *Tuskerslayer* consisted predominantly of boredom. From the patrol vessel's lowliest grunt laborer all the way up to its drech'tor, none aboard could deny that this was the simple truth of the crew's existence.

Perched in the center of the cramped command deck, Drech'tor Kreutz recalled a joke her predecessor had been fond of making: *Boredom, punctuated by tedium.* He'd repeated it often enough over the years—even on the very day she had killed him—to make the words all but unforgettable.

But Kreutz was too well trained an officer to give even tedium anything less than her full attention. Tonight, she presided over a third-watch skeleton crew, anticipating a long, plodding march through the ship's night, as was her wont whenever sleep proved elusive. *Tuskerslayer*'s current mission was shaping up to be a spectacularly uneventful patrol of the vast cometary cloud that bounded the far fringes of the Oghen system.

And what could this patrol possibly be other than uneventful? she thought. The most Aerthlike world yet discovered, the Coreworld of Oghen was the center of the vast Knownconquered Territories—the beating heart of the ever-expanding Neyel Hegemony. So close to the innermost enclaves of Neyel influence, the odds of encountering a significant threat were vanishingly small.

Certainly, Hegemony border ships were called upon to answer distress signals from other Neyel vessels from time to time. And they still occasionally came upon lone alien free-booters, or radiation-scorched indigie refugee ships, filled past their capacity with all manner of arguably semisentient M'jallanish trash. *Tuskerslayer* and her sister ships had made short work of such as these as far back as Kreutz could remember.

Kreutz began to fantasize about finding an indigie refugee ship; she didn't particularly care what kind of indigies were aboard. Such an encounter would make for a nice surprise. Mrony, the gunnery specialist, could use the target practice.

A sensor-klaxon suddenly blared, prompting the young officer in charge of *Tuskerslayer*'s remote-sensing apparatus to widen his sleepy, half-shuttered eyelids. His slack tail went rigid, as though he'd accidentally stepped into the ion grid.

"Report," said Kreutz, her training quickly dispatching her prior listlessness.

The young officer shook his head. "This makes no sense, Drech'tor. The scanners must be damaged."

Kreutz scowled. "Don't talk in riddles, lad. What do *Tuskerslayer*'s eyes think they've seen?"

"It looks like . . . It appears that a *seam* is unraveling across the cosmos."

She smacked her tail against the deck angrily. *First he spouts conundrums, then poetry.* "Still you make no sense."

The drech'tor's gesture seemed to have galvanized the young male. "Perhaps I can resolve an image that might render a better explanation than I can provide."

"Cause it to be so."

The lightless deeps of Far Oghen vanished, replaced by a highly magnified, computer-enhanced image of what seemed to be a long, slender worm of the purest liquid silver. The tubular shape seemed to twist as it advanced through the surrounding dark, apparently woven from delicate traceries of light. Several faint, tentacular appendages, like meandering river tributaries, branched off from the main body, losing themselves in the eternal night.

"I see it," Kreutz said, her breath catching in her steel-hard throat. "Now can you *explain* it?"

"As I said, Drech'tor, it seems best described as a seam. And a *torn* seam, at that. A juncture between two adjacent regions of space, that is somehow coming unraveled."

"It sounds like a description of the spreading boundaries between crustal plates back on Oghen's sea floor."

"A very good analogy, Drech'tor," said the young officer. "But an aerthquake fault might make for an even better one."

Her tail switching back and forth, Kreutz asked, "Might this effect endanger Oghen, or any of the other Knownconquered worlds?"

The officer nodded, looking as somber as death. "It may, Drech'tor, so long as it maintains its present heading. The phenomenon's apparent motion is determined by the direction, shape, and energy of whatever started the rent in the fabric of the universe in the first place."

"Source?"

"Indeterminate. It could be fairly close, within local galactic space. Or it might have originated quite far from Hegemony Space."

"How far?"

The young officer shrugged. "Perhaps from as far off as Milkyway, Drech'tor. There's no way to know."

Milkyway. Kreutz almost chuckled at that. The lad had

no doubt been reading too much romantic fiction about the Oh-Neyel of old. "Why have we received no warnings from the adjacent systems, or from the periphery outposts, of this thing's approach?" she said.

He shrugged elaborately, his tail forming an elegant question mark beside him. "The effect seems to propagate directly through subspace, Drech'tor. It may be forming simultaneously throughout Hegemony Space. Therefore, we may be among the very first to observe it."

"How long until the phenomenon reaches us? What is its speed?"

"Subspace interactions make its speed difficult to gauge. However, I believe I'm detecting boundary effects fairly close by."

She growled at his tentativeness. "How long would it take *Tuskerslayer* to reach the vicinity of those effects?"

He looked at her with apprehensive eyes as large as Oghen's moons. "Under ten mennets at Efti'el Factor Six."

Grasping the club-end of her tail with one hand, Kreutz stroked her unyielding gray chin with the other. Her bare feet entered a few quick notes into her log.

She paused, wondering silently what force might be potent enough to cause the very universe itself to begin coming unraveled. Might the repeated passage of Efti'el vessels through this region of space be the culprit, stressing the fabric of the cosmos? Or could the cause be some unanticipated consequence of the recent nearby test-firing of the Neyel Hegemony's newest weapons?

Or perhaps some hitherto unknown foe has deliberately created this phenomenon as a weapon, and has chosen this moment to loose it upon our coreworld.

That grave thought made her next decisions very simple indeed.

"Rouse the firstwatch crew. Lay in a course for the near

end of that . . . thing out there. Update my logs and transmit them to Oghen Central. We depart on my mark."

As the command deck filled with busy Neyel officers and the rumble of the Efti'el drive suffused the chamber, Kreutz sat back in her chair.

If this thing is indeed a weapon, she thought, *then* Tusker-slayer *may once again be called upon to earn the revered name she bears.*

Chapter 25

2294, Auld Greg Aerth Calendar

Helmrunner Baruclan rose from his station and faced the drech'tor of the Neyel Hegemony Fleet Cruiser *Slicer*. "We have just passed the last confirmed whereabouts of *Tuskerslayer*, Drech'tor."

Drech'tor Faraerth nodded silently, staring at the starscape displayed on the viewer before him. He'd been a soft-bellied stripling when *Tuskerslayer* had vanished nearly thirty oghencycles ago, and that lost vessel and crew had since ascended to almost legendary status. To be out here now, exploring in *Tuskerslayer's* very warpwake after so many years and so many tales, was an overwhelming honor.

Faraerth wished he'd taken the time to compose some clever turn of phrase, some brilliant utterance destined for the ages. But now that he actually faced the prospect of venturing where few, if any, Neyel had ever gone before, he came up dry. He felt no better able to conjure words than were the Devils the Rift had recently begun sending into Hegemony space.

Faraerth gave the helmrunner leave to return to the delicate business of conducting *Slicer* through this famously unstable region of space, then turned toward the sensorman. "Show me the Rift."

"At once, Drech'tor," said the sensorman, a compact, muscular female named Dayan.

On the screen, a tactical overlay appeared, tracing the outline of the inconstant spacefabric that bordered the Rift itself. This bizarre cosmological phenomenon—in fact a gigantic rent in the very stuff of the universe—had steadily faded into the background of space since its initial appearance mere lighthours from the Coreworld of Oghen. Many took heart in the gradual disappearance of the pars'x-long, silver-hued worm that had so unexpectedly riven the skies of the Neyel Hegemony two generations earlier.

For others, like Drech'tor Faraerth and his superiors in the Hegemony Fleet, this unforeseen change was merely a clarion call for greater caution. *It's difficult to avoid falling into a hole whose edges elude one's sight.* Fortunately, Dayan and her remote sensors had prevented *Slicer* from blindly stumbling over the hellhorizon that by turns either drove unlucky Neyel ship crews mad, or sent Devil ships out of the Rift and into Neyel territory. *Slicer*'s crew had been vigilant. And thus fortunate.

So far.

Faraerth rose from his seat, absently using his tail to brush a stray piece of lint from the sleeve of his crisp black uniform. He'd been aware ever since his earliest flight training of his tendency to sublimate stress and nervousness into excessive tidiness. Today, he felt ready to bring the Gran Drech'tor herself aboard for an inspection tour.

He approached Dayan, who was intent on her multifarious readouts and instruments. "Ready the probes for launch, sensorman," Faraerth ordered.

Dayan complied, three limbs working in speedy tandem to enter the complex string of instructions. The command deck shuddered in response. "Four sensor probes are now away. They should make contact with the Rift interior momentarily. The telly-eyes are already transmitting."

Faraerth nodded. "Show us what the telly-eyes on Probe One see," he said, crossing back to his chair.

The sensorman entered another command into her board, and the main viewer shifted the starscape's orientation, if only subtly. The great eye of Milkyway had moved slightly to port, though it remained impossibly distant, as unattainable as fabled blue Aerth itself, the Ur-world after which his parents had named him.

Staring into Milkyway, he revisited a romantic question that he had entertained in secret for most of his life: Might the other end of this Rift terminate within the ancestral galaxy, the home of the first Oh-Neyel to venture forth from timelost Aerth?

Suppose the Rift's terminus lies near to Far Aerth itself?

Dayan's report shattered Faraerth's reverie. "The probes are entering Riftspace now, Drech'tor."

Milkyway's brilliant swirl abruptly vanished from sight, replaced by a silvery wash of static. The electronic eyes remained blinded for perhaps a mennet, shedding no light whatsoever on the Rift's enigmatic interior. If *Tuskerslayer*'s bones were interred in the worm's depths, their recovery would have to wait for another day, another ship.

Then, as suddenly as it had come, the crackling interference cleared. The viewer displayed a starscape that Faraerth didn't recognize. All he could determine about it was that it harbored a far sparser array of stellar lights than any he had ever seen before, even in the vast, untrammeled hinterlands adjacent to the Knownconquered Territories.

It is just as an edgeward region of Milkyway might look, he thought. *If viewed from the* inside.

Emboldened by this idea, he stood and faced Dayan again. "Spread the probes out from one another to optimal survey distance. Keep Probe One posted near the Rift's far terminus to serve as a commlink for the other telly-eyes. Then run the whole assemblage in tandem to generate a pulsar map."

Dayan appeared puzzled, but complied quickly. Within moments, the viewer was displaying a detailed tridee pulsar map that centered on the volume of space surrounding the other end of the Rift. Blood-red icons, set against a dark blue backdrop, represented every pulsar the sensitive telly-eye probes had been able to detect.

"Now overlay this image with the pulsar map of Milkyway from our cartog computer," said Faraerth.

Though still obviously mystified, Dayan quickly did as she was bid. Within moments, a second map formed on the screen, appearing transparently atop the first. The sensorman massaged the two images until they were exactly alike in size and scale.

The two pulsar maps matched perfectly, point for point. Faraerth's insides went nullgrav.

"The Rift's other end really *is* inside Milkyway," Helmrunner Baruclan whispered. He, too, had evidently speculated along such lines, which really wasn't surprising. After all, scores of popular Neyel novelists and playwrights had advanced similar ideas for many oghencycles. But before today, no one had succeeded in putting the far-fetched notion to the test.

"It appears so," Faraerth said, his hands clenched behind his back as though each were trying to contain the other's excitement. With a flick of his tail, Faraerth pointed toward a flashing blue icon located near the edge of Milkyway's simulated disk. "And note the approximate position of Aerth relative to the Rift's terminus."

Baruclan gasped. "It lies only about sixty-two pars'x from the Rift's far end. Can it be?"

Faraerth laid a thick hand on the younger officer's shoulder. He did it as much to moderate his own mounting enthusiasm as the lad's. "Maybe. Maybe not. We will need to make many observations before we can be absolutely certain."

"Once we are, we may be able to actually reach Aerth," said Dayan, her rugged eyeslits opened up wider than Faraerth had ever seen them before.

"And enfold it within the Neyel Hegemony, where it belongs," Faraerth said, confident that he had completed her thought for her. Since he still had no words of his own, he quoted from the Sacred Writ. " 'The long-lost Coreworld from which all true sentients sprang, of which even Blue Oghen was never more than the palest of shadows.' "

An even older snippet of skiffy verse, which his grandfather had been fond of reciting, occurred to him then. It had been one of the very few pieces of digitized literature to have been recovered from the rad-stricken computers after Holy Vangar's tumultuous passage from its origin point to the edges of M'jallan's Cloud.

We pray for one last landing
On the globe that gave us birth;
Let us rest our eyes on the fleecy skies
And the cool, green hills of Aerth.

Standing in silence, Faraerth marveled at how much closer the ancestral world had suddenly come. *Sixty-two pars'x*, he thought. To be sure, sixty-two pars'x was no mean distance. But it was as nothing compared to the yawning gulf of Blackempty that separated even the most edgeward Neyel outpost from Milkyway's nearest spiral arm.

Faraerth's musings were interrupted by the klaxon that began blaring from Dayan's instrument array. She hastened back to her scanners to disable the intrusive sound, and immediately set about trying to determine what had triggered it.

"Well?" Faraerth asked, his impatience flaring like an old warwound.

The sensorman looked up from her readouts and displays. Confusion was written across her duty-roughened, hullmetal-hued face. "I've just lost contact with the two farthest telly-eye probes."

"Put Probe One's visuals up on the viewer," Faraerth said, still looking expectantly in Dayan's direction.

"Perhaps *that* is the reason for our difficulties," the helmrunner said, pointing forward. Faraerth turned toward the viewer, surprised that Dayan had managed to carry out his last order so quickly.

Looking through Probe One's unblinking telly-eye, Faraerth saw a trio of wedge-shaped, silver-and-scarlet spacecraft. Their precise size was impossible to determine. But the alacrity of their approach made their intent crystal clear.

"They're heading straight for their side of the Rift," Dayan reported, her voice quavering slightly. She, too, must have apprehended what they were about to face. "I'm picking up intense subspace interference from all three vessels. They must have either jammed our other telly-eye probes, or else they've destroyed them outright."

"Do we fight them?" Baruclan wanted to know. Faraerth noted the dread in the helmrunner's youthful eyes, a visual complement to the apprehension he could hear barely restrained behind Dayan's voice.

The drech'tor chose to overlook his crew's all-too-evident fear. It seemed perfectly rational, considering the nature of the monsters that now stalked them. Faraerth had never seen a Devil up close, but the few who'd survived such encounters had described them as crystalline killing machines, about as receptive to reason as the dead, dry stones of Oghen's airless moons.

"Alert status," Faraerth said, working hard to suffuse his voice with confidence. He hoped his crew would respond to it, draw strength and resolve from it. "Hard about, maximum Efti'el. Summon reinforcements from the fleet. The Hegemony will learn what we've discovered today about Milkyway and Aerth, but I don't want it broadcast over the subspace bands." There was nothing to be gained by allowing an implacable enemy to learn that a Neyel crew had apparently found a means of reaching Aerth.

No one on the command deck wasted any time carrying out Faraerth's orders. They all held fast to chairs or consoles, using feet, tails, or hands, as the velocity compensators labored to adjust to the ship's rapid change in course and speed.

The Rift had just set a pack of Devils hard on *Slicer*'s heels.

And now they stand between us and Far Aerth, the drech'tor thought, his righteous anger swiftly growing as hot as the densely packed suns of M'jallan's Core.

Chapter 26

2295, Auld Greg Aerth Calendar, the Neyel Coreworld of Oghen

The past oghencycle had been a most troubling one for Faraerth. His body had been rent asunder permanently; his right arm had stubbornly refused to grow back, despite repeated regeneration therapies. And ever since the day a Devil monofilament blade had maimed him and a Devil energy-net had crushed *Slicer*—killing most of Faraerth's crew—the Neyel Hegemony itself had suffered injuries on a scale not seen since antiquity, when the Tuskers had beheaded the First Drech'tor and made martyrs of so many others.

The first Devils to emerge from the Riftmouth into Hegemony Space had done so in a single battered ship. A handful of others soon followed. Within the span of one scant oghencycle, the Devils began arriving in steadily escalating numbers. Dozens. Hundreds. The Hegemony Fleet's drech'tors now likened them to clouds of Oghen cropshearers, the dread insects that had descended upon the Cultivations during the worst of the Coreworld's early famine years.

The fleet joined the battle immediately, for Neyel spacers were nothing if not ready and willing to defend their territory. Despite the suddenness and ferocity of the Devil assault, the ships and weaponry of both races quickly reached a rough parity. These days, neither side seemed able to maintain an advantage over the other for very long.

But during recent days, Faraerth had watched with his own eyes as the balance of power slowly tipped against the Neyel. Even now, the Devils continued to come across the Rift in ever-increasing numbers, apparently as determined as ever to kill as wantonly as the Tuskers of old had done, despite their apparent lack of language, culture, or any other observable evidence of sentience.

Save, Faraerth often thought, despite the horrors the Devils had visited upon him and his shipmates, *their ships and weaponry.* These, of course, the Alien Contact experts had always dismissed as the handiworks of other races, taken by the shrewd machinations of a ruthless, cunning, yet subsapient and instinct-driven species.

Faraerth wasn't so sure how to evaluate the enemy's sentience, nor if such questions truly mattered when the Devils were inflicting so much damage upon the Hegemony—and while such a hellish adversary stood between the Neyel people and the Riftmouth that could enable them to regain Auld Aerth.

And another problem had recently assumed an urgency far greater than the recovery of Aerth: Lately the now-all-but-invisible Riftmouth, the source of the increasingly perilous alien infestation, had begun drifting ever further downsystem from the outer comet cloud, falling inexorably—and at an apparently accelerating rate—toward the warm climes wherein orbited Oghen, the Coreworld to which all other Neyel Hegemony planets paid tribute in troops, raw materials, and finished goods.

Oghen, a planet nearly as revered among Neyelkind as was Far Aerth itself, might soon be utterly helpless before the Devil onslaught.

Gran Drech'tor Zafir had to redouble the fleet's efforts

not only to repulse the expanding Devil incursion, but also to seek to end it at its source.

And that was why, Faraerth supposed, he now found himself standing under the semicylindrical vault of the Great Hall of Oghen, in the august presence of the Gran Drech'tor Herself, along with some of her most senior visors. That she had called upon Faraerth's expertise in spite of his shamefully permanent injuries—and despite his having committed the even more outrageous offense of surviving the destruction of *Slicer*—spoke volumes to him about the fear and desperation that now reigned at Gran Drech'tor Zafir's court.

Why she believes I *can do anything to stem the Devil tide is Vangar's own mystery*, Faraerth thought, glancing down at his mangled stump of an arm. It was a brutal, unhealed scar that often served as a useful call to humility. *Such a talisman might serve some of Zafir's other visors even better than it serves me.*

Faraerth looked up across the cavernous hall, a space whose polished nickel-iron surfaces brought to mind the hallowed nullgrav Core Spaces of the Vangar Innerworld, the original Great Rock which even now stared down from Oghen's cloud-scudded sky like some beneficent deity, from the place where Drech'tor Wafiyy had parked it nearly a century earlier. His eyes lighting upon the broad, gleaming dais, Faraerth saw Gran Drech'tor Zafir, flanked by her guards. The guards were hard-pressed to keep up with her pacing, and to avoid being struck by the heavy club end of her anxiously switching tail.

Standing on either side of the wide, oblong table that lay between Faraerth and the Gran Drech'tor were Jerdahn, an expert in the Soft Sciences renowned across the Hegemony, and Loford, an equally well regarded, top-echelon military and technical visor whose hard-line views toward the Devils were celebrated across the Hegemony, thanks to her voluminous monographs and commentaries on the subject.

Splayed across the table, and the principal object of attention for the monarch and her visors, was a Devil. Or rather, the charred, cracked-open husk of one, the lifeless residuum of both battlefield and pathology lab.

"Behold the foe, Gran Drech'tor," intoned Visor Loford. She gestured toward the alien corpse with both hands and the distal end of her tail. "See that which stands between us and the Ur-world which is the birthright of all Neyelkind."

Zafir complied, her thick-lidded black eyes unfathomable. "This creature seems to be a thing of stone or crystal," she said at length, eyeing the neatly cleaved planes and angles of the dead creature's open thoracic cavity, the blocky heaviness of its rigid, semitranslucent internal organs. "It hardly seems real."

"It is unlike any exobiota we have ever encountered before. Yet it lived, right up until it fell in battle," Visor Jerdahn said. Faraerth suppressed a smile at the academic's froshclass lecture-chamber tone, no doubt an unconscious mannerism. Loford scowled noticeably, but the Gran Drech'tor seemed too absorbed by the dead creature that lay before her to pay any heed to the byplay.

"Even the Tuskers of antiquity bore at least *some* resemblance to us," Jerdahn continued, apparently not realizing that Loford had been about to speak. "Even they were constructed of nucleic acids and proteins. The Devils, by contrast, are crystalline mineral constructs, evidently the product of one of the harshest, hottest, highest-pressure environments imaginable. Even a species as adversity-hardened as we Neyel could not survive long unprotected under the atmospheric conditions that prevail within their war vessels. It may take us many oghencycles merely to begin fathoming their biotic processes."

"Such is the unknowable face of the Devils," Loford said. "Mindless beasts who would extinguish our way of life as though they were bred merely for that sole purpose. As they have already amply demonstrated, their continuation necessarily means the end of our race."

"Assuming, of course, that we continue to fail to communicate with them," said Jerdahn. Though Faraerth often harbored such thoughts privately, he was surprised to hear the academic give them voice in this chamber. Given the imperative for war that now suffused even the intelligentsia of the Hegemony, such a comment was tantamount to treason.

But Zafir seemed to take the scholar's remark in stride, her slate-gray countenance showing a thoughtful aspect. *The war must truly be going badly for us,* Faraerth thought, *if she is actually considering an attempt to parley.* Faraerth knew well that most, if not all, Hegemony citizens found the notion utterly unthinkable. Fighting for survival was too ingrained a Neyel characteristic to be headed off by even the wisest of leaders, or by the direst of consequences.

"We are better off devoting our resources toward studying and countering the instinct-ruled tactics and strategies of the Devils," Loford countered, a muscular sneer contorting her otherwise rigid face. "Only by pursuing such a course can we succeed in wiping out this scourge before it annihilates *us* instead."

Faraerth still said nothing, silently noting the irony of Loford's tuskish words. He knew that she had never taken up arms in the service of the Hegemony, nor braved the madness-inducing regions that bordered Riftspace, nor faced down the Devils' lethal energy webs as he had. The stump of his arm throbbed and a phantom itch crept across a nonexistent elbow as he considered these things. *What does she know of war?* he thought.

Jerdahn approached the table. With a theatrical flourish, he raised the Devil's severed head, reminding Faraerth of a scene from one of the ancient stage plays that had survived the exodus from Auld Aerth. A *Devil of infinite jest,* the maimed spacer thought wryly.

"We may be better able to anticipate and counter our attackers' moves," Jerdahn said, "if we first understand the contents of *this.*"

Loford snorted, her eyelids shuttering down to hostile slits, her gaze like a pair of particle cannons. "We understand *that* quite well enough, I think. The Devils exist only to kill us, and that is the only thing approximating thought in their hard, subsentient brains. They lack the wit even for intelligible language, and thus aren't fit even to be slaves, much less free sentients. There can be no coexistence with them."

Faraerth found himself growing irritated at this irrelevant line of reasoning. Intelligent or not, the Devils endangered the very existence of the Hegemony.

"They have sufficient wit to pilot starships, and to unleash terrible energies upon us," he said, no longer able to hold his tongue. "Their brainpower suffices to do things such as this." Using his one good arm and his scarred but unbowed tail, Faraerth pointed to the battle-ravaged stump on his right side.

Faraerth's outburst apparently brought Loford up short. She sputtered, obviously nonplussed that Faraerth, being a long-time member of the military—and one who had fought the Devils at close quarters—had not reflexively agreed with her.

"Hear, hear," Jerdahn said, his eyes alight.

Gran Drech'tor Zafir raised a hand for silence, and the conversation ceased. Faraerth worried for a moment that he may have fatally overreached himself, then decided he'd been on borrowed time ever since the glowing Devil webs had torn *Slicer* to pieces.

If the monarch was surprised by Faraerth's comments, she revealed no sign of it. "I summoned you here, Drech'tor Faraerth, because you have looked into the enemy's eyes and lived to tell of it," she said.

Faraerth bowed respectfully. *I survived in disgrace, you mean,* he thought, feeling a bloom of shame spreading slowly across the tough skin of his face. *Had I returned alive from an engagement with a lesser foe, your underlings surely would have executed me immediately on charges of cowardice.*

Then his embarrassment subsided as he reached the

sobering realization that the whole world was changing all around him. One way or another, for good or for ill, the Devils were forcing Neyel society to adapt itself to the vicissitudes of the current moment. *The Gran Drech'tor needs me alive more than she needs to hew to tired traditions, and she knows it.*

The thought prompted him to wonder if the danger posed by the Devils might not be even more dire than he knew.

Uncomfortably aware that everyone's eyes were upon him, Faraerth gathered his thoughts and spoke. "I fear that discounting the wiles of the Devils is to minimize the damage they can do us, Gran Drech'tor. How can creatures lacking minds as we understand them so thoroughly destroy a vessel as mighty as *Slicer?*"

"Solar flares are destructive as well," said Loford. "But I do not conclude from this that the stars have the intellectual wherewithal to draw clever plans against us. Such dangers can be outrun, and thus survived, as your presence in this chamber today so graphically demonstrates."

Faraerth grit his teeth, nettled. Loford had as much as accused him of cowardice. His left hand twitched, moving slightly toward his sidearm until he stopped it with a supreme act of will. He hoped no one noticed.

Ignoring Loford, Faraerth continued speaking directly to the monarch, who seemed anxious to hear what he had to say. "It is true enough that the Devils failed to kill me, Gran Drech'tor. But not because they are stupid, pliant beasts like the grazers who held sway on this world before Drech'tor Wafiyy claimed it."

Gran Drech'tor Zafir's eyes twinkled. "Then it must have been your own personal bravery in combat that secured your life."

Faraerth wondered briefly if she, too, was trying to shame him, then decided that it didn't really matter; his fate would be in her hands in any event. Shaking his head, he said, "No, Gran Drech'tor. I survived only because my crew was prepared to fight to the last man to defend their ship and their drech'tor. They did this because they are Neyel."

Zafir smiled approvingly.

"So despite your belief in the entirely undemonstrated intelligence of these unlettered Devils," Loford said, "you don't seem to consider it particularly relevant to the fate of *Slicer*."

Faraerth paused for a thoughtful moment, then said, "When the Devils attacked *Slicer*, we had time only to protect ourselves and wage war as best we could, taking care not to underestimate the adversary. Neither I nor my crew had time to debate philosophy." He wanted to tell Loford that he'd had time in abundance to consider such things during his oghencycle-long convalescence afterward. But he decided it would be a pointless exercise.

Loford turned toward the monarch, bowing deeply before addressing her. "Gran Drech'tor, as you have already seen, the massed forces of the Neyel Hegemony stand ready to bear any burden to destroy this enemy. Whether or not we agree on their lack of sentience, they will not cease their attacks and incursions until they overrun Oghen and seize Holy Vangar itself—unless we carry the war directly to the Devils *now*, and end forever their ability to make war. And the surest way to do that is to destroy them utterly, like the infestation they are."

Zafir stood in silence, considering Loford's words for nearly a full mennet before she resumed her pacing. To Faraerth's eye, she did not appear entirely sanguine about exterminating another race, even one as alien and implacably hostile as the Devils.

The monarch halted and addressed Jerdahn. "Is your institute still attempting to communicate with the Devils, Visor?"

The scholar looked embarrassed. Coughing nervously, he said, "Yes, we are, Gran Drech'tor."

"And has any progress been made lately?"

"The newest studies remain inconclusive," Jerdahn admitted. "We have never been able to develop reliable exotranslation algorithms suitable to even begin the task. And we're not even sure what sounds the Devils use to communicate. It's even possible that they employ some speech modality other than audible sound."

"Ridiculous," said Loford, sniffing. "They're clearly beasts operating on instinct, creatures who have come to possess high technology through some opportunistic happenstance."

"We invented neither the Efti'el drive nor the antigravity devices which make the Neyel Hegemony possible," Jerdahn pointed out, his tone eminently reasonable. "What is our acquisition of such things if not opportunistic?"

Gran Drech'tor Zafir held her hand up again, forcing Loford to fume in silence. Faraerth could only wonder how the military visor might have refuted the academic's excellent point. *Might we not at times seem like Devils to some of the subject races?*

Then the monarch lifted her eyes and stared off into the distance for a seeming eternity before shattering the quiet that had descended over the vast chamber.

"I have come to a decision. Regardless of the right or wrong of it, total war is now upon us. Whether or not the enemy reasons as we do, the Devils have left but one course of action open to us."

Turning her back on Jerdahn, she faced Loford and Faraerth, her obsidian eyes sad, her back bowed by an unimaginable burden of responsibility. "Assemble the entire War Council. Our race cannot survive and prosper while theirs does. They cannot be dissuaded from attacking, so they must die. *All* of them."

Loford looked triumphant. Jerdahn seemed to deflate, as if suddenly realizing that he had just wagered his career and lost. Perhaps he had.

Faraerth bowed before the Gran Drechtor, then began

slowly moving toward the chamber's exit to do as he'd been bid. Loford walked beside him, but would not meet his eyes. He wanted to ask her if she was pleased to have finally gotten her wish, but decided against it.

Faraerth searched his soul. Whatever misgivings he had developed lately about total war, he could find no fault with Gran Drech'tor Zafir's decision. *We must cling to life any way we can. Even if the cost is the doing of unpalatable things.*

Such had always been the price of Neyel survival. And Faraerth knew that he would never hesitate to pay that price in defense of his people, their Coreworld, Holy Vangar—and the distant, nigh-legendary planet Aerth.

Faraerth stepped into the gentle breeze of an Oghen afternoon and walked toward the squat buildings of the War Complex. He paused on the skystone steps, ignoring the busy crush of minor functionaries and office workers who stepped briskly past and around him.

He looked up into the deep blue-and-ocher sky toward where he knew the Riftmouth—and distant Aerth—lay. A faint but definitely visible aurora sparkled and shimmered in the distance. Such things had been occurring with increasing frequency of late, but no one knew for certain why. This particular display might have been a simple interaction between Oghen's energetic star and the planet's necessarily powerful magnetic field.

Or it might be Riftspace closing ever inward on us. A sign that even now the damned Devils are preparing to lower the Riftmouth into the very sky of Oghen and set their fleets upon us before we can react.

Faraerth recalled a time aboard *Slicer* when the Efti'el drive had malfunctioned, leaving the ship stranded in a fractured region of space that closely bordered the Riftmouth itself. Fully half his crew had begun to go mad during the half-day it had taken to repair the engines sufficiently to escape the Rift's pernicious influence.

Would such a fate eventually befall everyone on Oghen as Riftspace invaded the inner system? He imagined a sacred world transformed into a place fit only for madmen and Devils. The thought made Faraerth shudder.

Peering beyond the forest of spires that made up the great city's skyline, Faraerth lowered his gaze to the horizon. Although the sky was still bright, he could see Holy Vangar, the longtime home of all Neyel prior to the historic Oghen Planetfall, as a gleaming pinpoint. Lately he had begun fantasizing about piloting the Great Rock itself out of its current orbit. He vividly imagined attaching a forest of Efti'el nacelles to its surface in order to fly it back to its original place—the womb of Auld Aerth's stable Elfive Point.

The recurring fantasy buoyed Faraerth's spirits. *Maybe the unlikely survival of one named after Far Aerth is an augury*, he thought as he resumed his steady march toward the War Complex offices.

Should the Riftmouth set every Devil alive against us, Neyelkind will *regain the ancestral homeworld of Aerth.*

PART 9

RECONCILIATION

Chapter 27

"It's beautiful, is it not?" Jerdahn said, leaning on the railing that overlooked the aft observation deck's huge window. "Holy Vangar, the Great Rock, never ceases to inspire. For me, it symbolizes both the timelost past and a future in which that past might be regained."

Burgess couldn't help agreeing, and she was glad that Jerdahn had come aboard to view the famous O'Neill habitat with her. Though half an hour of watching the huge object's stately procession across Oghen's face had gotten her used to Vanguard's reality, she still felt like a medieval pilgrim who had just touched an aged sliver of the True Cross.

Though she was farther away from her birthworld than she had ever been before, she felt, paradoxically, as though she had come home.

It was time.

"Commander Rand, please hail Drech'tor Joh'jym," Sulu said.

"Aye, Captain." Rand set about her business in her usual efficient manner.

A second or so later the image of the Vanguard Colony vanished from the main bridge viewer, to be replaced by the faces of Joh'jym and Oratok.

"My thanks for allowing *Excelsior* to visit Oghen, if even for a short time," Sulu said. He knew it couldn't have been as simple as "allowing" *Excelsior* to orbit his homeworld; he had no doubt that Joh'jym must have convinced some very important and powerful people that *Excelsior* was not a threat or some secret weapon sent by the Tholians. Joh'jym had to be an influential figure within the Neyel power structure.

Sulu continued: "I regret that we lack the time to visit the surface of your world, and to get to know your people better." *I would have loved to get inside Vanguard, too,* he thought wistfully.

Joh'jym looked grave. At least, Sulu thought he looked graver than usual. "So *you remain determined to return to the Devils who would destroy you?*"

"I assure you, there are any number of things I would rather do than fight the Tholians," Sulu said. "But I'm afraid we can't stay here any longer. We must return to our own space."

He omitted mentioning that far more than the welfare of *Excelsior* was at stake. As slender as it was, the only hope for averting the bloodbath for which the Neyel were now preparing was to convince the Tholians to sue for peace. And only by meeting Yilskene in *truthcombat* would he have any chance of broaching the topic with the Tholian political and diplomatic castes.

Then, a way had to be found to convince the Neyel to call off the dogs of war. But even Joh'jym, as friendly as he had proved to be since Yilskene had trapped *Excelsior* and *Oghen's Flame*, seemed unable to consider any peace that wasn't preceded by the complete annihilation of the Tholians.

The current grim situation took him back to his Starfleet Academy days, when he'd taken the no-win *Kobayashi Maru* test. He had opted then to allow the few hundred personnel aboard the doomed freighter to die rather than risk war with the Klingons.

Compared to today's circumstances, that *Kobayashi Maru* scenario had been a picnic in Golden Gate Park. *Even if I manage to save the lives of my crew, war is still just about a foregone conclusion.*

Weariness and despair threatened to engulf him as he considered just how long the odds were, not just for himself, but also for two societies, and maybe even for Earth itself.

"Would that our invasion fleet was ready to leave this day," Joh'jym said, snapping Sulu back to full alertness. *"You would have aught to fear from the Devils on your way home."*

"Thank you. But my purpose here is to *prevent* a war, if at all possible."

Joh'jym laughed as though Sulu had just cracked a joke. *"I tried to convince my superiors to allow me the use of several warships to escort you safely through the Devil phalanx. I regret that I failed in that attempt. Some of the high drech'tors inside the War Complex distrust your motivations, it seems, in spite of my intercession on your behalf."*

Sulu nodded sadly, though he counted himself fortunate that the Neyel military hadn't tried to blow *Excelsior* out of the sky. "There's a war on," he said. "I understand your people's need for caution. *Excelsior* will depart as soon as your traffic authorities grant us clearance. In the meantime, we will return Jerdahn to your vessel with our transporter."

"That is premature, Hikarusulu. Jerdahn need not return to us until your vessel and mine are ready to part company."

Sulu blinked. "I don't understand."

"I said I failed to assemble an escort fleet. However, I still command Oghen's Flame. *Thanks in part to the assistance of your engineers, she is now quite spaceworthy."*

Sulu was incredulous. "We inflicted considerable damage on your ship, Drech'tor Joh'jym."

"We Neyel are long accustomed to dealing with far more catastrophic damage. Repairing our most critical systems was not difficult, especially with your Commander Azleya and her

crew helping us. Now we are ready. When do we depart for the Riftmouth?"

"We fired on you, remember?" Sulu said.

"And we fired on you," Joh'jym said with a shrug. *"But that was before we understood one another so well. You later saved* Oghen's Flame *from the Devils' trap. It is a debt I must repay."*

Sulu shook his head. "I can't allow you to put yourself and your crew at risk on our behalf."

A smile spread across Joh'jym's hard features. *"They are my lives to risk, Captain."*

Sulu wondered for a moment whether the Neyel commander was actually concealing a different, more sinister, agenda. Perhaps his real plan was to have another crack at the Tholian colony that Yilskene's ships had come to defend.

Then he decided to take Joh'jym at face value. Peace, after all, had to begin with trust. And if he returned to Yilskene accompanied by a Neyel drech'tor, perhaps Ambassador Burgess could at last find an opening to get a Tholian-Neyel dialogue started after all.

Hope rising within him, Sulu returned the Neyel commander's smile. "Thank you, Drech'tor. Take us out of orbit, Mr. Lojur. Lay in a course for the rift."

Anxious, Chekov watched the forward sensor displays carefully as *Excelsior* navigated the gray expanse of interspace. The vessel was nearing the interspatial aperture that opened up deep into Tholian territory.

"What's ahead of us, Pavel?" Sulu wanted to know.

"No sign of any energy webs," he reported to the captain. Relief washed over him; Yilskene hadn't barred the door, as it were. And in the absence of the Tholians' charged filaments, outrunning Yilskene's small flotilla was going to be easy.

"I confirm Commander Chekov's findings," Tuvok said

from sciences. "Unfortunately, I also believe I also can explain them."

At the same moment, Chekov's sensor display explained the situation to him as well. His heart went into freefall.

Chekov moved toward the bridge railing. "Captain, the reason Yilskene isn't bothering to lay energy filaments in our path is because he doesn't need to."

Sulu frowned. "Why?"

"Because it looks like he's summoned half the Tholian fleet as reinforcements."

Chapter 28

Seconds later, *Excelsior* and *Oghen's Flame* emerged together once again from interspace. Fortunately, Yilskene and his massed reinforcements—Tuvok had counted more than four hundred small but heavily armed Tholian ships, with more apparently on the way—did not immediately open fire.

Admiral Yilskene's multifaceted visage was up on the bridge viewer seconds after the arrival of the admiral's hail. Sulu imagined that if the Tholian's face could have registered human-perceptible emotions, it would have displayed a look of intense surprise at *Excelsior*'s sudden reappearance.

"*You escaped our energy web, Captain Sulu. And yet now you have returned. You have one of your minutes to explain yourself, or we will summarily destroy both your ship and the intruder vessel.*"

Sulu looked straight into his adversary's blank eyespots. "Admiral, I believe that you and I still had an appointment to engage in *truthcombat.* I have returned to you ready for combat, in order to lawfully win the freedom of my vessel—and that of the Neyel ship."

Yilskene's head moved slightly from side to side. "*Very well then, Captain Sulu. Your lawful challenge will stand, as scheduled. You will face your death—and the destruction of both your vessel and the intruder's—in twenty of your minutes.*" The screen abruptly went blank.

Sulu immediately rose from his command chair and stalked toward the situation room, calling on Chekov, Tuvok, Hopman, and Akaar to follow him. The group quickly entered the chamber, leaving Rand in charge of the bridge.

As the doors hissed closed, Sulu turned to Akaar and Hopman. "Have you found anything further that will help me gain an advantage in this fight?"

Hopman shook her head. "I'm sorry, Captain. I've already given you and Lieutenant Akaar everything I could dig up. The Tholians haven't been exactly forthcoming with information about their personal fighting styles. All I can really offer you now is the obvious: Yilskene will be going for the kill. It's hard to imagine him yielding. You may have no choice other than to kill him."

"My intent is to gain Yilskene's cooperation," Sulu said. "Even if I have to place him under physical duress to do it. I think the admiral is a pragmatist. He'll listen to reason if his alternative is dying on an alien's monoblade."

"You're assuming that you're going to win," Chekov said, his voice grave.

Nodding, Sulu matched his old friend's grim tone. "If I assume anything else, Pavel, then this mission has already failed." He trained his gaze next on Akaar. "Lieutenant, what can you tell me about the weaponry I'll be using?"

Akaar opened a canister that contained the monoblade used by Mosrene to assassinate Kasrene. He carefully removed the crystalline-hafted weapon, holding it horizontally. The molecule-thin blade would have been invisible but for the elusive glints of light it captured and reflected as it sliced the air.

"You will be using a weapon very similar to this, only longer," Akaar said. "Take great care. From what I understand of monoblades, it can cut through your environmental suit, flesh, and bone just as easily as it penetrated Kasrene's crystalline skin and organs. However, it is also my understanding that duelists are allowed the use of an energy shield capable of repelling a monoblade attack."

"That sounds encouraging," Sulu said.

Then Akaar's expression grew even more dour than usual. "Unfortunately, this shield can be activated only a limited number of times before it exhausts its energy reserves and leaves its bearer defenseless."

Sulu nodded, thinking it was still better than nothing. Then he turned toward Tuvok, who seemed beside himself with tension. "You have something to add, Lieutenant?"

Tuvok handed him a padd, and as he spoke, Sulu scrolled through the notes there. "You will be outfitted with a modified environmental suit, which will restrict your movements. While the gravity aboard Yilskene's ship is approximately one gee, the intense atmospheric pressure will further hamper your mobility. Additionally, if your suit is ruptured and not immediately repaired, your life will be further imperiled by the hot, anoxic atmosphere aboard the *Jeb'v Tholis.*"

"Thank you for all the good news, Mr. Tuvok," Sulu said as he handed back the padd. The science officer hadn't told him anything he didn't already know.

Tuvok's right eyebrow rose. "Captain, I'm not certain you fully appreciate the seriousness of this situation. In my opinion, you are walking to your death in defiance of all logic."

"That's enough, Lieutenant," Chekov said. It was plain to Sulu that his exec didn't seem any more enthused about the coming duel than Tuvok was. But Chekov was clearly committed to backing up his captain—at least in front of the junior officers.

Obviously not yet ready to back down, Tuvok glowered at Chekov. "I am merely attempting to point out that an attempt to outrun the Tholian fleet stands a far better chance of success than does personal combat with Admiral Yilskene."

Sulu held up a hand for silence. "Your objection is duly

noted, Lieutenant. And you're right. We *could* run, and probably elude the Tholian fleet. If their ships were fast enough to catch us at maximum warp, then it wouldn't have taken them so long to get here in the first place.

"But running back to Federation space won't help us make peace with the Tholians. And it won't do a damned thing to keep the Tholian Assembly and the Neyel Hegemony from trying to wipe each other out."

"Suppose Yilskene kills you, Captain," Tuvok said, clearly still not satisfied. "What then?"

"If that should happen, Lieutenant, then *that* will be the time to run." Sulu met Chekov's silently reproachful gaze. "If I can't overcome Yilskene, Pavel, you're to tell our Neyel friends to turn hard about and go home. Then outrun the Tholians, take *Excelsior* clear of any jamming by the Tholian fleet, inform Starfleet Command of the situation, and continue back into Federation space."

"Understood, Captain," Chekov said quietly.

Sulu realized then that very little else remained to be said. "Dismissed."

"Are you sure about this, Hikaru?" Chekov asked after everybody else had filed out of the room.

Sulu had been asking himself that same question for the past several hours. "Of course not, Pavel. On the other hand, the only ones who never have to sweat the outcomes of things are dead people."

Chekov chuckled in response to Sulu's gallows humor. "In that case, let's hope the outcome of all of this remains as ambiguous as possible—for as *long* as possible."

Lojur sat behind the navigation console on the strangely quiet bridge, contemplating the Tholian ships he saw on the main viewer. They hung ominously in the void, their wedge shapes looking like so many spear-points.

He hadn't felt so troubled since the Orions had laid waste

to Kotha Village all those years ago. His thoughts went yet again to his dear, dead Shandra. So *much blood has been shed already. And so much more is to follow if nothing is done to stop it.*

Some of that blood, Lojur knew, would issue from the veins of Captain Sulu, who would shortly be fighting for his life aboard one of those Tholian vessels out there.

There had to be a better way. Too many had died already.

The doors to the situation room hissed open, momentarily drawing Lojur's attention away from the viewer. He watched as Tuvok, Hopman, and Akaar stepped back onto the bridge, their expressions uniformly serious.

Lojur's gaze locked for a moment with that of Akaar as he made his way to the tactical station. *Thank you, my friend, for lending me some of your strength in my moment of weakness. Were it not for you, I would have become a murderer.*

Yet again, he considered what he'd nearly done: he'd tried to murder Jerdahn in cold blood, and would have succeeded if not for the Neyel's exceptionally tough hide. He had no choice other than to accept the bitter truth that he had yet to atone for that most grievous of sins.

Merely because Akaar hadn't turned him in.

I must atone, Lojur thought, recalling the Orion raiders who had died by his hand so long ago, in defiance of every Halkan tradition. *Perhaps I can do so in a way that will prevent still more bloodshed.*

The only action he could conceive at the moment lay, in its own fashion, utterly outside the bounds of propriety. But hadn't Commander Chekov taught him that failing to act could be as costly as acting incorrectly? Improper action might be precisely what was called for.

Lojur decided then that he had to seek the advice of someone neutral. Someone completely outside of *Excelsior*'s chain of command. Neither of his closest friends, Akaar and Tuvok, could help him this time.

He turned his chair toward the communications station, where Commander Rand appeared to be listening intently to something on her earpiece. She was also nominally in command of the bridge until the captain and Commander Chekov returned from the situation room.

"Commander?"

Rand looked up, quickly giving Lojur her full attention. "What can I do for you, Mr. Lojur?"

He regretted compounding his earlier sins by lying. But he felt he had little choice. "I feel . . . unwell. I request permission to leave my post."

"It's past time to take some decisive action of our own," Burgess said. "Nothing good can come of Captain Sulu's plan to duel with the Tholian admiral."

"I am forced to agree with your assessment," Jerdahn said, sitting cross-legged on the floor of the ambassador's VIP quarters.

Burgess was surprised at how quickly the huge Neyel officer had come around to her way of thinking. He was obviously a creature of discipline, a man used to following the orders of his superiors without hesitation. But he also just as clearly possessed a lively, flexible intellect that seemed at odds with his humble position as a sanitation worker aboard *Oghen's Flame.*

Jerdahn had evaded her direct questions about the "previous life" to which he'd referred after the boarding party had briefly been taken into custody aboard *Oghen's Flame.* While she could only speculate about the details of Jerdahn's mysterious past, it seemed to have given him a perspective on alien relations that was atypical of his species.

Or maybe he's finally realized that he's run out of options other than trying to make peace. Could that mean he's also coming to accept the Tholians as fellow sentient beings?

"All right, then," Burgess said, feeling truly hopeful for the first time in hours. "That just leaves us to work out the operational details. We've already tried asking Drech'tor Joh'jym nicely to consent to a meeting with the Tholians, and vice versa. That approach got us nowhere. So now we have to find a way to *force* your commander and Admiral Yilskene to sit down with me at the negotiating table."

Jerdahn's expression grew even more deadly serious than usual. "You understand that to do this will require us to kidnap both of them. They have already demonstrated that nothing less will suffice. But we will have to move quickly. My drech'tor grows impatient with waiting, and might soon take some precipitous action on his own."

Burgess sighed, well aware that she might be about to cross the Rubicon. "We'd have to move quickly in any case, with half the Tholian fleet ready to pulverize both your ship and *Excelsior* the moment Yilskene kills Captain Sulu. Under the circumstances, I think we can be forgiven for letting the ends justify the means."

"Perhaps Captain Sulu would also agree, in private, were he not bound by both honor and military regulations," Jerdahn said.

She laughed harshly. *If Sulu really thinks he can win a monoblade-duel against a giant hunk of sentient crystal, then he's bound more by testosterone than by Starfleet regs.*

The door-chime sounded, interrupting her reverie. "Come," Burgess said.

The door slid open, admitting Lieutenant Commander Lojur. The Halkan was clearly beside himself. Burgess supposed he was traumatized by the prospect of the extreme violence that almost assuredly lay ahead.

She decided it was best to give him a polite but firm brush-off. Though she had long admired the tradition of pacifism embraced by Lojur's people, she simply didn't have the time right now to let him cry on her shoulder.

"Lieutenant, I'm really quite busy at the moment."

For a Halkan, he was surprisingly direct. "None of us

has much time, Ambassador. I need to speak to you about the *truthcombat* ritual that the captain intends to undertake."

He surprised her again by stepping past her and entering the room unbidden. Before she could react, he walked straight toward Jerdahn, who eyed him warily.

Stopping within arm's reach of the Neyel, Lojur said, "I tried to take your life earlier because Neyel weapons fire took the life of someone I cherished. In my rage, I betrayed everything I grew up believing. I beg your forgiveness."

Jerdahn seemed surprised as well, but quickly recovered. "We were adversaries. You tried to kill me. Such is the way of the universe."

"Sometimes, yes," Lojur said. "But it shouldn't be." He suddenly seemed on the verge of tears.

Burgess felt her impatience beginning to boil over. "All right, Lieutenant, I hope you feel better now. But Jerdahn and I currently have more important things to do than help you redeem your honor. Now, if you'll excuse us—"

The Halkan surprised her yet again by turning toward her and interrupting. "We're about to be destroyed by an overwhelming force. So are the Neyel. I can't imagine what could be more important than *that*."

"Get *out*, Commander." Burgess pointed toward the still-open door.

But Lojur stood his ground. "Too many have already died. The two of you may be the only ones who can help me prevent still more unnecessary death."

Burgess's eyebrows rose involuntarily. After considering his words silently for a moment, she turned and placed her hand back onto the security keypad for a moment. The door hissed closed.

"He may prove useful," Jerdahn said. "Don't forget, Ambassador, that certain 'operational details' still remain to be worked out before we can proceed."

Burgess had to admit that Jerdahn was right. She and the Neyel officer could do little without the assistance of at least one member of *Excelsior*'s crew. Yet she remained uneasy about taking any Starfleet personnel into her confidence, given what she and Jerdahn were considering.

But she also knew she was all out of other options. It truly was time to cross the Rubicon. A plan, possibly an incredibly stupid plan, began coming together in her mind. *You always told yourself you wanted to do something bigger and nobler than simply fine-tuning agreements made by other people,* she thought. *It looks like it's finally time to put up or shut up.*

Burgess approached Lojur, stopping only centimeters away and never breaking eye contact with him. "Please have a seat, Commander. Tell me what's on your mind."

As the shimmering light of the transporter beam released him, Sulu took in his new surroundings. The decks and bulkheads were smooth and dark, as though cut from volcanic glass. Even in the relatively dim light, the atmosphere in the high-ceilinged chamber shimmered slightly because of its extreme heat and pressure. The environmental suit's thermal exchangers could handle 200° Celsius easily enough. But he could feel the dense atmosphere pressing down against his chest and shoulders. Fortunately, the newly modified internal servomotors in the suit's joints greatly ameliorated the overall effect.

Still, he felt a sensation uncomfortably like wading through gelatin as he took a few experimental steps. This was going to take some getting used to.

Several scantily attired Tholians were waiting to greet him on the broad chamber's opposite side. None appeared to be Yilskene, but it was difficult to differentiate between them, especially with the dense atmosphere that obscured each individual's distinctive coloration pattern. Without the encumbrance of pressure suits, these Tholians seemed a good deal more graceful than had their diplomatic-caste counterparts during the initial meetings between Kasrene and Burgess.

That wasn't an encouraging sign, with a monoblade duel coming up.

"Greetings, Captain," one of the Tholians said, its tail switching back and forth. It crossed its multijointed forelimbs in front of its chest, crossing them just below the claws. "I am Taskene. I am to be your *weaponskeeper*—your assistant and fair witness to your death during the *truthcombat*."

"Thank you, I suppose," Sulu said. He bowed slightly, glad that his modified environmental suit gave him greater flexibility than did the standard models.

As he straightened, he noticed a dull ache in his left shoulder, the one that the Losira-simulacrum's lethal fingers had brushed thirty years earlier. It might have been an artifact of his growing fatigue. Or perhaps his body was trying to remind him that it had been a very long time since he'd swept the Inner Planets championship fencing tournament.

Taskene gestured toward the wide door located at the far side of the chamber. "Through here, please. It is time for me to make you ready for *truthcombat*."

As they moved down a black glass-lined corridor, Sulu took in more of the ship. He assumed that the polyhedral outcroppings beside which many Tholians perched were computer system interfaces. The strange, corrugated metal designs placed at irregular intervals along the corridor walls might have been anything from security cameras to art objects for all Sulu could tell.

Finally, Taskene gestured toward another door set into the winding corridor, and Sulu entered. Sitting on a crystalline pedestal was a meter-wide hexagon that Sulu assumed to be his shield. Beside it lay a monoblade. From the faint glow the superheated atmosphere imparted to the whisker-thin blade, Sulu could see that it was at least as long as the shield was wide.

"I will advise you in the use of this weapon, and on the rules of the duel," Taskene said, lifting the haft of the blade. "You may be interested in the surrender-forfeit option. It may not save your life, but it might spare you from experiencing *this.*"

The Tholian then threw a stonelike object into the air, neatly cleaving it in two with the weapon.

In spite of the room's intense heat, Sulu felt a chill course down his spine.

Chapter 29

Chekov regarded the empty captain's chair for a protracted moment before taking a seat. *I sincerely hope Hikaru doesn't force me to keep this permanently,* he thought. *If he does, I'll never forgive him.*

"We're being hailed, Commander," said Janice Rand, who was seated at the communications console. "It's the captain of the Neyel vessel."

"Put him on the screen," Chekov said. A moment later, Drech'tor Joh'jym's face appeared on the main viewer, his hard brow scored by a look of worry.

"Commander, Jerdahn has informed me that your captain has gone among the Devils."

Chekov wondered how Jerdahn had learned about the *truthcombat.* On the other hand, the fact that the captain was off the ship at the moment wasn't exactly classified information among *Excelsior*'s crew.

"That's right, Drech'tor."

"Why aren't you aiding him? We can't simply leave him at their mercy."

"I'm afraid we have no choice. I have direct orders from Captain Sulu not to intervene." *At least, not before intervention becomes absolutely necessary,* he thought. "Please don't complicate things by getting involved in this."

After a pause, Joh'jym said, *"I am hardly less involved than you, Pavelchekov. But I will respect your captain's wishes. For now."*

"We're making preparations to withdraw, should the need arise," Chekov told the Neyel commander. "If we give the word, we want you to head straight back into the rift, to warn your people."

"My people are already well aware of the threat the Devils pose," Joh'jym said. *"I do not relish the idea of running from them a second time. Once was enough. Twice is cowardice."*

"Captain Sulu is convinced that he'll succeed," Chekov said. "But if you are ever to see Old Earth, it will either be because Sulu won the *truthcombat,* or because he has failed and we have escaped from the Tholians to fight another day."

Joh'jym nodded, though his expression showed that he still needed more convincing. *"Very well. In whatever fashion you intend to move, inform us when you are ready."*

After Joh'jym signed off, Chekov turned his chair back toward Rand, who was paying close attention to her console.

"What's the status of the transponder in Captain Sulu's environmental suit, Janice?"

She grinned. "Coming in loud and clear, Commander. According to his suit's biomonitors, he's fine so far."

"His heart rate is slightly elevated," Tuvok reported from the science station. "And he began consuming considerably more oxygen than normal forty-seven seconds ago. I believe this would signify that he has begun the *truthcombat* duel in earnest."

Chekov felt some measure of relief to hear that Sulu had already apparently survived nearly a minute of close-quarter combat against a monoblade-wielding Tholian. But his relief was tempered by an equal portion of apprehension. The captain was still in grave danger.

Pressing a button on the arm of his chair, Chekov said, "Transporter Room One, do you still have a lock on him?"

"Aye, sir," Ensign Prager reported over the comm. *"Standing by and ready to energize at your signal."*

"Very good. Keep monitoring the transponder transmissions and let me know about any changes."

Chekov was grimly aware, of course, that any sudden change in Sulu's bioreadings would very likely mean that the captain was either dead or had sustained a monoblade injury so serious that not even Dr. Chapel could mend it.

Let's hope I don't have to yank him out of there prematurely, Chekov thought. *Yilskene's bound to react badly to that.*

While each combatant's *weaponskeeper* looked on from his respective end of the oblong chamber, Yilskene advanced. He moved on four of his legs, his tail switching hypnotically from side to side over his head. Mirroring Sulu, he grasped a monoblade in one claw, and an energy shield in the other. While their shields were easily visible, the blades themselves betrayed their lethal presence only with a faint, heat-induced glow that grew elusive with motion.

Sulu waited for his opponent to strike the first blow, testing his balance. He was pleased to note that the artificial gravity seemed indistinguishable from that aboard *Excelsior*; it was the hazy, oppressive atmosphere that was affecting his moves.

Yilskene thrust forward with his blade, and Sulu barely managed to sidestep it, forcing the more massive but slower-moving Tholian to lumber awkwardly past him. But Yilskene recovered quickly, sweeping the weapon back around in a semicircle. When Sulu moved to parry with his own blade, Yilskene pulled back slightly, causing Sulu's weapon to slice vainly through the thick but empty air.

The Tholian thrust forward then, and Sulu brought his shield up in time to avoid a blow that would have cleaved his shoulder from the rest of his body. Yilskene's blade sizzled for a split-second as it made contact with the shield's energies. Then the Tholian retreated two steps, apparently looking for another opening.

Sulu pressed forward, feinting to the left as Yilskene answered, circling his blade around clockwise, then switching to a counterclockwise motion. As Yilskene moved, Sulu lunged forward as quickly as the atmosphere and his suit would allow, aiming the point of his blade above Yilskene's shield and stabbing the tip deeply into one of the admiral's forelegs.

The Tholian admiral let out a roar of pain and rage, and as Sulu withdrew his blade, brilliant turquoise fluid pulsed out from the wound. Sulu hoped he hadn't done any mortal damage.

He stepped back, catching his breath as Yilskene paused to bind his wound. "Admiral, I am willing to end the *truth-combat* now, and spare any further harm to either of us."

"I choose not to allow you to yield, Captain," Yilskene said, evidently misunderstanding Sulu's request. A millisecond later, he charged forward with his blade, releasing a ferocious sound that brought to mind erupting volcanoes.

Sulu moved to block the blow, but Yilskene reared up on his hindmost legs, and was suddenly taller than Sulu by at least a meter. The trajectory of the Tholian's weapon changed, and Sulu barely managed to raise his shield in time to absorb the lethal blow. The shield emitted a refulgent crackle of energy that made Sulu's left forearm go momentarily numb.

Yilskene rained three more quick chopping blows down onto the shield, each one releasing still more energy as it connected. Sulu could feel progressively more force behind each successive blow. He ducked to the side and stumbled, half-rolling out of harm's way. Trying to keep his balance, Sulu stabbed forward, missing one of Yilskene's rocky flanks by a hair's breadth.

I'm using up my shield's power too quickly, Sulu thought. *Maybe if I can find a way to separate him from* his *shield, I can gain an advantage. Convince him to yield.*

Sulu struggled to remain standing in the bulky environmental suit, even as Yilskene approached him again.

Yilskene slashed to the side, but as Sulu attempted to parry, the Tholian swept the blade up in an arc. Sulu parried again, and their weapons clashed this time. Yilskene attempted to disengage, but Sulu followed his blade around, pressing forward and forcing the Tholian to retreat toward the far wall.

Finally, to escape Sulu's blade, Yilskene batted it away using his shield.

Then, as Sulu tried to recover his balance, Yilskene stabbed forward, nearly skewering Sulu straight through the chest. Sulu arched his back, twisting his body as far away from the blade as he possibly could, then pushed Yilskene's blade aside with the lowermost part of his own, where he could put the most brute force behind the stroke.

The blow actually knocked the blade from Yilskene's grasp, and it skittered away across the obsidianlike floor. Sulu hoped the room didn't contain any external bulkheads; a stray monoblade slash could conceivably breach the hull.

Sulu was about to offer Yilskene another chance to withdraw, when he felt himself beginning to gag. A noxious, sulfurous odor suddenly permeated his suit.

He looked down to see if he could tell where the tear might have occurred, and saw a neatly sliced opening in the suit's chest-covering. Sulu's eyes began to water and his stomach heaved as he looked back up.

Yilskene was recovering his blade.

Aidan Burgess was proud to think of herself as one possessed of a great many skills. She also knew that piloting a Starfleet shuttlecraft was not among them. But thanks to the access codes, transporter and environmental preprogramming, and helm automation routines she'd just downloaded, she and Jerdahn had managed to finish their uncomfortably hasty preparations in just under twenty minutes. According to Janice Rand, whom Burgess contacted over a secure, Diplomatic Corps-issue communicator, Captain Sulu had just beamed over to the Tholian flagship a few minutes earlier.

It's time, Burgess thought as she sat in the darkened cockpit. She double-checked the settings on the faintly glowing helm, then entered the "initiate." command. A comforting chorus of bleeps and chirps came in response.

"Hangar doors opening," Jerdahn said, unnecessarily, from the chair to her right. She could see the doors for herself through the cockpit windows.

Seated on the left side of the small, deliberately darkened command center of the *Shuttlecraft Genji,* Burgess checked the automated departure procedure yet again. All the indicators remained green, and there was no sign as yet that her unauthorized launch of an auxiliary craft had been discovered. The observation deck that overlooked the main shuttlebay still appeared to be empty of personnel.

Burgess felt the craft shudder slightly as its antigravs lifted it above the deck. The motion immediately smoothed as the *Genji* moved forward, cleared the open hangar doors, and was enfolded in the infinite blackness of space.

But this region of space was far from empty. Though she could see only a handful of running lights near the orange crescent of the Tholian colony world, Burgess knew that she was surrounded by dozens of heavily armed Tholian ships.

As annoyingly phlegmatic as ever, Jerdahn said, "We're away."

And flying straight into the crosshairs of both the Tholians and the Neyel, Burgess thought, her hands unconsciously worrying the charm bracelet she'd kept with her since childhood. "Let's hope the computer can carry out its instructions before some alert weapons officer blows us out of the sky," she said.

She saw Jerdahn's answering shrug in the glow of the instrument panels. "Our lights are off. This vessel is small, space is large, and the planet's shadow conceals us. We will succeed."

Burgess knew that the *Genji* wasn't exactly small, at least for a shuttlecraft. Intended, ironically enough, for special diplomatic missions, the craft was wider and roomier than most shuttles she'd ridden in previously, no doubt to make room for the small transporter unit it carried, as well as for its multienvironment life-support equipment. This latter feature was evidently intended to allow sentients with radically different environmental requirements to travel together in close quarters on diplomatically sensitive missions.

And that's exactly how I intend to use it, she thought. *Sort of.*

Although the onboard inertial dampers suppressed all sensation of velocity, Burgess could see from the tactical displays that the *Genji* was moving swiftly toward the Neyel vessel, which was keeping station only a dozen or so klicks off of *Excelsior*'s stern.

Burgess rose, drew a phaser from the storage locker, and checked it to make certain it was locked on the heaviest stun setting possible. Then she handed it to Jerdahn.

"When your boss materializes here, he's going to be pretty unhappy with both of us," she said.

Bathed in the faint light given off by the transporter's targeting scanners, Jerdahn turned the weapon over and over in his large hands, studying it cautiously, as though it were a poisonous snake. She'd remembered then that he'd been on the wrong end of just such a weapon fairly recently.

"I will be prepared," he said simply, lowering the weapon to his side.

A short time later, and with some assistance from Jerdahn, Burgess locked onto the Neyel vessel's commander. A few seconds later, Drech'tor Joh'jym's tall, powerful form began shimmering into existence on one of the two transporter pads located in the shuttle's aft section.

Joh'jym touched his chest to make sure he was still in

one piece, then cast his startled eyes about the shuttlecraft's interior. Finally, his keen gaze lit upon Jerdahn and Burgess, whom he recognized immediately despite the darkness.

"Why have you brought me here?"

Burgess rose, smiling. "I wish to invite you to a . . . diplomatic meeting. I regret that I've been forced to use such extraordinary means."

The drech'tor's voice was a low growl. "You're trying to force me to parley with the Devils. Haven't you listened to anything I have said about them?" Then she saw a flash of movement in the near-total darkness as he lunged toward her.

Before Burgess could react, Jerdahn fired the phaser. He ended up having to repeat the procedure three times before his superior finally slumped insensate to the deck. Then, with surprising gentleness, Jerdahn carried the unconscious Joh'jym to a starboard-side seat and fastened him there with restraints he jury-rigged by taking apart one of the safety harnesses.

While Jerdahn secured Joh'jym, Burgess activated the next set of preentered commands. The *Gengi* responded by passing the Neyel vessel and tracing a long ellipse back toward the *Jeb'v Tholis.* According to the readouts, the shuttle was approaching the Tholian flagship at high impulse speed, while running a gauntlet that consisted of at least three dozen other armed Tholian vessels.

How much longer will our small size and lack of running lights protect us? she wondered uneasily, now that the *Genji* had flown clear of the planet's shadow.

Burgess was momentarily startled by the crackle of a forcefield behind her. Aware that she couldn't see it in the darkness, she didn't bother turning to look at it. Instead, she glanced at a glowing console before her and quickly confirmed that the entire aft portion of the cabin—the section that lay beyond the forcefield—was now hermetically sealed off from the forward section, as per her plan.

"Pressure and temperature are rising in the aft section,"

she told Jerdahn. "My board shows an N-class atmosphere forming behind the barrier."

Jerdahn grunted. "I will not raise an objection if our next 'guests' are made comfortable."

So Jerdahn had a sense of humor after all. Perhaps a human heart truly *did* beat beneath that gray, sequoialike exterior. She grinned in the darkness, which was gradually being suffused by a gentle, oven-like light coming from the superheated atmosphere trapped behind the force-field.

Perhaps two minutes later, the wedge-shaped Tholian flagship loomed before them, looking as large as a mountain. Just as it seemed that a crash was inevitable, either Jerdahn or the navigational computer—Burgess wasn't sure which—veered off from a direct collision. A bright pyrotechnic shower became visible through the forward windows as the shuttle's shields intersected with those of the *Jeb'v Tholis.*

An amber light flashing on her console told her that it was time to activate the transporter scanners. *They've* got *to know we're here* now, Burgess thought as she searched the Tholian vessel for her two Tholian targets. Ambassador Mosrene's profile was already stored in the transporter computer's active memory, so the system established a stable lock on him almost immediately. The display indicated that Mosrene and his diplomatic retinue were still aboard Yilskene's flagship, apparently ensconced in VIP quarters well away from the warrior-caste Tholians who comprised the bulk of the crew of the *Jeb'v Tholis.*

Unfortunately, Admiral Yilskene was proving somewhat more difficult to track down. Since he had never beamed aboard *Excelsior,* Burgess hadn't been able to upload a copy of his sensor profile to the *Genji*'s computer. But she knew that all she had to do was scan for Captain Sulu. By now, the captain should be in the midst of his ill-advised duel against the Tholian admiral. And unless Sulu was already dead, whichever Tholian life-sign registered as closest in proximity to him had to be Yilskene's.

There! Recognizing Sulu's distinctive human signature—he was the only human aboard the *Jeb'v Tholis,* after all—Burgess quickly established a lock on the Tholian signature nearest to him and entered the "energize" command for both Yilskene and Mosrene.

Then Burgess turned toward the figures that were taking shape within the forcefield barrier. She felt ready to face the greatest challenge of her diplomatic career.

Then, seeing by the dull glow of the confined Tholian atmosphere, she counted the figures who now stood disoriented behind the energy barrier.

There were three.

"Oh, crap," she whispered.

Chapter 30

Sulu's lungs felt as though they were on fire from the noxious gases, and the heat leaking into his suit was burning his skin as well. As Yilskene charged, Sulu parried the blow, ducked, and sidestepped. The momentum of his charge carried the scorpionlike Tholian warrior past Sulu and to the other side of the room, but not before Sulu's blade tagged the Tholian's shield again.

Setting his blade down so as not to slice himself with it, Sulu quickly pulled an adhesive emergency patch from the forearm pocket of his environmental suit. Applying it to the tear across his chest, he could feel immediately that the leak had been plugged.

But before he could purge the suit, Yilskene was back on the attack, lunging with his monoblade raised high. Sulu scrambled to recover his own blade, and just barely saved himself with a parry-sixte-and-disengage that would have done the Starfleet Academy fencing team proud.

Sulu feinted, lunged, and smacked Yilskene's shield, almost disarming him a second time. While Yilskene recovered, Sulu hit the purge button on the suit's belt, and was immediately rewarded with an invigorating blast of cool air. He still felt sick to his stomach, but at least he was no longer in immediate danger of toxic poisoning.

Sulu repeatedly advanced, feinted, advanced, retreated. Yilskene matched most of his movements with surprising grace, though the admiral's heavy crystalline body couldn't quite keep up with Sulu's speed.

Yilskene lunged again, and Sulu parried, then leapt to the side and riposted. Yilskene barely caught the blow with his shield. *Our energy shields have each taken about the same amount of punishment,* Sulu thought, wondering whose shield would fail first.

He hoped he could persuade the Tholian to at least call it a draw before both shields were exhausted, leaving "kill-or-be-killed" combat as the only other option.

Tuvok noticed an alarming change in the readings. "Commander, Captain Sulu's suit has been breached."

Chekov visibly blanched, and his finger hovered over the communicator on the chair arm. It was an unnecessary action, Tuvok knew, because the comm channel to the transporter room was already locked open.

"Is *he* hurt or is it just the suit?" Chekov asked.

"Biomonitors still show strong life signs, sir," Tuvok replied. "But he could easily have sustained a life-threatening injury already."

Chekov's leg bounced quickly. Tuvok had seen the commander exhibit this particular nervous tic before during times of high stress. Clearly, this was such a time.

The voice of Ensign Prager came over the comm. *"Should I beam him back now, sir?"*

The readings on Tuvok's monitors suddenly changed again. "Sir, the suit has been stabilized."

The commander let out an audible sigh. "Good. That means he really is alive and kicking." To the comm, he added, "Stand by, Ensign."

All at once, it seemed to Tuvok that again, the captain was about to triumph in spite of having gone about his mission in a highly unorthodox, utterly illogical manner. While he was gratified that the captain was evidently doing as well as he was in an extraordinarily unfavorable situation, Tuvok simultaneously found himself experiencing an uncomfortable sensation akin to frustration. He wondered why the captain bothered to consult him when he routinely refused to avail himself of his advice.

I simply have a fundamentally different approach to problem-solving than do most of the humans in Starfleet, he realized with the clarity of an epiphany. *Mother and Father were wrong after all. I do not belong in Starfleet.*

The moment was manifest. He had not experienced such hyperlucidity since the *tal'oth* ritual he had undertaken at the age of ten.

I do not belong here.

It was not an emotional thought born of fear or nerves or pride. Nor was it some residual shadow of the memories the Tholian ambassador had passed to him. Somehow, he knew that he responding to the cold, clear voice of logic itself.

I do not belong here.

Sulu lunged again. Then, as Yilskene attempted to parry, Sulu brought his blade around in a semicircle, redoubling his attack. His blade grazed Yilskene's body, chipping off a swatch of crystalline hide. A viscous, turquoise liquid seeped from the wound.

Sulu was winded now, but even as his body became more tired and his muscles fairly screamed for rest, he felt a state of calm enveloping him. The blade had become almost an extension of himself, its movements as natural as those of his arms and legs.

Yilskene had landed several more blows on Sulu's shield, but Sulu had matched his opponent strike for strike. The Tholian's shield had to run out of energy soon.

Still, Sulu remained wary. In fencing tournaments, he

had sometimes allowed pride to lull him into a false sense of security, and that had been his downfall. More than once he had been defeated by overcommitting to his attack, or by allowing his opponent's retreat to force him into chase and overextension, leaving him off-balance and vulnerable.

Here he could afford to make no such mistakes. Luckily, even as he became cooler and more controlled in his attacks, Yilskene seemed to become steadily more frenetic, even vicious.

Another thrust from Yilskene. Sulu parried and riposted. The admiral counterparried, then lunged again. Sulu again ignored the fact that a giant crystalline scorpion was angrily charging him, and met the blade with his own. Sparks skittered across the whisker-thin blades as they struck each other. Sulu used Yilskene's momentum to trap the Tholian's blade, forcing Yilskene to disengage.

Sulu pressed forward, and Yilskene brought his shield to bear yet again. Sulu slashed at it, prompting Yilskene to retreat shouting a Tholian curse.

Sulu advanced and feinted, then feinted a second time. As Yilskene attempted to block the initial false thrust, Sulu swung his blade around, knocking the Tholian's weapon from his grasp.

For a moment, neither of them moved. Yilskene's blade skittered onto the floor near him, slicing a long trench in the hard black floor before it came to rest. The Tholian stooped in an effort to regain his weapon.

"Admiral Yilskene, it appears that I have disarmed you," Sulu said, watching Yilskene stop in his tracks. "Though it is my right in this ritual to kill you, I choose *not* to exercise that right. It does not serve my needs to do so, nor does it serve the good of either the Tholian Assembly or the United Federation—"

As Sulu spoke, a familiar shimmering light began to envelop Yilskene.

Dropping his weapon, Sulu leapt toward the admiral, even as his foe began to dematerialize.

"Where have they gone?" Taskene asked, running to the room's empty center.

Crellene, Yilskene's *weaponskeeper* looked back at Taskene, her eyespots glowing a distressed purplish hue. "They've been *taken!*"

Taskene passed a claw over the crystal outcropping on a nearby bulkhead. She knew that sounding an alarm was likely unnecessary—the *truthcombat* had been broadcast, via the Lattice, to every ship in the fleet—but she knew that it was her duty to sound an alarm just the same.

A moment later her consciousness entered the SubLink of the Lattice. It was a cacophony of bright noise, with many minds conversing at once.

The consensus was rage at the perfidious Federation starship, whose transporter beam was the only possible culprit. In its reflexive, collective anger, the Lattice very nearly directed a devastating attack on *Excelsior.*

But Taskene and many others realized that such an attack would have killed Admiral Yilskene.

The Lattice's consensus quickly shifted from rage colors to hues of patient, vigilant waiting.

But Taskene knew that the colors could easily shift again should the waiting last too long.

Yilskene's memories will survive within the Lattice, should the admiral die aboard Excelsior, rang the rapidly darkening thoughts of Benrene [The Gray]. Taskene saw/heard other voices, members of various castes, flashing colors of agreement.

Suddenly, an alien gleam entered into the SubLink unbidden, and another bedlam of bright sounds and stentorian light assaulted the Lattice. When it receded, the SubLink's contact with Mosrene's mind had become strangely muted and misdirected, just as had occurred with Admiral Yilskene moments earlier.

Reacting to this new violation, the Lattice's colors shifted yet again toward passion and wrath.

Chekov saw Akaar looking up from his monitors. Alarm not only showed on the Capellan's face, but was clearly audible in his voice as well. "Captain Sulu and Admiral Yilskene have just been beamed off of Yilskene's flagship!"

Chekov swiveled in his chair. "By *whom?*" He directed his voice to the comm. "Transporter Room, have you beamed back the captain?"

"*No, sir.*" Ensign Prager sounded surprised.

His mind racing, Chekov turned back toward his science officer. "Where did that transporter beam originate, Mr. Tuvok?"

The Vulcan tapped his fingers nimbly over his console, his eyebrows knotted in deep concentration. "I am still attempting to determine that, sir. Scans show that the beam did not come from any of the Tholian vessels."

"What about *Oghen's Flame?*" Chekov asked.

"Negative," Tuvok said. "The Neyel vessel possesses no such technology. And the pattern of the beam is consistent with those of Starfleet transporters."

"Contact Yilskene's ship," Chekov said to Rand.

Rand turned, a hand on her earpiece. "They're hailing *us*, sir."

"On screen."

The image on the main viewer shifted again, displaying a Tholian whom Chekov didn't recognize. "*Your actions have violated the* truthcombat," the creature said. "*You will be destroyed.*"

Before Chekov could respond, the screen went blank.

"Shields to maximum! Red Alert!" Chekov said. "Hail the Neyel ship."

The angry image of Oratok, Joh'jym's visor, appeared on

the viewer. *"Commander Chekov, where has Drech'tor Joh'jym been taken?"*

Chekov barely had time to register surprise when Tuvok spoke up again. "Commander, I have located the source of the transporter signal. It is coming from one of our own shuttlecraft. And I am detecting the captain's transponder there as well."

Great, Chekov thought, putting aside his initial shock that somebody could take a shuttlecraft without being noticed. *And with the shields raised I can't just beam everyone off the shuttle.*

"The shuttlecraft is refusing my hails," Rand said.

"Several of the nearest Tholian ships are powering up their weapons," Akaar reported. "As is *Oghen's Flame.*"

Chekov's mind whirled. "Get me whoever's in charge of *Jeb'v Tholis* and *Oghen's Flame,*" he shouted to Rand, preparing to talk faster than he ever had before.

Chapter 31

Somewhat disoriented, Sulu rose from where he'd fallen when the transporter beam released him. Except for the faint glow coming from the superheated air around him, he was in darkness. Standing in his damaged, hurriedly patched environmental suit, he tried to get his bearings.

Then he noticed that the light levels all around him were quickly rising, and within moments had reached full illumination.

Beside him stood Admiral Yilskene and Ambassador Mosrene. Despite their expressionless faces, Sulu gathered that they were both at least as confused as he was.

Then he heard the voice of Ambassador Burgess. "It's good to have the lights turned up again. There doesn't seem to be much point in stealth anymore. Everyone knows what we've done by now. We're committed."

Sulu turned and saw that Ambassador Burgess and Jerdahn were both watching him from the cockpit of one of *Excelsior*'s shuttlecraft. A flashing light on a forward companel, indicating an incoming hail, was being ignored. Jerdahn was holding a Starfleet-issue phaser. And a semiconscious Neyel military officer—Sulu recognized him immediately as Drech'tor Joh'jym—was strapped to a chair near the boundary of a forcefield, which Sulu surmised must be maintaining a separate atmosphere suitable for the Tholians.

What the hell is going on here?

Sulu was relieved to learn that the Tholian military caste apparently wasn't as keen on assassinating higher-up as were their diplomats. So far, the Tholian ships visible through the forward windows hadn't opened fire on the shuttle. However, several of them displayed dully glowing weapons tubes, apparently making ready to vent some wrath. *They must be taking aim at* Excelsior, he thought, chilled.

Sulu's gaze fell back upon Burgess, and his anger swiftly rose to a flash point. *She's finally crossed the line. Now I'm party to three kidnappings. And worse, she may have just touched off a three-way interstellar war.* It would matter little to Starfleet Command and the Federation Council that she had acted both behind his back and without his knowledge. As commander of *Excelsior*, he was responsible for the actions of everyone aboard his ship.

With an extreme effort of will, he reined in his anger, keeping his deep voice as level as he could manage. "You've got some serious explaining to do here, Ambassador."

"Isn't my purpose obvious, Captain?" she said. "I'm trying to broker a peace between parties who've so far proved reluctant to talk."

"By *abducting* them? Listen to me, Aidan. You're about to throw your whole career away."

Her eyes narrowed. "This isn't about my career. Or yours. It's about a war between the Tholians and our own distant relatives. That war will inevitably drag Earth into it as well. Unless we act now to prevent it. We *have* to get a dialog going between influential parties on both sides. By whatever means are at hand."

"This certainly isn't the way, Ambassador."

"And a *swordfight* was?"

"The *truthcombat* would have settled everything without

bloodshed. You may have just tossed that out the airlock. Congratulations, Ambassador."

Coming from behind him, Yilskene's deep, multilayered voice interrupted Burgess's reply. "This display is a farce."

Sulu turned to face the admiral. Ambassador Mosrene, who stood beside him, seemed content simply to watch and listen.

Yilskene continued speaking before Sulu could respond. "Though you would pretend otherwise, Captain, your deceit is apparent. First, you ally yourselves with our most deadly enemies,"—he pointed a claw toward Jerdahn and Joh'jym—"all the while denying it. Then you conspire with those same enemies to obtain rescue from a lawful *truthcombat*."

Sulu decided he had finally reached his threshold for sanctimony. "What exactly does combat have to do with truth?" He was acutely aware of how easily Yilskene could kill him simply by ripping the patch from the front of his damaged suit. Though he could have backed away another meter toward the atmospheric forcefield, he stood his ground.

"Whatever deceptions you have attempted, human," the Tholian admiral said at length, "I grant that you have courage."

Sulu met Yilskene's gaze unflinchingly. "I'll admit that I wasn't completely candid with you in the beginning. I *did* order *Excelsior* deep into your territory without your government's authorization. But it was only to discover whether or not your Neyel adversaries might pose a threat to *us*. And I neither ordered nor approved your abduction."

Mosrene turned toward Yilskene, looking like a stone gargoyle that had suddenly come to life. "I believe the human is being truthful. Ambassador Burgess has exceeded her authority before."

"The captain *is* telling you the truth," Burgess interrupted. "And to demonstrate *my* good faith, I will agree to return you both to your flagship—on two conditions."

At that moment, some of the Tholian vessels that had

charged their tubes loosed their volleys of directed energy, split seconds apart.

"*Excelsior* has sustained a number of hits," Jerdahn said calmly, looking down at a tactical display on the console before him. "But I perceive no serious damage."

Her shields are holding, Sulu thought, his fists clenching involuntarily. *For now.*

He glared at Burgess. "You have no right to strike bargains that affect the safety of my ship, Ambassador. I want you to let them go *now.* Along with the Neyel commander. As a show of *my* good faith." Sulu reasoned that Yilskene didn't really want to kill him, or his crew. After all, the admiral had just walked away from an easy opportunity to simply rip open his environmental suit.

"I don't answer to you, Captain," Burgess said, her green eyes blazing. "And I'm holding all the cards right now."

Sulu glared silently at her, forced to admit that she was right, at least for the moment. There was nothing he could do except wait for an opportunity to gain control of the situation. And hope that she didn't bury them all in the meantime.

"Name your terms," Mosrene said.

"One," Burgess said, holding a finger aloft. "You both must agree to allow me to mediate a provisional truce between your forces and those of the Neyel commander, Drech'tor Joh'jym. And two, Admiral Yilskene must allow *Excelsior* and the Neyel vessel safe passage back to their respective territories."

"You ask much, human," Mosrene said.

"I ask you to consider a way to avoid an unnecessary war. You may destroy *Excelsior* and the Neyel vessel today. And they will be but the first small stones that will start the rockslide of war tomorrow. And that, I fear, will crush us all."

Several long, tense seconds passed while the Tholians turned toward each other, evidently conferring via the wordless ether of the Lattice. Sulu wondered if Yilskene was also simultaneously relaying orders to his crew in the same manner.

Finally, Yilskene turned to face Burgess, his rock-hard features unfathomable. But the universal translator picked up the anger in his voice. "Regarding your first demand: I presently have no alternative other than to listen to your words. My response to your second demand will be contingent upon their persuasiveness."

And with that, the admiral sat on the deck, suddenly becoming as motionless as a garden gnome. The Tholian ambassador followed suit.

Well, Scheherazade, Sulu thought. *We'll get to continue breathing for about as long as the sultan likes the tale you're about to tell.*

Turning to face Burgess again, he said, "Looks like it's your play, Ambassador. You'd better make it good."

Sulu heard Joh'jym groan, and saw that Jerdahn was rousing him with repeated percussive slaps to the face. Still tied to his chair, the Neyel commander lolled his head and blinked in the bright cabin lights as consciousness returned more fully.

"Jerdahn? What is this?" he said, looking around the shuttle. His speech was slurred, no doubt a residual effect of the phaser Jerdahn still held in his hand.

"Drech'tor," Jerdahn said to his superior. His tone was respectful, though Sulu noticed that he hadn't lowered his phaser. "I have helped to arrange a parley with our adversaries. I regret that circumstances prevented speaking to you about it in advance."

Joh'jym tugged at the tough crash harness that had been wound around his body to secure him to the chair. "So you say, Subaltern. But your abducting and confining me inspires little confidence." The commander of *Oghen's Flame* nodded toward the forcefield barrier, beyond which the two inert Tholians were clearly visible to him. "And how can one converse with Devils who lack even the rudiments of language?"

Apparently, Yilskene was not nearly so inert as he appeared. "We have often asked the same question about *your* species, biped. How is it possible for you to suddenly acquire the ability to produce intelligible speech?"

Burgess stretched her hands toward Neyel and Tholian alike. "We possess instantaneous translation technology. Neyel culture has nothing like it, and the Tholian equivalent evidently isn't yet quite as developed as ours. It is my hope that our translator will provide the basis for creating a new understanding between your peoples and ours."

Sulu began to feel an ember of hope burning within him. Perhaps there was indeed some method to Burgess's madness after all. "Perhaps we should start by clearing up the most urgent of the misunderstandings that divide you."

"Say on," Yilskene said.

"I refer to the weapons which your adversaries claim you have deployed against them, from your colony world."

Yilskene's multilayered voice grew sharply discordant. "Weapons? The settlement contains only peaceful members of various lesser castes, mainly builders and engineers. As well as equipment designed to seal the interspatial rupture through which the aggressors attack us. Because this task is large, and the colony has run this equipment continuously over a period of many years. We no longer send ships to the OtherVoid."

Burgess seemed to mull these facts over for a long moment before addressing the two Neyel. "I ask that you both consider the possibility that the damage the Tholians' equipment has caused to Neyel worlds on the other side of the rift may be entirely unintentional."

Joh'jym did not yet appear convinced. "You wish us to believe that the technology that has ravaged our worlds was intended only to close the rift? How could all of the war and suffering we Neyel have endured since our first encounters with these Devils have been a mere *accident?*"

Burgess now seemed to be in her element. Choosing her words carefully, she said, "Centuries ago, my home planet was plunged into a global war because of the assassination of a single man. A crime, a mistake, if you will, that was allowed to engulf an entire world. War can be the ultimate mistake, the last in a long, dreary series of errors."

Sulu thought he saw a subtle change in Joh'jym's gray eyes. "If mistake it is, it is a mistake to which two civilizations have already committed themselves."

"And both of those civilizations may cease to exist soon unless they both commit themselves to something nobler," Burgess said.

"How?" Mosrene said, his choir of voices sounding infinitely sad. Sulu surmised that, because he was a diplomat, issues such as the expanding Tholian-Neyel conflict must weigh heavily on his soul. "How can we do that, once hide has been sliced and ichor has been drawn?"

"We can start," Burgess said, "by examining and trying to put right all the mutual errors that have led us to the edge of this precipice."

Jerdahn laughed, but without mirth. "There seem to have been many. Where do we begin?"

Burgess looked pained. She didn't seem to have a ready answer. Sulu wondered if she was finally realizing just how enormous a task she had chosen to tackle. After all, even the Organians might have had some trouble sorting this situation out.

Sulu decided to jump in. "Let's start with the way both of your species simply assumed that the other wasn't even sentient. It seems to me this entire conflict was built on the assumption that the other side is an implacable foe that can't be reasoned with. Maybe once the word gets out on both sides that this isn't so, everyone involved will have to reevaluate the idea of war. And put a stop to it."

Silence reigned aboard the shuttlecraft for several minutes while everyone considered what had been said.

Then Mosrene spoke up, his chorus of voices far more pleasing and harmonious than before. "The Tholian Lattice has already been advised of what you and Ambassador Burgess have revealed to us today. Much will doubtless be reevaluated now, among *all* the castes."

"Do you think the Tholian Assembly's government will consider not reactivating the damaged equipment on the colony?" Sulu said. "If you were to cease your recent efforts to close the interspatial rift, the Neyel might regard it as a real sign of good faith."

"I can make no promises today," Mosrene said. "But I believe the Great Castemoot Assembly can be swayed. I will advocate a cessation of all activity in and around OtherVoid as long as invader hostilities cease. But there is much work ahead."

"I will authorize the release of *Excelsior* and the other vessel," Yilskene said. "As a gesture of good faith, the other vessel has my leave to enter OtherVoid to return home. *Excelsior* must get under way on a heading for Federation space in one of your hours."

Smiling, Sulu turned back to Burgess. "Then I think now would be an excellent time for *another* show of good faith, Ambassador. Don't you agree?"

Burgess nodded, evidently aware that if Yilskene and Mosrene had really just made contact with the Tholian Lattice, then continuing to detain them in the shuttle wasn't necessarily going to buy anyone's safety. She entered a series of commands into one of the cockpit consoles, then bid the two Tholians good-bye.

After Yilskene and Mosrene had vanished from sight, Burgess set about pumping out the noxious, Tholian-friendly atmosphere contained behind the forcefield barrier. Sulu glanced at his suit's telltales and saw that it had only minutes of breathable air left, thanks to all the damage it had sustained during the *truthcombat.*

As the atmosphere around him normalized, he glanced toward the two Neyel. Joh'jym, whom Jerdahn had just freed from his bonds, appeared thoughtful. Jerdahn, however, looked downright glum.

Burgess evidently noticed it as well. "What's wrong, Jerdahn?"

Jerdahn handed his phaser to Burgess. "I fear our 'reevaluation' will be a good deal less efficient than that of the Dev—the Tholians. Unlike them, we have no magical 'Lattice' we can consult in order to avert war."

"No, we do not," said Joh'jym, absently rubbing at his rough-skinned wrists. Evidently the tough crash harness material had begun to cut off his circulation. "But we may have something that will work at least as well. I have personally briefed the Gran Drech'tor of the Neyel Hegemony on three occasions since this conflict began. And Jerdahn once served as one of her visors, before he found himself on the wrong side of the issue of Total War against the Devils."

Sulu had wondered about Jerdahn's references to his "old life." The notion that he now held a humble job because he'd run afoul of Neyel Hegemony politics made an appealingly romantic sort of sense.

"I believe that I know the Gran Drech'tor's heart as well as anyone in my position can," said Jerdahn. "She has no true wish to wage Total War, in which one side exterminates the other."

That sounds promising, Sulu thought as he released the catch on his suit's neck ring and removed his helmet. "Will she listen to either of you? Do you think she can be persuaded to end the war?"

Jerdahn raised his hands in a comfortingly human gesture of uncertainty. "Who can say for certain? No one has demonstrated a viable alternative before. But I feel that when she learns that our foes are as sapient as we, much will change."

"Let's hope so," Burgess said.

"But what of those who seek Auld Aerth?" Jerdahn asked his superior. "Many Neyel will still want to pass into this side of the Rift to seek it out. That may spark further conflict."

Sulu was tempted to tell them both flat out that they had both already come into contact with denizens of their ancestral world. That he had seen that beautiful blue planet with his own eyes, that he had been born there. But Burgess had already pointed out that this might cause more harm than good, and might even damage his credibility in their eyes.

Joh'jym placed an iron-gray hand on his subordinate's shoulder. "Aerth exists primarily in our hearts and souls anyway. If the price of our survival is sacrificing the reality to the ideal, then so be it."

Earth is already only a legend to these people, Sulu thought. *Maybe it needs to stay that way. How well would the Neyel really fit in there anyway?*

Sulu felt a surge of shame at this last thought. Despite whatever horrors had shaped an entire branch of his own species into the battle-hardened race the Neyel had become, hadn't they proven today that their hearts were as human as his? Hadn't they transcended their environment and listened to the better angels of their natures? *Maybe I could stand to learn a thing or two from the Neyel.*

Sulu put aside his musings when Joh'jym approached him. "Like those you call the Tholians, we, too have much work to do, Hikarusulu."

Sulu smiled. "Then let's get you back aboard your ship and on your way." Moments later, it was done.

Afterward, Burgess sagged into one of the cockpit seats, evidently exhausted by the momentous events of the past few minutes. Gazing through the forward windows, Sulu could see some of the Tholian warships were pulling back from their attack postures. He didn't expect most of them to depart at once, however; as both Mosrene and Joh'jym had said, much work still needed to be done to forge a peace that both civilizations could live with.

"Congratulations, Ambassador," Sulu said, entering the cockpit and laying a hand on her seat's headrest. "Though I can't condone the way you did it, I have to admit that you may have just saved three worlds from war."

Burgess shook her head wearily. "No, Captain. I merely started a conversation. *You* made the sale to the Tholians, and you did it while you were just as much a prisoner as they were. Whether or not they sue for peace, my usefulness among them is at an end."

"Why do you say that?" Sulu said, his brow furrowing.

She glanced forward, her eyes lighting on the Neyel ship, which was beginning to get under way. Soon it would fly across the frayed edges of interspace and vanish from sight.

"As alien as the Neyel appear to be," Burgess said, "I think they resemble us far more than they do the Tholians. They're *human*, after all, and the Tholians are anything but. The Neyel can understand the human frailty that can drive someone to break the rules for the greater good. The Tholians won't be quite so understanding, even if they sign a peace treaty in the name of that same greater good. What I did today, I did in collaboration with people they considered enemies at the time."

Sulu understood her meaning. "Jerdahn and Joh'jym. You believe that by working with them you crossed the line in the Tholians' eyes. Even though the outcome may well be a Tholian-Neyel peace accord."

"I understand how the Tholians think. You may have been right about my having thrown my career away." She turned in her seat and entered a series of commands into the helm console.

"Maybe not," Sulu said as he sat down in the other cockpit seat. "Maybe the worst of this is finally over. I'll fly us back to *Excelsior*, Ambassador. Why don't you relax and—"

He felt the transporter's confinement beam suddenly surround him, a sensation like ants crawling on his skin.

"No, Captain," she heard Burgess say as the dematerialization process began taking him apart. *"I might not be of any use to the Tholians, but the Neyel* need *me."*

Chapter 32

Through the *Genji*'s forward windows, Burgess watched the Neyel cruiser, *Oghen's Flame*, as it made its way toward the interspatial rift. She wondered if the vessel might have taken its name from the nimbus of blazing light that surrounded its aft section as it moved forward on impulse power. It looked a bit like the fires of reentry she had seen engulfing prewarp spacecraft as they descended ballistically through Earth's atmosphere.

Another quick flash of light made her see spots as the ship went to warp.

Burgess reflected on the last few days, and on what she had accomplished . . . and had *failed* to accomplish. The mission had largely been a mess, and although she knew that most of the blame could be placed at the crystalline feet of the Tholians, a fair portion of the responsibility also lay with her.

Still, many of her decisions had been dictated by the actions of Captain Sulu. Even the decision to use kidnapping as a diplomatic tool.

"This job is certainly not what it once was," she said to herself with a chuckle. A line of verse came to her, from the nineteenth-century writer Isaac Goldberg: *"Diplomacy is to do and say, The nastiest thing in the nicest way."* It seemed a lifetime ago that her second husband, Shinzei, had engraved that snippet onto a piece of marble on Risa, where they'd vacationed after she had completed a particularly grueling assignment.

These days, it seems I've dispensed with the "nicest" part entirely.

As much as she had criticized Sulu for his own unorthodox tactics, she had proved herself at least as eccentric. She knew that what she was about to do would burn her last remaining bridges with the Federation.

The Federation held nothing for her. She realized now that she'd felt that for quite a while, though she'd never been truly honest about it. She wondered how other diplomats dealt with burnout; she wished she'd taken the time to discuss the problem with Sarek, or Curzon Dax, or C'letta Rinz, during one of their past meetings.

This was how she was dealing with her crisis of faith. But she looked on it less as an act of desertion—which is surely how the Federation Council would view it—and more as a *rebirth.* If her plan worked, she could create real, positive change for the Neyel.

Burgess tapped several of the controls, readying the shuttlecraft. The shields were up, preventing anyone from beaming her off the ship, and she would soon be out of the reach of Sulu's and Yilskene's tractor beams. She didn't expect pursuit from either *Excelsior* or the Tholians.

The incessantly blinking light on the companel signaled an incoming message. She decided to cease ignoring it and toggled it on.

"Captain Sulu," she said coolly as the image of *Excelsior*'s bridge came up on a small monitor screen.

"*What are you playing at now, Ambassador?*" Sulu asked.

"I'm not the ambassador anymore," she said. "My name is Aidan."

His eyebrows knotted as if he were perplexed. "*Aidan, you need to return to* Excelsior. *We are preparing to depart.*"

"I can't do that, Captain," she said. "I *won't* do that."

"Then what exactly are *you planning to do?"*

She smiled in spite of herself. "Captain, when I was a little girl, I met two people who spent their lives exploring. Not exploring in the way Starfleet does; they did it in the way that only one or two people can. Small stones creating a ripple in a larger pond.

"They called me a 'fellow traveler.' I don't know whether they knew the connotations of the phrase as it was used in the twentieth century, but I took it to mean they saw me as someone who was worthy of exploring on my own. For too long now, I have been a part of a larger force, an organized governmental unit. I've allowed rules and regulations and protocol to mold me, distort me, control me."

As she continued, she caressed the bracelet on her wrist. Some of the stones and shells had been worn smooth over time. "Captain, there is much work to be done here, and a new human culture to explore. The Neyel are prone to violence, and they will need help to mend their fences with the Tholians.

"And you and I both know that it is only a matter of time before the Neyel come fully into contact with Earth. If they are to learn to coexist peacefully with their human cousins, they will need someone who can help them bridge the gap."

Sulu leaned forward in his chair. *"I'm not so sure that the Tholians will let you go."*

"Maybe, and maybe not. But I think the real question is this: will *you* let me go?" She touched another few buttons on the control panel, hoping that the automated programs she'd downloaded would make up for her lack of real piloting skills.

"You won't be able to negotiate the rift," Sulu said. *"You'll be trapped inside it, like the* Defiant."

"I don't think so," she said, smiling again. "I can just follow the warp signature of the *Oghen's Flame* like a trail of bread crumbs. That should see me safely through to the other side."

Before Sulu could argue further, she held up her hand and continued. "Captain, I think this is what I was born to do."

She switched off the comm and moved her fingers onto the throttle control. The shuttle moved forward swiftly, and through the forward windows Burgess exulted as the auroral lights of the rift engulfed her.

Yilskene watched on his flagship's crystalline monitors as the Federation shuttlecraft moved toward the rift that led to the OtherVoid. He wondered if that unstable region of space had caused the vessel's pilot to go mad. Or were the Starfleet people attempting to deceive him again? He once again considered destroying both the shuttle and *Excelsior.*

The knowledge-caste officer working the sensors informed him that only one person remained aboard the shuttle—the human envoy, Ambassador Burgess. Additionally, *Excelsior* was not following the shuttle's course. It was puzzling.

Yilskene considered the human ambassador. He knew that even within the Lattice, there were certain individuals—especially those from the political castes—who would shut themselves off from the SubLink permanently to undertake a lifelong voyage of contemplation. It was alien to a warrior's way of thinking, and probably to most of the other castes as well. But Yilskene's best mate had done it, exiling herself to a lifetime of silence and solitude.

Perhaps that is the path the ambassador is following, he thought, deciding to stay his hand. *Or perhaps she is pursuing the departing invader ship for some reason. The Neyel. Will she continue to advocate peace among them?*

"What do *you* believe her motives to be?" Yilskene asked Mosrene, who squatted nearby, watching the image of the shuttle on the viewscreen.

Mosrene's eyespots flared for a moment. "She has been

erratic yet guileless. Of all the humans on *Excelsior*, she seemed most sympathetic to us. However, she also identified with the concerns of the Neyel. But I don't believe that this is because the Neyel are humans. I think it is because she is able to see many sides at once."

Yilskene looked away from Mosrene and back to the viewer. The shuttlecraft was nearing the rift. "The other humans displayed multiple facets as well. Even while they were deceiving us, they protected our settlements from attack. And when Captain Sulu had the opportunity to kill me, he displayed mercy instead."

"Perhaps it is not just the ambassador who is multifaceted," Yilskene continued. "Perhaps it a characteristic shared generally by all of her kind."

Mosrene tilted his head, signifying agreement. "That may be so."

Yilskene looked over at Mosrene. "Then perhaps we and the humans are not so different from each other." The notion struck the admiral as equal parts truth and heresy even as he gave it voice. Only the passage of time could determine the truth of it.

On the screen, the shuttlecraft became a bright pinpoint, then disappeared over the invisible horizon of the Other-Void.

PART 10

PRODIGALS

Chapter 33

Sitting with his two closest friends in *Excelsior*'s mess hall, Lojur found he wasn't surprised by Tuvok's announcement. It had been pretty clear to him that the Vulcan wasn't entirely happy aboard *Excelsior*, if the word *happy* could even be used to describe a Vulcan.

But he knew that he would miss the science officer's calming influence and sharp intellect. He looked away from Tuvok and regarded Shandra's conspicuously empty chair in grim silence.

"When will you leave?" Akaar said as he idly moved his food around his plate with a fork. Though his Capellan stoicism concealed it, the security chief had to be feeling Tuvok's imminent departure keenly as well. Lojur knew that the two young officers had worked closely together for more than three years now.

"*Excelsior* is due to stop at Vulcan next month," Tuvok said. "At that time, I intend to resign my commission, return to my betrothed, and then resume my *Kolinahr* training."

"Captain Sulu and Commander Chekov will no doubt try to talk you into remaining aboard *Excelsior*," Akaar said.

"They already have. As have my parents."

"They clearly were not successful," Akaar said.

"As I said, after the Praxis affair, I promised them I would complete my assignment here rather than resign immediately. They were quite persistent. But that period has elapsed. My tour of duty is nearly over. The time has come for me to move on."

Lojur knew that Tuvok had never been comfortable serving among beings who lacked the emotional discipline of Vulcans. That preference probably accounted for the bonds of friendship that had grown among Tuvok, Lojur, and Akaar over the years. Yet, despite misgivings that had nearly come to a head shortly after the Praxis incident, Tuvok had continued serving aboard *Excelsior* for another five years.

Lojur decided that Tuvok's decision to leave Starfleet *now* must somehow have been precipitated by the Tholian-Neyel affair. But he knew better than to ask him to reveal more than he obviously wanted to.

A heavy silence descended across the table.

Perhaps a minute later, Akaar turned toward Lojur. "You have uttered fewer words than even I have so far tonight," he said, speaking around a mouthful of meat of some sort. Lojur experienced an ingrained pacifist's revulsion every time the Capellan took a bite.

But he also knew that the taciturn security chief was right. Lojur usually spoke far more than he had so far this evening. Pushing his salad away, he leaned forward so that no one else in the mess hall would overhear him.

"I am . . . troubled," Lojur said, then lapsed once again into an uncomfortable silence.

"That much is evident," said Lieutenant Tuvok, raising an eyebrow. He was seated beside Akaar, across the table from the Halkan navigator, an abstemiously portioned meal of bread and *plomeek* soup set out before him. Lojur noticed that the Vulcan science officer also seemed to be going out of his way not to look at Akaar's food.

It's so strange that a Vulcan and I both regard this hulking carnivore as a friend, Lojur thought. But he also knew that a kind, wise heart beat beneath within the Capellan warrior's chest. Akaar understood the world in ways that Lojur doubted he himself ever could.

" 'Troubled,' " Akaar repeated, then raised his fork to his lips to take a small bite of animal flesh. He washed the morsel down with something foamy that he drank out of a glass that looked absurdly small in his hand. " 'Troubled' is a word that says little. It is like saying 'Klingons are violent.' It is self-evident."

Lojur's need to unburden himself was finally beginning to overcome his sense of shame and betrayal. "May I tell you something in confidence, L.J.? And you, too, Tuvok?"

Akaar stared across his cup into Lojur's eyes for a moment before responding. "I will betray no confidences. Provided what you are about to divulge does not compromise the security of the ship."

Tuvok nodded, setting his fork down. "Lieutenant Akaar speaks for me as well, Commander."

"All right," Lojur said, trying to decide where to begin. "I have a confession to make. It doesn't pose any threat to the ship. At least, it doesn't *now*."

"And what, specifically, do you wish to confess?" Tuvok said, prodding. Lojur knew that in addition to his scientific duties, Tuvok also maintained a keen interest in ship's security.

"I . . . am the one responsible for the theft of the *Shuttlecraft Genji*," Lojur said simply. He looked from Akaar to Tuvok and back again, waiting for their reactions. But neither face betrayed any hint of emotion.

"I was under the impression," Tuvok said at length, "that the *Genji* was stolen by Ambassador Burgess and our Neyel 'guest.' "

Akaar nodded. "But they had to have help to get away with it. Access codes. Prelaunch assistance. False messages to divert the attention of key personnel at critical moments."

Then Tuvok displayed an uncustomary emotion: incredulity. "You are a navigator, Commander Lojur. Such specialties lie well outside your purview."

Lojur felt himself blushing. "I like to cross-train."

"It seems to me that you have but one ethical option open to you, Commander," Akaar said.

Lojur could only nod. His appetite now gone, he pushed his tray toward the center of the table and rose. He paused for a moment beside Shandra's empty chair. "Please excuse me."

Commander Chekov sat behind the desk in his quarters, listening in silence as Lojur told him everything. His first reaction was one of anger.

But he reminded himself that because of the navigator's unauthorized actions, Ambassador Burgess had laid the groundwork for a rapprochement between the Tholian Assembly and the Neyel Hegemony. It brought to mind another young navigator's lapse in discipline.

"Captain," the young navigator said, "I wish first to apologize for my conduct during this time. I did not maintain myself under proper discipline. I endangered the ship and its personnel by my conduct. I respectfully submit myself for disciplinary action."

Captain James Kirk stood in silence briefly before replying. When he spoke, his tone was surprisingly gentle. "Thank you, Mr. Chekov. You did what you had to do, as did we all. Even your friends. You may go."

Chekov turned his chair away from his console, finally mustering the courage to face his captain. "Thank you, sir." He rose from his station and headed for the turbolift.

The doors opened as he approached them. His old flame Irina Galliulin stepped out onto the bridge, nearly melting him with her dark eyes.

"I was coming to say good-bye," he said, nearly tripping over his tongue.

"And I was coming to say good-bye to you," she said. "Be incorrect . . . occasionally."

He smiled. "And you be correct . . ." He trailed off.

"Occasionally," Irina said, grinning mischievously.

"Sir?" Lojur said, evidently expecting him to detonate any second.

"I have to inform the captain, Commander," Chekov said.

"I completely understand, sir," Lojur said. "My actions might have caused many unnecessary deaths."

"But it may also have prevented as many. In light of the positive outcome, I intend to recommend the lightest possible punishment. Dismissed."

Lojur rounded a corner in the corridor near Commander Chekov's quarters.

Akaar was leaning against a bulkhead, evidently having lain in wait for him. "Well? What did Commander Chekov say when you told him?"

Lojur shook his head in confusion. "I'm not sure I made him understand just how serious my actions were. He doesn't appear very eager to punish me."

"Perhaps that is because he looked at your face. It is a map of pain, my friend."

Lojur didn't doubt that for a moment. But it didn't make him feel any better. "I took a terrible risk with the lives of everyone aboard this ship. That is anathema to a Halkan."

"What you did was in the name of peace. Your entire species should be proud of that."

"They wouldn't be if things had gone differently."

Akaar's eyes widened. "There will always be an infinite number of ways that things might have gone differently. You must make peace with those might-have-beens. Then let them go."

"Shandra," Lojur whispered. "You're talking about Shandra."

Akaar nodded. "The most painful of your might-have-beens. You still mourn her, and you always will, I expect. Even for one bred to peace, it can be difficult to allow such a loss to go unavenged. You felt the need to act."

"And I nearly committed murder," Lojur said, shutting his eyes. He could never forget firing his phaser at the unarmed Jerdahn. Had Akaar not intervened then . . .

"But you did *not* commit murder," Akaar said, lancing him with his deep brown eyes. "Instead, you channeled your need to act into deeds that may have saved countless lives."

Was it my desire for revenge against the Neyel that saved the ship? Lojur thought, suddenly feeling as sick as he had after he had killed the Orions who had raided Kotha Village. *How could such an evil impulse ever serve a good purpose?*

Peace. War. Love. Dead Kothans. Green-skinned corpses. Revenge. They swirled about his consciousness kaleidoscopically. He felt estranged from Starfleet and its ideals, just as he had been shunned by the Kotha Village Elders.

More confused by his conflicting emotions than he'd been since on that horrible day in Kotha, Lojur realized that he had only one place left to turn.

"Come," Tuvok said in answer to the door chime. He rose from his meditation mat, taking care not to disturb the geodesic shape of a half-assembled *kal-toh* puzzle he'd left sitting on a nearby table. Tuvok had always found the game a highly effective aid to his concentration.

The door slid open, admitting Lojur. "I hope I am not interrupting anything, Lieutenant Tuvok."

"I was just finishing my meditations, Commander. How can I help you?"

Lojur seemed more tentative and hesitant than Tuvok had ever seen him. He was clearly in distress. Just as Tuvok was beginning to realize that he had no idea how to help his friend, Lojur broke the silence.

"Why are you leaving Starfleet, Tuvok? Really."

Tuvok looked his friend in the eye. Since this was not the mess hall, and since he knew he could count on the Halkan's discretion, he decided to be completely candid.

"This ship is constantly awash in emotions, Commander. Humans tend to treat important Starfleet protocols in an extremely lackadaisical fashion, as we have seen on this very mission. Logical counsel is rarely accepted, even by the highest-ranking officers aboard." Tuvok considered saying something disparaging about the captain's challenging Admiral Yilskene to a duel, but decided to hold his tongue.

"Tell me about the *Kolinahr* training," Lojur said.

Tuvok experienced some surprise at that. Halkans, he knew, were a disciplined people; following the narrow path of total nonviolence as they did required an extreme focus of mind and will. But however disciplined Lojur might be, he was not a Vulcan. Being a Vulcan, for that matter, was no guarantee of success at *Kolinahr.*

"Tell me first why you are interested in *Kolinahr.* Completely purging one's emotions is a radical step for any non-Vulcan to take."

Lojur took a deep breath. "When I was in my teens, I raised my hand in violence. Necessary violence, but violence nonetheless. Afterward, I had no home on Halka. Commander Chekov and Starfleet took me in. Now, I fear I may soon lose that as well."

Without warning, the Halkan collapsed onto his knees, weeping. "Shandra's death has brought that violence back upon me. If I do not learn to control it, it will overwhelm me."

Tuvok didn't hesitate to help his friend. Stepping over to the table, he carefully lifted the tangle of crystalline-metal *t'an* rods that comprised the *kal-toh* puzzle.

Perhaps on Vulcan, he thought, *we can both find a measure of peace.*

Tuvok set the puzzle before the distraught Halkan. "Then let us begin together."

Chapter 34

Sulu retrieved the glass of Merlot from the food slot and returned to the couch. Chekov sat on a chair across from him, nursing a small glass of vodka. Chekov hadn't changed to off-duty gear yet, but Sulu was in his white turtleneck undershirt, and he had kicked off his boots.

"I still feel as if it's my responsibility," Sulu said. "I was in command of the ship when Burgess took the shuttlecraft into the rift. I could have tried to stop her."

Chekov snorted. "Well, of *course* you feel responsible, Hikaru. You're a Starfleet captain. *Everything* that happens on this ship is your responsibility, whether you know it's going on or not. But that doesn't mean that you're to blame for her actions. *She* stole the shuttle all on her own—with a little unauthorized help."

Sulu knew that Chekov was referring to Lieutenant Commander Lojur. He was still uncertain as to exactly what punishment the navigator should receive. Perhaps it had been a mistake to allow Lojur to come back to duty so soon after the death of his fiancé. That thought brought with it, unbidden, a sad reminder that there were several dead crew members for whom he and Pavel had to plan memorial services.

Chekov interrupted Sulu's clouded thoughts. "Burgess was a real *styervo*, but I think that in the end, I can understand why she did what she did." He took a swallow of his vodka, then continued. "I don't think it was ego that drove her. At least not completely."

"Well, *she* didn't seem to think so," Sulu said. "So, what do you think it was?"

"Humanity has been unified for centuries," Chekov said. "But the Neyel have been left out of all of that, and they'll need a lot of guidance if they're ever to join the human mainstream. How many human diplomats ever get an opportunity to help unite mankind all over again?"

Sulu nodded. Put that way, Burgess's passion made a great deal of sense.

A chime rang out then, followed by Janice Rand's voice coming over the comm. *"Captain, I have Admiral Nogura on subspace for you."*

Sulu put his glass down on the table and walked over toward his desk. "Put it through to my quarters, Commander."

Back to the beginning, Sulu thought as he sat behind the desk and activated the terminal there. *This is where it all started.*

"Captain Sulu, I'm looking forward to reading your report regarding the situation with the Tholians."

Sulu swallowed. "Yes, sir. I've just finished it, but I haven't filed it yet. If you'd like to hear it now, I'm ready."

Nogura smiled as if he were indulging a request instead of making one. *"Please do, Captain."*

Sulu launched into a narrative of the past days' events, laying out the highs, lows, and middles, as well as the surprises along the way. He ended with his admission that only the most foolhardy of risks and the sheerest luck had prevented a war. And that because of his dereliction of duty, Burgess had stolen the shuttlecraft *Genji* and kidnapped key figures in the local Tholian-Neyel dispute in an effort to force a truce whose final resolution was still admittedly uncertain.

Nogura leaned back in his chair as he listened. When

Sulu finished, he sat back upright. "*Captain, let's deal with Burgess first. She revealed sensitive information to the Tholians without authorization. It sounds to me that her actions were beyond the pale long before she stole the shuttle.* No *matter* what *she ultimately accomplished, I can guarantee that neither the Federation Council nor Starfleet Command will look kindly upon her should she ever return.*" With a slight smile, he added, "*Not that I expect* that *to happen any time soon. Her career is finished.*"

Chekov moved around to the area behind the monitor, and Sulu saw that his expression was full of misgivings. *He's not happy about my taking responsibility for Burgess's actions,* Sulu thought. *But I have no real choice.*

"*Regarding your own actions,*" Nogura said, "*I'm not certain that I'd use a phrase like 'dereliction of duty' to describe them. True, the assignment I gave you* did *call for a 'discreet investigation,' and you do seem to have failed miserably at that.*" He smiled broadly then, as if to soften his last statement. "*But in the end, everything seems to have turned out very well indeed for all concerned, thanks in no small part to your own quick thinking.*"

Sulu wasn't aware he was holding his breath until that point, and he let it out in a rush.

"*From where I sit,*" Nogura continued, steepling his fingers in front of him, "*Ambassador Burgess seems far more deserving of blame for anything that went wrong on this mission than you are. So let me ask you this: when you file your official report, are you certain you want to include absolutely* everything *you've just told me?*"

Chekov cleared his throat, and held up a hand to get Sulu's attention. Sulu looked back down at the monitor. "Admiral, will you excuse me for a moment? Something urgent has just come up."

"*Certainly, Captain.*"

Sulu muted the audio feed on the subspace channel and

stood, moving around the desk and out of the visual pickup's field of view.

"What is it, Pavel?" he asked.

"Don't you understand what the admiral is telling you?" Chekov asked, scowling. "The Federation Council is going to pressure Starfleet Command to pillory *somebody* over the various breaches of diplomatic protocol that occurred during this mission. It'll be a lot harder for them to do that to Burgess *in absentia* than it would be for them to go after somebody else."

Sulu nodded. "I know that."

"Well, that *somebody* they're after doesn't have to be *you.*"

Chekov stepped forward and put his hand onto Sulu's shoulder. "You and I have been friends for a long time, Hikaru. I know you want to take full responsibility, the way you've always done. But sometimes the responsibility for a bad choice needs to stay with the one who made it. Don't put *your* career in jeopardy because of the things that *she* did."

Grinning, Chekov added, "Besides, I don't want to be the captain *that* badly."

Sulu recalled something that Pavel had said to him earlier: *Just remember that taking responsibility for a family member sometimes means having to decide against them when they go astray.*

Burgess's safety had been his responsibility. Perhaps he was punishing himself for having allowed her to persuade him to let her enter the rift and strike out for Neyel Hegemony space. There was no way even to know for sure that she hadn't developed interspace-madness during transit, or had simply gotten lost and joined the graveyard of ships that tumbled eternally through the interdimensional depths.

But making that journey was her *decision, not mine. Just as kidnapping Yilskene and Joh'jym was.*

Sulu returned Chekov's smile, then arrived at a decision of his own. Crossing back to his desk, he was relieved to see that Nogura was waiting patiently, apparently studying something on a padd. Sulu reactivated the audio feed and cleared his throat. "I'm sorry, sir. I didn't mean to keep you waiting."

"No problem at all, Captain," Nogura said. *"I was just reviewing some other reports here. And speaking of reports, have you made a decision about what's to be in yours?"*

Sulu looked back at him quizzically. "Report, sir? I'm afraid I haven't had time yet to complete it."

Nogura smiled, and pointed directly into the monitor. *"Very good, Captain. I'll expect to see it sometime tomorrow. Nogura out."*

Sulu stood and stretched. He turned to see Chekov staring out the cabin window, holding a newly filled glass of vodka on the rocks. Sulu picked up his glass of wine and joined his friend.

As the stars moved by at warp speed, streaks of light that appeared and were gone in a blink, Chekov hoisted his drink. "Here's to our next mission. May it be unsullied by both monoblades and diplomacy."

Sulu grinned, clinked his glass against Chekov's, then turned to watch the stars fly past.

Chapter 35

2298, Auld Greg Aerth Calendar, the Neyel Coreworld of Oghen

The long war to annihilate the Devils, which seemed to have been raging all her life, was suddenly done.

And Oghen endured, though it was more than a little worse for wear.

Still, Vil'ja could scarcely believe it, nor could most of her classmates. Even Father seemed to have given up hope of victory during the darkest hours before the Treaty.

It's over, Vil'ja repeated to herself over and over after Father had given her the news. She knew that war was a bad thing. Yet she was both frightened and exhilarated by the sudden wrenching change.

So what happens now?

Standing beside her father in the early morning chill, Vil'ja grew quiet, as did the rest of the crowd that had gathered today in the capital city's broad boulevards and courtyards. Virtually everyone was looking skyward, and Vil'ja and her father were no exception.

The compact white ship was landing, descending very slowly on its antigravs toward a wide, brick-paved plaza, which the crowd had sensibly decided to leave clear. Vil'ja's small, bright eyes were drawn irresistibly to the unreadable—yet somehow vaguely familiar—writing that adorned the sides of the small craft's spotless hull.

Nudging her father, Vil'ja pointed at the alien vessel. "Do the Devils ever fly ships that look like that?" she asked, feeling a sudden jolt of anxiety at the idea. When she'd first heard about the landing that was to take place this morning, she'd imagined a triumphant Neyel commander would emerge from the ship, holding aloft the head of the leader of the Devil forces. Then she'd had a disconcerting image of the reverse—a Devil brandishing a severed Neyel head.

Looking up at Father, Vil'ja squeezed his hand, drawing comfort from its rocklike solidity.

"No, that's definitely *not* what a Devil ship looks like," Father said, smiling down at her. "Remember what the newsnet said this morning? This ship is carrying a peace envoy who came all the way from Aerth."

Vil'ja nodded, even though the notion of a living person from Aerth was hard to accept. The idea of Aerth being tangible, something more than a setting for bedtime tales, would take some getting used to.

Even as the white vessel came to rest beside an ornate fountain carved from black volcanic glass, a pair of small Neyel patrol vessels came to ground nearby. Vil'ja found their presence reassuring, since each of the Neyel craft was much bigger than the compact white ship, and probably also better armed as well, judging from the way Father had always described them.

Hatches on both Neyel vessels quickly opened and several armed troopers stepped out. They marched briskly toward the white vessel, their limbs and tails coming to rigid attention as they took up positions beside what appeared to be a sealed hatch near the small ship's bow. Their brilliant silver sashes identified them as an official honor guard, as though the being inside the white ship were a high-ranking official from the Gran Drech'tor's court. But Vil'ja knew that if the creature from Aerth turned out in reality to be some sort of monster, perhaps a Devil in disguise, the troopers—all of them hard-eyed veterans like her father—would be ready for it.

Like many Neyel children, she was well acquainted with the muted yet omnipresent sense of dread and worry that always descended like a low fog whenever a parent was called up to defend Blue Oghen from the Devil scourge. Like so many other parents, Father had done his duty, and had come back to the family afterward with many stories, some of which Vil'ja knew he was withholding from her "for her own good." Mother, too, had taken her turn fighting the Devils during the later phases of the Rift War.

But Mother had not returned. She had not been so fortunate as Father. Or maybe, as Vil'ja sometimes wondered when Father was lost deep in his cups, it was the other way around.

Still holding tightly to her father's hand, Vil'ja looked up, half expecting to see a Devil ship come swooping down on the unassuming-looking Aerth vessel, intent on mindless destruction.

Instead, she saw only an azure, almost cloudless sky, now completely free of the intense auroras and magnetic storms that had lately disrupted the broadcast of so many of her favorite tridee programs. Father had blamed these troubles on the effects of Riftspace, from which the Devils had sprung. The Rift, he'd explained, had stirred up violence on the surface of the sun, which created some pretty frightening fireworks in the skies of Oghen. It had gotten so bad that Vil'ja had begun to resign herself to the prevailing belief that only the utter extermination of the Devils could save her people. And perhaps not even that.

Today, everything was different. Now Vil'ja took the sudden complete absence of atmospheric disturbances as a reassuring sign. It showed, as Father had explained, that the Riftmouth was sealing up. It meant that the very fractures in space that had created the Riftmouth were now closing, scabbing over and healing like a sewn and sutured wound.

But Vil'ja knew that this healing also meant that Auld Aerth was now once again out of the Neyel Hegemony's reach. Perhaps forever. The Aerth of the Neyel's ancestors would once again fade away into legend.

Except for the white ship. The alien vessel, the ship from the ancestral world of Aerth, was real. Almost disconcertingly so.

Continuing to scan the heavens, Vil'ja noticed something else: the sky contained only the merest hint of its usual yellow-orange discoloration today. Father sometimes called these ubiquitous sunset hues "the fruits of Neyel impatience," usually after he'd had too much to drink, or had spent too much time alone in his study staring forlornly at old pictures of Mother, or both. Vil'ja wasn't entirely certain what he meant when he described the sky in this way. But she had an inkling that it had something to do with the numberless resource extractors and foundries and smokestacks that had built this city and all the others that now sprawled across the globe, as well as the massed fleets of Neyel warships that protected the skies and expanded the Hegemony's reach in every direction.

Warships like the one Mother had died on.

A low murmur rippled through the crowd. Father pointed toward the Aerth ship, snapping Vil'ja abruptly out of her reverie.

The hatch on the Aerth ship began to slide open, and a narrow gangplank slowly extended downward past the ship's graceful engine nacelles to the plaza floor. Moments later, a figure appeared in the open hatchway. *The Aerth envoy*, Vil'ja thought.

The Aerthean was a female, Vil'ja surmised, judging

from its overall shape and proportions. But aside from its possessing a head, torso, and limbs, the creature was like no Neyel she had ever seen. The being was short in stature compared to her Neyel escorts, and had no tail. Though clothing covered most of the alien's form, Vil'ja could see that the Aerth woman's skin looked incredibly fragile, her face and hands apparently as smooth and vulnerable as those of a newborn Neyel.

But the Aerthean's crowning feature, literally, was the great shock of fine, red-hued fiber that grew from her head. The long, ruddy strands reminded Vil'ja of the fur that covered the heads and torsos of the indigies she sometimes saw on tridee, or the ones she'd seen mounted and stuffed in the Knowledge Museum. She had even once observed a few of the indigies alive, making their traditional ceramic housewares at a tourist attraction she had visited with Mother nearly three oghencycles ago. The indigies who lived in that place had not seemed very happy.

But unlike those indigies, who'd seemed to Vil'ja like walking ghosts, the Aerth woman was smiling. At the signal of the head of the honor guard—a one-armed trooper, who'd no doubt been maimed during the conflict with the Devils—the Aerthean spread her hands, evidently preparing to address the hushed, expectant crowd. After quickly touching a device on the collar of her garment—*a microphone or voicecaster,* Vil'ja realized—the Aerth woman began to speak, her warm, pleasant voice audible everywhere in the plaza.

"People of the Neyel Hegemony, my name is Aidan Burgess. And I bring you greetings and good wishes from your cousins, the people of Earth, and from the United Federation of Planets of which Earth is a part."

Earth? Vil'ja wondered as a gentle murmur passed through the crowd, then subsided. *Urth? Aerth? What a strange accent she has.*

Burgess continued: "You may ask why I have come here, especially since the peace treaty my people have negotiated on behalf of the Hegemony and its former adversaries prohibits all future traffic across the Rift. It is certainly fair to ask why I would strand myself so far from my own people.

"But the answer is a simple one: It is because my people are really not so different from yours. I have come to tell you that Earth, the fabled world of your ancestors, is no myth. It is a real place with a real history, filled with people as real as any of you. It is the planet of my birth, just as it was for your pre-Neyel ancestors of centuries past."

Vil'ja felt her father tense beside her as a renewed murmur moved through the crowd, like an insistent wind bending a stand of tall grass. She had always been taught that such talk of Auld Aerth was irreverent, disrespectful. Aerth was sacred, and thus best not discussed in overly concrete terms.

But today, with the Rift War finished and proof of Aerth's tangible reality now on display for all to see—escorted by one of Gran Drech'tor Zafir's own military honor guards, no less—the mood of the crowd seemed more tolerant. At least, that was Vil'ja's hope. She did not want to see the people grow angry, especially now that the Rift's closure gave them cause by precluding any chance of actually reaching Distant Aerth. She didn't want to endure any more fighting and strife, especially not among her countrymen.

The Aerth envoy went on, as though she'd read Vil'ja's mind: "I understand that the Neyel people are weary of war. It may encourage you to know that my people have learned, after many centuries of errors and misunderstandings, to live in harmony with many different species who now make up our peace-loving Federation. We have even dissuaded some of the less friendly peoples—such as the Tholians, a species known in your tongue as "Devils"—from further aggression. This tradition of peace is the birthright of all Neyel, a people as closely linked as mine to the Earth of your forebears. Your esteemed leader, Gran Drech'tor Zafir, has expressed a desire to learn all she can of this birthright, and I have pledged the remainder of my life to giving her, and all of the Neyel, every assistance in reaching that end.

"My reason for wishing this is as simple as my reason for coming among you. And it is this: However many centuries have passed since our common ancestors diverged, and no matter how many changes may separate us, my people and yours are indissolubly linked. We are all creatures of Earth, regardless of whether or not any of us—myself included—can ever return there. As branches of the same tree, our two peoples and cultures are stronger together than apart. Thank you, my friends, for allowing me to speak to you today."

And with that, Burgess bowed and walked down the gangplank, the one-armed honor guard leader at her side. Moving with purposeful strides, with the guards marching behind and beside them, they headed toward the Great Hall of Oghen, where Gran Drech'tor Zafir held court. The crowd, now once again silent, parted to make way for the procession.

Moments later, Vil'ja realized that she and her father were standing directly in the path of Burgess and her party. Father tugged gently on Vil'ja's arm, trying to coax her out of the way.

But Vil'ja could only stare at the approaching Aerth woman, transfixed. She pulled away from Father, but overbalanced and found herself tumbling arms over tail into a heap on the dew-damp bricks of the plaza floor.

She looked up. The Aerth woman was standing directly over her, staring down with a worried expression while Father and the Neyel military escorts looked on, each of them scowling the same military-issue scowl.

The one-armed trooper began to shoo Vil'ja out of the Aerth envoy's way, but Burgess held up a restraining hand.

The vigilant troopers withdrew slightly, moving two steps backward as the Aerthean woman crouched beside the girl.

"Looks like I've just made first contact," Burgess said. "I'm sorry to have been so clumsy. Are you hurt?"

The Aerth woman reached down to help Vil'ja reach her feet. As she grasped Burgess's soft arm with a tough-skinned hand, the Neyel girl noticed the strands of the multicolored bracelet the woman wore on her slender wrist. Small stones, shells, and charms of every description were strung like beads all around it, reminding her of an art project she'd done recently at school.

Vil'ja returned her gaze to the Aerth woman's impossibly soft, vulnerable face. Could such supple creatures as this truly be the fruit of the same tree as the battle-hardened Neyel?

Unless she could reach Aerth herself, Vil'ja realized, she might never know. And without the Rift, that simply wouldn't be possible.

It took an awkward few moments for Vil'ja to find her voice. "I am not hurt," she said simply.

Suddenly Vil'ja felt emboldened, perhaps by all the suffering and terror she had absorbed during the Rift War. So she added, very quickly, "But I do have a question."

From the corner of one hard-lidded eye, Vil'ja saw her father blanch. He obviously wanted them both to melt back into the anonymity of the crowd.

But she also saw the Aerth woman's smile return, and it encouraged her to stand her ground. "Please. Ask," the Aerthean said.

Vil'ja drew a deep breath. "Your people have driven the Devils away. For that I thank you."

She shuddered inwardly when she thought of the Devils. Even though her father, her teachers, and every other adult she knew all claimed that the Rift War was now a thing of the past, Vil'ja had no closure. She still feared and hated the

Devils and everything they had done. The war the crystal beasts had started had taken Mother from her. In a way, it had taken Father as well.

"You're very welcome," Burgess said. "By the way, what's your name?"

"Vil'ja," said the girl, flushing with embarrassment at her own atrocious manners. She thought the members of the honor guard were beginning to look impatient. Father appeared ready to slink away and hide, with or without her.

"And what was your question, Vil'ja?"

With an effort, Vil'ja gathered her jumbled thoughts before speaking. "Ending the Rift War meant sealing the Rift, which meant placing Aerth beyond our reach. How can your people and ours really know each other across such a great distance?"

"That's a very good question, Vil'ja," Burgess said as she slowly removed the bracelet from her wrist. "And I don't know if I have an answer. All I can say is that the question is the reason I had to come among you."

"Even though you can never get back?"

The Aerthean's eyes glistened with moisture. She nodded. "Even so. Now hold out your hand."

Vil'ja quietly did as Burgess asked. The Aerth woman placed the stone-and-shell-beaded bracelet into the palm of her hand and gently closed the girl's rough, gray fingers around it.

"This is a piece of Earth," the envoy said. "Actually, it's a whole lot of small pieces of Earth. Every one of these pieces tells a story of its own."

"Are they *your* stories?"

"Some of them are," the Aerth woman said. Vil'ja started trying to return the bracelet, but Burgess pushed her hands back, gently but firmly. "I doubt I'll ever be going back there, Vil'ja."

"Will you tell me some of those stories?" Vil'ja asked.

"I would be happy to do that a little later on, Vil'ja. If you will make me a promise first."

Vil'ja held the bracelet and nodded.

"Someday I want you to return the bracelet to where it came from," Burgess said.

The girl blinked in confusion. "To Aerth?"

"To Aerth," the woman replied, this time coloring the revered place name with a fairly good mid-southern latitude Oghen-Neyel accent.

"But without the Rift, a voyage like that would probably take a megajillion oghencycles," Vil'ja said.

The Aerth woman's smile turned almost playful. "Maybe even a gigajillion. But you Neyel are clever, patient people. It seems to run in the family. So if your generation doesn't find a shortcut to Aerth, then your children or your grandchildren almost certainly will. Or theirs will. The Neyel and my people won't remain isolated from each other forever. The universe simply isn't big enough to allow that."

"You're here," Vil'ja said, conceding the point. "I guess that proves you're right."

The Aerthean woman placed her hands on Vil'ja's shoulders. "Believe it. Your people will find Aerth, Vil'ja. It's only a matter of time. And my life's work is to prepare everyone for the day when that happens. We all have a lot to learn. Myself included."

Then Burgess nodded to her one-armed escort, and within moments she and the squad of troopers around her departed, the entire group quickly vanishing into the crowd as it resumed its course for the Great Hall of Oghen.

"Let's go," Father said to Vil'ja long moments later. His tail twitched spasmodically behind him as though he didn't know what to do with it.

Vil'ja ignored him. Standing stock-still, she held the bracelet in the flat of her hand and let the morning sun dance across its homemade beadwork of colorful, unfamiliar stones and weird, alien shells. *Every one of these pieces tells a story of its own.*

Vil'ja looked heavenward again. The largest of Oghen's moons was visible, and Holy Vangar lay beneath the horizon, out of sight. She concentrated instead on the section of the sky where the teachers had said that Milkyway—and Auld Far Aerth—could be found.

Clutching the bracelet tightly, she decided that one day she would contribute a story or two of her own.

ABOUT THE AUTHORS

MICHAEL A. MARTIN, whose solo short fiction has appeared in *The Magazine of Fantasy & Science Fiction,* is also coauthor (with Andy Mangels) of *Star Trek: Deep Space Nine Mission: Gamma, Book Three—Cathedral; Star Trek: The Next Generation, Section 31—Rogue;* and the forthcoming *Star Trek: Starfleet Corps of Engineers #30* and *#31 (Ishtar Rising Books 1* and *2).* Working with Andy, Martin has also coauthored *Roswell: Skeletons in the Closet; Roswell: Pursuit;* and *Roswell: Turnabout* (the last of which is forthcoming).

Martin was the regular cowriter (also with Andy) of Marvel Comics' monthly *Star Trek: Deep Space Nine* comic-book series, and has generated heaps of copy for Atlas Editions' *Star Trek Universe* subscription card series. He has written for *Star Trek Monthly, Dreamwatch,* Grolier Books, Wildstorm, Platinum Studios, and Gareth Stevens, Inc., for whom he has penned several *World Almanac Library of the States* nonfiction books.

Martin lives and works in an ancient house in Portland, Oregon, surrounded by his wife, Jennifer J. Dottery, their two boys (James and William), and much love and laughter.

ANDY MANGELS is the co-author of *Star Trek: The Next Generation, Section 31—Rogue; Star Trek: Deep Space Nine, Mission: Gamma—Cathedral;* and a number of upcoming *Star Trek* novels, e-books, and short stories, all written with Michael A. Martin. The pair have also written *Roswell: Skeletons in the Closet* and *Roswell: Pursuit,* with *Roswell: Turnabout* forthcoming. Flying solo, Andy is also the author of *Animation on DVD: The Ultimate Guide,* as well as the best-selling book *Star Wars: The Essential Guide To Characters,* plus *Beyond Mulder & Scully: The Mysterious Characters of The X-Files* and *From Scream To Dawson's Creek: The Phenomenal Career of Kevin Williamson.*

Mangels has written for *The Hollywood Reporter, The Advocate, Just Out, Cinescape, Gauntlet, Dreamwatch, Sci-Fi Universe, SFX, Anime Invasion, Outweek, Frontiers, Portland Mercury, Comics Buyer's Guide,* and scores of other entertainment and lifestyle magazines. He has also written licensed material based on properties by Lucasfilm, Paramount, New Line Cinema, Universal Studios, Warner Bros., Microsoft, Abrams-Gentile, and Platinum Studios. His comic-book work has been published by DC Comics, Marvel Comics, Dark Horse, Wildstorm, Image, Innovation, WaRP Graphics, Topps, MVCreations, and others, and he was the editor of the award-winning *Gay Comics* anthology for eight years. He has also written DVD supplemental material and liner notes for Anchor Bay. In what little spare time he has, he likes to country dance and collect uniforms and *Wonder*

Woman memorabilia. He lives in Portland, Oregon, with his longtime partner, Don Hood, and their dog, Bela.

Visit his website at www.andymangels.com

Look for STAR TREK fiction from Pocket Books

Star Trek®

Enterprise: The First Adventure • Vonda N. McIntyre
Strangers From the Sky • Margaret Wander Bonanno
Final Frontier • Diane Carey
Spock's World • Diane Duane
The Lost Years • J.M. Dillard
Prime Directive • Judith and Garfield Reeves-Stevens
Probe • Margaret Wander Bonanno
Best Destiny • Diane Carey
Shadows on the Sun • Michael Jan Friedman
Sarek • A.C. Crispin
Federation • Judith and Garfield Reeves-Stevens
Vulcan's Forge • Josepha Sherman & Susan Shwartz
Mission to Horatius • Mack Reynolds
Vulcan's Heart • Josepha Sherman & Susan Shwartz
The Eugenics Wars: The Rise and Fall of Khan Noonien Singh, Books One and *Two* • Greg Cox
The Last Roundup • Christie Golden
Gemini • Mike W. Barr
Garth of Izar • Pamela Sargent & George Zebrowski

Novelizations

Star Trek: The Motion Picture • Gene Roddenberry
Star Trek II: The Wrath of Khan • Vonda N. McIntyre
Star Trek III: The Search for Spock • Vonda N. McIntyre
Star Trek IV: The Voyage Home • Vonda N. McIntyre
Star Trek V: The Final Frontier • J.M. Dillard
Star Trek VI: The Undiscovered Country • J.M. Dillard
Star Trek Generations • J.M. Dillard
Starfleet Academy • Diane Carey

Star Trek books by William Shatner with Judith and Garfield Reeves-Stevens

The Ashes of Eden
The Return
Avenger
Star Trek: Odyssey (contains *The Ashes of Eden*, *The Return*, and *Avenger)*
Spectre
Dark Victory
Preserver
The Captain's Peril

#1 • *Star Trek: The Motion Picture* • Gene Roddenberry
#2 • *The Entropy Effect* • Vonda N. McIntyre
#3 • *The Klingon Gambit* • Robert E. Vardeman

#4 • *The Covenant of the Crown* • Howard Weinstein
#5 • *The Prometheus Design* • Sondra Marshak & Myrna Culbreath
#6 • *The Abode of Life* • Lee Correy
#7 • *Star Trek II: The Wrath of Khan* • Vonda N. McIntyre
#8 • *Black Fire* • Sonni Cooper
#9 • *Triangle* • Sondra Marshak & Myrna Culbreath
#10 • *Web of the Romulans* • M.S. Murdock
#11 • *Yesterday's Son* • A.C. Crispin
#12 • *Mutiny on the Enterprise* • Robert E. Vardeman
#13 • *The Wounded Sky* • Diane Duane
#14 • *The Trellisane Confrontation* • David Dvorkin
#15 • *Corona* • Greg Bear
#16 • *The Final Reflection* • John M. Ford
#17 • *Star Trek III: The Search for Spock* • Vonda N. McIntyre
#18 • *My Enemy, My Ally* • Diane Duane
#19 • *The Tears of the Singers* • Melinda Snodgrass
#20 • *The Vulcan Academy Murders* • Jean Lorrah
#21 • *Uhura's Song* • Janet Kagan
#22 • *Shadow Lord* • Laurence Yep
#23 • *Ishmael* • Barbara Hambly
#24 • *Killing Time* • Della Van Hise
#25 • *Dwellers in the Crucible* • Margaret Wander Bonanno
#26 • *Pawns and Symbols* • Majliss Larson
#27 • *Mindshadow* • J.M. Dillard
#28 • *Crisis on Centaurus* • Brad Ferguson
#29 • *Dreadnought!* • Diane Carey
#30 • *Demons* • J.M. Dillard
#31 • *Battlestations!* • Diane Carey
#32 • *Chain of Attack* • Gene DeWeese
#33 • *Deep Domain* • Howard Weinstein
#34 • *Dreams of the Raven* • Carmen Carter
#35 • *The Romulan Way* • Diane Duane & Peter Morwood
#36 • *How Much for Just the Planet?* • John M. Ford
#37 • *Bloodthirst* • J.M. Dillard
#38 • *The IDIC Epidemic* • Jean Lorrah
#39 • *Time for Yesterday* • A.C. Crispin
#40 • *Timetrap* • David Dvorkin
#41 • *The Three-Minute Universe* • Barbara Paul
#42 • *Memory Prime* • Judith and Garfield Reeves-Stevens
#43 • *The Final Nexus* • Gene DeWeese
#44 • *Vulcan's Glory* • D.C. Fontana
#45 • *Double, Double* • Michael Jan Friedman
#46 • *The Cry of the Onlies* • Judy Klass
#47 • *The Kobayashi Maru* • Julia Ecklar

#48 • *Rules of Engagement* • Peter Morwood
#49 • *The Pandora Principle* • Carolyn Clowes
#50 • *Doctor's Orders* • Diane Duane
#51 • *Enemy Unseen* • V.E. Mitchell
#52 • *Home Is the Hunter* • Dana Kramer-Rolls
#53 • *Ghost-Walker* • Barbara Hambly
#54 • *A Flag Full of Stars* • Brad Ferguson
#55 • *Renegade* • Gene DeWeese
#56 • *Legacy* • Michael Jan Friedman
#57 • *The Rift* • Peter David
#58 • *Faces of Fire* • Michael Jan Friedman
#59 • *The Disinherited* • Peter David, Michael Jan Friedman, Robert Greenberger
#60 • *Ice Trap* • L.A. Graf
#61 • *Sanctuary* • John Vornholt
#62 • *Death Count* • L.A. Graf
#63 • *Shell Game* • Melissa Crandall
#64 • *The Starship Trap* • Mel Gilden
#65 • *Windows on a Lost World* • V.E. Mitchell
#66 • *From the Depths* • Victor Milan
#67 • *The Great Starship Race* • Diane Carey
#68 • *Firestorm* • L.A. Graf
#69 • *The Patrian Transgression* • Simon Hawke
#70 • *Traitor Winds* • L.A. Graf
#71 • *Crossroad* • Barbara Hambly
#72 • *The Better Man* • Howard Weinstein
#73 • *Recovery* • J.M. Dillard
#74 • *The Fearful Summons* • Denny Martin Flinn
#75 • *First Frontier* • Diane Carey & Dr. James I. Kirkland
#76 • *The Captain's Daughter* • Peter David
#77 • *Twilight's End* • Jerry Oltion
#78 • *The Rings of Tautee* • Dean Wesley Smith & Kristine Kathryn Rusch
#79 • *Invasion!* #1: *First Strike* • Diane Carey
#80 • *The Joy Machine* • James Gunn
#81 • *Mudd in Your Eye* • Jerry Oltion
#82 • *Mind Meld* • John Vornholt
#83 • *Heart of the Sun* • Pamela Sargent & George Zebrowski
#84 • *Assignment: Eternity* • Greg Cox
#85-87 • *My Brother's Keeper* • Michael Jan Friedman
  #85 • *Republic*
  #86 • *Constitution*
  #87 • *Enterprise*
#88 • *Across the Universe* • Pamela Sargent & George Zebrowski
#89-94 • *New Earth*

#89 • *Wagon Train to the Stars* • Diane Carey
#90 • *Belle Terre* • Dean Wesley Smith with Diane Carey
#91 • *Rough Trails* • L.A. Graf
#92 • *The Flaming Arrow* • Kathy and Jerry Oltion
#93 • *Thin Air* • Kristine Kathryn Rusch & Dean Wesley Smith
#94 • *Challenger* • Diane Carey
#95-96 • *Rihannsu* • Diane Duane
#95 • *Swordhunt*
#96 • *Honor Blade*
#97 • *In the Name of Honor* • Dayton Ward

Star Trek®: The Original Series

The Janus Gate • L.A. Graf
#1 • *Present Tense*
#2 • *Future Imperfect*
#3 • *Past Prologue*
Errand of Vengeance • Kevin Ryan
#1 • *The Edge of the Sword*
#2 • *Killing Blow*
#3 • *River of Blood*

Star Trek: The Next Generation®

Metamorphosis • Jean Lorrah
Vendetta • Peter David
Reunion • Michael Jan Friedman
Imzadi • Peter David
The Devil's Heart • Carmen Carter
Dark Mirror • Diane Duane
Q-Squared • Peter David
Crossover • Michael Jan Friedman
Kahless • Michael Jan Friedman
Ship of the Line • Diane Carey
The Best and the Brightest • Susan Wright
Planet X • Michael Jan Friedman
Imzadi II: Triangle • Peter David
I, Q • John de Lancie & Peter David
The Valiant • Michael Jan Friedman
The Genesis Wave, Books One, Two, and *Three* • John Vornholt
Immortal Coil • Jeffrey Lang
A Hard Rain • Dean Wesley Smith
The Battle of Betazed • Charlotte Douglas & Susan Kearney
Genesis Force • John Vornholt

Novelizations

Encounter at Farpoint • David Gerrold
Unification • Jeri Taylor
Relics • Michael Jan Friedman
Descent • Diane Carey
All Good Things... • Michael Jan Friedman
Star Trek: Klingon • Dean Wesley Smith & Kristine Kathryn Rusch
Star Trek Generations • J.M. Dillard
Star Trek: First Contact • J.M. Dillard
Star Trek: Insurrection • J.M. Dillard
Star Trek: Nemesis • J.M. Dillard

#1 • *Ghost Ship* • Diane Carey
#2 • *The Peacekeepers* • Gene DeWeese
#3 • *The Children of Hamlin* • Carmen Carter
#4 • *Survivors* • Jean Lorrah
#5 • *Strike Zone* • Peter David
#6 • *Power Hungry* • Howard Weinstein
#7 • *Masks* • John Vornholt
#8 • *The Captain's Honor* • David & Daniel Dvorkin
#9 • *A Call to Darkness* • Michael Jan Friedman
#10 • *A Rock and a Hard Place* • Peter David
#11 • *Gulliver's Fugitives* • Keith Sharee
#12 • *Doomsday World* • Carter, David, Friedman & Greenberger
#13 • *The Eyes of the Beholders* • A.C. Crispin
#14 • *Exiles* • Howard Weinstein
#15 • *Fortune's Light* • Michael Jan Friedman
#16 • *Contamination* • John Vornholt
#17 • *Boogeymen* • Mel Gilden
#18 • *Q-in-Law* • Peter David
#19 • *Perchance to Dream* • Howard Weinstein
#20 • *Spartacus* • T.L. Mancour
#21 • *Chains of Command* • W.A. McCay & E.L. Flood
#22 • *Imbalance* • V.E. Mitchell
#23 • *War Drums* • John Vornholt
#24 • *Nightshade* • Laurell K. Hamilton
#25 • *Grounded* • David Bischoff
#26 • *The Romulan Prize* • Simon Hawke
#27 • *Guises of the Mind* • Rebecca Neason
#28 • *Here There Be Dragons* • John Peel
#29 • *Sins of Commission* • Susan Wright
#30 • *Debtor's Planet* • W.R. Thompson
#31 • *Foreign Foes* • Dave Galanter & Greg Brodeur
#32 • *Requiem* • Michael Jan Friedman & Kevin Ryan
#33 • *Balance of Power* • Dafydd ab Hugh

#34 • *Blaze of Glory* • Simon Hawke
#35 • *The Romulan Stratagem* • Robert Greenberger
#36 • *Into the Nebula* • Gene DeWeese
#37 • *The Last Stand* • Brad Ferguson
#38 • *Dragon's Honor* • Kij Johnson & Greg Cox
#39 • *Rogue Saucer* • John Vornholt
#40 • *Possession* • J.M. Dillard & Kathleen O'Malley
#41 • *Invasion! #2: The Soldiers of Fear* • Dean Wesley Smith & Kristine Kathryn Rusch
#42 • *Infiltrator* • W.R. Thompson
#43 • *A Fury Scorned* • Pamela Sargent & George Zebrowski
#44 • *The Death of Princes* • John Peel
#45 • *Intellivore* • Diane Duane
#46 • *To Storm Heaven* • Esther Friesner
#47-49 • *The Q Continuum* • Greg Cox
#47 • *Q-Space*
#48 • *Q-Zone*
#49 • *Q-Strike*
#50 • *Dyson Sphere* • Charles Pellegrino & George Zebrowski
#51-56 • *Double Helix*
#51 • *Infection* • John Gregory Betancourt
#52 • *Vectors* • Dean Wesley Smith & Kristine Kathryn Rusch
#53 • *Red Sector* • Diane Carey
#54 • *Quarantine* • John Vornholt
#55 • *Double or Nothing* • Peter David
#56 • *The First Virtue* • Michael Jan Friedman & Christie Golden
#57 • *The Forgotten War* • William R. Forstchen
#58 • *Gemworld, Book One* • John Vornholt
#59 • *Gemworld, Book Two* • John Vornholt
#60 • *Tooth and Claw* • Doranna Durgin
#61 • *Diplomatic Implausibility* • Keith R.A. DeCandido
#62-63 • *Maximum Warp* • Dave Galanter & Greg Brodeur
#62 • *Dead Zone*
#63 • *Forever Dark*

Star Trek: Deep Space Nine®

Warped • K.W. Jeter
Legends of the Ferengi • Ira Steven Behr & Robert Hewitt Wolfe
Novelizations
Emissary • J.M. Dillard
The Search • Diane Carey
The Way of the Warrior • Diane Carey
Star Trek: Klingon • Dean Wesley Smith & Kristine Kathryn Rusch
Trials and Tribble-ations • Diane Carey

Far Beyond the Stars • Steve Barnes
What You Leave Behind • Diane Carey

#1 • *Emissary* • J.M. Dillard
#2 • *The Siege* • Peter David
#3 • *Bloodletter* • K.W. Jeter
#4 • *The Big Game* • Sandy Schofield
#5 • *Fallen Heroes* • Dafydd ab Hugh
#6 • *Betrayal* • Lois Tilton
#7 • *Warchild* • Esther Friesner
#8 • *Antimatter* • John Vornholt
#9 • *Proud Helios* • Melissa Scott
#10 • *Valhalla* • Nathan Archer
#11 • *Devil in the Sky* • Greg Cox & John Gregory Betancourt
#12 • *The Laertian Gamble* • Robert Sheckley
#13 • *Station Rage* • Diane Carey
#14 • *The Long Night* • Dean Wesley Smith & Kristine Kathryn Rusch
#15 • *Objective: Bajor* • John Peel
#16 • *Invasion!* #3: *Time's Enemy* • L.A. Graf
#17 • *The Heart of the Warrior* • John Gregory Betancourt
#18 • *Saratoga* • Michael Jan Friedman
#19 • *The Tempest* • Susan Wright
#20 • *Wrath of the Prophets* • David, Friedman & Greenberger
#21 • *Trial by Error* • Mark Garland
#22 • *Vengeance* • Dafydd ab Hugh
#23 • *The 34th Rule* • Armin Shimerman & David R. George III
#24-26 • *Rebels* • Dafydd ab Hugh
#24 • *The Conquered*
#25 • *The Courageous*
#26 • *The Liberated*

Books set after the series
The Lives of Dax • Marco Palmieri, ed.
Millennium Omnibus • Judith and Garfield Reeves-Stevens
#1 • *The Fall of Terok Nor*
#2 • *The War of the Prophets*
#3 • *Inferno*
A Stitch in Time • Andrew J. Robinson
Avatar, Books One and *Two* • S.D. Perry
Section 31: Abyss • David Weddle & Jeffrey Lang
Gateways #4: *Demons of Air and Darkness* • Keith R.A. DeCandido
Gateways #7: *What Lay Beyond:* "Horn and Ivory" • Keith R.A. DeCandido
Mission: Gamma
#1 • *Twilight* • David R. George III
#2 • *This Gray Spirit* • Heather Jarman

#3 • *Cathedral* • Michael A. Martin & Andy Mangels
#4 • *Lesser Evil* • Robert Simpson

Rising Son • S.D. Perry

The Left Hand of Destiny, Books One and *Two* • J.G. Hertzler & Jeffrey Lang

Star Trek: Voyager®

Mosaic • Jeri Taylor
Pathways • Jeri Taylor
Captain Proton: Defender of the Earth • D.W. "Prof" Smith
The Nanotech War • Steve Piziks

Novelizations

Caretaker • L.A. Graf
Flashback • Diane Carey
Day of Honor • Michael Jan Friedman
Equinox • Diane Carey
Endgame • Diane Carey & Christie Golden

#1 • *Caretaker* • L.A. Graf
#2 • *The Escape* • Dean Wesley Smith & Kristine Kathryn Rusch
#3 • *Ragnarok* • Nathan Archer
#4 • *Violations* • Susan Wright
#5 • *Incident at Arbuk* • John Gregory Betancourt
#6 • *The Murdered Sun* • Christie Golden
#7 • *Ghost of a Chance* • Mark A. Garland & Charles G. McGraw
#8 • *Cybersong* • S.N. Lewitt
#9 • *Invasion! #4: The Final Fury* • Dafydd ab Hugh
#10 • *Bless the Beasts* • Karen Haber
#11 • *The Garden* • Melissa Scott
#12 • *Chrysalis* • David Niall Wilson
#13 • *The Black Shore* • Greg Cox
#14 • *Marooned* • Christie Golden
#15 • *Echoes* • Dean Wesley Smith, Kristine Kathryn Rusch & Nina Kiriki Hoffman
#16 • *Seven of Nine* • Christie Golden
#17 • *Death of a Neutron Star* • Eric Kotani
#18 • *Battle Lines* • Dave Galanter & Greg Brodeur
#19-21 • *Dark Matters* • Christie Golden
#19 • *Cloak and Dagger*
#20 • *Ghost Dance*
#21 • *Shadow of Heaven*

Books set after the series

Homecoming • Christie Golden

The Farther Shore • Christie Golden

Enterprise®

Novelizations

Broken Bow • Diane Carey

Shockwave • Paul Ruditis

By the Book • Dean Wesley Smith & Kristine Kathryn Rusch

What Price Honor • Dave Stern

Surak's Soul • J.M. Dillard

Star Trek®: New Frontier

New Frontier #1-4 Collector's Edition • Peter David

#1 • *House of Cards*

#2 • *Into the Void*

#3 • *The Two-Front War*

#4 • *End Game*

#5 • *Martyr* • Peter David

#6 • *Fire on High* • Peter David

The Captain's Table #5 • *Once Burned* • Peter David

Double Helix #5 • *Double or Nothing* • Peter David

#7 • *The Quiet Place* • Peter David

#8 • *Dark Allies* • Peter David

#9-11 • *Excalibur* • Peter David

#9 • *Requiem*

#10 • *Renaissance*

#11 • *Restoration*

Gateways #6: *Cold Wars* • Peter David

Gateways #7: *What Lay Beyond:* "Death After Life" • Peter David

#12 • *Being Human* • Peter David

Star Trek®: Stargazer

The Valiant • Michael Jan Friedman

Double Helix #6: *The First Virtue* • Michael Jan Friedman and Christie Golden

Gauntlet • Michael Jan Friedman

Progenitor • Michael Jan Friedman

Star Trek®: Starfleet Corps of Engineers (eBooks)

Have Tech, Will Travel (paperback) • various

#1 • *The Belly of the Beast* • Dean Wesley Smith

#2 • *Fatal Error* • Keith R.A. DeCandido

#3 • *Hard Crash* • Christie Golden

#4 • *Interphase, Book One* • Dayton Ward & Kevin Dilmore
Miracle Workers (paperback) • various
#5 • *Interphase, Book Two* • Dayton Ward & Kevin Dilmore
#6 • *Cold Fusion* • Keith R.A. DeCandido
#7 • *Invincible, Book One* • Keith R.A. DeCandido & David Mack
#8 • *Invincible, Book Two* • Keith R.A. DeCandido & David Mack
Some Assembly Required (paperback) • various
#9 • *The Riddled Post* • Aaron Rosenberg
#10 • *Gateways Epilogue: Here There Be Monsters* • Keith R.A. DeCandido
#11 • *Ambush* • Dave Galanter & Greg Brodeur
#12 • *Some Assembly Required* • Scott Ciencin & Dan Jolley
No Surrender (paperback) • various
#13 • *No Surrender* • Jeff Mariotte
#14 • *Caveat Emptor* • Ian Edginton
#15 • *Past Life* • Robert Greenberger
#16 • *Oaths* • Glenn Hauman
#17 • *Foundations, Book One* • Dayton Ward & Kevin Dilmore
#18 • *Foundations, Book Two* • Dayton Ward & Kevin Dilmore
#19 • *Foundations, Book Three* • Dayton Ward & Kevin Dilmore
#20 • *Enigma Ship* • J. Steven and Christina F. York
#21 • *War Stories, Book One* • Keith R.A. DeCandido
#22 • *War Stories, Book Two* • Keith R.A. DeCandido
#23 • *Wildfire, Book One* • David Mack
#24 • *Wildfire, Book Two* • David Mack
#25 • *Home Fires* • Dayton Ward & Kevin Dilmore
#26 • *Age of Unreason* • Scott Ciencin
#27 • *Balance of Nature* • Heather Jarman
#28 • *Breakdowns* • Keith R.A. DeCandido

Star Trek®: Invasion!

#1 • *First Strike* • Diane Carey
#2 • *The Soldiers of Fear* • Dean Wesley Smith & Kristine Kathryn Rusch
#3 • *Time's Enemy* • L.A. Graf
#4 • *The Final Fury* • Dafydd ab Hugh
Invasion! Omnibus • various

Star Trek®: Day of Honor

#1 • *Ancient Blood* • Diane Carey
#2 • *Armageddon Sky* • L.A. Graf
#3 • *Her Klingon Soul* • Michael Jan Friedman
#4 • *Treaty's Law* • Dean Wesley Smith & Kristine Kathryn Rusch
The Television Episode • Michael Jan Friedman
Day of Honor Omnibus • various

Star Trek®: The Captain's Table

#1 • *War Dragons* • L.A. Graf
#2 • *Dujonian's Hoard* • Michael Jan Friedman
#3 • *The Mist* • Dean Wesley Smith & Kristine Kathryn Rusch
#4 • *Fire Ship* • Diane Carey
#5 • *Once Burned* • Peter David
#6 • *Where Sea Meets Sky* • Jerry Oltion
The Captain's Table Omnibus • various

Star Trek®: The Dominion War

#1 • *Behind Enemy Lines* • John Vornholt
#2 • *Call to Arms...* • Diane Carey
#3 • *Tunnel Through the Stars* • John Vornholt
#4 • *...Sacrifice of Angels* • Diane Carey

Star Trek®: Section 31™

Rogue • Andy Mangels & Michael A. Martin
Shadow • Dean Wesley Smith & Kristine Kathryn Rusch
Cloak • S.D. Perry
Abyss • Dean Weddle & Jeffrey Lang

Star Trek®: Gateways

#1 • *One Small Step* • Susan Wright
#2 • *Chainmail* • Diane Carey
#3 • *Doors Into Chaos* • Robert Greenberger
#4 • *Demons of Air and Darkness* • Keith R.A. DeCandido
#5 • *No Man's Land* • Christie Golden
#6 • *Cold Wars* • Peter David
#7 • *What Lay Beyond* • various
Epilogue: Here There Be Monsters • Keith R.A. DeCandido

Star Trek®: The Lost Era

2298 • *The Sundered* • Michael A. Martin and Andy Mangels

Star Trek® Omnibus Editions

Invasion! Omnibus • various
Day of Honor Omnibus • various
The Captain's Table Omnibus • various
Double Helix Omnibus • various
Star Trek: Odyssey • William Shatner with Judith and Garfield Reeves-Stevens
Millennium Omnibus • Judith and Garfield Reeves-Stevens
Starfleet: Year One • Michael Jan Friedman

Star Trek® Short Story Anthologies

Strange New Worlds, vol. I, II, III, IV, V, and VI • Dean Wesley Smith, ed.
The Lives of Dax • Marco Palmieri, ed.
Enterprise Logs • Carol Greenburg, ed.
The Amazing Stories • various

Other Star Trek® Fiction

Legends of the Ferengi • Ira Steven Behr & Robert Hewitt Wolfe
Adventures in Time and Space • Mary P. Taylor, ed.
Captain Proton: Defender of the Earth • D.W. "Prof" Smith
New Worlds, New Civilizations • Michael Jan Friedman
The Badlands, Books One and *Two* • Susan Wright
The Klingon Hamlet • Wil'yam Shex'pir
Dark Passions, Books One and *Two* • Susan Wright
The Brave and the Bold, Books One and *Two* • Keith R.A. DeCandido